THE BUDDHA TREE

FUMIO NIWA

The Buddha Tree

A NOVEL

TRANSLATED BY KENNETH STRONG

CHARLES E. TUTTLE COMPANY
Rutland, Vermont & Tokyo, Japan

UNESCO COLLECTION OF CONTEMPORARY WORKS
This volume has been accepted in the
Translation Series of Contemporary Works
jointly sponsored by the International PEN Club
and the United Nations Educational,
Scientific, and Cultural Organization (UNESCO)

Originally published in Japanese as *Bodaiju*

Published by the Charles E. Tuttle Company, Inc.
of Rutland, Vermont and Tokyo, Japan
with editorial offices at Suido 1-chome, 2-6, Bunkyo-ku, Tokyo, Japan
by special arrangement with Peter Owen Limited, London

Library of Congress Catalog Crad No. 74-157259

International Standard Book No. 0-8048-0995-X

First Tuttle edition, 1968
Fifth printing, 1974

0293-000110-4615
PRINTED IN JAPAN

The translator wishes to acknowledge much valuable help received from Mrs Tomio Kawarasaki, of Tokyo, and Professor Michio Watanabe, of Tokyo Women's Christian College.

The translator wishes to acknowledge much valuable help received from Mrs. Fumi Kawamoto, of Tokyo, and Professor Mieko Watanabe, of Tokyo Woman's Christian College.

Introduction

Niwa Fumio, one of contemporary Japan's most prolific novelists, was born in 1904 in surroundings that have exercised a decisive influence on all his work, and especially on *The Buddha Tree.* His father was the hereditary priest of Sogenji, a temple in the small port of Yokkaichi, on Ise Bay not far from Nagoya. Niwa grew up in the priest's quarters adjoining the temple, which remained his home for twenty-eight years. Much of the background to the narrative of *The Buddha Tree* is transcribed directly from the author's own experience. Not only is this true of the detailed descriptions of the temple itself, of the various religious observances and the routine of life in a priest's house. The Tan'ami of the novel is Niwa's home town of Yokkaichi, together with its immediate surroundings—the fields, for instance, of the first chapter, and 'Heron's Forest', with its old Shinto shrine, where the boys play among the camellia trees. Sometimes the correspondences carry a significance beyond the vividness or detail that derive from personal recollection. The new road running through Tan'ami is the modern, macadamized form of the old Tokaido or Eastern Highway that linked the feudal capital of Edo with the old imperial city of Kyoto. In feudal times Yokkaichi was one of the famous fifty-three post-towns or stages on the Highway; and the dull rumbling of long-distance trucks or buses passing through Tan'ami, as the priest of the story hears it from the quiet of the temple compound, is a subtle symbol—perhaps unconscious on Niwa's part—both of continuity with the past and of the modern, industrialised Japan, the complex background against which the priest struggles to realise in his own life the meaning of an inherited religious faith.

As with so many ancient occupations in Japan, the priesthood has frequently been a hereditary office. The Niwa family provide a remarkable example of this—no less than fifteen Niwas had been priests of Sogenji before the novelist's father. Over more than two centuries they built up the temple to a position of considerable influence and wealth. During the upheavals of the Meiji Restoration, however, the parishioners of the temple scattered, and its status declined. Many stories are told of those troubled times. At one time the Niwa family was in such financial straits that the priest took to keeping pigs in the temple compound, and even attempted to sell the temple bell, dragging it on a handcart down the Eastern Highway to a scrap-dealer's in the middle of the night till he was seen by a shocked parishioner and compelled to turn back. But by the beginning of the twentieth century, largely owing to the efforts of the novelist's father, Sogenji had been restored to some at least of its former glory.

At the age of eight Fumio Niwa was ordained as a novice-priest in preparation for his eventual succession to the hereditary charge of Sogenji. In the same year his mother, whom he adored, absconded with a lover—inflicting on the boy an emotional wound that did not heal for many years, and conditioned all his subsequent development. After graduating from a local Middle School, Niwa studied in Tokyo. By 1929, when he graduated from the Japanese Literature department of Waseda University, he was no longer interested in the hereditary priesthood he was expected to assume, and wanted only to write. Failing to find any means of supporting himself in the capital, however, he reluctantly returned to Yokkaichi to serve as deputy priest of Sogenji, holding the regular services and visiting members of the congregation in their homes.

Two years later, encouraged by the phenomenal success of a story he had published in a Tokyo magazine, Niwa finally decided to abandon the priesthood. He has left a vivid account of how he walked out of Sogenji on the night of 10th April 1932, eager and excited, yet wondering whether he could really bear to leave the temple his family had served for two and a half centuries, and remembering inevitably his mother's flight of twenty-one years before.

Arriving in Tokyo once more, but this time penniless and without the support of his family, Niwa turned for help to a woman barkeeper with whom he had lived while still a student; and for three years, until shortly before his marriage in 1935, this woman kept him. The relationship was evidently a strange one. Not infrequently she would bring her bar-customers home to her one-room apartment in the middle of the night, forcing Niwa to withdraw. At once his mistress and his only source of support until he could establish himself as a novelist, to Niwa the writer she was at the same time a 'case', in whom he could study at leisure the workings of feminine psychology and its physiological basis. From his observation of her and from memories of his mother derives Niwa's obsessive concern with woman as a creature of instinct, at the mercy of her sensual nature. Some Japanese critics regard this concern as the product solely of Niwa's personal experience: others trace it to a deeper source, the traditional Buddhist feeling that women are *a priori* more liable to sensual temptation, more 'sinful', than men.

At the time of its publication much of his early work attracted severe criticism from the authorities for its supposedly immoral tendencies. During the war two of his books were banned, and he wrote little apart from some rather half-hearted reporting from China and New Guinea, where he was sent as a war-correspondent. Since 1945, however, he has poured out in rapid succession more than fifty novels and stories, treating with sharply critical realism a wide range of aspects of contemporary Japanese life—but always with his characteristic interest in the sensual side of womanhood, together with an underlying sense of the ultimate futility of all human aspiration.

The Buddha Tree[1], first published in serial form in 1955-6, represents a major landmark in Niwa's development. For a western reader there is a special interest in the frank account, not before attempted in Japanese literature, of certain aspects of contemporary Buddhism—the general decline of traditional religion, the round of 'services' in temple and home, the interaction in the lives of priest and congregation of feudal and modern influences. As with so many Japanese novels, the immediate inspiration is autobiographical. Soshu, the priest of Butsuoji Temple, is modelled in part on Niwa's father—who is said to have divided his leisure between carrying on affairs with women of his congregation and copying out ancient Buddhist writings in the most exquisite calligraphy—and Renko on his mother; while the boy Ryokun is a straight recreation of the author's own childhood. Yet apart from these general correspondences, the book is very far from being a record of actual events. Nor is it primarily concerned with the spiritual struggle of its central character. There is no 'hero'. Soshu may appear as such in the earlier chapters, perhaps, and the characteristically Japanese way in which he wrestles with his weakness alone, shut up inside himself, with the possibility of sharing his troubles with a fellow-priest or other friend never even mentioned—this might attract the sympathy of a non-Japanese reader to the exclusion of other aspects of

1 The phrase is a synonym for 'enlightenment' or 'Buddhist wisdom'. It derives from the bo-tree or bodhi-tree under which the Buddha sat in meditation for forty-nine days before his final enlightenment.

the novel; but the emphasis on Soshu's weakness of character is so continual that an interpretation of the story as essentially the record of one man's lonely pilgrimage towards enlightenment cannot be sustained.

The Buddha Tree is not a 'religious' novel in the propagandist sense, though here again some passages dealing with the timeless quality of the doctrines of Pure Land Buddhism might suggest this interpretation. The author's purpose is literary—to dramatise in novel form the inherited religious awareness he had consciously rejected in youth as incompatible with an artistic sensibility, but which returned of itself in middle age, too deeply engrained to be forgotten or ignored. 'I did my best to forget I had once been a priest,' Niwa has written of the first fifteen years or so of his literary career, 'out of the shallow notion that memories of that period of my life would hinder my work as a novelist. But underlying all my writing has been an awareness of human sin, deriving entirely —though it took me many years to realise this—from the experience of growing up in a temple and the specific religious teaching that was a natural part of daily life in such surroundings . . .' 'Awareness of sin' has obvious affinities with the traditional Christian doctrine of original sin; and True Pure Land Buddhism, with its belief in salvation and translation into a Western Paradise through utter faith in Amida, the (non-historical) 'Buddha of Boundless Light', has often been called the most 'Christian' of the Buddhist sects. Every human being, according to the doctrines of Shinran (1173-1262), principal founder of the sect, is of necessity the prisoner of his passions. Salvation is possible; its single, inescapable condition is the abandonment of all attempts to save oneself, symbolised in Pure Land theology as the sincere acceptance of Amida's 'Vow' of mercy.

In his early work, when he was still pursued by bitter childhood memories of his mother's flight, Niwa's 'awareness of human sin' finds expression in a cynical bitterness.[1] But 'The Buddha Tree' goes deeper. All men's lives are in some degree sordid, the inevitable result of the sins they are bound to commit; but for this very reason all men are to be pitied rather than condemned. 'My novels have been criticised for their detachment, or lack of human feeling,' Niwa

[1] In 'The Hateful Age', for example (in *Modern Japanese Stories*, Eyre and Spottiswoode, London, 1962). In this powerful story attention is directed entirely to the old woman's unpleasant habits as they appear to the younger generation: there is no sympathetic attempt to enter into *her* feelings—indeed, the implication is that she has long since lost the ability to have *any* feelings other than greed. In this case, of course, the limitation of the point of view enhances the effect of the story as an attack on the traditional respect for the aged in Japan.

has remarked, 'but that is not the effect I have sought. For me, detachment is a means, not an end—a state of mind closely connected with the awareness of sin.' If detachment is the means, to be achieved—paradoxically—by the recognition that the observer is no more free of human weakness than the sinning men and women he observes, a compassion akin to charity is the end. There is thus no final condemnation even of Mineyo, the aging woman whose sensuality drives her even to hate her own daughter, nor of Yamaji, the upstart financier whose brutality and shallowness epitomise the worst side of modern Japan, nor of Tomoko, who surrenders to Yamaji in spite of her love for the priest.[2] A western writer, working from a longer tradition of the novel as a philosophical criticism of life, might have made these victims of their own sensuality into universal symbols of human weakness. Niwa does not achieve this: he is still too closely involved with the experiences out of which the book grew. Nor is he interested in working out all the implications of his theme. We are not told how Soshu fared after his eventful public confession, nor given any clear idea of the reaction of his congregation. If *The Buddha Tree* retains the power to move, it is because it reflects with great sincerity a view of life which has been held for several hundred years by innumerable adherents of the most popular form of Japanese Buddhism and is deeply rooted in Niwa's own consciousness.

Niwa's somewhat slow-moving and discursive style is characteristic of much Japanese writing. In part it probably reflects the conditions of publication, reminiscent of nineteenth-century England—*The Buddha Tree* was originally written in fifty-three instalments for a popular magazine, while Niwa was simultaneously engaged on another novel of similar length for serial publication in a newspaper. More essentially Japanese is the lack of concern with tidy plot structure, even in a novel which does not pretend to be anything but traditional in form. The abrupt introduction and equally sudden disappearance from the story of the business-man Ifukube, for instance, will probably strike a western reader as otiose: he may wonder too why the (from a western point of view) potentially interesting relationship between the priest Soshu and his Communist parishioner Tachi is not developed further. As in Japanese films, incident is freely used to accentuate a mood rather than to advance or expand the plot—sometimes almost to the point of sentimentality.

2 It is, perhaps, something of this Buddhist charity which has enabled Niwa to create, without shame or self-consciousness, a series of sensual women openly modelled on his mother, whom he greatly loved.

On occasion this method can be peculiarly effective, as for instance in the vivid interludes describing the escapades of the boy Ryokun and his friend. Less attractive to a modern reader is the author's unashamed use of his characters as mouthpieces for musings of a purely historical or sociological interest.

For most readers, whether western or Japanese, the interest of Niwa's subject will outweigh any deficiencies of style. On the one hand there are the unvarnished descriptions of contemporary temple religion: on the other, the evocation of the 'feel', in the lives of priests and laymen, of their inherited Buddhist faith. Such uniqueness as 'The Buddha Tree' possesses derives from the successful fusion of these two elements—the modern critical spirit and the sombre yet compassionate view of life nurtured by centuries of popular Buddhism.

K. S. 1965

Principal Characters in the Novel

THE GETSUDO FAMILY

Mineyo	Widow of the late priest of Butsuoji, mistress of Soshu
Soshu	Adopted son of Mineyo; present priest of Butsuoji
Renko	Wife of Soshu
Ryokun	Son of Soshu and Renko
Shoju, also referred to as 'the old priest' and 'the old man'	Brother of the late priest of Butsuoji

THE OTHERS

O-Sugi	Maid to the Getsudo family
Yosuke Tachi	A factory worker
Mosuke Yamaji	A company president
Tomoko Komiyama	A widow
Shoko Komiyama	Her daughter
Sumi	Her maid
Naka Mimori	Keeper of a geisha establishment
Naota Ifukube	A business-man
Tsuruko Yamashiro	Mistress of Ifukube
Tanomi Hoshina	A young widow

Much of the action of the novel takes place in the Temple of the Merciful Buddha, a temple of the True Pure Land Sect of Japanese Buddhism. For the sake of brevity, the temple is referred to throughout this translation by its Japanese name, Butsuoji.

1

Once outside the school gate, his friends scattered, some to the right and some to the left. Ryokun Getsudo was the only one to keep straight on across the road. As he ran under the two-storeyed gate of the Temple of the Merciful Buddha, his little satchel on his back, you might have thought he had come to play in the temple grounds on his way home.

The house where he lived was directly opposite the primary school, and the two gates, of the school and temple, faced each other. A little way back from the temple gate, and overshadowing it, stood the main hall of the temple. Ryokun's steps suddenly slowed down when he was through the gate; it had happened like that every day for some time now. In the dead silence that lay over the temple and its grounds, the boy seemed reluctant to enter the priest's house. He was unhappy, with an aching sadness that made him forget he was walking, even. Every afternoon when he passed through the gate on his way home from school, it came over him, like the sudden recollection of something important that he had forgotten. Every day this feeling of loneliness and unhappiness seemed to be waiting for him at the gate. How to explain it, or how it had started, he did not know. Butsuoji[1] and the whole compound had turned into a vast, dark cave, and though he could not understand the cause of his unhappiness, the weight of it crushed him.

Mother's going away—that was it. . . . It was a month ago now. They had not even told him where she had gone. 'You'll find out, all in good time,' was all Soshu, his father, had said when Ryokun asked him, and from the way he said it, the question seemed to be unwelcome. Soshu was not so upset as Ryokun at Renko's disappearance, so he probably knew where she was. In reply to the

1 Butsuoji. Temple of the Merciful Buddha. Every Japanese temple has its own name.

same question Mineyo, the boy's grandmother, merely said, 'A fine mother she's been to you, Ryokun—running off and leaving you like that . . .' She herself, however, did not seem very bitter against Renko, for all her running off and deserting her child. O-Sugi, the old servant, whom Ryokun went to next, would only say, 'I don't know anything about it,' avoiding his eyes for some reason as she spoke.

'Shoju, do you know where Mother's gone?' Shoju, the younger brother of the former priest of Butsuoji, was sixty-six now. He had never married, and lived alone in a little house in the middle of the cemetery on the hill, from which he came every day to work in the temple. People said he was weak in the head. He had been ordained once, but had never actually served as priest; he worked as a kind of inferior curate and general handyman. Everybody despised him except Ryokun, who loved the old man. He would trim the hedge round the compound like a professional gardener. In midsummer snakes four or five feet long would hide in the hedge, looking like branches, and Shoju would talk to them as if they were human: 'Shoo! Shoo! Get away with you—the shears'll have you if you're not quick about it! What did I tell you—nearly snipped you in two then!' Peremptory taps on the hedge from Shoju's long shears usually succeeded in driving the reluctant snakes to shift their positions; and if they didn't move, the old man would pick them up carefully by the neck and deposit them on a part of the hedge that he had finished cutting. He wasn't in the least afraid of snakes. Sometimes when he picked one up he would show it to Ryokun, saying what a pretty little fellow it was. Ryokun thought Shoju was strong and brave, because he could do things that other people couldn't. But the old man had one weakness. The same Shoju who thought nothing of snakes would hobble away yelling with terror if you produced a frog. Even little tree-frogs were too much for him. It was a mystery to the boy that he should be so frightened of them, when he didn't mind picking up snakes and even nestling them against his chest. But he liked him all the more because of it.

'You want to know where your mother is, eh? I don't know . . .' Shoju, at least, would tell him the truth, Ryokun thought. So there was nobody who would tell him where she had gone. Even the elders[1] of the temple and their wives seemed to take special care

[1] The office of 'elder' in a temple congregation is a hereditary one, concerned more with the running of temple affairs than with any spiritual or pastoral responsibility. The word translated here and subsequently as 'elders' wives' refers to the group of women members of the congregation whose primary duty is to assist at special temple functions. Some of them might not, in fact, be the wives of elders: but it would probably be even more misleading to translate the word as 'women's group', in view of the quite different connotation the phrase would have for readers with a Christian background.

to avoid the subject. Ryokun was only eight; how could *he* find out where she was, if none of the grown-ups would tell him? His school-cap tilted back slightly, he stopped for a moment in the middle of the compound. There was no sound of any kind from the house. The sun shone directly on the lower half of the massive sliding doors of the main hall, bleaching their paper panels dazzling white. The boy's eyes wandered to the bell-tower, and then to the well of holy water nearby, with its row of little wooden buckets on the shelf. Between the tower and the well, in the distance, he could see the cemetery and the gleaming white of the newest gravestones. At midnight, he had heard, the dead come out of their graves to talk to each other. To a Shinto shrine, night brings only a deep, peaceful silence; but a Buddhist cemetery awakes to a strange life in the dark hours. Not that there is anything you can see, people said; but you can *feel* them there, talking. Ryokun was afraid of the cemetery.

Leaning on one of the heavy sliding doors of the living quarters, he pushed it open, and felt the cool air from inside gently brush his cheek. 'It's me—Ryokun!' His voice was swallowed up by the high ceiling. But somebody was coming; he could hear the soft swish of footsteps hurrying over the floor-matting. 'Hallo, Ryokun!' All smiles, his grandmother Mineyo took the satchel off his back. Ryokun made no attempt to help her. It hurt him that she seemed not to notice the unhappiness and emptiness he felt. All of them—his father, his grandmother, O-Sugi and Shoju—seemed to be doing their best to forget that his mother had disappeared. He himself was the only one who clung to memories of her.

'What did you do at school today? Did you eat your dinner up properly?' With one arm round his shoulders, his grandmother went with him to the study-room. As she took his lunch-box and schoolbooks out of the satchel and arranged them neatly on the desk, he was aware of her make-up, of the scent surrounding her. She was tall, with unusually sloping shoulders; but for Ryokun, her broad forehead, and the old-fashioned way she wore her hair, tied back and bundled on top of her head, made her somehow severe, more like a man than a woman. He knew how different she looked when she was just out of bed and when she had been at her mirror. She was fifty-three, and had a bad complexion. Early in the morning her face was full of blotches and wrinkles. But once her make-up was finished, everyone said she couldn't be more than forty-five or six, an estimate of which she seemed to be proud. 'Your Granny ought to be ashamed of herself, putting on all that rouge and powder at her age!' his mother had complained sometimes. Mineyo's taste in dress and make-up infuriated her. Even now, his grandmother wore a pink under-kimono, and was careful to let it show at the neck.

'Where's father?'

'Pastoral duty, dear.' 'Pastoral duty,' Ryokun had been told, meant visiting parishioners' homes and reciting the sutras for them.

Ryokun had always asked about his mother and father the moment he came home from school. Not that he needed them specially for anything; he just wanted to make sure where they were. If he was told they were busy, or had gone out, he was quite happy. But since his mother had disappeared, he had stopped asking where she was. He felt that for some reason it was wrong to ask, and was even afraid to speak about her at all. Strangely, he had never asked 'Where is Granny?' He didn't mean to ignore her, but something inside him always seemed to prevent him from asking about anyone other than his father and mother.

As usual, Mineyo had been waiting for him to come back and had got his biscuits ready, wrapped in rice-paper. Stuffing them in his pocket, he ran out of the house. In the corner of the garden on the south side of the temple, in front of the shed, the old priest was chopping firewood. For work like this he wore a faded cotton *hakama*[1] over his white robe. But the robe itself was never really white—Shoju had to do everything himself, including his washing.

He looked up as Ryokun came running from the house. They smiled at each other. For a moment the old man looked as if there was something he wanted to say, but he did not say it and with a sigh, began swinging his chopper again. There were signs of blood on his left leg, where a flying splinter must have struck him.

Ryokun went round to the open space in front of the main hall. Occasionally a lorry would pass down the road outside the great gate, but that was all. The road looked forlorn now—the buses and lorries had begun to use the new road away behind the temple as soon as it was completed. Ryokun waited to see if any of his friends would come to play, but there was no sign of anyone, so he went back to the old priest, who was still chopping away. O-Sugi was working too, cutting up some vegetables by the well. Otherwise the temple grounds were as quiet as ever.

'When are you going home, Shoju?'

'When I've finished the firewood. The old man's tone was polite and humble, like that of a servant addressing his master. He was always humble like this, because people said he was weak in the head; though in fact he belonged just like the rest of them to the Getsudo family, hereditary priests of Butsuoji. Perhaps after all, such humility was proof of his stupidity. 'I've got through my work

[1] A divided skirt worn over the kimono: traditional wear for men.

sooner than usual today. The bath water's drawn, and Father Soshu says he'll lock up the hall, so I'm going home early.'

'I'll go to the hill with you.'

'Did your Granny say you might?'

'No. I don't care what she says, anyway.'

'Then you mustn't come.'

'I'm not afraid of Granny, even is she does get angry.'

In order to stifle the sadness and loneliness he had felt for a month now, Ryokun had been tempted two or three times to disobey his grandmother. But if he went to the little house on the hill this afternoon without her permission, it was Shoju who would get into trouble afterwards. Mineyo would assume he had taken the boy with him without troubling to ask her. Ever since she had come to the temple as a bride, she had regarded Shoju—her husband's younger brother—as if he were a personal enemy. She would seize on every little example of the old man's forgetfulness to abuse him, and over the years had finally succeeded in reducing him to a mere servant. It was she was was responsible for the contempt in which he was generally held; and Shoju himself seemed to have too little spirit to oppose her. Once he had had a little room in the temple house, but before long she had driven him out to the lonely little cottage in the cemetery on the hill. Twenty years had passed since then.

When Shoju had collected his firewood into a pile, the old man and the boy left the temple grounds together, though they knew very well the scolding they would have to face from Mineyo later. Shoju was tall, and walked with a stoop. His shoulders protruded sharply under the white robe, like a pair of sawn-off logs.

The temple was on the outskirts of the town of Tan'ami, and the hill with the cemetery about three quarters of a mile further out. The 'road' to the cemetery had only recently been marked out, in a rearrangement of the fields and their boundaries; but it was little used, and already the weeds were sprouting over its surface. Two faint ruts showed where the farmers' carts sometimes passed. On either side of the road white and yellow butterflies hovered over a faintly-scented carpet of rape-flowers. Ahead rose the hill, with Shoju's cottage in the middle of the cemetery, looming unexpectedly large among the scattered gravestones. Both cemetery and cottage belonged to the temple. New housing had begun to spread towards the hill—another five or six years would see it swallowed up in the expanding town. No one, however, wanted to live too close to the cemetery; and there was a belt of trees, recently planted at some distance from the foot of the hill, which guarded it for the time being from further encroachments.

The two walked on without speaking. Behind them, Butsuoji stood out among the houses, floating on a sea of yellow flowers. The massed colour seemed to pierce the eye with its brilliance. Ryokun drank in the scent.

'Your mother will not come home again.' Shoju said suddenly. Ryokun stopped, just by a night-soil tank, and stared at the wrinkled face of his companion.

'Why not?'

Shoju shook his head. 'Last spring she didn't come home for five days—d'you remember?'

Ryokun had forgotten. Miserable, of course, he had been then, when she had disappeared without a word; but until now she had never been away as long as a whole month, and this new unhappiness had made him forget about last year. Suddenly he had a feeling that she would never come back. The smell from the tank made him shiver slightly.

Ryokun's eyes were big like his father's, but he had his mother's mouth.

'How do you know?'

Shoju started to walk again. Ryokun knew for himself that Shoju was right about his mother; But grown-ups lived in another world, and he wanted to know in the same way as Shoju knew.

'You're only eight yet, Ryokun. You'll find out for yourself when you grow up.'

There was a deep sadness, even despair, it seemed to Ryokun, in the old man's voice. Still the sea of yellow enclosed them. Shoju said no more; and when a grown-up shuts up like that, there is nothing an eight-year-old can do. Ryokun hardly came up to Shoju's waist; but he walked on, hands in pockets and head bent forward, looking as if life had taught him all its secrets already. One hand was clutching the packet of biscuits.

They climbed the hill. Shoju's house, which was about eight yards by twelve, had no shutters, no ceiling, and not even proper foundations—the threshold was raised off the ground, without the usual supports. Ryokun had to jump up on to it, as if he were mounting a horse. The main part of the house was walled only on one side, so that it was open to all the force of the strongest winds that swept across the hill. A shelter, four posts and a roof, it was no more. The sliding doors were falling apart with old age and use. One corner of the house had been made into an eight-mat 'living-room'. It was like a room on a stage; there were groves for the doors, but no doors to run in them. Walls on three sides gave it something of the look of a real room. A closet occupied one side; on the wall opposite hung a cheap scroll with a portrait of St

Shinran.[1] Below the scroll, on a small sutra-desk, shabby with peeling paint, were a candlestick, an incense-burner, a china vase and a sutra-bell. A black priest's robe and stole hung on a hook on the third wall, the former too worn-out to attract even a thief. To imagine the kind of life Shoju led here was painful for Ryokun; it was so remote from the comfort of the Butsuoji house. He could not believe a life like this was to be humbly accepted, just because people said one wasn't clever.

Shoju sometimes cooked and ate his meals at home. A charcoal brazier, two saucepans, a rice-bowl and a single pair of chopsticks lay on the floor beside the desk.

'Aren't you afraid, with the house open all round?'

'Only people who have things worth stealing are afraid. There's nothing like that here—a thief'd have to be pretty cracked to burgle a place like this. I do have company now and then, though, on wet nights; it's shelter for them, and they don't care who lives here.'

'Thieves?'

'Dogs. Human company is better than staying out all night alone, I suppose. They're not shy anyway—walk calmly in and sleep with me as if they lived here.'

The boy smiled. 'Big ones?'

'Big enough to jump up on to the floor, like you did. They couldn't get in otherwise.' When Ryokun was standing outside, the floor was level with his chest. Sometimes, Shoju told him, a dog too small to jump into the house would bark and howl outside the whole night long.

'Your mother was always giving me extra food, Ryokun; though she took care your Granny never knew about it. I shan't get enough to eat if she doesn't come back to Butsuoji any more.' As Renko's uncle by marriage, Shoju should never, of course, have been treated as anything less than a respected member of the family. 'Father Soshu himself has been very good in that way sometimes, though it's not been easy for him. . . .'

'I know, it's Granny who's so spiteful—'

Instead of answering, Shoju took an old broom and went out into the cemetery to sweep between the gravestones and collect the withered flowers from the graves. Ryokun followed close behind, like a dog. The sweepings served instead of firewood for Shoju's little cooking brazier. Below the cemetery wave after wave of yellow flowers seemed to roll towards the hill. Beyond them, in the distance, was the temple.

—Mother isn't there—

A gust of wind blew across the yellow sea. There were tears now

1 Founder of the True Pure Land Sect (Jodo Shinshu) of Japanese Buddhism early in the thirteenth century.

in Ryokun's eyes. Somewhere out of sight, an aeroplane was droning its way across the sky. 'Things will be easier when the warm weather comes,' said Shoju, still sweeping. 'The Jumannin services start on the 6th of April.' A few extras always came the old man's way when special services were held at Butsuoji, though the treatment he received from Mineyo made him nervous about accepting even a box of matches.

'What shall I do if mother doesn't come back. . . .' A surge of longing for his mother flooded Ryokun's throat. Shoju seemed not to have heard; he was busy with his broom among the gravestones.

Suddenly feeling less sorry for himself, Ryokun began to run down the hillside—then stopped; the temple was waiting for him there beyond the flowers. He walked on slowly. On the hilltop behind him, a couple of hundred yards away, Shoju stood motionless, his grimy robe showing white now among the darker gravestones. Leaning on his broom, he stared after Ryokun. Ryokun waved; but Shoju did not move. He looked steadily across the great field of flowers, that all but submerged the slowly receding figure of Ryokun; as if watching something invisible suspended in the air above the boy. Perhaps it was the tragedy of Ryokun's motherless future that he seemed to see so clearly. Still without moving, in his eyes the gleam of an old man's wisdom, he watched Ryokun's figure growing smaller in the distance.

The road was deserted. At its edges spring grasses were pushing their way through the withered matting of last year's weeds. The sky seemed more lofty and remote than usual; only the violet silhouette of the mountains to the west broke into its cloudless expanse. Four crows were flying westwards, for all they were worth, as if afraid of returning late to their nests. The boy stopped to watch them.

Noiselessly, a bus crossed the bridge some way ahead of him, a thick red stripe painted along its side. Around Ryokun the air was laden with scent. The flowers themselves were small; but so many of the plants had grown to the same height that leaves and stalks were hidden under the densely packed blossoms, through which Ryokun's head and shoulders moved, a tiny swimmer through a yellow sea.

He remembered how they had gone by bus and train and then another bus, to a town he did not recognize; his mother did not tell him where they were going. After leaving the bus they walked for a while, and came to a residential street with big houses lining both sides. A big new *torii* led to a Shinto shrine; beyond it was a broad river, like the sea. Through a newly-built gateway, Renko and Ryokun entered an imposing house.

The upstairs room they were conducted to was small, but overlooked the river. Leaning on the handrail outside the sliding window, Ryokun looked across to the opposite shore, a hundred yards or more away. No waves lapped either shore; the river was flowing too fast. A few thatched cottages rose up out of the profusion of reeds opposite, giving the impression that the ground they stood on was lower than the level of the river.

A woman of about his mother's age came into the room and the two began to whisper to each other. Without showing any special consciousness of the boy's presence, they evidently did not want him to overhear their conversation. His mother seemed worried, her companion sympathetic; and as they talked on, his mother's distress grew. Ryokun had often seen her like this at Butsuoji; he was not too young to understand that look, listless and weary, as if with some incurable pain she could no longer bear. But what made her suffer like this he did not know. At home in Butsuoji he had never heard her laugh.

Night fell. For a while the river stood out bright against the black sky, then it too gradually melted into the surrounding darkness. Ryokun's mother said nothing about going home. The house grew more noisy; it was a restaurant, Ryokun realized now. The woman his mother had been talking to went out, and a maid brought in supper.

'I'm so sorry to give you all this trouble.' Apologetic, almost obsequious, Renko told the maid they would serve themselves; and the two began to eat.

'When are we going home?'

His mother was silent; apparently all thought of returning to Butsuoji had left her. She seemed lonely and sad, yet calm, as if she had come to some great decision. The woman she had been talking to before now came back in a new kimono.

'You'd better take things easily—stay here four or five days. You'll be making yourself ill if you can't get away from all that worry for a bit. It'll give you time to decide about the future, too.'

'Can you forgive me—coming and throwing myself on you like this?'

'Nothing to forgive—and it's not as if I could look after you properly anyway. I ought to apologize for shutting you up in this tiny room.'

'I never stopped to think how busy you'd be: I just came. . . '

'Busy's the word all right—we're always busiest after dark, and then we get so rushed, we hardly know what we're doing. Still, we'll have time for a proper talk tomorrow. You'll ask the maid if there's anything you want, won't you?' She stroked Ryokun's head as she left the room.

'There's a good quiet boy!'

'Who was that?' asked Ryokun the moment the sliding door closed behind her.

'Someone I knew at school,' Renko looked him in the eyes. 'She was my best friend—we two used to talk about everything together. Her husband runs this place.'

Ryokun heard the twang of a *samisen* from one of the other rooms.

'It's a restaurant, Ryokun—that's why they have the *samisen*. Lots of pretty geisha come here.'

'I've seen a geisha.'

'Of course—there are some who belong to the the Butsuoji congregation, aren't there?'

'They come to worship at New Year, all dressed up.'

Every year, on the first of January, a yellow curtain was hung all round the main hall, and from early morning Ryokun's father, sitting at a desk outside, would receive the New Year greetings of the worshippers. He was thirty-eight. Tall, not tonsured like most priests, he had a broad forehead that gave him an air of wisdom, and large, rather melancholy eyes. Always he wore a robe of pure white, which in his case, as he was extremely particular about his appearance, seemed to reflect his character. In the black gown and stole of gold brocade that he wore over the robe, he somehow gave the impression of an actor playing the part of a priest. Though he had dressed like this for twenty years, he had none of the priestly air that one expects from Buddhist divines. There was a look of newness about his gown, as if he turned priest in middle age, after half a lifetime as a layman.

The maid came in to lay the *futon*[1] earlier than usual; her mistress had evidently given special instructions.

'Will you take a bath, madam?'

'No, I won't, thank you—I have a cold coming on, I think.'

Ryokun began to feel sleepy. Nestling in bed with his mother, he slipped his hand into her breast between the folds of her gown. There was no brother or sister for him to sleep with, and so he had always slept like this, even after starting primary school. When he came running home from school in the afternoon, he would throw away his satchel and press his face against her breasts. It did not

1 Thick quilts which take the place of bed and mattress in Japan. They are kept in cupboards during the day, and spread on the floor each night.

matter that they had given no milk for years now, and that the nipples were small and shrunken; for Ryokun his mother's breasts were toys to play with.

'Ryokun! Aren't you ashamed of yourself—a big boy like you!' So his grandmother had scolded him once, but he had only glared back at her, his mother's nipple firmly in his mouth. A parishioner who happened to be visiting had looked scandalized. Smiling, Renko had taken off Ryokun's school cap—he was still sucking at her breast—and stroked his head. Evidently it was hard for her, too, to break the habit of eight years; in spite of the discomfort that Ryokun's sucking of her milkless breast caused her, she wanted the feeling of physical contact with her son to last for ever.

They could hear the *samisen* still, and several voices singing. Ryokun's fingers clutched at his mother's breast as it slipped from his lips; he was half asleep. Renko put her arm around his neck. He knew nothing of what his mother went through now, long after he was asleep; even after all the noise from the restaurant had died away and the river could be heard once more against the stillness of the night, she lay awake and restless.

Except that it was certainly more than two or three days, Ryokun did not remember how long they had spent there. Perhaps Renko had intended this visit, and others like it which she had made, as preparation for her final flight from the temple. Ryokun could not remember clearly the particular sound of the river that flowed beneath the windows of the restaurant, because it was merged in his memory with the sounds of similar nights spent at another inn. On these other occasions, Renko had taken him with her on the train, without saying where they were going. She could not bear Butsuoji any longer, evidently—why, Ryokun did not know; but she made several of these journeys, and always took him with her. The second inn where they stayed faced a broad river-bed, most of which was dry white shingle. A hill dominated the opposite bank; to the right, an iron bridge carried a stream of cars and trams. The river itself pounded so swiftly along its narrow central channel that anyone falling in would almost certainly have been drowned. It frightened Ryokun. As he stood watching it from the inn window, he fancied the inn itself was moving, and then the whole river-bed and the hill opposite, caught up in its irresistible flow.

It was a western-style inn, and some of the guests were foreigners. Ryokun and his mother took their meals at fixed times in the big dining-room. The bedrooms, however, were all Japanese-style—except that each one included a western bath, which Ryokun thought very strange. He fell asleep early that night, while still playing with his mother's breasts; but after a while he woke up again suddenly. Someone was talking close to the bed. 'Can't you sleep, dear?' His mother spoke gently. She had been talking with a man. Ryokun had never seen him, nor had he noticed him come into the room that evening. The stranger smiled at him, and his mother too, which surprised him greatly; it was so long since he had seen her smile. Her companion's arrival had given her such delight, that a new tenderness revealed itself in every movement she made; a side of his mother Ryokun never saw at Butsuoji. Picking up a bar of chocolate from the little table, she put it beside his pillow.

'Tomorrow morning, mind—you mustn't eat it now! I'll leave it here, ready for you when you wake up!'

Wondering when she had bought it, Ryokun clutched the bar of chocolate with one hand, and was soon ásleep again.

Next morning the stranger was gone. Who or what he was, or whether he had spent the whole night in their room, were questions that did not occur to Ryokun. He went out into the garden, which stretched almost to the riverbank, and sat on a bench. Cars were passing along the road that occupied the narrow strip between the end of the garden and the river. A foreign couple sat down on the next bench, smiled at Ryokun, and said something to him he could not understand. His mother, who was looking fresh and happy, smiled back; Ryokun wondered whether she had understood.

That night Ryokun slept till morning without waking. Two nights later, he woke up again, this time in the middle of the night; the stranger of the first night was in the room again. Evidently he took great care not to disturb the boy when he came in. Reassured when he saw who it was, Ryokun soon went to sleep once more.

If he had known how make-up can alter a face, Ryokun might have recognized the man when he first came to the inn. He was an actor of some repute in the Kansai Kabuki company, and Renko had taken Ryokun to the theatre with her when the company came to play for a week at Tan'ami. She took him on the second day, too, and again on the third and fourth. The theatre had come through the war undamaged; the pit was a swept earth floor strewn with thin mats, and there were still some of the old-style tea-booths. One of the attendants, who appeared to be almost all middle-aged women, was a member of the Butsuoji congregation, and through her Renko was able to get tickets for the whole week. Every night they sat on the same mat in the pit. Every night Renko had eyes only for one actor. Always she kept her gaze fixed on him, as if obsessed; and from the third night he began to take notice of her. Ryokun saw the same play three times. The screams and killings in the play would make him bury his head in fright in his mother's lap, but she never lowered her eyes from the figure on the stage. On the last night the attendant who belonged to Butsuoji took Renko to visit the actor in his dressing-room, and they arranged that she was to wait for him at an inn in each town the company visited.

If life in the temple household had been depressing before, after Renko's visits to the theatre began it became unbearable. When the family met at meals Renko scarcely spoke to her mother; but Mineyo, undeterred, chattered on alone.

There were no rooms in the house smaller that ten mats.[1] Two rooms, though part of the same building, formed a kind of annexe, separated from the main quarters by the kitchen. Originally used as a maid's room and storeroom, they had been converted into proper living-rooms, and were now occupied by Renko. Mineyo had taken the room with the family shrine for herself; Soshu, the Lute Room, a twelve-mat room, so called from a lute stand in one corner. The shrine-room and Lute Room were separated only by their sliding doors and a few yards of corridor; but to get from there to Renko's room one had to go from one end of the house to the other, down the whole length of the corridor and across the kitchen. Most of the time Renko shut herself up in her retreat, alone with Ryokun. The boy was only eight, so it was hardly surprising that he could not understand the tension between the grown-up members of the family. 'Who ever heard of someone in a priest's family chasing after an actor? What do you think the congregation will say when it gets about, eh?' Ryokun had heard Mineyo say to his mother, wondering what she meant by "chasing after an actor." Renko hated Mineyo. Not that she ever answered her taunts; but Ryokun could feel the hatred boiling inside her. Without knowing why, he sided with her against his grandmother. Yet even at his age he was aware that she was not altogether in the right. It was certainly wrong of her to leave the temple for days on end—which made him think it all the more strange that his father never said anything to her about it. Only Mineyo scolded her.

'It would be too much for your mother altogether if there wasn't an actor or somebody like that for her to go after now and again. It'd be unnatural otherwise.' the old priest had said to Ryokun.

'Why unnatural? I went to the plays with her, Shoju.'

'You don't understand yet, Ryokun. You will later on.'

'If she's doing something wrong, why isn't father angry with her?'

'He was only adopted into the family, you see.'

'Is that why he can't be angry with mother—because he was adopted?'

'You'll find out, Ryokun, all in good time. . . .'

Even Shoju would not tell him what he most wanted to know. But Ryokun felt no strong desire to insist on answers to his

1 The size of Japanese rooms is always measured by the number of standard-size mats required to cover the floor.

questions. He was conscious of some mysterious, malignant force disrupting their lives at Butsuoji; that was all. To learn the secret of the mystery, he had decided, there was nothing for it but to wait till he was older.

For a while things were almost normal again. The grown-ups seemed somehow to have made up their differences, and Renko no longer spent nights away from home. Then, as if to prove that the mystery Ryokun had felt and feared was as virulent as ever, his mother disappeared altogther. Nor had she given him the least hint of her departure beforehand. A whole month passed. When Ryokun came home from school, no mother was waiting for him to run to her and bury his head in her breast. She would never welcome him any more. Mineyo tried very hard to lessen his misery. She was delighted to have him to herself again, and came every night to sleep with him in his bed in the annexe. Ryokun hated her coming; he wanted passionately to defy her. 'If you insist on being so disobedient, I shall tell your father,' she threatened, and accused Soshu of being too lenient when she found he made no attempt to scold the boy. Since Renko's disappearance, Soshu seemed to be avoiding his son's eyes.

About a third of the field of flowers still lay before Ryokun. Looking back, he could still see the white figure of Shoju, sweeping among the tombstones; his movements seemed slower than usual, though he was too far away now for Ryokun to see his face clearly, or even shout to him.

The yellow of the fields was overpowering. Rainwater was still lying on the black soil between the ridges. A sudden wild urge sent Ryokun running headlong among the flowers, jumping from ridge to ridge. The yellow pollen was all over his clothes at once, clinging to them obstinately as he rushed about among the flowers; even his face and hands were yellow. Missing his footing on one of the ridges, he landed in a shallow pool of rainwater. Mud streaked his shoes, which annoyed him vaguely for a moment, he didn't know why—then he was off again, dashing across the field and whirling his arms more madly than ever.

2

Mornings began early at the Temple of the Merciful Buddha. The new state highway through Tan'ami was busy day and night, but in the Butsuoji district, which had grown up by the outskirts of the town, along the old road, the traffic ended with nightfall. Half the households were farms, so that the days started earlier here than in the town proper.

O-Sugi got up before sunrise, unlocked the back door, and lit a fire in the big stove. In the kitchen, darkness began its retreat from the morning, of which the young flames, visible through the firing-holes of the stove, were the first sign. White smoke curled out of the holes, and drifted, as if sucked upward, to the roof—there was no ceiling; only an old-fashioned bare roof, supported by four massive, soot-blackened beams. Inside the stove, O-Sugi's sticks crackled. The Butsuoji family and its secret tragedy slept on undisturbed. Every morning at first light, Shoju would appear at the back door. It was still night when he came down from the house on the hill, past the graves, to the fields below, but the darkness did not trouble him; the long years had made him familiar with every step of the way.

Snuffling in the cold air, Shoju went to open the outer door of the temple house. It was heavy, and rumbled as he pushed it to one side along its groove. Then he crossed the courtyard, opened the folding sections of the main gate, and hurried back again to the house; a lean, worn figure with jutting angular shoulders. The same figure might have been seen at the same work a year before—or three or ten years before. Shoju, brother of the late priest of Butsuoju, had been opening and shutting the gates for more than sixty years, like a robot, every day and in every kind of weather. Recently he had begun to find it difficult to climb up from the kitchen on to the corridor leading to the living rooms. It was higher even than the floor of his own cottage; there were three steps, each one a foot high.

Going back to the door of the house, he undid the heavy shutters round the porch. The porch was very large, like a vestibule in an Imperial Palace, with a wide wooden platform before you stepped up on to the floor proper. Next came the shutters along the corridor leading to the big hall, and then the massive doors of the hall itself, each one of which folded in two and had to be hooked back to prevent a gust of wind from blowing it to. As Shoju opened these doors one by one on three sides of the hall, the darkness seemed first to retreat to the sanctuary, then to the corridor behind. Shoju knelt before the shrine, palms pressed together and head bowed, and recited a deep, hoarse *nenbutsu*.[1] The gilded doors of the feretory on the altar were shut tight.

As he passed the shrine containing the picture of Shinran he held his breath and walked with special care, as if the portrait were a living being whose sleep must not be disturbed. Once past the two gilded pillars behind the altar, he relaxed again. Behind the sanctuary and the recess was the corridor, whose single tiny window Shoju opened, though it was too small to lighten the corridor much. It looked out over the original Butsuoji cemetery, which had served for more than three hundred years, until at last there was no more room, and a new burial-ground had to be opened on the hill. Shoju's morning duties in the temple were now ended—he was not allowed to open the altar feretory, or the little shrine with the portrait of Shinran. He went back now to the house to open the rest of the shutters, trying not to disturb the still sleeping family as he did so, though the noise usually woke them. Next he swept the temple compound. The old man had repeated these morning tasks for so long that he did everything automatically; time was forgotten in the steady movement of his broom. All the sixty-six years of his life had been so uneventful, and to watch him at work now was like looking at a picture of some aged priest who had cut himself off from all attachment to the world. Even the terrors of the war had been unable to disturb the calm of his existence. Every morning he swept the compound clean of a day's accumulation of dust and rubbish; and the bare earth, after his broom had passed across it, looked somehow lonely and decayed, like the life he himself led on the hill.

Rice was bubbling on the kitchen stove by now—Shoju could smell it as he went past the back door to put his broom and dustpan away in the shed. Washing his hands by way of purification, he

1 An invocation, or prayer, much used in Pure Land Buddhism. It consists of the three words 'Namu Amida Butsu', sometimes translated as 'Homage to Amida Buddha'. (For 'Amida' see Introduction.)

set about preparing the morning offerings. The bubbling had finished when he took the lid off the pot, leaving only the holes where the water had evaporated. Filling ten bowls with rice, Shoju then emptied them on to tiny little tables, making a little conical mound of rice on each one. The tables for Amida, to whom the temple was dedicated, and for Shinran were twice as big as the others, and more richly engraved.

Soshu and Mineyo were up by this time. 'Get up, Ryokun, you'll be late for school!' Mineyo would repeat again and again until Ryokun got out of bed. After putting on a faded black gown and threadbare stole over his dirty white working clothes, the old priest disappeared in the direction of the temple hall with the box containing the ten brass tables, which clinked against each other to the rhythm of his walk—there were special holes in the box, one for each of the one-legged tables, so that they could be carried without fear of shaking them and spilling the sacred rice. Shoju deposited the box in a corner of the recess, and went behind the altar to start lighting the candles—first the taper, then the hanging oil-lamps; then the candles in the big crane-shaped stands. The candles were so many that merely to light them took some time; and in addition there were always several wicks to be trimmed, as it would have been extravagant to renew the candles every day. It was forbidden to touch the wicks with the fingers, and Shoju duly used the special trimmer, for he was incapable of skimping any of his duties just because no one happened to be watching him. He would extinguish all the candles with the trimmer, too; to blow them out, even by waving a hand, was irreverent. After the candles came the censers. Their columns of white smoke began to rise as he lit the incense sticks and arranged them in their places. Last of all, he distributed the rice-offerings.

A moment later Soshu appeared, looking strangely depressed. Opening the doors of the shrines of Amida and Shinran, he dropped incense powder in the burner, bowed with clasped hands, and took his place directly before the altar. To his right, at right angles to him, sat Shoju; erect and solemn as he faced the sutra-table and gong.

Soshu's profile, as he looked up at the statue of Amida, gleaming darkly within the shrine, had the clarity of a sculptured head. The nose was prominent, the forehead high; about the lips, however, there was a trace of melancholy, of an almost feminine softness. His voice, as he now began to repeat the *nenbutsu*, was different from usual, as if some powerful but long-repressed emotion was at last finding expression in the speaking of the prayer. Shoju picked up the wooden hammer, but something kept him from striking the gong immediately. Long use had worn down the wood, even though it was wrapped in leather, but it was still almost too thick to hold in one hand. He's worried about something, Shoju thought, gazing at the priest. Shoju, Soshu's uncle by marriage, had never made any attempt to resist the gradual process which had turned him into little more than a menial, nor did he feel, even now, any sense of defeat or inferiority. His nephew was learned, popular among his fellow-priests, respected by his parishioners—and handsome; and Shoju was secretly proud when people said the priest of Butsuoji looked like a distinguished actor. In any gathering of priests his good looks were conspicuous, and this too gave Shoju nothing but pleasure. At Senshuji Temple, the headquarters of the Takada branch of the True Pure Land Sect, to which Butsuoji belonged, the affairs of the sect are administered by a priestly equivalent of a cabinet and parliament, whose members are selected from time to time at a conference of priests from the branch temples. Soshu's popularity was such that he was invariably nominated as a candidate at these elections, even though hitherto he had always refused to stand on account of his youth.

The gilded pillars flickered with the reflected light of row after row of candles. From behind a thin line of incense-smoke St Shinran looked Soshu calmly in the face; from above, the bronze Kamakura-style Amida, blackened by the smoke of incense, gazed down at him with its glittering, all-seeing eyes, demanding insistently to know what had made his wife desert him and abandon their child. . . . From those eyes there was no escape; their light pierced into the obscurest regions of Soshu's heart. Shoju was aware this morning of an intense sincerity in his superior's prayers, a heart-felt quality which they usually lacked. The sutra readings which Soshu and Shoju used at these brief morning and evening services were simple and straightforward; they did not include any gathas, for instance. These gathas, which appear in the Chinese translations of the sutras, are rhymed songs or poems, with from four to seven words in each line. Their function is to tell a congregation which sutra it is that is being read. At Butsuoji, it was the custom to use only the Amida Sutra. The old priest struck the great gong before him as Soshu intoned the ancient text.

In the house, as the two men were beginning morning prayers in the temple, Mineyo took their place at the family shrine. The dark, twelve-mat room containing the shrine was sometimes called the 'altar-room'; the altar itself, normally hidden behind the doors of the closet where it was kept, was about six feet wide, a perfect replica on a smaller scale of the great altar in the temple. Mineyo arranged the rice offerings on their little tables—which looked like a child's toy meal set—lit the hanging oil-lamp with a candle, and burnt some incense.

Sitting on the floor in front of the altar, Mineyo began to read the Shoshingé. The book was torn and curled at the corners from long years of use. Mineyo read fast. It had never occurred to her to ask what the words on the page meant, nor did she know that the Shoshin-nenbutsu-gé scripture, to give it its full name, had been written by Shinran himself as the conclusion of the section on 'Conduct' in his book, *Doctrine, Works, Faith and Attainment*. For Mineyo, the morning and evening offerings and scripture reading were merely a duty that had to be fulfilled as part of the inevitable routine of life in a temple. After thirty years of daily reading, she practically knew the Shoshingé by heart.

> Let the sinner with his burden call upon Amida: it is all that that is needful. For He will save me, even me, with His loving mercy; though my eyes are darkened by lust so that I can no more behold Him, yet with love unwearying He will lighten my way for ever.

The words were to be intoned: Mineyo did not understand what they meant. In thirty years she had never dreamt of trying to apply them to herself. It was enough if she could finish each morning's duty in good time. The fact that she had never once missed a morning seemed to her proof of the depth of her faith; and being convinced of her own saintliness, she convinced others of it, too. 'What a pity Renko's such an unbeliever, in spite of being born a priest's daughter and brought up in a temple,' she was fond of saying. Renko would clasp her hands before the altar, but had never recited the Shoshingé or sung a hymn; so in Mineyo's eyes she was impiety personified. Coming to the end of the Shoshingé, Mineyo tapped the sutra-bell three times, and began to recite the five morning hymns, beginning with

> All ye who would not delay
> But long for assurance now
> Praise Amida's holy name
> With humble and reverent heart

—her favourite; she felt she intoned the words with such expression. Ryokun knew the hymns by heart, without understanding them. He had listened so often to Mineyo reciting them, ever since he was a baby nestling in her lap.

Prayers finished, Mineyo took down the rice offerings, banged the cupboard-door to, and went to the living-room. 'Ryokun!' she called; but there was no sign of him getting up. One word from his father, and he would jump out of bed immediately; but if

Mineyo called, he would not move—it was a silent struggle, his will against Mineyo's.

'Be quick and get up now! You'll be late for school!' Ryokun heard her coming to pull back the bedclothes, and wrapped himself in them more tightly. He could smell her scent as she came into the room. She never let anyone see her face before she had put on her morning make-up; Soshu, in particular, she was always anxious to avoid before her toilet was complete.

The tiny sound of brass vessels clinking together was heard again. Morning service in the temple was over. Carrying the big wooden box as before, Shoju came back to the house. The family started breakfast, Shoju, as usual, eating with the maid in the kitchen. Breakfast at Butsuoji was vegetarian, as they always ate the rice that had been offered on the altar at morning prayers. Ryokun hated it; the little conical heaps were cold and hard now. 'Ryokun's getting naughtier and naughtier—I can't manage him any more. Only yesterday he was up at Shoju's again, when I don't know how many times I've told him not to go there. And then on his way home he has to go rolling about in the fields, covering himself with yellow from head to foot—and mud all over his clothes, too. It's time you spoke to him, Soshu! What's going to happen if he goes on like this, I'd like to know?' Soshu looked at Ryokun for a moment, but said nothing. Mineyo's words hurt Ryokun, and he was glad he did not have to face a scolding from his father as well. She appealed to Soshu again; still he did not reply—and Mineyo seemed all along not to expect any answer, as if merely to complain was satisfaction enough.

Putting on his cap and satchel, Ryokun ran across the temple compound and out into the road, leaving little footmarks among the lines that marked where Shoju's broom had swept.

In the third lesson, a little while before midday, one of the school porters came to the classroom and exchanged a few words with the teacher in a whisper. The teacher looked at Ryokun; the boy knew they were talking about him. 'Getsudo!' Ryokun jumped up and went with the porter to the porters' room in a separate building. The porter, who was a member of the Butsuoji congregation, said nothing. Ryokun entered the room. Renko was waiting for him, sitting by the sliding door. Nothing about her had changed since her disappearance from Butsuoji a month ago. Meeting her here, at school, dressed in her best kimono, was like a dream for Ryokun.

'Mummy's coming here is a secret, darling. Granny's not to know about it.' Ryokun nodded solemnly. He loved making this promise of secrecy to his mother. The porter's wife brought them tea, but did not stay to talk; she seemed anxious to leave them alone together.

Many of the temple congregation, though not all, knew why Renko had left her home, and sympathized with her. Even her visits to the little theatre, and her passion for the Kabuki actor, were common knowledge. In Tan'ami and in the country round about, the relationship between temple and parishioners is very close. The parishioners are responsible for the upkeep of their temple, and each of them regards the temple itself as a kind of extension of his own home, where he can drop in any time, not necessarily on temple business, but just for gossip and a cup of tea. Whenever any of the Butsuoji congregation had a fresh crop of vegetables, he would always bring some to the temple, before eating them himself; anything special, in fact they made a point of sharing with Butsuoji first. Through these connections, they had come to feel a personal interest in the domestic affairs of the temple household. For longer than anybody could remember, too, it had been the custom to consult the priest about all their own family problems. The parishioners were distressed, therefore, at Renko's disappearance, and there was much talk about what had happened, though none of it came to Ryokun's ears. People were waiting anxiously for the next parishioners' meeting, which was due very soon.

'What would you think if Mummy were to change her name, darling?' Renko asked Ryokun.

'Change your name, Mummy?'

'Yes, darling—it would mean I'd never go back to Butsuoji again.'

Already, less than a month after leaving home, Renko had to face the decision whether or not she would remarry. Not knowing how to explain the situation to Ryokun, she spoke about it only briefly. as if it were nothing unusual. For Ryokun, the final separation at which she was hinting was unimaginable; and even Renko herself did not fully realize what marriage would mean, or how she would suffer if she could not see Ryokun frequently. Mother and son sat quietly sipping tea, as if they were merely calling on a neighbour.

3

Night came early to Butsuoji. After evening prayers Soshu closed the shrines of Amida and Kannon and left the sanctuary, Shoju standing with head bowed until the priest had gone. The candles and oil lamps burned fitfully still. Shoju went round putting them out with the wick-trimmer, unconsciously murmuring *nenbutsu* as he did so. As the last light died, the sanctuary vanished in a cavern of darkness. 'Namu-Amida-Butsu, Namu-Amida-Butsu . . .': the murmured invocation moved slowly to the room behind the altar, then to the corridor at the back of the hall. It took Shoju some time to close all the doors and shutters. Coming to the last door of all, he looked out across the courtyard, and wondered vaguely why the strip of sky above the great gate should be so green. Across a sea of roofs came the roar of trucks on the national highway. Shoju put up the shutters of the connecting corridor, and of the big porch; darkness drifted through the house.

Crouching at the fuel-hole in the wall, the old man lit a bundle of rape-stalks and husks to heat the bath. When the flowers are past and the seeds ripening, rape-stalks grow tall and thick and tough, tougher than you would think any plant could grow. When the farmers have cut them at the root and shaken the pods free of their cargo of tiny, dark-purple seeds, these stalks might be withered branches, except for their weight, which is next to nothing. Tied into bundles as big as a man can hold, they are stored in great piles for the winter. Some of the parishioners would bring cartloads of them to Butsuoji, taking the temple nightsoil by way of payment. There was no room for a fuel store in the shed, so the farmers would come in a group of three of four, pass the bundles to each other up a tall ladder and stack them under the roof of the house.

Sometimes Ryokun came across Shoju lowering fuel from the loft by a rope with a wooden hook tied to it. It was strange to see him up there, and the big bundles swaying on their way down. 'Any snakes up there, Shoju?' he called up to the roof.

'Ay, and big ones, too.'

'Don't they make you afraid?'

'They behave themselves, snakes do—go away quietly if you ssh them a bit.'

'Is there one there now?'

'There's always one or two.'

'How big?'

''Bout so big . . .,' said Shoju, illustrating with both hands. To Ryokun he was like a magician, moving unafraid among the snakes. Perhaps he could even talk to them. They must grow fat on the rats under the roof . . . how had they found their way into the house? There were snakes in the hedge outside, and in the bushes round the pond behind the temple, too, attracted by the frogs; and now snakes up there in the loft.

'Why does a temple have so many snakes?' he asked Shoju with a puzzled expression.

'We're not allowed to take life in a temple. The snakes like to live here—they know nobody will do them any harm.'

So even snakes can feel where it's safe and where it's dangerous, thought Ryokun; but he hated and feared them still.

The family of three sat down to supper in the living-room. Only Mineyo talked. Occasionally Ryokun said something to his grandmother; but Soshu was silent.

'The reverend's been miserable ever since his wife left him—maybe there's something big he's got to make up his mind about,' Shoju was thinking as he fanned the dried stalks. Soon they were burnng furiously. As usual, Soshu took the first bath. Always he wore a white robe, as spotless as if it were brand-new; even on the hottest days he would never come from the changing room even half-undressed. Ryokun would often run about naked before going to the bathroom, and sometimes even Mineyo would sit cooling herself on the verandah with bare shoulders. When Soshu had finished his bath, he retired to the Lute Room for the night. The radio was silent now; it had not been touched since Renko's disappearance, except by Mineyo, who would invariably switch it on when Soshu was out visiting a parishioner.

The moment Mineyo and Ryokun went to take their baths, the silence was broken, with Ryokun refusing to be washed, and Mineyo insisting that there was no point in having a bath at all unless one scrubbed oneself first. It had always been Mineyo who had bathed Ryokun, even before Renko left. 'The boy must have his bath early and get to bed before his mother,' she would say, and there was no arguing with her.

It was Mineyo who went to bed with Ryokun now, to help him to get to sleep, for though he was eight, he still could not sleep alone, any more than he could have stopped himself running to his mother and nestling in her breast when he came from school. But it was his mother's fault and Mineyo's, not his, that he could not grow out of these habits.

'Your mother's a wicked, wicked woman,' Mineyo would suddenly say, when they were in bed. Her breast replaced his mother's, for the boy to rest his hand upon; his loneliness vanished with the feel of its warmth, and sleep came easily.

'How could she run away and leave such a lovely little boy—Granny can't get over it . . . you must forget all about her, Ryokun, that wicked mother of yours. . . .' He had to be careful, Ryokun thought. Had she heard about the meeting at school? He did not know the ways grown-ups have of keeping things secret from each other.

In the porter's room, Renko watched him silently as he ate the *kintsuba* cakes she had brought him. Then she got up to go.

'I'll come again darling! Be a good boy and do what Granny tells you.'

She seemed to feel guilty towards Mineyo for what she had done, and Ryokun, in spite of his ignorance of what had driven her to leave Butsuoji, sensed vaguely that his mother was in the wrong. But he was on her side, however wrong or wicked she might be, and longed to defend her; he was so much closer to her than to Mineyo.

'You won't be lonely, Ryokun, darling: Daddy and Granny will look after you.' Ryokun shut his eyes and tried to sleep. Mineyo certainly believed she was capable of taking Renko's place, and that the boy could not be lonely so long as he had his grandmother. It was she who had always looked after him; as a baby he had scarcely ever left her arms, except at feeding-time, and after he was weaned there was even less for Renko to do. All this did not mean that Ryokun himself became more attached to her than to his his mother; but Mineyo thought of him as entirely hers, and was convinced nobody could have raised him but herself.

A few nights before Renko's disappearance, when the two women were alone together, Mineyo had repeatedly complained about her daughter's conduct. 'There isn't a soul in the parish who doesn't know about your goings-on. Just how humiliated do you think Soshu feels when he goes visiting? It's time you thought about him a bit—and there'll be trouble if you don't, I can tell you!' Mineyo was referring to Renko's succession of visits to the theatre. 'Not that you were a very virtuous wife even before . . . disappearing without telling a soul and staying away for two or three nights like you did. It wouldn't matter so much if it were a layman's family—but living in a temple, depending on the parishioners for everything, even for food, so that we can't lift a finger without wondering what their gossip'll make of it—anybody would think you've been doing your best to make enemies of the lot of them!'

Pale but determined, Renko sat with bent head, making little attempt to defend herself. 'And then your shameless chasing after that actor—that's no secret, either. . . .' Mineyo was in a hurry to force a crisis between them. 'You didn't even have the intelligence to be careful about it—seven nights watching the same play from the same seat . . . as if you wanted everybody to know you were being unfaithful!' Of any mention of the real causes of trouble in the family—what domestic unhappiness it might be that tempted Renko to seek relief outside her home, why she had followed the Kabuki actor from theatre to theatre, and why Soshu was so deeply distressed—Mineyo seemed afraid; she dwelt only on the consequences of Renko's love affair, never on its origin. 'A grown woman, too . . . it's not as though you were just a chit of a girl any more. You know what that means, don't you? You've made your own bed and you'll have to lie on it.' Mineyo's manner was unusually tense and strained, as if it was a stranger whose conduct she was denouncing, and not her only daughter. Diffident by nature, Renko had never been good at putting her own point of view; a weakness of which Mineyo now took full advantage.

'I've made up my mind . . .' Renko murmured. Mineyo was careful not to push her abuse to the point of telling her openly what she was impatient for her to do. It was enough to goad her until she made the decision herself. To remove Renko, to cut her off utterly from the family, was Mineyo's object. To wreck Renko's life, to destroy her even—but not by lifting a finger against her. She must merely be driven by degrees to desperation, forced to tie the noose herself. . . .

'And what might that mean?' Mineyo pretended not to know what was going on in her daughter's mind. Renko was silent for a while. It would have been dangerous to torment her further, and Mineyo merely stared coldly at the tired face opposite her, aware of Renko only as a being she hated, no longer as a daughter—hardly even as a woman; Renko was nothing to her now but a creature, a rival animal of her own sex, with no weapon but her youth. Age apart, Mineyo knew she suffered little by comparison with Renko. The two women might be sisters, people were always saying; Mineyo looked so much younger than her years.

'If I go away now, there'll be nothing for the parish to get upset about, will there?'

A reaction almost physical in its intensity prevented Mineyo from replying at once.

'So I've decided. . . .'

Mineyo was calm and serene now, as before. 'Well! So you've really made up your mind that's the only way?'

Triumph in her eyes, she looked at her daughter who was trembling slightly. Of her own free will she had spoken the words Mineyo had determined to make her speak; and Mineyo tasted a victory she had begun to dream of nearly twenty years before.

Soshu was only twenty, and still a student, when he was adopted into the temple family. It was Mineyo who paid his fees and enabled him to finish college. Mineyo, who had lost her husband a year earlier, was thirty-four, and Renko a school-girl of eleven, with no idea of course, that Soshu was intended for her husband. The young widow's beauty was striking enough to be admired even by other women. It was her habit to emphasize her attractions by always wearing long and unusually close-fitting kimonos, which led to murmurs that she was no lady for a temple.

She often went to see Soshu in his lodgings in Kyoto, ostensibly to see how his studies were going, but in reality to indulge the tempting visions that his good looks—he might have been a film star—and the knowledge that he was soon to come to Butsuoji as her son-in-law excited in her. One meeting had been enough for her to decide on the adoption. Soshu, the second son of a priest of an important temple of the Takada branch of the True Pure Land Sect, to which Butsuoji also belonged, was a quiet and pleasant, but weak young man. Mineyo was told by some of his friends, students older than himself, how he had come to them in distress, much to their amusement, because a girl student at a sewing school near his lodgings had sent him an anonymous love letter, and he didn't know what to do with it. One day when Mineyo was visiting Kyoto, she had to send for a doctor and have an injection for a sudden attack of stomach pains. Soshu spent the evening nursing her. The pains came on again in the middle of the night, but this time Mineyo would not let Soshu send for the doctor. Her lovely face twisted in pain, she insisted he himself should massage her stomach. It was not long before Soshu suspected the genuineness of the pains Mineyo had complained of; but their secret intimacy had begun that night.

When Renko was eighteen, the parishioners urged Mineyo to make arrangements for her marriage to Soshu, but she said it was still too early. To similar hints a year later she gave the same answer. Another year passed, and as Renko was twenty and Soshu twenty-nine, Mineyo could no longer find an excuse to put the wedding off. She herself was now forty-three. Renko, who had grown up knowing nothing of the world or of men, became the young priest's wife. Mineyo began to hate her daughter.

'You could blame it on my being so young, I suppose—but that doesn't make what I've done any less wrong. . . . I'll take whatever punishment I deserve. I can't go on deceiving her any longer,' Soshu said to Mineyo repeatedly; but this only inflamed her the more against Renko.

Ever since his student days the Lute Room had been Soshu's. Mineyo and her daughter had always slept together in the annexe that had once been a storeroom, but after the wedding Mineyo moved to a room in the main part of the house, across the corridor from the Lute Room. Renko still slept in the converted storeroom, alone. Soshu knew he was being watched, like a prisoner in a cell; yet he could not bring himself to say in so many words that he wanted to go to his wife in her room at the end of the long corridor and sleep with her. Every night the newly-married Renko slept alone—marriage was always like that, for all she knew. Mineyo spent more time than ever on her toilet. Such maternal feeling as she had left was steadily fading, and the outward gentleness she still showed towards Renko merely served to veil a burning hatred. But of this only Soshu was aware. Under silent pressure from Mineyo, Soshu's behaviour towards his wife grew cool. Inwardly, he longed to tell her of the real state of his feelings; but it would have meant confessing the whole story of his relations with Mineyo since his student days, and this he had not the courage to do.

In the middle of the night a soft, scarcely audible footfall from the corridor would wake Soshu, and plunge him into a trough of dark, conflicting feelings. Silently the door slid back. Scent filled the room; behind it, provocative through the darkness, a figure moved across the mats towards him. Not knowing how to get rid of her, Soshu pretended to be asleep; but once she lay down beside him he could resist no longer. A helpless prisoner of the lust she had inflamed, his body no longer his to control, he lacked the courage even to cry out against his seducer. Self-disgust, remorse, shame, fear of the future, guilt towards his wife—all such feelings were swallowed up in the fires of lust, whose steady devouring of his body he could sense, but never stop. Mineyo knew Soshu's weakness perfectly. He had always been like that, surrendering instantly to her stronger will, ever since she had first known him as a student. She was convinced she could do whatever she pleased with him.

The stillness of the small hours at Butsuoji was profound. Filling the whole expanse of buildings and compound, for any member of the temple household who chanced to wake in the middle of the night it was like a sudden breath of icy air, chilling mind and body alike. Renko slept with Ryokun. Sometimes a strange cry, apparently from an inner room in the main part of the house, would wake her suddenly. She shivered; it was like a moan of pain. In a temple, concerned in an almost professional way with death, occurrences remote from the everyday world are not necessarily to be wondered at, as Renko knew. When a parishioner was ailing, so Mineyo had often told her, his spirit would visit the temple to report his coming death. In the night, steps would be heard along the corridor; and the following morning news of a death would invariably be brought to Butsuoji. But of this Renko had no personal experience.

The first night she heard the moan, it was not repeated. Perhaps it was an illusion, she thought. Next morning, when she spoke about it to Mineyo and Soshu, Mineyo merely laughed, saying she must have been hearing things in her sleep. Soshu turned away. No secret can be kept in an ordinary house of three or four rooms. The temple house, however, with its long corridor that was dark even in the daytime, its many rooms, including some not in everyday use, and its unusually small family, was ideal for intrigue; and so the hidden relationship could be continued and deepened. For more than ten years Butsuoji enabled Mineyo to keep the secret, its old-fashioned style of architecture a silent spur to her desires. No one discovered the truth. No one resisted Mineyo's domination of Butsuoji, and by her management of the temple household she made sure that nothing interfered with her. Shoju had been in the way; he was forced to go and live in the little house in the cemetery. Soshu's occasional moods of self-reproach, far from weakening her passion for him, merely made it burn more intensely. 'Which of us has known you longer?' she would ask him, as if she had some natural right to urge her claim against Renko's. Haven't I known you for ten years, and done more for you than she ever could?' At last Soshu began to speak of the horror he felt at his sin, but Mineyo insisted that such talk was nothing but selfishness on his part. Soshu's marriage and the birth of the child belonged only to the world of appearances, of conventional morality, whose claim made it necessary that Mineyo should have a grandchild; but neither of these two events made her feel that she was beaten. Soshu and herself were bound by deeper, older ties.

But Ryokun was certainly a delightful child, and Mineyo determined to make him her own. Taking advantage of her own experience as a mother, and Renko's ignorance and uncertainty as to how to treat her first child, she succeeded completely in attaching him to herself while he was still little more than a baby. A grandson, at least, could never be a rival, or harm her in any way; he was a speaking toy, a doll with wants and feelings, no more. Of rights as a person, Ryokun had none whatever, as far as Mineyo was concerned.

Until the baby was born, Mineyo was content with Soshu alone. Anyone else was unwanted. But when Ryokun appeared, he became as necessary to her as Soshu himself. She was convinced, too, that Renko was not to be trusted with his upbringing: only she herself could manage him properly. Mineyo's constant dream was to find some way of driving Renko away. If she did go, she was young enough to be able to start a new life on her own. For Mineyo, however, Butsuoji would be her last home, and she wanted to make sure now that she would be able to live on there undisturbed until her death. With Renko out of the way, father and son would support her, if only for form's sake, so that once she established her power over Soshu and Ryokun, there could be no anxiety about the future.

Yet she could not openly persecute Renko. The girl, after all, was her own and only child; whatever coolness or even hatred or actual clashes there were between them could have been ten times worse if they had been related merely by marriage and not by blood. They would quickly forget all about the moments of friction, too, where a mother and her daughter-in-law would have hoarded every detail of the most trivial quarrel. Mineyo could not get rid of Renko by sheer cruelty.

One night Renko was woken up again by the moaning sound from the direction of the Lute Room. She had heard it several times before, but it was only now that she recognized it as her mother's voice. Ryokun was three then.

'It's unnatural for a husband and wife to sleep apart like we do, at opposite ends of the house. Ryokun would be happier if his Mummy and Daddy were together,' Renko said to Soshu, using Ryokun as a pretext; she could not bring herself to question him directly about the voice in the night. I'll ask Mother what she thinks—it's the same to me either way,' was all Soshu would reply. Renko felt as if she were standing on the edge of an abyss, in whose dark depths her words were lost before they could reach him.

'But we are husband and wife, aren't we? What concern is it of Mother's?'

'I've always discussed things with her, that's all. I've no objection myself—but I wonder whether Mother could sleep if I went to your room; she'd be all alone in the main building, and in that big shrine-room, too. . . .'

The words gave Renko the feeling that Soshu could only see things from Mineyo's point of view; she and Ryokun were secondary now. She tried to think when this change in him had taken place. He seemed afraid of Mineyo—it wasn't that he meant to neglect his wife, but Mineyo's domination of Butsuoji was so complete that he was no longer free even in this respect. But of the real nature of Soshu's feeling of constraint towards his mother-in-law, Renko remained unaware.

'Then Ryokun and I will come and sleep in the Lute Room. . . .' Short, simple words. For Renko as she spoke them, they seemed to represent a decisive, almost a desperate step, a choice from which there could be no going back. Soshu turned his eyes away, unable to conceal his sense of guilt. Mineyo could not, however, resist Renko's and Ryokun's move to the Lute Room, the ostensible reason being that Ryokun had asked for it. To speak out against her daughter, to bring their quarrel into the open, might be fatal to herself, and this she was determined to avoid. She said nothing, therefore, though inwardly furious at what she told herself was Renko's spitefulness. From Renko's own point of view, of course, her appeal to Soshu had been merely an act of protest against treatment she could no longer bear; but for Mineyo it was perverse, unnatural, a revolt against her maternal authority.

When Renko, now in the Lute Room, woke in the middle of the night, she would sometimes hear Mineyo walking past the half-transparent sliding doors, on her way to the toilet at the end of the corridor. Her footsteps were careful, almost soundless, but not because she was anxious to avoid disturbing Renko and Soshu in their sleep: her movements silhouetted dimly on the paper of the doors, showed that she was spying on the couple.

'It's her turn to be watched now,' thought Renko. But in fact Mineyo was still the real watcher, crouching in her nightdress in the corridor. One night, after Soshu and Renko had gone to bed, Mineyo came to their room, a gaudy coat thrown over her nightdress.

'There was a strange noise from the temple just now. It might be a burglar—won't you go and see, just to make sure?' she said, addressing Soshu.

'Did you hear anything, Renko?' said Soshu, turning to his wife.

'No, nothing—Mother must have imagined it.'

'There *was* something suspicious, I tell you, and it makes me nervous—I can't sleep. I'll go and have a look myself—'

Soshu had to get up. 'I'll go and see.'

'I'll come with you, then,' said Mineyo. Sitting up in bed, Renko listened to their footsteps as they walked along the corridor to the temple. Away in the distance there was a faint hum of truck engines—the night traffic on the new highway. She heard Soshu and Mineyo cross into the temple, and then all was silent. They must be trying to find where the noise had come from. In former times they would have had only candles to light them, but now there were five electric lights in the temple hall, controlled by a switch in the corridor, and others in the dark passage behind the alter. They must be turning on all the lights, Renko supposed, and looking in every corner.

She sat on the bed, smiling at her mother's imaginings. But—they were taking time, it struck her; they should not have taken so long, even if they were checking every part of the building. She turned pale, an ugly suspicion flickering at the back of her mind. Getting up from the bed, she walked noiselessly down the corridor as far as the entrance to the temple. They had not switched on the temple lights, then. There was no sound from the hall, whose interior lay hidden in a profound, oppressive darkness. Where could they have gone? There was no sign of them anywhere, no whisper, even. Renko's heart beat violently; a choking sensation made her want to cry out. Feeling as if her feet could scarcely support her, she walked back along the corridor, reached the Lute Room at last, and sank down limply on the bed, as if abandoning her body to an endless yielding darkness. It was some time later when she heard Soshu and Mineyo returning. Their footsteps were quiet and unhurried, as though they had found nothing amiss in their search.

'It was just my fancy after all, I suppose.'

'It must have been—there certainly wasn't anybody there.'

'Sorry you had to get up!'

'That's all right. Goodnight.'

Mineyo went back to her room. 'It was Mother's mistake—there was nothing,' said Soshu to his wife, coming in from the corridor; but Renko lay on her side, apparently asleep. For a while Soshu stood looking down at her shoulder, but said no more. Her pretence of sleep had not deceived him.

It was after this incident that Renko began to make frequent visits to her high-school friend, sometimes staying overnight, and sometimes taking Ryokun with her, too.

'Renko knows—of course she does, and has done for a long while. It would be impossible for her to speak about it to any of the parishioners, and that's why she goes and visits this friend of hers. It's too horrible—we can't hide it any longer!' The feeling that a crisis was inevitable tortured Soshu. Yet he could not wrench himself free of the idea that it was Mineyo, not himself, who must find a solution.

'What do you mean—what does Renko know?'

'It's my cowardice that's the trouble. . . .'

'Are you going to tell her everything, then? *Can* you—*can* you tell everything?—the whole story, starting when you were still a student in Kyoto—when she was a girl of ten?'

'I am a servant of the Buddha,' said Soshu with a faint, bitter smile. 'And a slave to the lust of the flesh. I admit it. But isn't it just such people as us that St Shinran longs to save?'

A very convenient argument, thought Mineyo. But as far as Soshu was concerned, there was something else, something which she herself possessed, of greater power and offering more bliss than the promises of St. Shinran. More than ten years had slowly matured her ascendancy over Soshu. Better than Soshu himself, she knew his weakness; how much more susceptible he was to an appeal to the reasonable, the practical, common-sense view of things, than to the claims of the religion he professed.

'We must let Renko do exactly as she wants. If she finds something or somebody to make her forget her troubles for a bit, that will suit all of us.' Mineyo seemed to be certain that no crisis would ever disturb their existing relationship. Perhaps because she foresaw what was soon to happen, she made little attempt to scold Renko for her conduct. Renko, moreover, would never have the courage to question Soshu and herself outright; of this Mineyo was perfectly aware. She was confident, too, that she knew what outlet Renko's resentment would find when her suspicions became too strong for her to ignore. Renko's nights away from home merely confirmed her expectations.

'If by any remote chance she ever does say anything to me, I shall simply deny it—she's never seen us together, after all. The same thing applies to you—promise me you'll deny everything, no matter what she says!'

Though she scolded her to her face, Mineyo was secretly pleased when Renko got to know the Kabuki actor and began to follow him from theatre to theatre.

'I've no right to blame Renko—it's my sin that's driven her to it.'

'Another of your cowardly moods! Now things have gone so far, all we have to do is to make up our minds to do without her; and that shouldn't be difficult. She's not wanted here any more. Suppose you blurt out everything—do you think it wouldn't affect the temple? You should have told her about it when you got married, if you were going to tell her at all. To talk about confessing everything *now*, when you were quite content to keep it a secret then and have been ever since—it's too selfish altogether. And anyway, even if Renko goes, there'll still be Ryokun. It's him we must think of; it's our duty to bring him up properly.'

It would have been easy to point in turn to the selfishness behind her plausible reasoning; but Soshu's weakness, like an evil spirit whispering always "Save thyself", kept him silent. His impulse to confess was certainly genuine, but he had not the courage to carry it out; he was terrified of the congregation getting to hear of what he had done, for it would obviously jeopardize his whole position at Butsuoji. The fact that he was a priest made it all the worse, a disgrace that would stick to him for the rest of his life. Soshu was very conscious of this, and from fear of such exposure he let the days go by without saying anything to Renko. To confess now would be like tying a noose round his own neck, and would need no less courage. In spite of a continuous longing to tell the truth, he could not bear the thought that it would mean his own extinction from the world of which he had grown to be a part. He would never be able to attend any meeting of priests again, people would jeer at him, it would become impossible to show himself anywhere, in the end he would be driven to suicide. . . . The urge to save himself—it was always a match for the conscience that tortured him with the knowledge of his sin. Popular with his congregation, respected by his fellow-priests; fine-looking, so that girls could not help looking round when he passed them in the street—he was all these things; other people besides the parishioners felt an interest in the handsome priest of Butsuoji. How could he throw away the good opinion people had of him? His authority would vanish, of course, immediately the secret was known. The way they would treat him then, that would be so hard to bear; like a dead rat tossed into a ditch. . . . Forced to leave his temple, exiled to some remote spot where he knew no one—suicide would be no worse. Even in the temple where he had been brought up they would probably refuse to have anything to do with him. To yield to his impulse to confess was impossible. It was easier after all, to side with Mineyo, to keep up the pretence that there was nothing between them. He had done this for nearly twenty years; there was no reason why it should suddenly become more difficult now.

On the nights when Renko did not come home Soshu was drawn irresistibly to her mother's room, as if he had been merely waiting for the freedom her absence brought. Yet it was with disgust at his own weakness that he went. Night after night with Mineyo corroded his determination to confess; it gave way by degrees to a brazen readiness to abandon himself wholly to his lust. The poison had been working in his system for so long. Had the affair begun after his marriage, he might after all have found the courage to make a clean breast of it to Renko. But now long habit had produced its own inertia, and after all these years it seemed ridiculous that he should suddenly reveal the secret now. Gradually the inner tension that had kept his spiritual life from decay began to slacken.

On her return from a visit to the actor, Renko of her own accord went back to sleeping in the converted store-room. Nobody said anything, which made her feel more than ever that she could no longer bear to live at Butsuoji. Of all this Ryokun knew nothing; he slept as before with his hand in her breast.

'There's no point in talking it over with the congregation now,' said Mineyo to Renko on the evening before she left for good. 'It would only lead to trouble. You'd better leave quietly, without telling anybody outside—people will forgive you once they're faced with the fact that you've actually gone. Nobody will run after you then—there'd be no point in it, anyway. But you said you were going to settle things your own way, and I can't tell you what to do. You can do as you please, I won't interfere.'

If she had chosen to defy Mineyo, Renko would have been in a stronger position than her mother. The two hundred families that made up the congregation would have taken her part. But Renko had already given herself to another man, and it was her own guilt that she felt most keenly now.

I shall have to leave the temple—there's no other way, she thought. It never occurred to her that her mother had driven her to take this decision; she only felt that there was no tie of affection to keep her there any longer.

'I'll go to one of my school-friends for the time being.'

'You'd better leave at night when you do go.' Mineyo had made sure that Soshu was not present at this conversation. There was no knowing what he might have said when confronted with his wife's decision. Nor did she have any intention of telling Soshu that she herself had all but forced Renko to take it. Like all weak men, he was capable of sudden bursts of courage that even he himself could not understand; and however short-lived such a mood might be, her plans would be irretrievably damaged if it impelled him to tell Renko the truth. 'It's Ryokun I'm worried about. . . .' Slipping her hands from her knees and placing them side by side on the floor-matting in front of her, Renko sat with bent head, as though asking forgiveness. Her body was shaking.

'Please . . . please look after him!' She could hardly force the words out.

'Don't worry about Ryokun. I'll bring him up a fine boy, I promise you.'

'It's only Ryokun I'm . . . Ryokun. . . .'

Renko's hands would no longer support her, and she fell forward on to the floor, sobbing violently. Unmoved, Mineyo stared coldly at Renko's slender neck, as if her eyes could push it away from her. As always, her pencilled eyebrows and faintly reddened lips gave her a youthful appearance and charm that clashed oddly with the harsh realities to which their conversation was directed.

'Ryokun will wonder where I've gone, he'll look for me . . . it's that I . . .' stammered Renko, the words breaking through her tears.

'It's not as if he wasn't used to your being away at night, anyway. Don't worry, I'll have him to sleep with me.'

'Ryokun . . . I can't help worrying. . . .'

'Ryokun will succeed Soshu as priest here. Butsuoji's the most important thing. You really ought to think a bit more about the temple—you were born here after all. Don't let what you've done hurt the temple and spoil its good name! It's easier to say now you've made up your mind to leave. I'm asking you seriously, Renko—when you go, go quietly, without any fuss or upset. Remember that, please!'

So Mineyo got her daughter to leave their home after her adultery with the actor—for the sake of the temple and its good name. Renko did not stop weeping that night till long after Ryokun was asleep.

4

Punctual to the minute, Father Soshu entered the house of Yosuke Tachi, one of his parishioners. The little single-storey house consisted of only three rooms, one behind the other, with an earthen passage running along one side; kitchen, lavatory and store-room were in an outhouse. A tiny strip of soil served for a garden. Tachi's neighbours were a *senbei*[1]-seller on one side and a teacher of Japanese dressmaking, who taught about twenty pupils in his two-storey house, on the other.

Soshu was shown to the middle of the three rooms. Tachi had been working in the garden, but the moment Soshu arrived he washed his hands and came to join him. He was still in his working clothes, black trousers and a jacket buttoned up to the neck.

'It's good of you to come.'

Tachi was a slightly-built man of fifty, with a lean, taut-looking face, and white hair which he kept cut short in workman's style.

'I suppose you've taken a day off from the factory today?'

'Just the afternoon, that's all.' It was the twenty-third anniversary of his father's death—Whenever I'm with this man I feel I'm in debt to him somehow. . . . I wonder why, thought Soshu. At twelve Tachi had left school to take a job in a porcelain factory, in order to help support his family, and had worked there ever since. During and since the war he had served continuously as Chairman of the union which the workers in the factory, of whom there were about three hundred, had formed before the war. Yet there was nothing of the belligerent or fanatical union leader about him; he was pleasant and friendly, and one would not have taken him for anything other than an ordinary worker. Popular with his fellow-workers, he was respected and trusted by the management. People

1 Japanese crackers.

were always surprised at his lively intelligence and remarkable fund of knowledge, which enabled him on occasion to carry on a theoretical argument for hours on end.

While his wife was serving tea, Tachi opened the family shrine which was kept behind the sliding doors of the cupboard, lit the candles and began to burn incense. A devout and wholly sincere believer, one would say. 'Perhaps it's his being a Communist, one of the chief Communists in Tan'ami, that makes me feel not quite easy with him,' Soshu thought. There were a great many types of people in his congregation, but Yosuké Tachi gave him the impression of being different in kind from all the others. This was partly due to Soshu's ignorance of Communism, and if he felt constraint in Tachi's presence, it was largely because he never knew what Tachi—a materialist, presumably—thought about the spiritual truths with which Buddhism was concerned.

After burning incense, Tachi sat before the shrine in silence, his hands clasped in reverence to the dead, then bowed to Soshu as the latter put on a ceremonial stole marked with the Butsuoji crest. Tachi's son, his only child, had not yet come back from school. As always, the house was quiet and tidy.

Soshu turned to face the shrine. Holding his rosary so that the single big bead was uppermost and the tassel hung down over the back of his left hand, he placed his hands together in the attitude of worship. Behind him Yosuké and his wife murmured a *nenbutsu.* What did these services with the long scripture readings mean to Tachi, as a Communist Party member? He would ask him some day, Soshu thought.

Two accounts are given of the meaning and purpose of such services. According to the first, the relatives ask the priest to come and read the sutras for the benefit of the deceased. For this service —reading the sutras in the prescribed manner—the priest receives money offering from the family. The absolute purity of body, mouth and mind which is required of a priest on such occasions is not easy to attain, and Soshu was painfully aware that his life was a continual negation of this threefold demand. Especially since Renko had left him, his sense of guilt had become almost unbearable. At Butsuoji he bowed each day before the statue of Amida and the portrait of Shinran, to all appearances still the saintly priest. But on his visits to members of the congregation, he felt as if his very body was foul, exuding corruption.

The efficacy of the scripture readings is held to increase according to the rank and standing of the priest who performs them. Soshu still belonged to the lowest rank.

He began with the Three Sutras of the Pure Land Sect. Altogether the readings took about two hours. Usually there would be a pause in the middle, while the priest rested and sipped a little tea to keep his voice fresh. Yosuké Tachi and his wife sat listening till the end, Yosuké without once relaxing his erect, formal posture. The first of the Three Sutras, The Book of Eternal Life According to Buddha, is a translation from the Sanscrit original made by Sogi, Tenjiku Sanzo and Kosogai. It is always intoned, in the manner peculiar to the reading of the Buddhist sutras, and to Tachi, therefore, sitting behind Soshu, it was wholly unintelligible. To have to listen quietly for two hours must have been a considerable physical strain, but Tachi did not seem to find it difficult.

The curious doctrine that the efficacy of scripture reading varies with the rank of the priest-reader is said to be derived from the theory of *jiriki eko*. According to this belief, one seventh of the merit acquired by a memorial service of sutra-readings accrues to the soul of the dead for whom the service is held, the other six sevenths to the mourning relatives—on the analogy, perhaps, of the practice, common in ancient times, of pilfering en route sums of money despatched to an exile, so that the exile himself received only a small fraction of the original amount. The 7:1 proportion is purely arbitrary.

The other interpretation of these services is that they are expressions of gratitude to Amida Buddha for his mercy. There is no suggestion of acquiring merit for oneself by holding the service. The anniversaries of the death of a relative are regarded simply as occasions for deepening one's faith and giving thanks to Buddha for his infinite grace; and on these days, if the souls of the dead should chance to have fallen into the River of the Three Ways, Amida in his compassion will send his glorious light to shine upon them and help them in their distress. This salvation does not depend upon the merit of the reader of the sutras, or of whoever pays the offering to the temple for the service. It is wholly due to the grace of Amida.

The *nenbutsu* which Yosuké and his wife, sitting behind Soshu, murmured from time to time were like a refrain to the long intoning. Soshu had a fine voice, merely to listen to which was a sensuous pleasure, however incomprehensible the words themselves might be; a perfect instrument for intoning the scriptures.

A truck rumbled past along the old highway. Recognizing the priest's voice as he came home from school, Yosuké's son tiptoed into the room and sat down between his parents. Even passers-by on the road outside could hear Soshu. In this room Tachi and his fellow-workers would often spend all night discussing union business, yet nothing about the normal appearance of the room suggested that it was used for such a purpose. The sliding doors, with their paper panels, may have been old; but the house always had an atmosphere of order and cleanliness that harmonized perfectly with the intoning of the scriptures. Tachi's neighbours, who would hear both the union discussions and the sutra-readings, felt the latter suited the house far better than the former.

After the Three Sutras, Soshu began the Monruigé scripture, Tachi and his wife joining in as he did so. Soshu himself, of course, knew the text by heart, and so did they, having recited it, in Tachi's case at least, at regular intervals for twenty years or more. Nowadays fewer and fewer of the members of the Butsuoji congregation who lived in the commercial part of Tan'ami could remember the scriptures well enough to recite them together with Soshu; but in the farming households even the children knew them still. Tachi and his wife joined in again, though rather uncertainly, in the final hymns after the scripture. Their son sang, too. In the same way, Ryokun at Butsuoji had learnt the Monruigé and the Buddhist hymns from hearing them repeated night after night, sitting on his grandmother's knee. 'A shop-boy living near a temple learns to chant a sutra,' one of the Japanese alphabet cards says; and the boys had learnt sutras and scriptures such as these long before they were old enough to know what religion is—the more readily because of their simple musical settings, which are used to make chanting in unison easier.

"He looketh in mercy on all that call upon His Name, in every corner of the earth; He turneth not His people away, but watcheth over them with loving care. Let us worship Him, the Lord Amida is His name . . . ."

Finally, Soshu read from one of the Senshuji religious commentaries. His copy, which was paper-covered and bound with cotton thread in the old style, had been used by generations of Butsuoji priests; the cover was torn, and the faint smell of incense that clung to the pages made the book itself seem somehow holy. As the text was short, Soshu would often read it on his regular monthly visits to members of the congregation, when it was usual to choose a short sutra, too, such as the Amida-Sutra. The first section was by Abbott Gyoshu.

"Hear first the teaching of the holy Saint, our founder. Revere the laws of the Emperor and respect the Shogunate; obey the decrees of the governors of provinces, and of the lords of manors; perform faithfully your allotted part in public works; be unswerving in loyalty to your lord, fail not in duty to your parents. He that would escape the snares of the world, let him honour all Buddhas and Bodhisattvas, all spiritual beings; let him not speak evil of other ways there may be to salvation. What is the way to peace? Hear now the teaching of our master. To call on Amida with one's whole soul, casting upon Him and the power of His Original Vow[1] all our fear of death and the hereafter; to repeat His holy name of Amida in unwavering faith by day and by night, as long as our lives shall last; this is the true peace of the soul. Amen. Amen. . . ."

Ridiculously out-of-date the words must seem to a layman nowadays—especially when he is a Communist. . . . Soshu had never read from this particular book at Tachi's house before. Such words and style may have been current in Gyoshu's time, but "laws of the Emperor", "Shogunates", and "governors and lords of manors" meant nothing in twentieth-century Japan. To go on woodenly reading the same text generation after generation as the priests of Senshuji and all its subordinate temples did—such traditionalism was absurdly remote from real life, Soshu felt. It was one thing to preserve a text like this for its historical significance; but to recite it to members of a temple congregation, let alone to this particular member, was ludicrously inappropriate. When he reached the twenty-fifth chapter, Soshu moved a little to the left, so that he was no longer directly in front of the shrine, bent his head slightly, raised the book reverently to his forehead, and began to read again, holding the book now with both hands just below the level of his eyes:

"If we look earnestly upon the shifting vicissitudes of the world, whose sleeve will not be filled with tears? If a man ponder in silence this floating life of ours, sorrow will be engraved upon his heart. Is it not written in the sutra, 'All the manifold changes of Karma are but the passing phases of a dream'?" These, too, were the words of Abbott Gyoshu. "Ever-recurring are the seasons of the year, endless the passing of men through the cycle of birth and death. Truly all creatures, animate and inanimate, are bound by this law. He who sports with flowers on a spring morning, at evening he is laid low, as the north wind withers the pampas-grass; he who views with delight the autumn moon, at dawn he is hidden from sight in the clouds. . . . Ah, the sadness of things! For no man is his desire fulfilled: the tree would be still, but the wind never ceases; the father stays not in this world for his son to cherish him. . . ."

Tachi and his wife and son listened with bowed heads. Soshu turned to face them when he had finished reading, and after Tachi had thanked him formally for performing the rite, began to take off his stole. Mrs Tachi went to prepare a meal for him. In all the households of the temple congregation, it was customary to invite and entertain all the relatives to these memorial services, which are held on the seventh, thirteenth, seventeenth and twenty-third

[1] The Vow in which Amida is said to have declared that he would not accept enlightenment for himself unless he could be sure that all sentient beings would be saved by faith in him.

anniversary of the death of a member of the family. On this occasion, the twenty-third anniversary of his father's death, Tachi had invited no one outside the immediate family; but even so, there was no question of omitting the meal that was always offered to the officiating priest. Soshu merely tasted the food briefly, for politeness' sake. Afterwards, as was the custom with families living near Butsuoji, the dishes would be taken, just as they were, to the temple, an unexpected treat for the priest's family—yet not so unexpected either, since with two hundred or so families in the parish, one such meal would be brought to Butsuoji practically every week. Formerly the meal offered to the priest had been more lavish, and not strictly vegetarian. Even *saké* had been served sometimes. In those days Soshu had taken off his priest's gown and sat down in his plain white robe to take the meal in the house where he had held the service.

'Have you heard anything of Mrs Soshu lately?'

Soshu swallowed his embarrassment. 'I'm sorry the parish has had all this worry on my account—most distressing. . . .' It was six months now since Renko had disappeared.

'It may be only a rumour, of course—but I heard something about her having married again. . . .' Soshu felt as if the steady, deep-set eyes were reading every corner of his mind.

'Haven't you heard anything about it, sir?'

'Yes, I did hear something . . .' murmured Soshu, without mentioning who his informant had been.

'As far as the parish is concerned, the sooner she settles down the better for everybody, if she no longer has any connection with Butsuoji. . . . All the same, it's a bit strange she hasn't let the temple know, one way or the other.' Renko was incapable of supporting herself. She would have gone on visiting one friend after another, a burden to every family she appealed to; so everyone would be relieved if she found a permanent home, not least the family she had left. As it happened, a friend was found to make enquiries on her behalf, and finally she was married to a widower, the headman of a village about thirty-five miles from Tan'ami. The widower, who had been left with a baby boy, raised no objections about the way in which she had left her former home. A messenger from his family called at the temple one night. Mineyo received him, and sent him home without telling Soshu. 'Renko has nothing to do with Butsuoji now,' she explained. 'As far as I'm concerned, and so long as she doesn't trouble us here at the temple again, I haven't a daughter any more.'

No one was told of this visit. But somehow it had become known; the parishioners were beginning to ask Soshu about it when he visited them, though he said nothing about this to Mineyo. Gradually, during the six months since Renko's flight, a new purpose had been shaping itself in his mind, and the news of her remarriage made him long more than ever to carry it out.

'I wonder how her mother feels about it all,' said Tachi with a rather strained smile—to Soshu, the smile was sardonic, complex. 'She has very good health for her years, of course. It would hardly do, though, for a priest to go on indefinitely without a wife: we must think about that, after all. . . .' Mechanically, without the slightest desire to eat, Soshu took up the chopsticks. 'I ran into Mosuké Yamaji the other day. He was very worried about our priest having no lady.' Mosuké Yamaji, a stock-jobber who had built himself a palatial house, was the second most influential member of the congregation. His elder brother had a farm near the temple, and was one of the elders.

'There's talk of holding a general meeting about it; but they could hardly do it entirely on their own, without a word from you first.'

'Yes, I've been thinking I would need to consult with you all, when the time comes. . . .' At general meetings, by long custom, the parishioners sat in a fixed order. Without any word from the priest, it always happened that the wealthiest supporters of the temple, including, of course, Mosuké Yamaji, sat at the top, in an order which seemed to depend on the amount of local tax each paid. This group would include some who were no longer well-off, but came of old and well-known families. Yosuké Tachi invariably sat at the bottom, as the one who made the smallest money contribution to Butsuoji. Yet his voice carried weight, was decisive even, at every meeting. The others seemed to acknowledge tacitly that as a Communist he was in some way superior to themselves; but he was so gentle, so obviously honest, that everybody liked him. His family had belonged to Butsuoji for generations, and Tachi himself had been a member of the temple community since his childhood.

'It's your boy Ryokun I feel so sorry for. His Granny looks after him well, of course—a little too well perhaps—but there has been a real gap at Butsuoji since his mother went; such a lot depended on her. Even the temple has something dark about it now, it's not bright and cheerful like it used to be. Everybody in Butsuoji seems uneasy somehow—and that makes us feel awkward, too, when we go there.'

How sensitive they were to the changed atmosphere, Soshu thought. But the gloomy, oppressive feeling did not really belong to the temple—it was in himself; the darkness of his own spirit, communicating itself to the house. For Ryokun's sake, for his own sake, and for the good name of the temple, he would have to find some way out; to go on like this would never solve anything. What could he do? Soshu could think of no plan that he would have the courage to carry out. Schemes flashed through his mind, but they were all too fantastic—or too evil—to contemplate seriously.

When he returned to Butsuoji from Tachi's house, the old priest was sweeping up the withered leaves that had fallen on the mound in front of the porch. Acknowledging his greeting only with a nod, Soshu pushed back the heavy sliding door of the house. At once, as if in answer to the noise, footsteps came hurrying across the floor-matting. Mineyo took from him the purple crêpe wrapper containing the sutra books—the eager wife, welcoming her husband home. . . .

Soshu went to the little vestry next to the shrine-room to unrobe. Mineyo stood behind him to take his gown. 'Did you hear anything when you were at Tachi's?'

'Hear anything?'

Soshu turned round. 'No—nothing.'

'One shouldn't say anything bad of any of the Butsuoji people, of course—but I must say I've never liked Yosuké Tachi. One doesn't feel one can trust him, somehow. Some of the congregation detest him, too—some of the elders, even.'

5

A carpenter, one of the congregation, came to Butsuoji to remodel Mineyo's room. The idea was Mineyo's, and it was she who made all the arrangements. The carpenter and his men were in the house for about a month. Ryokun was delighted. Every day when he came home from school he went to where they were working and collected the chips and shavings, not to use them for anything, just for the fun of collecting. 'You'll get yourself covered in dust, boy!' the foreman would say, but Ryokun took no notice. They were putting in a new ceiling of elaborately carved ornamental planks on two levels, like the ceiling of an old-style Japanese restaurant. Fascinated, Ryokun watched the planks being nailed in position from above one by one, each one overlapping the next, till the carpenter came to the last one, which he slipped into place from below, without using any nails.

When the new cupboard was finished, the special sliding doors which had been ordered for it arrived. All the other cupboard-doors in the house were set in heavy wooden frames, but these had no frames at all. Ryokun had never seen such doors before. Mineyo explained that frames weren't fashionable now; but without them the doors looked naked, forlorn. The lower half of each was painted dark blue, which gave the room a smart and elegant look.

'Is this room going to be for you and me, Granny?'

'Yes, dear. I wanted to have the whole room remodelled. It'll feel quite different when it's finished. Just because it's a temple house, there's no need for every room to be bare and dull, and we might just as well as have *one*, anyway, that's not religious-looking, and that doesn't forever remind one of the temple. It's going to be lovely!'

Ryokun could not imagine what a room 'that wasn't religious-looking' would be like. As the doors and fixtures were finished, the whole atmosphere of the twelve-mat room was transformed: it was cheerful, dainty and attractive now. There was a big window looking on to the garden behind the temple, with a little cupboard below it, the top of which was low enough to use as a window-seat. Two chests of drawers—Mineyo's and Renko's—stood along one wall, together with a new tea-cabinet, and next to the window was a mirror-stand of the latest fashionable design. The middle of the room was occupied by a portable foot-warmer, covered with a gaily patterned silk eiderdown, and so placed that it was easy to make tea without getting up. Near it was a hexagonal iron *hibachi*[1] of Chinese make, much shallower than the usual type, with a silver *yakan* or kettle. Ryokun hated the noise this kettle made when it was boiling—it was not the thin, clear hum of an ordinary kettle, but a confused, agitated bubbling. Mineyo was very proud of her silver *yakan*.

Mineyo seemed to change together with the room. Now she was really young again. All the gnawing anxiety of years had been swept away, her desire achieved at last. Every night Soshu went to bed in the Lute Room just across the corridor from Mineyo and Ryokun, who slept peacefully with his hand in the fold of his granny's night-gown, touching her sagging breasts, as if she were really his mother. Nothing remained now to hinder her doing as she wished, no one whose presence was a constraint. She had Soshu entirely to herself. There was no longer any need to feel ashamed of her fifty-three years, and her complexion now was that of a woman of forty. To preserve the youthful texture and brightness of her skin, every night after bathing Mineyo rubbed her whole body with cream—first under her breasts, then her sides, buttocks, thighs and knees, and finally her breasts again, squeezing them with creamy hands as though to milk them. Five or six years ago, her age had begun to tell, and inevitably she had lost flesh about the hips and waist; but she had conceived the idea of massaging herself with cream before that, when she had happened to look at herself naked in the mirror one day. The skin at the back of her thighs, she had noticed then, hung loose, and looked somehow worn and faded. This sudden realization of the secret approach of old age had frightened Mineyo. In the mirror she saw too clearly how the years had begun to wither her. Ever since then she had struggled by nightly massage to reverse the process of decay and give her body back its youthful lustre.

Mineyo was sitting by the foot-warmer, listening to the radio.

'Madam. . . .' It was Shoju's voice, from behind the sliding door.

'Yes, what is it?'

1 A brazier, in which charcoal is kept burning on ashes. The *hibachi* is the usual form of heating in a Japanese house.

Still sitting respectfully in the corridor, Shoju slid back the door.
'A Mrs Tomoko Komiyama has called to pay her respects. I haven't seen her before.'
'Komiyama? I don't think I know the name. She doesn't belong to Butsuoji, does she?'
'She says she thinks Mr Yamaji may have mentioned her name.'
'Oh, yes, I remember. . . .' Mineyo's face took on a different expression—that of a shop-keeper preparing to welcome a customer. The visitor wanted to join the Butsuoji congregation. Apart from occasional applications from people with no previous connection with the temple, the only way in which Butsuoji acquired new members was when young people in the families of existing members married and set up new households. To canvass for new members was unthinkable, it was, in fact, forbidden, by agreement among all the temples. Occasionally a death in a family that had moved to the neighbourhood of Butsuoji might lead the surviving members of the family to join; but from whatever cause, increases in the congregation were extremely rare.
'She's brought her little girl with her.'
'Oh, I remember now—Father Soshu did tell me Mr Yamaji had spoken to him about her, but I'd forgotten all about it.' Mineyo showed no more interest in the visitor. Strictly speaking, if it was someone who wanted to join Butsuoji, Soshu or herself should have gone to the door in person to thank her for making the call; but the radio programme was amusing, and Mineyo did not want to get up from the foot-warmer.
'She says she would like to worship in the temple for a little while, but Father Soshu is out—'
'Then you'd better take his place, Shoju.'
On hearing from Shoju that the priest was not available, Mrs Komiyama crossed the courtyard and went up the steps into the temple with her little girl. She was wearing expensive high-soled leather sandals. Shoju went inside again, put on his robe, and hurried along the corridor, murmuring *nenbutsu*. When he came to the temple, mother and daughter were sitting side by side, looking forlorn and lonely in the emptiness of the great hall. The little girl seemed to be about seven or eight, her mother about thirty. The girl was staring in wonder at the unfamiliar world around her: the gilt on the massive pillars, the hanging oil-lamps and crane-shaped candle-stands, the shrine of Amida. Above them hung the great lantern. Still murmuring *nenbutsu*, Shoju lit the lamps behind the shrine and the candles in front, and taking two or three sticks of incense from the smoking bundle in his hand, set them in their stands. Then he sat down, a little to the right of the shrine, not directly in front of it, and began to chant *nenbutsu* in a louder

voice. Nudging her daughter to do the same, Mrs Komiyama put the palms of her hands together in the attitude of worship, the red coral beads of her tiny rosary shining like tiny points of fire against her kimono. Her hair, which was abundant, was parted down the middle, and showed a faint but distinct wave on either side, suggesting a love of order and neatness. Her eyes, and her daughter's, too, were unusually large. Shoju began to read a sutra. Such a visitor was a rarity nowadays. People would come to the temple only when they had to, on special occasions. 'Special occasions' meant mostly funerals, and the temple was felt to be of use only when somebody in one's family died. Otherwise people forgot about it completely, as they forgot about death when it was not confronting them directly. Gradually temples such as Butsuoji have come to be regarded as institutions existing for the soul purpose of holding funeral services. St Shinran, the founder of the Pure Land Sect, was concerned throughout all his agonizing struggles with the attainment of true enlightenment and spiritual peace in this life, rather than with the problems of death. Who has limited temples to their present role? Partly, perhaps, the ordinary laymen have been to blame; but far more so have been the priests.

The sutra-reading lasted nearly an hour. When he had finished, Shoju put out the candles and went and sat down beside Mrs Komiyama. 'I think you said you lived somewhere along Kiyota-cho.[1] May I ask just where?'

'You know the mud bridge, perhaps?' The slight unconscious smile that accompanied everything Tomoko Komiyama said reflected an innate gentleness. There was a feminine delicacy and grace, as of a flower waving faintly in a summer breeze, about her figure, but a hint of firmness, too, in the straight white line of the parting of her hair and the almost too close-fitting neckband of her kimono, precisely matching the shape of the neck.

'It's the second house from the bridge, on the bank.' Shoju tried to remember. The houses backed on to the river, which was quite narrow; along the other bank ran a road lined with willow-trees. He thought he knew the house. It was near the centre of the town. What was the relationship between this lady and Yamaji, he wondered. But there was no need to trouble himself with such questions. Mineyo's mind would instantly have begun working in that direction; but Shoju made a habit of suppressing any interest he might feel in the kind of things that Mineyo wanted to know. He would have to visit her house later, in any case, and would no doubt find out something about her then.

After thanking Shoju once more at the bottom of the steps, she

[1] A cho is a small subdivision or section of a Japanese town.

walked across the compound towards the temple gate. Shoju went back along the corridor to the house. Just then Soshu, dressed in the light robe a priest wears for travelling, entered the compound from the road. Mrs Komiyama passed him as she went out; they exchanged glances. So that's the priest of Butsuoji, she thought, and bowed, but without speaking. Soshu, who had never seen her before, returned the bow, and walked on towards the house. A strange face was no surprise; relatives of the parishioners would visit Butsuoji from time to time, and Soshu decided that that was what the woman and her little girl must be. Mrs Komiyama stood by the gate looking after him with a puzzled expression. The man she had met was not at all the kind of priest she had expected. Can it really be he whose wife ran away? she wondered. Mosuké Yamaji had told her what had happened at Butsuoji. That sort of thing was common enough in ordinary life, but in a temple . . . she had not been able to forget it.

Lonely, he seemed. The impression was a strong one, though he had merely passed by with a bow, hardly looking at her. How different he was from what she had imagined!

'Come *on*, Mummy!' Her daughter Shoko was tugging at her hand. For a moment she was flurried—then suddenly amused with herself for dwelling on Soshu's loneliness. The two walked away from the gate, leaving the temple compound to its spacious silence. Soshu heard from Shoju about the visit. 'So she's the lady Yamaji spoke of. You should have given her more of a welcome—asked her in to tea, at any rate. . . .'

Soshu knew no more than Shoju what connection there was between Yamaji and Tomoko Komiyama. Yamaji had merely said that she and her daughter had recently come to live in Tan'ami, and had asked him to introduce them to a temple of the Takada branch of the True Pure Land Sect, to which her family had always belonged. 'It's good when somebody as young as that comes to the temple of her own accord,' said Soshu.

'Her parents must be alive still, I suppose.'

Shoju explained where she lived.

'Kiyota-cho—isn't that near where Mrs Mimori lives?'

'Yes. I wonder what she does for a living. She can hardly be just an ordinary resident—all the houses round there are geisha-houses.' Mrs Naka Mimori, a widow of fifty-three, kept a geisha-house called the Mutsumi-ya.[1] She was an active member of the temple congregation.

Mineyo was calling Soshu. Taking off his stole, he went to her

[1] The name 'Mutsumi-ya' might be translated 'House of Harmony' or 'House of Friendship'.

room, where she was waiting to give him tea, and sat down by the foot-warmer, without changing his travelling robe. He always wore this robe when he had to go by bus to visit a Butsuoji family in an outlying district of Tan'ami—when a family lived near the temple, he would walk in his full priest's robes and gown.

Soshu looked at Mineyo as he sipped his tea. She was smiling. Always she would give him the same affectionate welcome, her expression seemed to say. Sadly, Soshu drank his tea.—Baldpated fool!—

Suddenly Soshu felt he knew the horror at his own weakness that had driven Shinran, the saint, to utter that agonized cry against himself. 'Fool'—sheer stupidity, imbecile weakness. "Baldpate"—the sign of failure to keep the commandments. . . . After Renko had gone, there had been a subtle change in Mineyo's voice when she came to his room at night; it made Soshu incapable of resisting or even of reproaching her. The fire of lust within him burned still more fiercely—yet the more fiercely it burned, the sharper his sense of loss and loneliness; as distant mountains show black under a fiery sunset sky.

He took up the newspaper, so that she could not see him. Mineyo poured him another cup of tea. Soshu did not read his paper. Thanks to the agony Shinran had been through, for seven hundred years priests like himself had been allow to marry and to eat flesh . . . they had taken advantage too easily of the faith that had cost the saint such great suffering. What brought this home to him now so powerfully was the presence of the creature before him, hiding her fifty-three years behind the youthful smile, the carefully rouged lips; more subtly seductive even than the mistress of the Mutsumiya geishas, conscious and proud of her sensuality, lust incarnate. Yet if her life was hardly more than animal, the same was true of his own. They were both loathsome, foul. He remembered a passage from the letter to the Corinthians:

> Now concerning the things whereof ye wrote: It is good for a man not to touch a woman. But because of fornications, let each man have his own wife, and let each woman have her own husband. . . .

Sex was a diabolic power, Paul had known; a power that no man could defy, however holy. De Gourmont had proclaimed in *The Physiology of Love*: 'To the authority of sex every son of woman must bow—saint and rake, ascetic and pervert.'

Buddhism recognizes five sins: the taking of life, theft, fornication, lying, and intemperance, or transgressing the prohibition against drinking and the eating of flesh. One can hardly live without ever committing any of the five—and today, even to mention such a possibility is to invite a derisive smile at one's inhuman notions. Man cannot escape from his earthly limitations by any efforts of his own—everyone accepts that nowadays; it is only common sense. But seven hundred years ago in Japan it was not so.

Shinran suffered because man cannot live without sin. 'Alas, I have learnt the truth,' he confesses in the *Doctrine, Works, Faith and Attainment*:

> The truth about Shinran, foolish baldpate that I am; how I foundered in the waters of passion, and wandered lost on the mountain of vainglory. I rejected the joy of the blessed, the delight of the knowledge of truth. How great is the pain, how bitter the shame!

The ordinary priests of Shinran's time were imprisoned in a rigid code of conventions and illusory doctrines. It is easy to imagine how infuriated they were by his marriage, which they denounced as a brazen sin. Many of them were committing the very same sin, but never openly. Shinran boldly showed the real power of sex in a man's life; by his own frankness and honesty he initiated the long fight for an honest view of every aspect of human nature. The spiritual struggle he experienced was something altogether different from the comparatively brief stage of temptation and resistance which every young priest has to go through.

Modern priests of the True Pure Land Sect like himself, thought Soshu, took it for granted that they could marry and have families. But to win that right for them Shinran had had to shed blood; it was his sacrifice alone that had made it possible for Soshu and his colleagues to lead normal lives. Soshu knew he must never again forget to be grateful to the saint. Till now he had been living in a dream. Seven hundred years earlier, what was accepted as normal now had been dangerous heresy.

—Yet the pain of what I have done is even greater than his, the shame more bitter. . . . He suffered so much just to marry, while I—my sin is his, but beyond that. . . . I drove her to leave me and took a woman who . . . who. . . . That he had chosen her, his wife's mother, to be the partner of his lust, made his sin far more deadly.

Soshu folded the newspaper and stood up.

6

Fire was burning merrily behind each of the five fuel-holes in the big kitchen stove at Butsuoji. Ten or twelve women were busily cooking a vegetarian meal and preparing *saké* for between thirty and forty people. More than half of the women were farmers' wives from the centre of the town. The occasion was the last autumn service in memory of St Shinran, which was now being held in the temple hall. The women were too busy cooking even to go and listen to the sermon. They were giving their services free, of course, and had contributed the rice they were boiling in the great pot. All the other expenses of the meal were taken from the money offerings the parishioners had made for the services. The meal itself, which was intended to celebrate the conclusion of the series of services, would be held in the big room of the temple house, and attended by the elders and their wives. A week before the services began the elders, each taking a part of the town, visited every family that belonged to Butsuoji, urging them to attend, and collecting contributions from those who would be unable to do so. Most of the elders were farmers who could not leave their fields in the busy season, so at Butsuoji the autumn services were held in the slack time after harvest.

For many years it had been the custom for the services to be organized in this way. The elders and their wives were the real managers of the temple affairs. They were also the link between Butsuoji and the two hundred families associated with it, and were therefore often in and out of the temple. Gradually, no one knew exactly when, such duties had become hereditary. From generation to generation the head of a family would be one of the elders, while his wife would have a natural authority among the women.

In both groups age carried the greatest weight.

'It's such a bad thing for the temple, too! They can't go on like this—something'll have to be done about it,' an old woman kneeling in front of the stove was saying to one of the tradesmen's wives, who was filling a big saucepan with vegetables. 'It's Ryokun I'm sorry for.'

'You're not the only one—and his being so small and innocent makes it all the more pathetic.'

'It'll be even worse for him when he grows up and gets to understand what's happened. He's the only son, after all, so he'll be the priest when his father dies.'

Miso soup was boiling in the big saucepan. The tradesman's wife who had been watching it knelt down by the old grandmother in front of the fuel-holes; their faces almost touching, the two chattered on, watching the hissing, crackling firewood. Appetizing smells drifted from the saucepan and the great rice pot up to the high beams and rafters, all of which were black with the soot of seventy years or more.

'Mrs Renko's leaving him was partly our fault, when you come to think of it.'

'That's right—all that talk of her mother's didn't seem to make sense then; the way she kept on saying it was too early, when anybody could see it was just the right time for them to be married. But we were wrong after all. If only we'd realized then. . . .'

The old woman looked up from the stove and glanced round the kitchen. Mineyo, she knew, had a habit of suddenly appearing at the most unlikely times and places; she was on her guard still, and listened intently to everything the elders and their wives said. They knew this, and were careful to say nothing pointed to Mineyo in person, though there was plenty of talk behind her back. Another reason for caution was that one of the women would secretly pass on to Mineyo what the others were saying—she alone had access to Mineyo's room, whether on temple business or not. Mineyo felt she could hardly lose by having such a contact, and accordingly her manner towards her was ingratiating. At least the woman might give her presents now and then. . . . If Mineyo was the secret autocrat of Butsuoji, she had an autocrat's weakness.

'Ryokun seems to have forgotten his mother.'

'He's only a child, after all. I expect he remembers her sometimes, though, even if he daren't say so. . . .'

'Maybe—he's a smart boy.'

'Clever at his books, too. He's got her face, hasn't he?'

'His eyes are his father's, though.'

Ryokun was a favourite with all of them. They pitied him for the blows they saw too clearly were in store for him, the inevitable suffering of which the boy himself knew nothing. Everybody was specially kind to him—even families that did not belong to the temple knew his story, and treated him with a gentleness they did not show to other children. Ryokun thought it was because he was a priest's son; but he was wrong. He was already the hero of a tragedy.

'If only Mineyo had been older, all this would never have happened,' murmured the old woman. 'She's too young and healthy altogether—lost her husband too early.'

'Even the elders are complaining. . . .'

'We haven't heard the last of it yet, that's certain.'

'Butsuoji means a lot to ordinary folk like you and me, whatever Mineyo has up her sleeve.'

'Aye, and our ancestors, too—they kept the temple going, I don't know how many hundreds of years. It's true, it means a lot to us: we haven't heard the last of this business yet.'

The tradesman's wife got up. 'He was playing here just now, wasn't he?'

'He went to the big hall.'

'Perhaps he wanted to hear the sermon.'

'The sermons are so beautiful, I dare say he can get something out of them. Even a child loves to hear a sermon when he's sad and lonely.'

Ryokun had certainly gone to the temple hall, but not to listen to the sermon—he would not have understood a word of it in any case. But these services made him happy in another way. While they were being held, the temple seemed less vast and lonely. Even Shoju was rejuvenated by the excitement, though he had more work to do during the services, and slept at Butsuoji, without going home to the cottage on the hill.

The day before the services were due to begin, Shoju put up a curtain of light yellow cloth over the steps in front of the hall, and another, of purple crepe and bearing the Butsuoji crest, at the entrance to the house. The house curtain hung down from the roof of the porch, heavy and impressive, with a white and gold plaited cord by which it could be raised and lowered. Another of Shoju's tasks was to hang ten paper lanterns in the compound between the temple and the road. There were special poles for the lanterns, each one with a tiny roof at the top, which Shoju fetched from the shed behind the house. Ryokun was too small to carry any of the poles; but he was content to follow Shoju with one or two of the folded lanterns, which was all he could manage. When they were drawn out to their full height, these lanterns were big enough for Ryokun to have hidden in. At nightfall Shoju lit them.

During the five days of the services, of which this was the last, the house was crowded from morning till night with leading members of the congregation. Ryokun wanted to eat with the women in the kitchen, but Mineyo had forbidden it, he could not understand why.

Two or three days before the services, the guest-room at the back had been swept and cleaned for the visiting preacher, who was to stay there till the services were over. To have a guest in the house was quite a thrill for Ryokun, and now and again during the five days he would go and peep into the preacher's room. The women took it in turns to wait on him.

The sanctuary and recess were brightly decorated, changing the whole atmosphere of the hall. Normally only three objects—an incense-burner, a lotus-vase, and a crane-shaped candle-stand—were placed on the offertory shelf in front of the shrine, but an extra vase and stand were added for the period of the services. Strictly speaking, three were all that was permitted in the Takada branch of the sect, to which Butsuoji belonged. In the *Takada Book of Observances* it is laid down: 'In our worship only three ornaments shall be allowed; the use of more than one vase or candle-stand is forbidden.' But at big services in memory of the founder, five were now normal, as an extra mark of respect. Gradually, in the generations following Shinran's death, forms and ceremonies had come to acquire an exaggerated importance in the temples.

Ryokun never tired of looking at the altar cloth hanging down in a triangle from the offertory shelf. Used only at the big memorial services, it was of red brocade, emblazoned with a dragon holding a jewel. The dragon, which stood out in relief from the cloth, was embroidered in gold thread from head to tail; its bulging eyes were of glass, its claws of shining metal. One clasp of those barbed silver claws could have throttled Ryokun. . . . There was terror in its lifelikeness, yet awe and splendour, too.

The cloth covering the offertory table under the portrait of Shinran was much smaller. It bore the figure of a phoenix, embroidered in red, blue, white, gold and silver. Under the portrait of St Shin'e was another table with a similar cover.

Over the shoulders of the crowd of seated worshippers Ryokun gazed at the embroidered dragon in the distance. Its claws gleaming, the dragon seemed to glare back at him.

After a while he raised his eyes to the shrine itself. On little wooden stands lay the flower offerings—two on each of the three shelves. Again the *Book of Observances* prescribes how the offerings shall be chosen: 'In the case of flowers and all other offerings for the shrine, reverence is the first principle. Only rice cakes and dumplings that are clean and pure may be offered. It is prohibited to offer cakes bought from common shops, or cakes of more than one colour.' But here again the ancient rules had been forgotten when the temples came to substitute the form of religion for the reality. They had not been faithful to their founder, to whom such formalism was anathema. Butsuoji was no exception. The glutinous red and white cakes that were stuck one above the other round hexagonal mounts on the three shelves were duly stamped with the crest of the Takada sect, but they were of poor quality, like the cheapest kind of *rakugan*.[1] Two other such mounts were stuck with small strips of red and green and white *mochi*,[2] each two inches long, carefully arranged in order so that no one colour predominated. There were also offerings of fruit on trays. Ryokun liked the cakes with the Butsuoji crest—they had a faint sweet flavour. The *mochi* was tasteless. After the services were over, the elders would distribute both cakes and *mochi* among all the members of the congregation, and since they were divided equally, irrespective of the size of each member's contribution to the expenses, no family would get more than two or three. On receiving these cakes, every family, including that of the Communist Yosuke Tachi, would first lay them for a while on the offertory shelf of its own shrine.

Ryokun was sitting in the shadow of one of the great pillars. Around him sat the worshippers, their faces sunburnt and deeply wrinkled. Resting their hands on their knees—earthy, peasant hands with the big nails that work in the fields develops—they were listening intently to the sermon. The preacher was a well-known priest, still in his thirties. His stole was constantly slipping off his thin shoulder, and he kept nervously pushing it back into place.

His pulpit was a small platform raised about three feet above the floor of the hall, covered with a half-size floor-mat. He moved continuously from one position to another, leaning now to his right, now to his left, waving the big sleeves of his gown and looking as though he were about to tumble at any minute into the crowd of worshippers below him. Clicking the wooden beads of his rosary with his left hand, he was intoning his sermon. The high-pitched chant reminded Ryokun of the *naniwa-bushi* he had heard on the radio in Mineyo's room—which was not surprising, as *naniwa-bushi* ballads originally developed as a popular version of the Buddhist religious songs. He had never heard his father intone from a platform, as the preacher was doing now. Perhaps his father could not preach like this, he thought.

This preacher was held in special respect even among his fellow-priests. His *naniwa-bushi*-like chanting of the sermon, Ryokun could see, was delighting the congregation. The rich, musical voice gave them a feeling of physical well-being. Their eyes fixed on his

1 A kind of dry cake.

2 Rice-balls made from a special kind of rice, pounded and steamed.

face, the rows of old peasant men and women swayed from side to side, following exactly every movement he made. He was a brilliant actor, a master of the technique of leading his hearers little by little to a state of ecstasy. Of all the great crowd packing every corner of the hall, not one looked anywhere but at the figure on the platform; they were hypnotised, spellbound, adoring . . . whenever he paused, as though it had been waiting for precisely that moment, a wave of murmured *nenbutsu*, like a great involuntary sigh, swept up towards him. Suddenly he would begin again, deliberately silencing the *nenbutsu* before they died away; after each pause his chanting would raise the emotions of his hearers to a new pitch of intensity.

The old farmers and their wives had no chance to think critically of what he was saying. Indeed such criticism would have been out of place—if they had listened with intent to criticize, they would never have experienced the blessedness of absolute trust in Amida. Sometimes the voice from the pulpit would be stern, reproachful. The preacher did what he liked with them—scolding, soothing, plunging them alternately into doubt or sadness or despair, giving sudden hints of glory, piling up arguments, or sweeping forward with a speed that left all argument behind. The evil spirits in their hearts were lured by his eloquence from their hiding-places, and driven away. Doubts were scattered; all were convinced, and felt themselves at peace.

The sermon was divided into three parts. With the handing round of collection bowls at the end of the first part, the atmosphere suddenly changed. The mood of exaltation induced by the sermon, the sense of doubts and anxieties dispelled—these were forgotten; as the bowls went round, men whose very faces had been serene and gentle a moment before resumed their usual expression of cunning. Each man wondered whether so-and-so had put more in the bowl than himself, whether he himself had given more than he need have done; noticing how cleverly so-and-so slipped the bowl to his neighbour without putting anything in at all . . . a sudden flash of materialism, like a spark from a smouldering fire.

The sermons were not free, after all. The preacher was paid according to the amount collected before and during the services. A famous preacher received more than one who was unknown. Many more people would come to hear him—the hall would be filled to over-flowing, so it was obvious that the collection would be substantial. The priest who was giving the sermon at Butsuoji had preached at each of the big services there for two or three years now. Those few of the congregation whom the sermon in the temple had left unsatisfied accompanied the priest, after it was over, to his room in the house. There were usually three or four who pursued him with questions. One of the group, however, followed him from the hall for another purpose. Mrs Kushimoto, a widow, and a member of the Butsuoji congregation, invariably went to his room the moment he had finished his sermon. She was a small woman of about fifty, too timid to express her opinion on anything, let alone question a preacher. She would serve him tea and fuss about his room in a vague pretence of looking after him, which was entirely unnecessary, as the elders' wives were waiting in the house for that very purpose. People soon began to talk about it.

'Haven't you heard—about the widow Kushimoto? It's been going on quite a while now. . . .'

'She might just as well be his wife, the way she insists on doing everything for him—it's ridiculous.'

'They can't even keep it a secret—everybody knows about it.'

From the widow's attitude when she listened to the priest answering questions, and from his own attitude while he was doing so, it was obvious enough that neither of them had freed themselves from the bondage of the passions. Obscurely, perhaps unconsciously, the widow was seeking something other than the words of grace; so intense was her expression as she gazed at the preacher on the platform.

That night, the elders and their wives took supper together in the temple house. Soshu ate with them for a while, but presently got up and left. Ryokun was in Mineyo's room. Mineyo called Soshu to her.

'The widow Kushimoto's still in the guest-room, you know.' The preacher was to leave early next morning. Soshu made no answer.

'Like a cat in the mating season! Aren't you going to say anything to her?' said Mineyo, hate in her voice. 'It's disgusting, really—and everybody knows about it, too. She makes herself a laughing-stock every time that priest comes, her eyes change colour, they say. . . .'

7

In spite of his being more than ten years younger than herself, the widow Kushimoto had fallen inexplicably under his spell—the expression is appropriate enough, for nothing in her past life as a tradesman's wife in Tan'ami had been in the least abnormal or given rise to any comment. Since her husband's death she had been known merely as an honest, rather timid and not very attractive widow; incapable by nature, one would have thought, of doing anything interesting enough for people to talk about. But even if she appeared to behave now with a forwardness that she had never shown the slightest sign of before, she could hardly be held responsible for her actions. She did not realize what she was doing.

Mineyo saw into the widow's feelings better than anyone else. An obsession that took absolute control of one's life—with painful clarity, Mineyo understood the woman's crude approaches, so disgusting at her age. While the preacher was stopping at Butsuoji the widow could not bring herself to stay quietly at home. She would come into the compound, though she had no business with anyone in the temple, stand looking at the hall, wander into the cemetery behind it and stare at her family grave, or walk up and down the roads on the east and south sides, peering through occasional gaps in the hedge at the guest-room on the other side of the garden. There was nothing unusual about her dress; to all appearances she was merely out for a stroll. But her eyes were feverish, with a strange fixed expression. It was really absurd, passers-by thought, stopping to look round as they noticed her peering through the hedge—all very well in a child; but for a widow of fifty-three. . . . She was unconscious of their stares, however.

The timid, quiet and steady widow was changing in her very nature. Her face took on a youthful gloss, as though from some inner secretion. From his room, the preacher would sometimes catch sight of her looking through the hedge, and call out to her to come to the house. Her family said that they had told her not to go to Butsuoji while the priest was staying there, except during the sermons. Her eldest son, in particular, was worried about what people were saying, but his mother would not listen. Some said he had even tried to confine her to her room. In fact, however, it was impossible to control her movements strictly enough, and she was still free to go out whenever she wanted. The family had had enough of scolding her—when they did so, she merely burst into tears; and they could hardly use force to keep her at home.

One would have thought she would understand the looks people gave her in the hall during the services; but she was oblivious, sitting in the shadow of the big pillar to the left of the door, gazing always at the preacher's face, carried away by his voice. For her, the figures of Amida and Shinran on the altar no longer existed. She listened only—listened with an intensity of which the rest of the congregation were incapable.

'Fancy those two using Butsuoji of all places, for their—assignations,' said Mineyo to Soshu, no longer mincing her words.

But there was nothing Soshu could say to the widow. She was drawn irresistibly into depravity, like a pretty schoolgirl lured by a gang of hoodlums, regardless of pleas from her parents or teachers. The violent change in her, together with the absence of any experience of a similar kind in her life hitherto, made her seem literally 'possessed'.

'You'll have to be firm with Mrs Kushimoto—tell her straight out that she's not to come to the temple any more!' Soshu was frightened by Mineyo's vehemence. She was overflowing with the righteous indignation that is common in such cases—the beam in her own eye forgotten.

'Perhaps we'd better ask somebody else to take the services next time.'

'No, that would be stupid—it's because of him the collections are so big. We can't sacrifice him for the sake of the widow. The only thing is to speak to her—and if you won't, I will.'

'Would you dare?' Soshu retorted, with a twisted smile.

'She won't listen to anything her family and relatives say, apparently. They'll be delighted if somebody from Butsuoji has the courage to speak to her. Of course if they will only go and hold their rendezvous somewhere else, it won't be any concern of ours any longer.' Mineyo appeared to have no intention of letting the affair settle itself quietly.

Ryokun heard the grown-ups talking about the widow. Without having a very clear idea of what the trouble was all about, he gathered that she was doing something very, very wrong. Soshu did not conceal his annoyance at the way Mineyo would deliberately raise the subject in front of the boy, but such moral delicacy was lost on Mineyo. He felt it was somehow wrong to feel even curiosity about other people's loves, and would try to forget about any that were mentioned to him; besides, to show interest in such matters was to betray himself. . . . When he heard about Mrs Kushimoto, his first wish was to keep it quiet. If only the gossips did not get hold of the story—but nothing could induce Mineyo to drop the subject of the widow. Why did she get so worked up about it?

'The women say they've had enough of it. The preacher's finished his supper, and had his bath, they've laid the bedding out for him—and that woman is still there in the next room. She treats it as if it were her own home—refuses to budge, once she's sat down.' Mineyo's abuse grew steadily more vehement.

Soshu wondered if this woman really managed to forget what she herself was constantly doing. If anyone could throw stones at the widow, it was not Mineyo. But to blame Mineyo, to sneer at her hypocrisy, was merely to deepen his condemnation and scorn of himself. Even before the Kushimoto affair Mineyo was always twice as much interested as anybody else in sex stories and would avidly read all she could find in newspapers and magazines. As far as she was concerned, political and economic events, or international affairs, belonged to another planet. Soshu began to feel a new interest in Mineyo's character, in the remarkable ability she possessed of distinguishing so clearly between her private affairs and those of the temple, with which as one of its inmates she supposed herself to be concerned. For the moment she was so busy defending an outrage involving the latter that the former were pushed out of sight, or simply ceased to exist. If she had been aware of her own conduct, her conscience would surely have troubled her, even though, if asked, she might still have given the conventional judgement on the widow's conduct. Everyone has the right, on occasion, to judge others by some external, public standard that may at the time have little bearing on his own case—but not if he invariably refuses to apply any such standards to his own shortcomings. Mineyo's brazenness in this respect had long amazed Soshu. But she was so glib in her conversation that he could never be sure whether she really felt what she said or was merely adopting for the moment the conventional, public attitude. She had a kind of genius for alternating imperceptibly between the conventional and the personal.

Sometimes during the period of the services she would attend for the sermon—and then take two or three old peasant women back to the house and give them a sermon of her own, copying the technique and way of reasoning from the preacher. The women thought she was wonderful, and brought others to hear her.

'They say the widow goes stupid, out of her mind almost, for days on end when the preacher goes!' There was passionate hatred in Mineyo's voice. 'If she were a pretty girl of twenty, one could understand her falling for a man like that and fluttering round him—but what sort of appeal does she think *she* can have for him, the conceited fool! She never knew how to make up even when she was young—her only idea of making herself smart is smearing cream on her hair. And that priest, he's just as bad; making love to a woman like her, fifteen years older than he is, and not even pretty at that—what taste the man shows! . . . But he's such a good preacher we'll have to turn a blind eye, I suppose.'

Soshu remembered the words from St John's Gospel:

> And the scribes and Pharisees brought unto him a woman taken in adultery: and when they had set her in the midst, they said unto him, Master, this woman was taken in adultery, in the very act. Now Moses in the law commanded us, that such should be stoned: but what sayest thou? This they said, tempting him, that they might have whereof to accuse him. But Jesus stooped down, and with his finger wrote on the ground. So when they continued asking him, he lifted up himself, and said unto them, He that is without sin among you, let him first cast a stone at her. And again he stooped down, and wrote on the ground. And they which heard it, being convicted by their own conscience, went out one by one, beginning at the eldest, even unto the last; and Jesus was left alone, and the woman standing in the midst.

Perhaps, thought Soshu, the reason why Mineyo kept harping on Mrs Kushimoto was that she had two selves, one of which was identifying the other with the widow in order to be able to blame it for her secret sin. Of course there was no comparison between Mineyo's actions and those of the widow. Mineyo was perfectly aware of the depravity of what she had done—and wasn't that precisely why she could not bear somebody else doing the same thing? Perhaps all her talk was only a roundabout way of attacking herself.

In her sermons to the old women Mineyo was fond of expounding karma. She would explain how utterly impossible it is to free oneself from one's past actions, and how no one can expect to go to the Paradise of the Pure Land who does not strive his utmost to acquire merit. Always she stressed the absolute power of karma. On these occasions she liked to quote a section of the Tannisho:[1]

> Even when I recite *Nenbutsu* I feel no joy welling up in me,

[1] Tract outlining the main points of Shinran's teaching, written by his disciple Yui-en. It is still widely read in present-day Japan.

nor do I feel a desire to be immediately reborn in the Pure Land. I wonder why.' This is the question raised by you. I, Shinran, like yourself have had this same doubt, Yui-en. When you consider it deeply, however, precisely because you don't feel like dancing and leaping for joy you have greater assurance of being reborn in the Pure Land. It is the tormenting cravings of the self that inhibit the feeling of joy in reciting *nenbutsu*. Amida, foreseeing this, has accepted us with all our tormenting cravings. Hence his Compassionate Vow was proclaimed for every sentient being. Having awakened to this reality, I feel firmer in the faith of Amida.

Again, it is because of the torments of the self that we worry about death at the slightest illness, feel helpless and forlorn, and lack the urgent desire to be reborn in the Pure Land. How truly flourishing are the cravings of the self when we cling to the abode of our long-cherished sufferings through interminable transmigrations without longing for the Pure Land of Peace and Contentment into which we are not reborn! We are reborn into that land when our karmic relation to this life of suffering expires and we die, however reluctantly, the self exhausted. Amida is especially compassionate toward those who have no urgent desire to be reborn in the Pure Land . . .

At fifty, the widow had succumbed to passions that had been dormant all her life. She was now one of those who would 'not long eagerly for the Pure Land' till she had fulfilled what fate was demanding of her, nor could she see the merciful hand Lord Amida offered to her to make easy her journey to Paradise. On such as she, Amida had 'special compassion'—Mineyo might have used her as a living illustration of her text; but she did not. The parallel between Mrs Kushimoto's conduct and her own was too close; the old women knew Mineyo's secret and would have resented any reference she might have made to the widow.—She doesn't know what shame is, thought Soshu, beginning to be afraid of Mineyo. She's brazen enough to pretend lust is inevitable, karma from a past life. . . . But the thought of such karma had no terrors for Mineyo; of fear she was apparently incapable.

'Ryokun—where are you off to?' said Mineyo sharply to the boy, who had suddenly got up to go.

'Heron Forest.'

'You're not to go alone!'

'Nobu'll come with me.'

'Don't go climbing any big trees!'

The moment Ryokun ran off, Soshu burst out, 'Why do you have to keep on talking about Mrs Kushimoto in front of him?'

'Why not? He doesn't understand, he's only a child.'

'He understands a lot more than we think, in his own way. I'm afraid for him.'

'If it's Ryokun you're worried about, I know him better than you do, after all. . . . You'll speak to the widow, won't you, when you visit the Kushimotos next?' Mineyo changed the subject, as if Soshu's concern meant nothing to her.

'What can I, of all people, say to her?'

'What can you say—?' Mineyo did not understand at first what Soshu meant. Then she pretended surprise. A look of disapproval followed; she was putting on her 'public' face.

'It would be different if her husband were alive still. As it is, she isn't causing anybody any great trouble. I'm inclined to think the best thing is to say nothing—just to keep a quiet eye on her.'

'What *are* you saying? Have you completely forgotten you have a responsibility as priest of Butsuoji?'

'My responsibility . . . do I really have any? And suppose I do, what right do I have to interfere with her life if that's the way she wants to live it?'

'You must think of all the worry it's giving her family. They're sure to come and see you about her soon, anyway—what are you going to tell them?'

'There's nothing I can say about her—nothing. . . .'

'Oh, you are so . . . cold!' Mineyo was staring at him, tears in her eyes. 'You're always like this nowadays, so cold and cruel. You hate me now, that's what it is . . . you haven't any idea how I think and think and worry my head off for your sake. . . .'

Tears were running fast down her cheeks, but Mineyo's eyes did not redden, nor her eyelids swell. She lost none of her composure. After some moments, like an actress on the stage measuring the effect of her weeping, she quietly drew the hem of her under-kimono from her hanging sleeve and dabbed away the tears. For a woman of her age, a grandmother, and of a priestly family at that, her under-kimono was too brightly-patterned—more so than even a showy tradesman's wife of that age would wear. Mineyo went to a lot of trouble choosing gay cheerful colours for her under-kimonos; but all such efforts, like the massage she still gave herself every night, were lost on Soshu.

'I adopted you, I know—but thousands of men marry women older than themselves, don't they. . . . I'm not too old for you . . . it tortures me now that I adopted you—you'd never have come to Butsuoji otherwise, that's the only reason I did it. . . . The moment I saw you, I knew I had to make you come. When I think I'm supposed to be your mother, it drives me mad. . . . Mother, mother,

mother . . . I've had no peace ever since, never even for a moment. . . . You can't begin to know what I suffer, the misery. . . .'

She was still weeping, and wiped her eyes with her sleeve as she spoke. Soshu was pale. He was remembering the scenes she made when he refused her, as he had done for a good many nights now; wondering how many more of them he could have to endure. And he a priest, he thought with more than the usual self-disgust. The fact that he was a priest meant that, terrible as his present situation was, to escape from it would mean something worse—hell itself. . . . There were footsteps coming along the corridor. They stopped outside the closed door.

'Excuse me, Father.' It was Shoju.

'Yes?' said Soshu mechanically.

'You promised to visit Mrs Komiyama about now.'

'Oh, yes, of course; I must go at once.'

Soshu hurried to the vestry and put on his travelling-robe, wondering as he did so whether there would ever come a time when he was strong enough to break free of his bondage.

As he was walking across the compound towards the gate, he met Ryokun pulling a long bamboo behind him.

'Visiting?' Ryokun asked his father.

Soshu nodded. 'What are you going to do with that bamboo?'

'Make a pop-gun.'

'Don't hurt yourself—bamboo's sharp, you know. Better get Shoju to make it for you.'

'I can make it.' Ryokun ran off towards the house, the leaves of the bamboo trailing along the ground behind like a broom. Soshu looked after his son.

—A motherless child. . . .

It was no terrible accident that had robbed him of his mother. His own father had driven her away; assured the boy in advance of years of doubt, suspicion and anguish.

A *nenbutsu* rose unsummoned to his lips, as he saw his son suffering the misery the years would bring. Before going into the house, Ryokun stood his bamboo on the ground and tore off some of the leaves, unaware that his father was watching him.

For Ryokun, the *nenbutsu* was like a cradle-song he had heard ever since he was a baby. Without understanding it, without even wondering what it meant, he himself would repeat it unconsciously in front of the shrine. The words alone were engraved deeply on his childish mind. So it had been with Soshu in his boyhood. Year after year, as a child, he had listened to it till it seemed almost a part of his physical self. There was always a sadness in the murmured prayer, as of an echo of the voices of past generations; their aspiration was his inheritance. Now, at thirty-nine, he would find himself uttering it spontaneously, an expression of his own need.

Suddenly he seemed to hear a voice warning him, shrill, insistent. His heart beat violently. Jolted by the lurching of the bus, he thought of Ryokun still.

8

Soshu got down from the bus. The long, black travelling-robe attracted no glances; it was a familiar sight in Tan'ami, which had twelve or thirteen temples, besides several preaching halls. There was a religious atmosphere in the town, one might say. In spite of the bitter disputes between employers and workmen that took place every year now and were given prominence in the local press, at a deeper level a concern for religion was still alive; it was something of which people were hardly conscious, a part of their inheritance from their ancestors. The new religious movements that were now fashionable everywhere had penetrated to Tan'ami, too, but made little headway. Some temple priests nowadays could even be seen going to visit their parishioners by bicycle.

The river near Kiyota-cho was not more than twelve feet wide and very shallow, but its waters were clear and beautiful. Houses backed on to one side, a paved road lined with willow-trees ran along the other. The neighbourhood was occupied almost entirely by houses of the 'three trades',[1] and its life began at night—in the daytime it was silent, as if the inhabitants had suddenly fled. Many of the buildings looked like private houses, but here and there were restaurants of various sizes.

Three young girls, probably geisha on the way home from lessons, were walking along the road, laughing and chattering. As they passed Soshu, they suddenly put on a serious expression.

'Good morning!'

Soshu returned the greeting. He recognized them as geisha of the 'Mutsumi-ya.' On his visits there he would hear them dancing or practising songs upstairs while he was reciting the scriptures at the house shrine. The three girls turned and looked after Soshu. Smiling, they whispered to each other.

[1] i.e. geisha-houses, 'tea-houses', and restaurants.

He walked on, looking at the name-plates, and it was not long before he found 'Komiyama' on a brand-new plate. He had passed the house a good many times before, though without ever noting who lived there. The neighbouring houses on either side looked like private houses, but one of them, with a name painted on the gate-lamp, was a geisha-house. On Mrs Komiyama's gate-lamp there was no lettering. The house was quite a big one, with two storeys, and expensive lattice doors. Soshu pushed back one of the doors.

'Mrs Komiyama? I've come from the temple.'

The room to the right of the porch was the living-room, Soshu gathered; the one opposite would be the kitchen. A passage ran straight through to the back of the house. Dividing it from the porch was a half-length curtain, not of the ordinary kind that tradesmen use for shop doorways, but such as are sold in department stores, with an elaborate, beautifully-coloured design. The house was silent. After a moment a screen door somewhere to the right slid back; there was a rustling of kimono.

Tomoko Komiyama knelt before him, bowing very low with both hands touching the floor-matting. From the quiet colours of her kimono, Soshu guessed she must be about seven or eight years younger than himself. He had hardly noticed her face when they met under the temple gate.

She took him to an eight-mat room with *tokonoma*[1] and double cupboards. Sitting in front of the *tokonoma,* Soshu noticed that the house seemed oddly dark—and realized at once that all the partitions dividing the rooms from each other were opaque *fusuma*; there were no half-transparent *shoji,* such as most houses have. The tea-room was evidently behind the *fusuma* nearest him—he could hear someone preparing tea. Footsteps sounded on the concrete floor of the passage. He heard no voice; but there was obviously someone else living here besides Mrs Komiyama.

She served him tea, and then for the first time they looked at each other. As before, he was struck by the perfect neatness of the parting that divided her hair, exactly at the middle, with a gentle natural wave on either side. Her hair was tied in a simple knot at the back of her neck, hiding its abundance, so that from the front it even seemed thin. There was no permanent wave—the style was of a simplicity unusual nowadays. Her eyes were gentle, yet there was depth in the gentleness, as of one who had suffered; the whole expression of her face had both dignity and charm, an impression which the slight tracing of rouge on her lips did not in the least spoil.

1 The alcove or recess in a Japanese room, in which a scroll is usually hung. A guest is always asked to sit with his back to the tokonoma—i.e. 'in front' of it, this being regarded as the seat of honour.

Her complexion fascinated Soshu. The delicate white, blended with a hint of the palest blue, could not be more tempting; which made the absence of any such expression in her face the more remarkable. But there was about the face a faint air of loneliness, something suggestive of hidden powers of feeling. Soshu had never before met a woman who aroused in him such a complex reaction.

'I'm so relieved to be able to join Butsuoji. My mother and father would be so happy.'

'Your mother and father . . . ?'

'My father died twenty years ago, my mother two years ago.'

'Does your husband work somewhere near?' She must be thirty-one or thirty-two, thought Soshu. A younger woman did not have such poise.

'My husband and I are separated—for various reasons.'

Apparently she was unwilling to say any more at present on that subject, so Soshu asked no further questions. That was probably why she seemed lonely. A woman like her—perhaps she was a teacher of tea-ceremony, he thought.

She opened the cupboard where her family shrine was kept, and prepared it for Soshu while he put on his stole with the temple crest. It was easy to see from her movements that the shrine and its observances had been familiar to her from childhood. Probably she worshipped before it every day.

Tan'ami had five or six shops selling shrines and their fittings. It was still quite easy to make a living in this way—evidence, up to a point, of the living interest of the people of Tan'ami in religion. But most of the customers were farming families. Perhaps the shopkeepers were too busy nowadays to find time for such things—at any rate, few of the younger families in the busy part of the town would think of having a family shrine. But the farmers still bought elaborate expensive ones, quite unsuited to their style of living, as if a shrine were the one piece of property that mattered.

Soshu knelt before Mrs Komiyama's shrine, placing his hands reverently together. The memorial tablets for her mother and father were in their places. His professional eye noticed that the shrine was a rich one, and beautifully made, like a miniature of the big shrine at the temple. The gilt was almost dazzlingly bright. In relation to the general appearance of the house, the shrine was too elaborate. It was not new; probably it had been her parents' before her, and had been brought to Tan'ami with special care when its owner moved. From its splendour, one could imagine what her former life had been.

Soshu began the readings, Tomoko Komiyama sitting behind him. She was the only other person in the room, he felt as he read, but now and then he heard steps from the passage again. A maid perhaps. There was no sign of anybody else sharing the house.

The readings lasted about an hour. Outside, passers-by heard the priest's voice. Girls' voices would stop as they recognized it, so that only the patter of their clogs told of their passing.

Somebody opened the gate of the house while he was reading, but he heard no voice. A moment later he was aware of someone tiptoe-ing into the room and sitting down behind him. When he had finished reading from the Senshuji book, he turned to face Tomoko Komiyama again. Her daughter, the little girl with such big eyes whom he had seen with her at Butsuoji, was sitting beside her. She stared at Soshu as her mother bowed to him. Tomoko Komiyama went to prepare tea.

'You're at school, I suppose?' Soshu asked the girl as he was taking off his stole.

'Yes, first grade.'

'What school?'

'Kiyota Elementary.'

She was in the same grade as Ryokun, though they went to different schools.

Her eyes were like her mother's, but even bigger—unnaturally so. A few more years would soften the impression of irregularity and mould the face into one of unusual beauty.

'You have a pretty daughter,' said Soshu to Tomoko Komiyama, 'and so quiet and well-behaved, too. Has she any brothers and sisters?'

'No, she's the only one. We had to move before she'd really got used to school, and she hasn't made many friends at the new school yet, so it's rather lonely for her.'

The colours the girl was wearing were gay and fashionable. Only the most superior of the Butsuoji people dressed their children like that; the farming families could not and would not imitate such smartness. It was not that they could not afford it—many of them were richer than anybody in the town—but they stuck to their simple ways. To be able to buy her daughter such clothes, thought Soshu, Mrs Komiyama must have inherited a good deal, or perhaps her husband made her a generous allowance.

'It was Mr Yamaji who first told me about you. Might I ask how you came to know him?' He had to ask her this. When he next visited Yamaji, he would have to thank him for introducing a new member to Butsuoji.

A sudden flicker of embarrassment showed in her eyes. Aware of this, perhaps, she blushed slightly. Her face recovered its usual poise immediately, leaving Soshu, however, with the feeling that somehow his question had hurt her.

She hesitated, as if to speak of Yamaji was painful—Soshu could not imagine why. After a moment she seemed to have come to a decision.

'There's something I ought to speak to you about. . . .' She faltered, and did not go on. Soshu began to feel interested.

'You must have some tea . . . do you prefer lemon, or milk?'—with a slight, forced smile as she changed the subject.

'Thank you—no special preference.'

'Shoko, dear—run and tell Sumi to make the tea with lemon.' The little girl went out. Again her mother smiled uneasily.

'Please say nothing about me when you visit Mr Yamaji.'

This was unexpected. That smile, apparently, was all the explanation of her words she was willing to give. Unwittingly, Soshu felt, he had opened a door on to the real secret of her life. 'I'm sorry . . . I didn't know. . . .'

'Father was in the same business as Mr Yamaji . . .'

Yamaji had made most of his money as a rice-broker, though now he was president of a securities company.

'There's something . . . it won't be long before you find it out for yourself anyway . . . ,' she went on, avoiding his eyes. Something behind the words made them painful to listen to.

Among the two hundred Butsuoji families there were men and women with every kind of problem, and often, like Christians in the confessional, they would pour out their troubles to Soshu. What he heard on these occasions he told no one, not even Mineyo.

Suddenly he found himself imagining . . . Tomoko Komiyama had come to ask his advice; she was revealing the whole story of her past life, pleading with him to tell her what she should do. Soshu was conscious of a secret excitement. To hear a confession from such a beautiful woman, to penetrate her deepest secret, would be a very agreeable duty. He was frequently called upon for advice and assistance—in arranging marriages, for instance, when he would sometimes act as a kind of behind-the-scenes go-between; or in helping young people to find jobs. Unhappy lovers would come to him for a cure for their troubles, and wives distracted by persistently unfaithful husbands. Sometimes parents even tried to use him as a private tutor for their children.

'After Father died, mother became more and more devoted to religion.' Tomoko began again. This time the smile was natural; she herself seemed unaware of it. 'She belonged to the Takada branch, and was such a strong believer. I remember she took me with her two or three times to worship at the big central temple at Isshinden. For myself I don't think it matters so much what temple I join, so long as it belongs to the Pure Land Sect. But mother would be unhappy if I didn't go to a Takada priest. Yamaji—' she had dropped the title; her breath caught for a moment, then she hurriedly corrected the mistake. '—Mr Yamaji laughs at me.' But the slip had revealed clearly enough what her relations with Yamaji were. Soshu pretended not to have noticed anything. 'He says twenty years from now will be soon enough for me to start getting religious—he's joking, of course; but it's my mother's blood in me, I suppose; her tablet's always there on the shrine, and if I feel her spirit is happy and at peace, then I'm happy, too.'

She tried to correct the impression the slip had made, but it was too late.

'There are just the three of us here, Shoko and I and the maid, so I have lots of time to think. I suppose I'm more like an old woman inside, in the way I think and feel. Mr Yamaji laughs when he sees me kneeling before the shrine. . . .'

So Yamaji was a frequent visitor to the house, thought Soshu.

He thanked her and got up to go. He had finished the sutra-readings, which were all he had come for, and decided not to stay any longer. Tomoko looked up at him as she knelt to open the sliding door.

'It must be difficult for you, too, Father . . .'

Soshu was startled. What did she mean? Without answering, he walked to the front door and slipped his feet into the white leather thongs of his clogs. So even she, the newest member of the temple, already knew the sordid story. 'Mr Yamaji told me. . . .'

'I see,' said Soshu, with a faint ironic smile. How could he help other people in their trouble when he was so deep in his own?

'I can imagine the burden it must be for you. . . .' Her voice was full of sympathy.

'It's my boy I think of—he's about the same age as your little girl. A child's happiness depends so much on its mother.' With feelings that would have been hard to define, the father and the mother looked at each other for a moment, conscious of how similar their situations were.

The maid, a red-faced country girl of seventeen or eighteen, appeared as Soshu took his leave.

He walked down the road under the willow-trees, thinking of Tomoko's last words. 'What a burden it must be'—the words were a natural expression of sympathy. It *was* a burden, certainly. Yet only a man who was struggling for real freedom could speak honestly of 'burdens'. Soshu had no such right; he had long ago abandoned the search for freedom.

When he first came to Butsuoji, Renko was only eleven. It seemed little more than a joke then that she was to be his wife. They were like brother and sister, often quarrelling—he remembered how more than once he had made her cry. Even after she had grown up and was old enough to marry, he found it difficult to think of her as an adult with a personality of her own; and was neither surprised nor distressed when Mineyo kept postponing their wedding. He had never loved Renko, never thought of her as a young and charming girl. Their marriage had been no more than an animal mating. If he had accepted her flight with relative calm, when Mineyo finally drove her from Butsuoji, it was partly because his conscience told him he had only himself to blame, but partly also because the brother and sister relationship they had known before marriage was all that had ever existed between them. His insensitivity went back that far—to her childhood. For nearly twenty years, too, Mineyo had blinded him to so much—he had never fully realised it, but all through the years Renko had been little more to him than a vague, feminine presence existing only in her mother's shadow.

Renko's feelings towards himself had apparently not been very different. Ryokun was the only tie that held her to Butsuoji.

Sitting in the jolting bus, Soshu reviewed his impressions of Tomoko Komiyama. Ashamed and afraid though it made him, the picture would not fade from his mind; he wanted passionately to know her secret. With all his contacts among the two hundred families of the congregation, none of his parishioners had ever excited him like this. She was about the same age as Renko, yet utterly different from her; different again from the seven or eight beautiful geisha of the Mutsumi-ya, though where exactly the difference lay, Soshu found it hard to define. Why did he find her so fascinating, he kept wondering.

The reason did not lie merely in her beauty. It was her suffering, the deep pain he was aware of in her life, that drew him to her.

9

Soshu had recently developed the habit of not looking at Mineyo when he spoke to her, and of not speaking to her at all unless it was essential. His refusal of all the conversational trivialities of which most of their daily intercourse had consisted made it seem to her as if he was constantly in a bad temper; but he had decided to ignore any such reaction. Tea was ready, she called from her room. Soshu excused himself, saying he had some work to do. He was determined that as far as possible he would not go to her room any more.

It was soon obvious to Mineyo that he was trying to keep away from her. Then again—it's too selfish to begin to avoid her so suddenly, he would remind himself. Yet he no longer felt the temptation to take the easiest way, to give way wholly to his lust till it should free him at last by burning itself out. There had been other such moments of repentance in the past; but on every occasion his courage had failed him, even when the break would have been easiest—at the time of his marriage. That was why he was still so weak even now, when his wife's flight, the result of all his previous failures, was forcing a decision upon him.

Soshu was incapable of arriving at a firm, irrevocable decision by some sudden emotional upheaval, corresponding to those sudden disturbances in the world of nature by which a new mountain can be thrown up overnight. It would take shape very slowly in his mind and heart, accumulating its different elements and gathering strength little by little; but when at last he was ready, it would be rigid, utterly immoveable.

Gradually, Soshu found himself able to treat Mineyo with greater coldness. In the end, he knew, it might mean he himself would be driven to leave the temple. But for this he was prepared. Till now it had been the one thing he feared most, such was his morbid terror of exposure, and had always deprived him of the courage to act.

To a certain extent Soshu was able to analyze and understand his changing feelings. Why they had begun to change, what was responsible for his growing sense of strength, was a different matter. It was as if a long fuse had been laid and lit in his heart—whether this was merely a chemical change taking place in himself as he grew older, or the stimulus of outward experience, he did not know—and was burning steadily towards its charge.

He longed now for innocence and purity of heart. But at the same time the thought of purity disturbed him. It meant chastity—and who could have been less chaste than himself as a husband? To think of chastity now seemed absurd. But at least he was seeking it only for himself, not demanding it of others. The longing grew stronger.

In the daytime it was not difficult to keep Mineyo at a distance. When night came, however, he was less certain of himself. As soon as he was in bed and had turned out the floor light, he began to listen uneasily for any sound in the house, nervousness almost stifling his breathing. At such moments, more than at any other time, the veils were torn away and his weakness laid bare. Because of the size of the old house, the darkness itself seemed abnormally profound, and expanded the rooms to a vastness that bore no relation to daylight reality. In the daytime the house was quiet enough, so few were its inhabitants; but from the twilight hours the stillness was absolute. Soshu could not sleep. Tense and restless, he wondered again and again what he should do if she forced herself upon him—imagining the crisis closer wth each moment. Worn out by such nervous anticipation, he would finally doze off, only to wake with a start a few moments later.

He listened continuously for any sign of movement from Mineyo's room, his whole body suddenly turning rigid at the least sound. Sometimes she would go to the toilet, but without switching on the light; every inch of the house was so familiar that she could pass from one room to another as freely in darkness as in daylight. Pretending to be asleep, Soshu listened to her footsteps. If he heard them returning to her room, the tension in his body would suddenly collapse. Only then would peace come.

Short of a direct clash, there was no way of making her understand the change that had taken place in him.

One night Mineyo got up to go to the toilet, and then went back to her room. Soshu fell asleep. Sometime later he woke up, feeling suffocated. It was Mineyo. . . . she lay sprawled across his bed, breathing jerkily.

Not all his listening, then, had prevented her from entering his room without his knowing it. Soshu felt outwitted. Her body seemed twice its normal size, and her short, quick breaths like spurts of flame. It was not only Mineyo who was thrusting herself upon him, Soshu thought. Not her body only oppressed him now, but all the burden of their past, of the years of his own weakness and indecision, of the inertia of his long-repeated sin. Mineyo said nothing. Soshu squirmed under her weight. It was no unknown woman, after all, but Mineyo; and even as he was twisting himself free of the bed, lust fought in the darkness with the longing to resist. When he did struggle free of the *futon,* she still clung to him. Breathing hard, he tore her hands from him and stood up, knocking against the sliding door behind him; it clattered in its groove, and nearly toppled into the corridor.

He stared down through the darkness at the panting figure as it crawled after him. Perfume, the sweet-sour scent of her body pervaded the room; but panic had dulled his senses.

Soshu pushed back the door. He made his way to the robing-room, groped in the dark for his gown, stole and rosary, and started to walk towards the temple, bumping into the door of the corridor before he managed to open it. The creaking of the wooden floor broke sharply into the deep night silence of Butsuoji. He switched on the light; back from madness to the familiar world. . . . Under the lamp, he saw how dishevelled he was, and hurried on into the great hall. Passing from the recess into the sanctuary by the door behind the shrine, he opened a small sliding door in the back of the platform on which the statue of Amida stood, and took out some candles. His hands were shaking.

His footsteps on the bare wooden floor of the sanctuary echoing through the deserted hall, Soshu lit the two hanging oil lamps and the candles on the sutra-table. Then he opened the door of the shrine of Amida, and sat down directly under and in front of it. Unless he looked up, he could not see the statue. With feverish intensity, he began to read a sutra. Intoning in the resonant voice that even his fellow-priests praised so highly, he forgot it was night; striving by the rich beauty of the sounds to calm his agitation, to escape. . . .

Once he had begun to intone, there was no need to read each one of the big characters in the old, woodblock-printed text. He knew the scripture practically by heart. Yet doubts suddenly attacked him. The reading worked like a charm on his feelings, and gradually his fear disappeared. He could recall now without agitation how he had wrenched himself free of Mineyo and fled panting from the room—could even visualise the figure of Mineyo herself, as she had struggled with him, frantic with desire. He remembered that neither he nor she had spoken; two animals squirming in the dark. . . .

The reading went on without interruption. From the shrine above him the face of Amida, pitch-black with age, looked down on Soshu, on the same body that a few moments before a woman had clung to in a fury of passion, and that was now suddenly innocent, sitting before the altar in its priestly gown, calmly reciting scripture.

The voice stopped. The hands that had been holding the sutra up reverently before the shrine dropped limp.

—Let not a Buddhist ever hide his faith.—The phrase had flashed suddenly on his consciousness. Soshu looked up into the eyes of the statue; and trembled in spirit before their clear, piercing gaze, as if accused. 'Let not a Buddhist ever hide his faith.' The words were those of Rennyo, urging all Buddhists to let their religion appear in everything they thought or did. Shinran, too, had striven to show himself always a true Buddhist, whether in his inner struggles, his conflict with the world, or in the austerities to which he bound himself. Yet Soshu was seeking peace for himself in escape, simply by reading a sutra in the 'religious' atmosphere that as a Buddhist priest he could create at will. The reading was a trick, a device for lifting himself out of the mire of human passion. The scene was appropriate enough for an act of repentance—reading the holy book in the middle of the night, alone in the great hall. Soshu was trying to save his soul by forcing himself to intone the whole of the Three Sutras. He was determined to stay in the temple all night—to sit there alone hour after hour could surely be called a true penance, if a minor one. But supposing he had been an ordinary layman, not a priest—what would he have done then, after such an experience? Run out into the street, in the middle of the night—and upset everybody in the neighbourhood? Only a priest, it struck him suddenly, could do what he was doing now; only a priest had this privileged way of strengthening the will to resist, of aspiring to purity. What did other men do? With nowhere to escape to, was there nothing for them but endless, unaided struggle with passion?

He was a coward, then—using his position as a priest, merely, seeking peace cheaply in an atmosphere where repentance, penance, strength of will came ready-made. And the scriptures did give peace of a kind. To an observer, Soshu's 'penance' would probably have seemed exaggerated, too dramatic to be genuine. Just like a priest! he might have said.—Just like a priest!

It was true, Soshu saw clearly, that as a priest his life had been very different from a layman's. Even in regard to material necessities he belonged to what was in its way a privileged class. Which had not prevented him from succumbing to a mad infatuation, and driving his wife away. . . .

—Certainly it was just like a priest . . . 'never hiding his faith' . . .

Again he began to read, but with less spirt than before. His voice lost its tension, as if he had even forgotten that his purpose in reading was to preserve his mind from relapsing into agitation.

At the beginning of his *Doctrine, Works, Faith and Attainment*, Shinran wrote: 'If we consider reverently the Sect of the Pure Land, we find that it offers two ways. One is called *oso,* the other, *genso.*'

Man thinks there is nothing he cannot conquer with his intellect; but is human ability really the measure of all things? Wars hitherto have only served to deepen men's illusions in this respect. The world in which we live is ever-shifting, a kaleidoscope of perpetual change. To realize for oneself the uncertainties of this life, and then to free oneself from them, is the way of *oso,* the first way of which Shinran spoke: *genso,* the second, is to return to ordinary life after attaining enlightenment and strive for the salvation of others, a wanderer for ever in the world of men.

It should have been clear to Soshu that he was taking neither of the two ways. Unable to realize fully his own instability and lack of faith, he was therefore far from a true awareness of the shifting, restless nature of man himself. Even the idea that had taken hold of him now—that these midnight readings would somehow preserve his inner purity—was absurdly shallow. Perhaps he was convinced for the moment that he would never repeat the sin again, that he could clear his soul once and for all of all danger. If so, he still had a long way to go to understand the treacherous depths of his own nature.

Suddenly he was aware of someone behind him. Without faltering, the voice continued its reading. Mineyo had come silently into the hall and was sitting behind him. Her eyes, red with weeping, were fixed on Soshu. Her hair was dishevelled; the neck of her gown disordered, showing the soft flesh unnatural for her years. She did not clasp her hands in worship, nor utter any *nenbutsu.* No gleam from the statue high up in the shrine was reflected in her eyes. With shoulders heaving, she sat riveted, her ears absorbing the even flow of Soshu's voice, her face burning with the feverish light of one blinded to everything but lust.

How long she had been sitting there, Soshu did not know. A slight creaking from the door into the corridor told him she had gone. He went on reading.

One of the big candles burnt itself out. Soshu looked up; dawn was showing through the chinks between the shutters.

Soshu left the hall feeling his determination had been renewed. He would take refuge in the temple, he decided, whenever she came to tempt him. A selfish enough plan, of course; protecting himself with his priesthood. . . .

The house was still dark when he returned, though the sun was already up. But a light was burning—Mineyo must have left it on for him. Shoju would be coming any minute from the cottage on the hill.

Soshu went to bed and fell asleep immediately. He did not hear Shoju opening the shutters, and was still sleeping under the white quilt, his face a shade paler than usual, when the sunlight covered every panel of the *shoji*.

'Where's Daddy?' Ryokun asked Mineyo when Soshu did not appear at breakfast.

'I don't know.' Her reply was abrupt. Ryokun knew his grandmother was upset and angry, but had no idea why.

When he came back from school, the packet of biscuits was lying on the desk where he did his homework. Mineyo, usually so eager to welcome him home, was nowhere to be seen.

That day was the anniversary of the death of Yamaji's father, so Soshu had gone to read the scriptures at his house. Yamaji was normally occupied all day with his business, but today he was at home waiting for the priest to come. As they met, Soshu thought of Tomoko's beautiful face, then he remembered he was forbidden to mention her. Even to think of her when he looked at Yamaji seemed a kind of treachery towards her.

After Soshu had finished reading the sutra and exchanged his formal stole for the smaller one a priest normally wears, Yamaji showed him to another room. Tea was served, and for a while they talked of unimportant matters. When the conversation lapsed for a moment, Yamaji said in a casual tone, 'Something will have to be done about Butsuoji, won't it?' He smiled pleasantly. Soshu felt a sudden shock of fear. 'What's past is past, of course—but all of us in the congregation are so anxious to have things settle down again there, you know. . . .'

'Yes, I am sorry, entirely my own—' but Yamaji brushed apologies aside.

'We would like you to consider the possibility, at least, of marrying again.'

'Marrying again?' Soshu was dumbfounded. Preoccupied so intensely with his immediate danger, the question of a second marriage had never occurred to him.

'It would hardly do to leave Ryokun's upbringing entirely to his grandmother, I suppose? Anyway, if you're thinking about it, as I imagine you are, the parishioners are very willing to make all the usual arrangements. . . .'

'But. . . .'

Yamaji's eyes took on a sharper expression. 'All that's needed is your decision. The rest you can leave to us.'

Yamaji was referring to Mineyo, Soshu knew; he could not speak of his relationship with her directly, that was all. Feeling himself reddening, he looked away. His cheeks had sunk a little—the melancholy expression might have been that of an actor impersonating a youth driven haggard by some importunate middle-aged beauty. . . .

They knew about it, then; they're planning to settle it all so simply—and I, the subject of all their plans, I can't break free, still torture myself . . . why can I never grow beyond such weakness?

He had no affection left for her, only hate and fear; yet still when she forced her body upon him, he could not bring himself to reject her harshly. Her body knew his weakness, and fastened upon it. Not all his maleness could make him use violence on her—yet neither was there anything he could say, that would reach the soul in that lust-tormented body. If there was preaching to be done, Mineyo was better at it than he.

10

Ryokun and his friend walked along the path between the paddy-fields. Ahead of them stood the dark, luxuriant Heron's Forest. It was about a kilometre from where the houses ended, and stood out like an island among the fields—in the time of the rape-blossom, an emerald island floating on a sea of yellow; in the barley season, an island in a green sea, itself a richer, more brilliant green.

A plan to make it the centre of a new park for the town had been drawn up, but nothing had been done yet to carry it out. Even at a distance, the wood looked old and mysterious, as though it had a history of its own. It was surrounded by paddy-fields. Just before reaching it, the path was cut off by a ditch, dug centuries ago to protect a fortress in the wood. The ditch had been filled in, but a perennial spring turned most of it into a bog, into which a man could sink up to his chest.

Ryokun loved the forest. Day after day he came back to it, as though to store up memories of his childhood. To his childish imagination it was huge—it covered about five acres—and reminded him of some vast, far-stretching range of mountains. Within its depths were valleys, hills, open spaces, hundreds of giant trees hiding the sky—cryptomerias, that even Ryokun and two of his friends together could hardly reach round. A Shinto shrine lay hidden in the dense foliage, deserted except on festival days, when the priest would come from Tan'ami. No sound but the chirruping of birds disturbed the silence. Before them stood the stone *torii* of the shrine. With a shout, Ryokun and his friend dashed into the wood, making for a huge cryptomeria that grew aslant, at an angle of nearly thirty degrees, as if it was falling over. It had been blown down by a typhoon long ago, and had grown that way ever since. The first boy to reach the tree would climb up it; then the game was to see who could climb higher.

Ryokun was first at the trunk. Shouting with excitement, he ran fourteen or fifteen feet up it and then, the impetus of his dash from the edge of the wood exhausted, stopped dead, gravity pulling him back. This was the moment to bring his muscles consciously into play—to spin round the instant his body came to a standstill, without stopping to breathe, and race down to the ground. The least slip ment a fall, or at best slithering down the trunk, one's arms round it to avoid toppling off. It was perfectly smooth; even the rubber sports shoes the boys always wore had been enough to peel off the bark. A boy who was clumsy or frightened or hadn't perfect control of his muscles would fall off the trunk, or slip and collapse astride it, before he was six feet up.

Ryokun loved the thrill of the rush up the tree, the sudden turn, the dash to the bottom again. His feelings during those few seconds were complex. The moment of turning, when his body had lost its impetus, brought a stab of despair; for a split-second his head felt empty, like a passenger in a aeroplane the moment it leaves the ground. Involuntarily, in that moment of panic, he would cry out, 'Mother. . . !'

Then once more the headlong run down, carrying him thirty feet beyond the bottom of the tree.

Ryokun loved the thrill of the rush up the tree, the sudden turn, him feel lonely or sad or uneasy—such feeling, whatever its immediate cause, resembling his original sense of desolation at losing his mother, so that it always made him think of her. At other times she no longer existed for him.

Straining to beat his friend, Ryokun raced up the smooth round tree. At the end of the run he was suddenly afraid. Till then, there had been nothing but the thrill of the race; now, the height of the tree terrified him—if he let go his hands, nothing could stop him falling. Below, his companion was still shouting, egging him on. Clinging desperately to the trunk, Ryokun tried to look triumphant. He wanted to cry, but of this his friend knew nothing. How could he get down?

It seemed impossible now. He could not move. Gradually his fingers were growing numb, and the bare foot he had pressed against the underside of the trunk. Even if he managed to keep holding on for a while, his hands were losing their strength, and were bound to start slipping soon. The voice below was still shouting its admiration. . . . Hot and red-faced, all confidence drained out of him, Ryokun held on grimly with both hands and feet. He looked up; a small patch of sky peered down through the trees.

'Mother!'

He was sorry he had come so high, and told himself he would

never run up the tree again, or if he did, only so far, so that he would not have to go through this again.

Still he could not move. The shouting stopped. At last his companion had realized, apparently, that he was in difficulty. Holding his breath, he stared up, suddenly aware of Ryokun's terror.

'Ryokun!' The half-whispered exclamation showed his own fear.

Ryokun began to slip. It was up to his hands and legs now to save him. Little by little, a few inches at a time, the rigid body slipped. Only his head moved freely, as if with a separate life of its own, looking to right and left, then straight down, trying to guess his height. Slowly, cautiously, he came down, not controlling his own descent so much as letting gravity take him down, in short, sharp pulls on the slackening muscles of his hands and feet.

At last he was standing on the grass at the foot of the tree. His friend was relieved, but did not speak for a while. Nor did Ryokun. He was flushed and tense; too agitated even to look up at the tree he had climbed. He felt strangely uneasy, too, towards his friend, as though he had been deceived in something they had both expected. By every law of probability, he should have fallen from the tree; the fact that he had not seemed a kind of betrayal. Yet his friend, of course, had not wanted him to fall. A lucky betrayal, then; it was puzzling. . . .

The two boys walked away quietly from the tree, leaving to silence the awkward feeling each sensed in the other.

Then suddenly one of them was running up a hill. 'Ya—a—a—ah!' The other followed, shouting. In a moment they had raced to the top. Here and there below them camellias were in flower, scattering dots of fire in a carpet of deep green. Chasing each other down the slope, the boys were soon clambering up two big camellia trees. Close-packed branches made climbing safe all the way up.

'Oo . . . sweet!'

'Lovely!'

'Sweeter than anything!'

Tearing flowers from the branches, they sucked the pistils noisily. The camellias, a haunt of bees and butterflies, tasted like honey, but with a special sweetness of their own; cool, fresh, containing the very essence of a flower's life. Ryokun chewed the white tip of each pistil. Sucking, chewing one camellia after another, again he remembered his mother. There, perhaps, in the fugitive sweetness of each dying flower, was the taste of a child's loneliness, to which his mother had abandoned him.

11

Settling his massive body comfortably, Naota Ifukube turned a florid face to Soshu. 'Shocking business I've come to see you about today,' he said cheerfully, looking round the room as if wondering whether anybody would hear their conversation. The Lute Room was hardly the best place for a private talk, so Soshu, remembering that Ifukube was fond of tea-ceremony, took him to the Butsuoji tea-room.

Ifukube's family had belonged to the temple congregation for generations. He himself was director of a fertiliser company and auditor to a warehousing firm, and lived in a big house in the centre of Tan'ami.

The floor of the corridor had creaked under Ifukube's footsteps, and the tea-room seemed to shrink suddenly as he entered it. Ifukube looked at the scroll hanging in the *tokonoma*.

> A calm sea
> Over the bay
> A gentle breeze
> A single sail

—a poem by Taiga, written in vigorous, flowing characters.

Quietly, Soshu put the iron kettle on its brazier. 'We shan't be overheard here.' Ifukube must be afraid Mineyo would hear—which probably meant that what he had come to talk about concerned himself. Soshu was alarmed. He was still upset by the shock Yamaji's talk of remarriage had given him. An invisible hand seemed to be torturing him. 'It's a serious business I want to ask your advice about, though—hardly the sort of thing to talk about over a cup of tea. . . .'

Then it wasn't about himself, thought Soshu with relief. He was nervous about his secret nowadays, no matter what company he was in. Strangely enough, during all the years his liaison with Mineyo had continued, he had not felt the slightest sense of shame in front of the parishioners, but since Renko had left him, and particularly since he had ceased to be able to satisfy the demands of Mineyo's passion, either a new weakness or an increased awareness of his own responsibility was making him worry more and more about what they said of him—especially the elders. That Mineyo was no longer his accomplice made it worse; it is easier to cheat one's conscience if one is not alone in a crime.

'It's about a woman, as a matter of fact—' The fourteen stone in front of him shook with quiet laughter. Soshu remembered that Ifukube must be about fifty-four. His son had already graduated from the university.

'A woman . . . I'd be grateful if you would see her and explain to her what I feel. The whole affair's got beyond me. I just have to have somebody's help. It's not everybody one can turn to in these matters, of course, and I worried a great deal; I didn't know what to do—till I thought of you. It's not exactly pleasant to come to you for help over a woman, I must say, when I'm always lecturing them on morals at the office. Still I'll have her come here to the temple, and if you could tell her my side of the story—'

'Does she live in Tan'ami?'

'No, in M—.'

'Is she young?'

'Thirty-eight—one child.'

This was not the first time he had had to deal with this sort of problem. Soshu wondered uneasily whether he was capable of being of any use, when he had failed so ignominiously in his own case. Self-distrust was suggested in the stiff formal position in which he was sitting, hands laid formally on the knees of his white robe.

'Tsuruko—that's her name, by the way—won't take the slightest notice of anything anybody says, hasn't up till now, anyway. If a priest were to speak to her, though, she might calm down a bit and think what's for her own good. She's convinced I love her, and nothing anybody says makes any difference.'

Soshu tried to listen dispassionately. It was hardly likely he could do anything with a woman only a year younger than himself if she was too much for a man of Ifukube's age. To such a woman the authority of the priest of Butsuoji would mean little.

The town of M—was half an hour from Tan'ami by the express. Tsuruko Yamashiro, it seemed, was a war-widow. Less than three months after her marriage, her husband had been sent to the front, where he was killed a few weeks later. She was pregnant when the news of his death came, and soon afterwards gave birth to a baby girl.

She and her daughter managed to survive somehow through the difficult years after the war. Leaving the child with her dead husband's family, Tsuruko supported herself by teaching Japanese dancing to a number of girls in the neighbourhood. To eke out her knowledge of dancing, which was limited to the elementary pieces she had learnt as a child, she worked part-time in a small inn in return for lessons from the proprietress, who was a qualified teacher. This enabled her to keep one or two steps ahead of her own pupils.

Ifukube always stayed at this inn when business took him to M—, and it was there that he and Tsuruko had met. At first, Ifukube said, it had been nothing more than a light-hearted flirtation. That was two years ago. For Tsuruko, Ifukube was the means of her awakening to sex—he was the first man she had had anything to do with since her husband's death; and in any case three months of marriage had left her still ignorant and inexperienced. Ifukube himself was attracted by the almost girlish immaturity of this woman of nearly forty.

After a while she had asked to be employed as a regular maid at the inn, so that she could meet Ifukube more easily. The proprietress, however, had refused.

'I might think about it, I dare say, if you weren't mixed up with Ifukube, but seeing it's how it is, and I know all about it, I could hardly take you on as a proper maid. Coming in part-time just to help, that's a different matter.'

Tsuruko changed completely. She could think of nothing but Ifukube day and night, with the single-minded intensity of a teenage girl. For three or four days after seeing him, she was cheerful enough, but would turn haggard and thin with sleeplessness and loss of appetite if ten days or more went by without a visit. Ifukube had kindled sensual fires in her body which were uncontrollable and gave her no rest.

She would appear suddenly at the inn and plead with the proprietress to arrange for her to meet him. 'He'll let you know himself when he's coming, won't he? I only give him the room when he asks for it—anything else is none of my business,' was the answer. When she could not see him for three weeks or more, Tsuruko imagined it was because the proprietress was jealous. 'I only want to see him now and then, not to ask him to marry me or anything like that . . . just see him, that's all. . . .' She would talk as if the proprietress was responsible for all the pain and frustration she felt. The proprietress told Ifukube; 'It's really too much when she makes out I'm responsible for your not seeing her . . . what have you done to make her so infatuated? It's very awkward for the rest of us, you know.'

'And for me, too. . . .'

Sometimes Tsuruko complained to Ifukube himself that his visits were getting less and less frequent. At first he rather enjoyed these outbursts, taking them as the quarrels inevitable in any love affair; but when she began accusing him of coldness every time they met, he did not know what to say—if he met her as often as she wished, his business would suffer. Ifukube realized the mistake he had made in starting his little flirtation, and repented of his stupidity. He wished she had been a prostitute.

Her simplicity and innocence, and the genuine love that no prostitute could have offered, had charmed him. But when he found she was incapable of controlling her passion, he was merely embarrassed; her very goodness became a torment instead of a delight.

He decided he would break it off. One day he gave her six times the usual monthly allowance he had been making to her till then, and told her he would be too busy to see her for the next six months. It was a clear enough indication of parting. The money would enable her to keep herself till she could settle down and earn her own living again.

From then on Ifukube stayed elsewhere when he visited M—. Tsuruko had taken him at his word and used the money simply as the usual living allowance. At the end of the six months she appeared at the inn, ostensibly to ask for work again. The inn happened to be busy and took her on, but the next day she complained of sickness and went to bed, where she stayed for three days—though she seemed to be in no particular pain and refused to see a doctor.

On the fourth day she got up, not looking in the least as if she had been ill, spent a long time making herself up, and put on a new kimono. Late that night, Ifukube came to the inn. 'Of course he arranged it—says he's had enough of her, but you can never believe a man,' the maids told each other. But Ifukube sent for the proprietress.

'What's that woman doing here? I finished with her six months back—you were there when I gave her the money, weren't you?' She saw from his expression that there had in fact been no prearrangement.

'But how can she have known you were coming?' The proprietress realized now that Tsuruko's illness had been a sham.

'You're the only thing she lives for, by the looks of it.'

'It's not love, anyway.'

'Oh, yes, it is, she says so herself—says she's always loved you, but never had a chance to show it.'

'Stupid woman—she's got big ideas, I suppose. Anyway I've done with her—why can't she have the sense to realize it?'

'Stupid if you like, but it's because she's a decent woman; they're more troublesome than the other kind.'

Ifukube was in a quandary. There was no going back to Tan'ami; the last train had already left.

In the story as he told it to Soshu, he himself was the central figure—naturally enough, from his point of view. If anything, Soshu felt himself siding with Tsuruko; he had never met her, of course, but understood her position so well. Yet even while he sympathized with her, there was enough similarity between his own dilemma and Ifukube's to enable him to see the other side equally clearly.

'When the proprietress talked like that, I began to suspect *she* must have been waiting for me to come, too, out of sympathy for Tsuruko.' Ifukube smiled bitterly.

Tsuruko's love for him was intense. Such single-minded love had delighted him for a while; but as it grew deeper, more demanding, delight gave way to embarrassment and annoyance. Not that she herself was at fault in any way; only his masculine selfishness was to blame.

'I know very well it's my own selfishness that started all this. But when I've admitted that, it's only words, and words won't help now. She's so obstinate . . . too much of a good thing all together.'

Soshu could no longer listen with detachment. What Ifukube was saying sounded too much like a cynical comment on his own case.

'If Tsuruko were a prostitute, she'd be more independent, and think more about her appearance—she wouldn't let her face show anything, even if she was boiling over inside. Prostitutes cool off quicker than we do. Or if she were a girl of twenty-two or three, now—'

Soshu wondered what the conclusion would be. It turned out to be simple enough.

'—she'd probably go on the streets, or commit suicide and have done with it.'

Ifukube was hoping, apparently, that Tsuruko would do something of the kind. The man was not to suffer, only the woman, taking revenge not on her partner but on herself.

'Nothing makes a man so mad as having a woman stick to him who's no self-respect nor will of her own, nor guts enough to drown her sorrows by going to the devil—and can't summon up courage to kill herself, either. Of course you wouldn't know how it feels,' said Ifukube, staring at Soshu, who had happened to look up at his last words. 'One couldn't expect you to understand—but it makes a man so ashamed, I can tell you. There's no escape; try and throw her off or let her have it the way she wants—one's caught either way.'

In the formal manner prescribed for the tea-ceremony, Soshu placed Ifukube's cup before him. Ifukube took it up with a movement that was easier, more casual, but still correct.

Soshu closed his eyes, suddenly afraid that Mineyo might be eavesdropping.

—Even so, you can stay away from her as long as you like, if you don't want to see her—. But for himself it was different. Under the same roof, day and night, meeting at every meal.

'I decided to stay the night at the inn, anyway, and have it out with her one way or the other.' Ifukube went on, with an air of relishing this part of his narrative. The kettle hummed gently, as if to soothe the listener, for the crude sensuality of the story clashed with the refined atmosphere of the tea-room.

'I went to bed in my usual room, rather keyed-up, and sure enough, when everybody else was asleep she came to me. I pretended to be surprised, and asked what she wanted. . . . "Just let me stay with you," she said—this woman of thirty-eight—as if it wasn't obvious what she'd come for. She thought I couldn't resist her for long, I suppose. But I knew perfectly well what she wanted, of course, and had made up my mind she shouldn't have her way. Then she got into the bed.'

Soshu glanced at Ifukube. He knew, then? Was he aiming all the time at Mineyo and himself, while pretending to be concerned only with his own affair? The stories were too alike—you could have changed the two couples round, and it would have made no difference.

'Did you tell her in so many words you were tired of her?' Soshu asked, to counter a feeling of desperation. He must steady himself, keep listening calmly.

'That's just the trouble—I never had the chance . . . she got so worked-up and tragic, I couldn't bring myself to say it. And that's why things are so difficult now.'

'She still believes you love her, I suppose?'

'She's convinced of it. She won't take seriously what I say—thinks I'm just teasing her. It's nonsense, of course. If only I could tell her exactly what my real feelings are towards her, it wouldn't be so bad—but I can't do that now, it's too late. . . .'

Tsuruko had told him how miserable she had been during the six months they had not met.

'I resisted. If I give in now, I thought, there'd have been no point in avoiding her all those months.'

Finally, to prevent her embracing him, he had been forced to lie on his stomach.

'Lying there in that absurd position, and shaking my head every time she tried to plead with me, I couldn't help remembering Kiyohime and her passion for Anchin . . . how she turned into a snake when Anchin tried to escape from her down the river—, and then wound herself round the temple bell he had hidden under, spitting flames. . . . Tsuruko didn't spare the tears, either. Weeping, squirming, pleading, her whole body on fire. She didn't get her way, though. I kept on refusing, till finally she was worn out.'

'Till she was worn out'—to judge from his expression, Ifukube was proud of this single 'victory'. Soshu despised him. He was angry at the cheap reference to the Kiyohime legend, and at the complacency of his whole attitude to the woman who was pursuing him. How to protect himself was Ifukube's sole idea; he made not the slightest attempt to see their relationship from Tsuruko's point of view. Ifukube had expected her to come to his room that night. What had happened was embarrassing enough, of course, but it was a far cry from such embarrassment to the terror Soshu himself had to face when he was visited in the night. He would be seized with a trembling so violent that he could hardly breathe, the knowledge that he would sin once more tearing his very soul apart. He could not keep Mineyo from him simply by lying still on his face, as Ifukube had done. They had both sinned, not he or she alone. No sudden penitence or decision to reform on his part would save him; the shared sin of nearly twenty years made any such one-sided repentence impossible. And he himself was to blame for the passion with which Mineyo still clung to him.

'It's these ordinary decent women that get so upset—you'd never have trouble like that with a girl off the streets. Tsuruko's taught me that much, at any rate. I've never taken love affairs too seriously, myself—but these moral women won't have anything to do with you unless it's serious. No lightly come, lightly go for them.'

He had never taken love affairs seriously—because he despised his partners, apparently. That, in so many words, was what it really meant when a man imagined that because his affair with a woman wasn't serious he had no responsibility towards her. When Ifukube found to his annoyance that Tsuruko's passion for him was deep and genuine, he thought he could simply drop her—because he wasn't serious. 'Tsuruko was married, of course, and has a child, even—but she keeps saying I was the first man to make her know her womanhood, and how she can't even think of any other man but me now. But it's not real love. If somebody else turned up and made love to her—even against her will at first—she'd forget all about me and be swearing in a couple of days he was the only man who existed for her.'

'Is she that kind of person?' Soshu was surprised.

'I've told the landlady I'll pay her if she can find a man who'll tame Tsuruko.'

'Do you really despise her that much?'

'Despise her?' The suggestion was evidently something of a shock to Ifukube, but he seemed to realize its truth. 'After all, for a woman of thirty-eight, love isn't the naive devotion it is for a young girl. Maybe you think her love is pure and passionate, Father—the kind you get in novels and films. It isn't. It's a delusion, and a self-centred one at that—an obsession with what she's at last found out about her sex, in middle age. If it really means so much to her, she might just as well think about suicide—but she never even hints at such a thing; it's never occurred to her.'

'Wouldn't it be awkward for you if she did start talking about suicide?'

'If it was a question of a love-suicide, yes.' Ifukube laughed. 'That would be too much of a good thing. But with her it's not love, it's just plain sex, and nothing else. She won't see it for what it is, that's all.'

'You think she'll forget you if another lover comes along. That may be all very well for you—but will it make things any better for her?'

'It won't make any difference. She's never been made love to before—there's nothing more to it than that. Not that she's specially virtuous—a woman of thirty-eight just doesn't get much opportunity. It came her way this time because she was working in the inn—and if she goes on working there, she'll have plenty more chances.'

'If you despise her as much as you say, there isn't much point in having her come here just for me to tell her it's all over. You've made up your mind, and that'll be more effective than anything I can say.'

'But if things go on as they are, I can't make a real break with her. Of course *my* mind's been made up all along—and that's what I want you to tell her, if you'll be kind enough to let me send her here—so that she can hear it from somebody else besides me.'

'Don't you think she'll get over it, without anybody else interfering?'

'Not a hope. She's got such ideas in her head. . . .'

'Perhaps she might decide to kill herself after all.' Soshu shuddered inwardly as he spoke. Would Mineyo kill herself? It was likely enough, if she was driven to desperation; her obstinacy would give her the courage. Then the agony of his sin would be without end.

'Her love isn't the pure, single-minded love that drives people to suicide. She'll live to seventy or eighty. She won't have any difficulty in supporting herself. None of the helpless romantic maiden about her—she's smart enough, and no weakling, either.'

Ifukube looked at his watch.

'Another cup?'

'No more, thanks.'

Soshu had had enough of Ifukube's story. He found it impossible to feel any sympathy with him, parishioner or no parishioner. Nor could he face the prospect of having to administer another blow to Tsuruko. At the same time he envied Ifukube the ease with which he could disparage the woman while ignoring his own shortcomings in the affair. Yet he despised him for it, too.

'One can't talk to anyone about an affair like this, of course—and if one doesn't get it off one's chest, it pretty soon gets unbearable. I was really depressed, I can tell you, till I came to see you—hardly knew what to do with myself.'

Soshu showed him out to the small porch at the side of the house. Mineyo did not leave her room.

When he came back to the Lute Room, however, she was sitting at the table waiting for him. Perhaps she had been there all through Ifukube's visit? Soshu suddenly felt confused. He wanted to avoid Mineyo now.

'Soshu!'

He stepped out into the corridor. She did not call again, and he went back to the tea-room, trying to understand more clearly his reactions to Ifukube's story while he put away the tea things and tidied the room.

Ironically, Ifukube's account of his affair with Tsuruko had been like salt on Soshu's own wound. Soshu had always explained Mineyo's behaviour to himself by assuming that she was somehow exceptional, unlike other women; but now this idea turned out to be an illusion. There were other women very like her—and for all he knew, there might be plenty of men like Ifukube, too. Maybe he himself was the exception. . . . But it was wrong to compare oneself with others.

'He thinks a lot of himself, doesn't he? Anchin and Kiyohime, indeed!' came a voice from the corridor. Mineyo entered the tea-room.

So she had heard the whole story—must have been sitting with her ear to the wall of the little cupboard to the right of the tea-room.

'There's no need for you to meet this woman Tsuruko.'

'No, I don't think there is.'

'If she does come, I'll see her and find some way of getting rid of her.'

'I've no particular desire to meet her.' Soshu wiped the tea-cups without looking at Mineyo. Her eyes were fixed on him. 'The woman's a fool. As if Ifukube's intentions weren't clear enough!'

'She's unfortunate.'

'I've no sympathy for her. She's the kind of woman a philanderer like that deserves—there's nothing to choose between them.'

Was she totally incapable of seeing an exact reflection of herself? Soshu wondered. He could not understand how she could have the nerve to criticize Tsuruko so coolly, as if there was not the remotest resemblance between the other woman's conduct and her own. What had she felt when Ifukube described Tsuruko's forcing herself on him—when she herself had done the same thing over and over again? She would weep when he repulsed her, as Tsuruko did, and leave in the end with the same bitter reproaches. Hadn't she even pursued him to the temple hall in the middle of the night?

Through the tea-room window he saw Shoju. The old man was on his way back from the garden behind the temple.

'You're too good-natured—otherwise you wouldn't listen so patiently when people insist on telling you about their petty love affairs. That's all it is, this business of Ifukube's; it's not as if it were a matter of life and death. He should have had more respect for the temple than to bring his sordid story here, anyway.'

Soshu looked out of the window at the camellia tree that grew nearby. The garish red blossoms seemed tinged with the brilliant yellow of the stamens.

The old priest appeared again. He was looking for Soshu, and came up to the tea-room.

'What is it, Shoju?'

'The Mutsumi-ya—shall I go?'

'The Mutsumi-ya? Oh, of course, I'd forgotten.'

'If you are busy, I'll go instead of you; but the lady said she particularly wanted the priest.'

'I'll go myself.'

'Silly woman!' exclaimed Mineyo as Soshu got up to go. 'What does it matter who goes, if it's only to read a sutra or two? It's always "the priest", "the priest" with her—she must have the priest, and nobody else. . . .'

'It's a good thing the temple means such a lot to her.'

'She's too fond of you, that's what it is—as if it wasn't disgusting, at her age. . . . I noticed it a long time back. People of that kind of profession don't like to be thought religious—it's bad for the trade, and they never call in a priest unless it's something really serious. When this woman keeps sending for you on some pretext or other, not just once a month, like any respectable household, but twice, if you please, it's beginning to go too far.'

'She's very devout, and I admire her for it. Her kind of profession may not seem to have much in common with a temple—but from one point of view, perhaps, it brings people closer to religion than any other. A geisha's life is full of uncertainty, and it's left its mark on her. She always sits behind me, quiet and reverent.'

'Really!' Mineyo was bitterly sarcastic. 'What do you imagine she wants from you? The religion is all a sham. She's a disgusting old hypocrite, and a crafty one, too. She makes a fine show of piety, bringing all those girls of hers to worship here at New Year—but Amida means nothing to her, she's just using him to cover up her own wickedness, that's all.'

'We mustn't say such things about a parishioner.'

'It's true, I tell you! You're too kind-hearted altogether.'

Mineyo followed him as he left the tea-room.

'Let Shoju go—there's no need—'

'I shall go myself.' Soshu had reached the room where he kept his robes.

'All those young girls she keeps—they're the attraction, I suppose. . . .' Mineyo's voice pursued him still, muttering now, as if she were talking to herself.

Soshu stood for a while before the rack where his robes were hanging, his eyes closed. Why could he never think of Mineyo with detachment? Her sudden bout of jealousy, groundless though it was, and her sneers at Ifukube and Tsuruko might be due in a way to his own inner weakness. A part of him seemed bound always to share her emotions, to feel responsible for her as for himself. Or perhaps such 'sympathy' was merely the psychological product of their having sinned together so long?

The bus jolted along the bumpy roads. Mrs Komiyama's house was near the Mutsumi-ya, Soshu remembered. A wave of melancholy overcame him, as he recalled the impression he had formed of her. She reminded him at first of the beautiful, shallow stream that flowed past the Mutsumi-ya. But no, he decided—the image was wrong; it ignored the turbid depths her life seemed to hide within itself.

—Trouble for the parishioner is trouble for the priest, thought Soshu.

In which he was not mistaken.

12

The geisha-houses, restaurants and tea-houses of Tan'ami were concentrated in Kiyota-cho, near the Mutsumi-ya. The predominance of such establishments gave the district a peculiar atmosphere, and Soshu could not help feeling out of place whenever he walked down its narrow streets.

The Mutsumi-ya was slightly different from the usual run of geisha-houses. Between the beautifully designed entrance, with its lattice-work gate, and the porch of the house, there was a path of stepping-stones, which were kept constantly sprinkled with water. One might have mistaken the place for a restaurant or a tea-house. It was kept by 'Mrs' Naka Mimori, an ex-geisha of forty-five with three children, who had been the mistress of the richest man in the town.

A geisha of seventeen or eighteen came to the door.

'*Oka-san*!'[1]

Mrs Naka Mimori appeared at once in response to the girl's hurried summons, as if she had been waiting for Soshu's arrival.

'So good of you to take the trouble! Do come in, please.'

To reach the place where the shrine was kept, they had to go through a large room of unusual design, like a big parlour. The house had two storeys, except for this one room, which covered both floors. A staircase in one corner led to the second floor. The room reflected the taste of Mrs Mimori's former patron, who was now dead. With its heavy carpet and luxurious armchairs, it contrasted strongly with the pure Japanese design and furnishings of every other part of the house. The high ceiling made remodelling of the room impracticable.

The shrine-room was Mrs Mimori's own parlour, and the shrine

[1] Literally 'Mother,' the form of address used by young geisha to their mistress.

itself, small but very expensive-looking, was fitted into a corner of the cupboard.

Tea and cakes were brought, and Soshu chatted for a while with Mrs Mimori. She was the only person he spoke to on these visits. He had to forget the time; she would not light the altar-lamps without a long talk first.

The whole house was quiet until Soshu had finished the scripture readings. The girls, he knew, were specially careful not to make any noise while he was there. In spite of her years, Mrs Mimori herself was remarkably youthful, Soshu thought whenever he looked at her. She was unusually tall for a Japanese, and plump and fair-complexioned still, without a single wrinkle; thirty-four or five, one would have said. Nor did she give the impression of clumsiness in her movements that one associates wth women of such large build; she was even expert in Japanese dancing, in which she had achieved the rank of *natori*. Emotionally, she was as placid as her skin was smooth, and in conversation diffused an air of affability that was almost overpowering. Her size seemed also to emphasize the fairness of her complexion, making it exceptionally attractive.

'You look younger and more handsome every time I see you, Father!'

Soshu did not know what to say.

'May I ask your age?'

'Forty-three.'

'Nobody would think you were out of your thirties. So handsome! They say you've always been famous for your good looks. But tell me,' she added, as if an idea had suddenly struck her, 'Which school of tea-ceremony do you follow?'

'*Ura-senke*.'

'Really? I'm *Ura-senke*, too. I never went very far with it, unfortunately, and I've begun to feel lately I'd like to take it up again. At my age, though, I can hardly go to a class with a lot of young girls—and I don't know any teacher well enough to ask him to come and give me lessons here. So it's been difficult to know how to go about it. Might I come and have lessons at Butsuoji, perhaps?'

'I'm hardly competent to teach; I don't follow the rules very strictly, I'm afraid.'

'Nobody would say anything if I came to the temple. Or perhaps you could teach me when you come here?'

'There are plenty of people who could teach you much better.'

'I have a complete set of tea things here—I'm not a good judge of such things myself, but my husband was very proud of them. The bowls are really quite valuable, but—well, it's like pearls before swine, you know, if nobody but me uses them. . . .'

The young geisha kept coming in one after another, a different one each time, bringing green tea and various kinds of fruit, till the table was covered with dishes. Scarcely touching the food, Soshu watched the girls. They looked demure and solemn enough; but it was for the chance of seeing him that they came. They never tired of telling each other how their mistress would change almost out of recognition on the day when a visit from Soshu was due, taking elaborate care over her make-up, and refusing all engagements.

'You'll excuse me this afternoon, I'm sure—the priest is coming, you know.' They would nudge one another when they heard her on the telephone.

The service began, with Mrs Mimori sitting immediately behind Soshu. Sliding back the door quietly as they could, the girls entered one by one and sat at the back of the room. They came not out of reverence or piety, but to enjoy the spectacle of Mrs Mimori listening so intently to Soshu intoning; and went out again when they had had enough of sitting still. The whole room smelled of rouge and powder. Sometimes the scent was the same as Mineyo's.

Today was the ordinary monthly service, so the sutra-readings were short. Invariably, when Soshu had finished, *o-sushi*[1] was brought in. He did not particularly welcome such generous hospitality on what was only a regular visit. However, she would insist on joining him in a meal, and it had become a habit with them to take *o-sushi* together, talking as they ate. Soshu often had to eat alone, while other people watched, and was used to it; but even so he felt more at ease when the parishioner who had sent for him was willing to keep him company.

'I know you have so many calls on your time, Father; but what do you think about the tea lessons—can I take them as fixed?'

'I should think you're busier than I am, aren't you? You haven't time for lessons, surely.'

'We don't really get busy till the evening. If it's not too inconvenient for you, I can come to Butsuoji in the morning.'

'Well—'

'Are you giving lessons to anybody else at present?'

'Not now—I used to have a class of two or three girls, but I've given it up recently.'

'Once a week would be enough, if you would be so kind.'

'Will you let me think it over? I'm not at all sure I'm competent to teach, as I said before.'

As soon as the service was over, the Mutsumi-ya reverted to its normal state. Somewhere a girl began to practise a song, accompanying herself on the *samisen*. She made no attempt to moderate her voice, and Soshu could not help listening.

[1] Slabs of boiled rice topped with raw fish, or stuffed with vegetables and wrapped in fine seaweed.

Empty are a man's words of love—
Yet of parting's sweet sadness
How can I weary?
Even in dreams, from a sorrowing heart,
From a longing unguessed—
A river of tears.
Brief shadow of wings on the water
As a lone bird flies
At evening bell.

He might have been born in a remote village and never left it, Soshu thought, for all he knew of geisha and their ways. He smiled sardonically.

'What song is it?' he asked. Mrs Mimori listened.

Wild and cruel now is the winter wind—
Yet how can I hate him
Whom I love?

'Midnight Moon,' she said.

This meant nothing to Soshu, but he tried to look as if he remembered the song.

'*Samisen* music and songs like that may seem like a world apart to a man of your profession, Father. But it seems to me a priest more than anyone else should know all types of people and understand how they think and feel. A practising specialist in men and women, if you can call it that—that's what a priest should be.'

Soshu hated being put in a special category just because he was a priest—but there was truth in what she said.

She came to the door to see him out. As she knelt and bowed to him, her fine complexion and big build gave Soshu yet another impression, as of a different woman from the one he had just been talking to; she seemed like an actress now, alert and under perfect control. Her training in Japanese dancing showed in the smooth, effortless grace of each movement.

Mrs. Mimori was one of the more eccentric of the Butsuoji people. If she did decide to come to him for lessons in tea ceremony, there would be trouble. Uneasily, Soshu wondered how he could tell Mineyo.

13

When he was within a few yards of Mrs Komiyama's, her daughter ran out of the house, but did not recognize him. Soshu pictured Tomoko's face to himself as he watched the little girl go past; he found himself turning and looking after her. A few steps beyond him she, too, stopped and looked back, bobbing her head in a childish bow as if she had suddenly remembered who he was. Soshu smiled, and she ran off.

'I just met your daughter,' he said to Tomoko by way of greeting. The shrine had been prepared already, and a cushion placed in front of it for Soshu. The altar-lamp had been burning all the morning. With Tomoko sitting behind him, Soshu began the service.

After finishing the Amida-Sutra, he closed his eyes and began to recite the *Shoshinge*. Tomoko joined in softly.

Suddenly the heavy glass door of the house slid back with a clatter. There was no sound, however, of a visitor announcing his presence. Yet it could hardly be anybody belonging to the house; there were only Tomoko's daughter and the maid, neither of whom would be likely to make such a noise when they opened the door.

Soshu had left his clogs at the entrance. From their special thongs of white leather, they were at once recognizable as the clogs a priest wears.

Without looking round, he was aware of Tomoko standing up. A noise from the hall sounded like western shoes; it must be a visitor for her, and she had gone to receive him. But still he heard no voice.

Shutting his eyes again, Soshu went on with the *Shoshinge*. After a while it seemed as if the visitor were going upstairs, but very quietly, as if on tiptoe. A moment later he heard Tomoko's footsteps on the stairs. Once or twice there was a muffled sound from somewhere on the second floor, almost directly over the shrine; then all was quiet. He continued to intone.

Tomoko came down before long, but avoided the shrine room. Soon she went back upstairs, carrying the tea the maid had been preparing.

Mosuke Yamaji was sitting with arms folded, leaning against the *tokonoma*-post.

'It would be awkward if we ran into each other on the way out—I'd better not stay long,' he said in a low voice.

'He doesn't know you're here.'

'Has he finished?'

'He won't be very long now, I think.'

'Give me my things!'

After a moment's hesitation, Tomoko opened one of her drawers and took out a man's padded kimono and cotton bathrobe. Sitting on the floor-matting, she began to fit the sleeves of the bathrobe into the kimono. She was pale now, her eyes dulled with resignation. Yamaji was taking off his clothes.

'Thank heaven it's warmer again.'

Both of them were careful not to raise their voices. When Yamaji had thrown his clothes on to the floor, Tomoko helped him on with his kimono.

'He doesn't know I come here, I suppose?'

'No.'

'You mustn't tell him.'

Tomoko nodded.

'Not that I should mind very much if he did know; but it's different for him; he comes to see me now and then, and he'd probably feel embarrassed.'

Tomoko kept thinking of the shrine-room, but tried not to show her uneasiness. Opening the cupboard as noiselessly as possible, she took out the bedding. The room was bright with the sunlight of early afternoon, diffused through the window of frosted glass.

'Having to whisper like thieves makes it all the more amusing, don't you think?' Yamaji stretched himself out on the bed. 'I've got a meeting at four. It's a nuisance the road is too narrow for a car.'

Tomoko did not reply. Slowly and with resignation in every movement, she picked up Yamaji's clothes and hung them on the rack.

'He didn't ask any questions about how I came to introduce you to Butsuoji?'

'No.' Tomoko lied, but not for Soshu's sake; it was simply that she disliked telling the truth about herself to Yamaji. In response to some inner need there were things she had kept secret from him from the beginning of their relationship.

'He didn't ask any personal questions about your parents, for instance?'

'None at all. Your introduction was enough, apparently.' Kneeling by the end of the bed, she took off her *tabi,*[1] and began to undo her sash.

'Listen—that's his sutra-bell, isn't it? He must have finished.'

Tomoko's hands were suddenly still, her sash half-untied.

'You can't go down now—let the maid see him out.'

'I think I ought to go. . . .'

'You can't, I tell you—I have first claim on you! It isn't as if I came every day, either.'

'He'll suspect something if I let him go without even seeing him—'

'Well—and why not? He's not blind after all, and he'll probably suspect something anyway. Anybody would, when you're living all alone in a house like this, with nobody to support you. He'll realize how it is, and think no more about it. A priest gets to know all sorts of homes. . . . What about his own family, come to that—he's not such an innocent himself. Don't tell me you haven't heard the stories about him and his mother-in-law, and his wife running away?'

Tomoko did not answer his question. 'I suppose the maid will think of some excuse,' she said without conviction. In contrast to her brilliant under-kimono of white patterned with plum-blossom, her face was tense and stiff, as if suddenly drained of its power of subtle expression.

Soshu had just begun the six *Shoshinge* hymns. His chanting sounded sleepy. Its slow rhythm suspended thought: but he was aware that Tomoko had not returned to join him in the service. When finally he came to the Senshuji Commentary, it seemed odd to be reciting alone; this scripture was intended for the living believer, not for the dead.

As soon as she heard him finish, the maid brought in tea, with an envelope containing the temple offering on a separate tray. She left the room at once, evidently afraid of being questioned about her mistress. Soshu drank his tea. There was nothing to keep him any longer, but before getting up to go he put out the candles, leaving only the altar lamp burning. The maid appeared again when she heard him step down into the porch. There was no sign of the visitor's shoes; they must have been hidden.

A few moments after the door had shut behind him, Yamaji began to put on his clothes again, the floor creaking under his weight as he no longer made any attempt to conceal his presence. Still in her under-kimono, Tomoko helped him dress.

[1] Japanese socks, worn by both men and women.

'Looks as though I'm going to be late for that meeting.'

'The car's waiting as usual, isn't it?'

'It's supposed to be.' Telling her not to see him out, he clumped down the stairs to the porch, where his shoes had reappeared. Pulling the glass door back with a clatter, he hurried out.

The moment she heard him go, Tomoko sank down on to the bed, exhausted beyond tears. One hand unconsciously coaxing her dishevelled hair back into its habitual faintly-waving lines on either side of the parting, she looked wearily around the room for a while. Then she got up to finish dressing, and after opening the window just long enough to change the air, put the bedding back in the cupboard.

Yamaji was always in such a rush, she was thinking. It was absurd, no doubt, to be so sensitive about this peculiarity of his, when he had been coming and going like that for so long; but still she could not get used to it. Yamaji never seemed to sense what she felt.

Tomoko went downstairs.

'Father Soshu has gone home.'

'He didn't say anything, when he left, I suppose?'

'No, nothing.'

The feeling of shame before the maid was something else she had never been able to get used to. The altar-lamp was still burning. Pushing aside the cushion Soshu had been sitting on till a few moments before, Tomoko sat down before the shrine and clasped her hands in worship. No *nenbutsu* came to her lips.

'Unclean—unclean . . . forgive me!'

Shinran would forgive her, if what she had learnt of him were true. Perhaps Father Soshu would understand. To feel drawn to St Shinran at such moments, when she had been forced to surrender to a man's lust, was humiliating—yet there was joy, too, at the heart of the pain.

Sitting with clasped hands, the tears beginning to gather in her eyes, Tomoko still forgot to recite the *nenbutsu*.

14

'Would you mind . . . Tomoko dear . . . going to Hakurei Spa, and staying for a while at the Shichisai Inn. . . . I'll look after Shoko.'

Her mother had tried to say it casually, as if the visit she was suggesting was of no special importance; but to Tomoko the words sounded peremptory, like an order. Swallowing her feelings, she looked at her mother. A host of conflicting emotions crowded into her mind when their eyes met. She was conscious of an insistent pressure, forcing her slowly to the point where she would have to abandon the only way of life she had known for all her twenty-five years. The Tomoko she had been was being denied the right to exist.

Her mother looked away. In her eyes Tomoko read the cry of despair, the agonized plea for forgiveness that she could not utter. Mother and daughter had never discussed the plan; but Tomoko knew how her mother was suffering. How much it must have cost her, to ask her in so many words to go and stay at Hakurei. . . . When Tomoko's husband, who had been adopted as the head of the family, was killed in a car accident, they had been left in very difficult circumstances. Yamaji had called on them to express his condolences, and from that time began to come to their house frequently. It was obvious enough that with no one to support them, their only prospect was to sell what possessions they had and live on the proceeds; and for a year they managed in this way. Tomoko did not know what had passed between her mother and Yamaji, but it was from the end of that first year that she began to be conscious of her mother's tortured pleading, never voiced but forcing itself upon her without words, till it became a part of the atmosphere of their life together, surrounding and constraining her whole body, even, as if with a physical presence. Her mother seemed to be waiting for her to answer the question that could not be asked.

Tomoko could think of nothing else but the continuous unspoken dialogue that went on between them.

When her mother spoke of the visit to Hakurei, she merely bowed. To all appearances, her mind was made up. With no trace of agitation, she arranged her hair and powdered her face in preparation for the journey.

'I wonder if the inn is easy to find,' she said, as she was changing.

'It's not more than a minute or so from the station by taxi, I understand.' Her mother was holding Shoko on her knee.

'I'll be going, then. . . . Good-bye. . . .' Tomoko paused for a moment, her mother bowed without speaking. Shoko was asleep.

Her mother did not move till Tomoko had left the house.

Sitting in the train, and recalling that her mother had never mentioned the name of the person she was to visit at the Shichisai Inn, Tomoko felt utterly forlorn, as if she had been driven forcibly from her home. She realised now for herself the anguish her mother must have suffered.

Her face gave no sign of emotion, but the delicate, girlish complexion had paled. The lobes of her ears, plump and slightly larger than average, were bloodless, white like an apple peeled before it is ripe; colourless, as her life was to be. Even the neat line of the parting down the middle of her head showed pale. Her abundant hair had no wave. It was tied simply, in a knot which lay somewhat heavily over her neck. Trying not to think, she stared blankly at the moving landscape.

As she walked under the bridge at Hakurei station, Tomoko seemed just another visitor come to take the waters. But it was if the taxi she took were transporting something other than herself, a body that had been hers and was suddenly dead, severed from all power of feeling.

Lifeless, she stood in the porch of the Shichisai Inn.

'Is Mr Yamaji staying here, please?' she had all the poise of a young woman already a mother and widow.

'Yes, madam; he is expecting you. This way please.'

No fear or hesitation showed in her walk as she followed the maid upstairs. As a lamb to the slaughter, Tomoko thought. Indifferent, as though what she saw could have no relation to herself, she watched the maid kneel outside one of the rooms and announce her arrival.

'Come in!' It was Yamaji's voice, gross, heavy. Tomoko knelt in the little ante-room, bowed, drew back the *fusuma,* and entered the inner room. Shutting the *fusuma* behind her, she bowed formally to the man opposite her.

What could she say? A casual 'Good afternoon' would have

sounded unnatural; 'You sent for me, I think?'—ridiculous. Tomoko suddenly realized how unprepared she was, even for this first moment.

Yamaji got up from the low table in the centre of the room. The cane chair on the balcony creaked under his weight as he sat down. He motioned her to the chair opposite.

'I was beginning to be afraid you'd stay at home after all. Come and sit down,' he said with an air of intimacy he had never shown before. Tomoko stood up. A thin film seemed to be drawn over her face, concealing its expression; as an actor's make-up masks his real self and enables him to face an audience with composure.

'I hate fuss, especially where women are concerned. We're neither of us children, who have to learn their ABC before they can go any further. I don't want any pathetics, either—weeping and whining. . .'

Tomoko sat opposite him, her eyes lowered. She heard sounds from the ante-room; the maid had brought tea.

'Your bath-robe is ready, madam.'

'You'd better take a bath right away—freshen you up,' said Yamaji. 'Have a bath first,' he repeated when the maid was gone, 'we'll talk afterwards—you'll feel different then, anyway.'

He got up from his seat. If either of them needed freshening up, as he put it, it was Yamaji himself, not Tomoko; he had been in such uncertainty, wondering whether or not she would come, and her arrival still did not put him wholly at ease. That was one reason for his sending Tomoko to have her bath—he wanted time to recover his self-possession.

Tomoko was in no particular hurry to take a bath; but Yamaji, standing in the middle of the room and waiting pointedly for her to change, left her no choice. As she was passing him on her way out he seized her in an abrupt and violent embrace. Her whole body cried out in terror. Again, she was wholly unprepared. Perhaps if they had both been young—but that a man thirteen years older than herself might treat her like this had seemed impossible. Her limbs were suddenly lifeless, and consciousness all but died within her, useless now except as an agent of pain. Tomoko could hardly stand, even; she was inert, a mere passive register of whatever suffering was to be inflicted on her. Pale, with closed eyes and only the faintest trace of breathing, her face was cold and still, like a smooth sea at dawn.

The big bathroom was empty. With quiet, unhurried movements Tomoko entered the bath. For some time she sat in it without moving, staring at her body through the clear water, feeling still the pressure of his embrace.

Her marriage had been merely a matter of accepting what her parents arranged for her. Marriage itself was no more than a general custom, a traditional observance, which she had no choice but to follow. She had had no very strong feelings, good or bad, towards her husband; not because she had never thought about family or conjugal love, but because her husband had died before such love had had a chance to develop between them.

Now she was going to give herself to another man, to this Yamaji. She ought to have resisted more, of course; but resistance would mean starvation for her mother and Shoko and herself, and for that she had not the courage—not the mad, passionate courage such a sacrifice would have demanded.

The bathroom window was not quite shut. A clump of bamboo trees grew just outside; their leaves rustled in the breeze. The sacrifice had to be made—it wasn't that she felt so deeply, but the thought of having to go through life without love. Perhaps she was incapable of loving? There could be nothing more desolate, more empty than a woman's life undisturbed by any deep passion till it was time to die. . . .

Perhaps it was just because something remote from love was awaiting her that Tomoko's thoughts wandered in this direction. Something which should be unthinkable without love, yet which for Tomoko was to destroy her belief in the very possibility of love.

Eventually she left the bathroom, after taking all the time she could, and walked back up the stairs and along the corridor. Through the windows, quite close, she could see an island, whose name she did not know. The inn was quiet. There were no casual visitors, and none of the guests who had booked rooms for the night seemed to have arrived yet.

Wiping a few drops of sweat from the back of her neck, Tomoko entered Yamaji's room. Her legs faltered suddenly. The white curtains had already been drawn; with the afternoon sun shining full through them, the room was like a glass-house. It was dominated by the bedding set out on the floor-matting; luxurious *futon* of blue *Yuzen* silk, worked with a pattern of wistaria flowers. Yamaji was lying on the bed on his stomach, smoking.

Determined to show nothing of what she was feeling, she walked across the room and knelt in front of the mirror. But she was trembling with shame at this turning of day into night. What had he said to the maid when he asked her to lay the bedding? The brazenness of it! And she herself, against her will, was forced to seem half responsible. . . . For the first time she saw Yamaji as he really was. The humiliation was unbearable. This time, at least, she had wanted him to show her some little consideration, for all that she was only selling herself to him—but now even this hope was gone.

In his childish impatience to make sure of his new possession, Yamaji ignored her feelings. By forcing her to surrender without protest, he thought he could break down the barrier between them —so that besides satisfying the desire for Tomoko that had possessed him ever since he had known her father, he could escape from his feeling of guilt at having taken advantage of her helplessness when she had lost her father and husband.

Tomoko lingered at the mirror.

'Pretty long about your bath, weren't you?' Tomoko did not answer.

'Why not lie down for a bit?' Again she was silent.

'It'll be quite a while till supper—time for a nap, anyway.'

This time she spoke, as if to her own reflection in the mirror. 'It's so light still—the inn people will talk. . . .'

'That's nothing to get excited about. The maid'll think nothing of it—she's used to laying beds, it's her job. Plenty of people send for the masseuse and have themselves rubbed in the middle of the morning, after all. Let the maid and the rest of them think I'm having a massage, if they're interested.'

'I. . .'

'Don't be ridiculous—worrying about such things!'

Tomoko did not move. It was her final act of resistance.

'You want to have things cut and dried, I suppose? Well, you won't want for anything, I promise you that.' He turned towards her, half rising from the bed. 'And if you want to work, I'll find you a job. You'd hardly earn enough to support the others, though, Tomoko. . . .' It was the first time he had called her by her name. Tomoko listened, as though their relationship was already decided.

'I'm a stock-jobber, and stock-jobbers live pretty well. They get badly hit when the market crashes, though. Your father helped me out more than once in bad times; I owe him a lot.'

To force himself on Tomoko, in other words, was his idea of repaying his debt to her father. Ridiculous enough, but he seemed to think it merely reasonable. Suddenly the wistaria flowers of the bedcover lay in a crushed heap; he was trembling as he leant towards her—then he gripped her by the arms.

'Shy as a little schoolgirl, eh?' He was smiling; the smile of a murderer before he stabs.

'I made up my mind when your father died. What do you think I kept calling on you and your mother for, when I'm always so busy? It was you I was after—your mother saw it at once; and you were such a child, you were the only one who didn't know what was going on.'

Like a hunter kicking a helpless animal before he kills it—or a cat pawing a half-dead rat when it no longer has the strength to bite.

The thick, soft arms held her in their embrace.

'Later on, I shall bring you over to Tan'ami; but for the time being you'd better stay where you are. The glass in the front door is broken, isn't it? You must have that seen to as soon as you get back. The floor-matting'll propably have to be changed, too. It's a rented house, isn't it?'

Tomoko made no answer.

'There's no point in doing any major repairs if it's rented. You must make it look respectable enough for a car to stop at without making people talk, that's all. A tumbledown house makes visitors look like paupers, as well as the people who live in it.'

The glare of sunlight from the curtained window was growing slowly less intense. Now and again there were voices from the corridor, as the maid showed a guest to his room.

'Let's have another bath,' said Yamaji, in a tone that left her no choice, and pushed back the bedclothes. A moment or two after Yamaji had gone down, Tomoko walked along the corridor, with an odd feeling that she had lost her identity, and was impersonating the woman who had finished her bath and gone upstairs only half an hour before.

'The small bathroom, madam, over here—.' The attendant showed her the bathroom Yamaji was using. From the little dressing room next door, she could hear him busily pouring water over himself. Making a last effort to leave all feelings behind, she opened the door and went in. Yamaji was sitting in the water up to his neck.

'Wonderful skin—like a girl's . . . you must have been born with it, I suppose, and then they brought you up in a glasshouse . . . wonderful!' he said, staring at her in fascination, as she bent down to step into the bath.

'You must take special care from now on: keep your nails cut perfectly, see your feet are always clean and wholesome, no smell between the toes, hair always in place, no matter what time of day. I don't like the smell of sweat, either. You'll have nothing much else to do, so there'll be plenty of time to keep yourself the way I want you, neat and fresh, every inch of you, mind. You're going to be a pet of mine, Tomoko, a kind of toy, if you like; and you mustn't forget it.'

Tomoko listened, hardly breathing.

'You mustn't tell anybody about me, either—or if anybody asks why I come to see you, you can say it's because I had business connections with your father—which is perfectly true, anyway.'

Tomoko nodded faintly.

'I heard a story the other day about a girl in the same sort of position as you; a clever girl, and pretty, too. Whenever the man who kept her went to see her, everything in the house was perfect—he could tell at once the trouble she'd gone to to please him. It was her job to give him pleasure in every way, not just by making herself beautiful, and she knew it. She never complained or wept or got jealous of other women, till finally he took her out of the house and married her.'

Tomoko heard only half this speech; she was thinking of her mother standing in the kitchen at home, with Shoko on her back. Still talking, Yamaji climbed out of the bath, washed his face again, and blew his nose noisily with his fingers. 'I've had a few women depend on me before. One of them smelt of the lavatory once. . . . That was the end of her, as far as I was concerned.'

When they came back to their room, the bedding had been cleared away. Tomoko felt she could not look the maid in the face again; the shame she could not suppress would give her away.

She stayed at the inn for three days. To her relief, Yamaji let her return alone. Her mother did not ask what had passed between him and herself. She merely said how good Shoko had been—which was not true. The little girl had cried without ceasing the first night. Her granny had tried to soothe her, first by carrying her pickaback about the room and then by taking her outside; but still she cried and screamed in a way she had never done before, as if her childish spirit was somehow aware of her mother's tragedy. But perhaps it is only grown-up sentimentalising to attribute such sensitivity to a child. The worst of Tomoko's suffering was over by nightfall, and only sentimentality would feel a deeper sympathy for her merely because it was dark.

Shortly afterwards a van from Tan'ami's big department-store delivered a set of luxurious *futon,* with Tomoko's name given on the invoice as the purchaser. Mother and daughter avoided mentioning Yamaji's name as they unpacked the big parcels.

Then one day his car drove up. 'You haven't had that door seen to yet—better have the glazier at once,' he said in the porch, looking at her sternly, as if he had discovered she was incorrigibly careless. Like a trainer with a new animal, determined to be strict from the start, Tomoko thought. She was no more considered than a dog on a leash—less, in fact; the dog was to be envied.

He would drive up to the house without any warning, like a stone dropped suddenly into the placid flowing of their day. But the ripples would spread and grow more agitated instead of dying away, till all the stream was turbid and chaotic.

Once Tomoko did not hear the car approach. 'The car's outside!' her mother called—and the whole atmosphere of the house was transformed, Tomoko herself growing suddenly tense, and her mother dropping everything to pick up Shoko and hurry out by the back door.

Nervously tidying her hair and adjusting the collar of her kimono,

Tomoko went to the porch. In the tension the shock of the car's arrival had generated, there was no excitement; only the dull anticipation of new suffering.

The moment she heard her mother go out from the kitchen with Shoko, Tomoko opened the front door to Yamaji. He came in at once, in a great hurry.

'*O-kaeri nasaimase*!' It was an odd greeting for her to use, since he came only two or three times a week. In the same way, when she saw him out she would say '*Itte irasshaimase*!' Both were a wife's greetings to her husband, implying that the house was his home. At first she had merely said '*Irasshaimase*,' but Yamaji had told her she must use the other form. He never enquired about her mother or Shoko. They seemed not to exist for him, not because he had forgotten they were always there in the background, but because he was determined to spare himself the embarrassment of mentioning them—just as Tomoko's mother was careful never to meet or speak of Yamaji.

'Busy today—got a meeting at four o'clock. Can't spare more than half an hour.' Yamaji invariably began by saying he was too busy to stay long. Tomoko had come to know what he meant: it was only for her body that he came. They never talked. She gave him nothing except her body; her feelings led a separate, secret existence of their own.

Even a few moments spent over a cup of tea with her made him impatient. Indifferent to what she might think of him, he made no attempt to appear attractive, his interest in her never seeming to extend beyond the idea of getting satisfaction for the money he paid her every month. On that first occasion, at the inn in Hakurei, there had been some real feeling in the way he tried to draw her out of her shell of mistrust—one-sided, as always with him, but at least they had managed to have something resembling a conversation.

After about two years he seemed to have lost any desire to talk to her or to regard her as anything but an instrument in a business transaction. The visits grew less frequent; he came only once a week now instead of two or three times. Neither had anything to say. At their first encounter Yamaji had cut himself off from any understanding of her feelings, and of the subtle torture she was now undergoing he had no idea.

Sometimes he would give her the money for her living expenses properly wrapped, sometimes just the cash, without even an envelope. The humiliation of knowing that she was selling herself was perpetually renewed in this way, for he was incapable of casually slipping the money into a drawer, or leaving it on top of the chest of drawers when she was not looking, and would always insist on her taking it directly from him, never realising that every time he did so he was inflicting a new wound. 'Don't I do enough for her already?' he would have retorted angrily if anyone had suggested that he might be hurting her. 'Wouldn't she have been driven on the streets anyway if I hadn't picked her up? As if she oughtn't to get down on her knees and thank me, after all I've given her!'

If Tomoko could have had even the slightest affection for him, perhaps even the act of accepting the money might have grown less painful. But affection was impossible. Instead of fading, the pain of what had been forced on her at Hakurei grew continually deeper; Yamaji's treatment of her might have been designed expressly to make her suffer more. That the outrage became habitual made it no easier for Tomoko to get used to. She would still feel sick at the sound of the car; the moment he had gone, she despised and hated herself. No longer able to justify even to herself what she had done, for some time she would sit like a cowed animal, refusing to speak to anyone. Sometimes, in a rush to keep some appointment, he would tell her not to see him out, and as the car drove off, she would still be sitting in the room upstairs where he had left her, in an agony of despair and self-disgust.

Shoko was still very young, which made it easier. Soon, however, she would be old enough to understand what was going on around her, and already Tomoko was oppressed by the thought of the ordeal it would be to find some answer to her daughter's questions.

It was only on that first occasion that Yamaji had invited her to a hot-springs resort. Nor did he ever ask her to go with him on the business trips he made fairly frequently to Tokyo and Osaka. If only she had joined him for two or three days on one of these trips, she might perhaps have seen another side of the man, and been able to feel a little differently towards him as a result. Or perhaps the experience would only have intensified her misery.

One afternoon is early summer, her mother came back to the house after hearing the car depart. Yamaji's visit had been even shorter than usual. She found the sliding-doors of the living-room closed, and could hear no sound from inside.

'Tomoko!'

There was no answer. She looked into the room from the little round window at one end, and started. Tomoko was lying on her back on the floor-matting.

'Tomoko!' The figure on the floor did not move.

Her mother caught her breath. The little rosewood desk had been pushed over to the wall, otherwise everything in the room was as usual . . . there was no sign even of the silk cushion that Yamaji always used, nor of the tea-ceremony things: evidently Tomoko had not even begun to prepare tea. And where was the bedding that had been sent from the department store—Tomoko had put it away in a hurry, perhaps . . .

Tomoko was lying with her head on the ledge of the *tokonoma*.

'What's happened—what's the matter, dear?'

Clasping her knees with one hand, and supporting herself against the *tokonoma* with the other, Tomoko pulled herself up to a sitting position. The pale, lifeless face tried to twist itself into a smile.

'It was so quiet, I got quite frightened!'

Like a flower torn roughly from a tree, the life ebbing out of its petals. Every part of her suggested weariness—of the spirit, not of the body.

She could not speak of what had happened, even to her mother. From the moment he entered the house, Yamaji had been in a hurry to leave, repeating again and again how busy he was. When Tomoko got up to prepare tea, he had slid the door to and grabbed her by the arm. His departure afterwards had been equally abrupt. Tomoko was left lying where he had thrown her, without the strength to rise, stunned by the sudden violence of Yamaji's assault. She wanted only to be left to herself, to lie there alone for a while, sullen in her misery. He was so brutal. She would have still responded to a gesture of tenderness, to the least sign that he was not insensitive to all her feelings; but he gave her no chance. Even a prostitute who sold herself at so much an hour, she thought, had a right to expect a show of such tenderness from her clients. She herself, however—and this hurt her most of all—was treated as if she were a mere object, an animated puppet, incapable of sensation.

Once she had told him she would like to study flower-arrangement and tea-ceremony. 'If you studied with a teacher, it would mean your being out sometimes, I suppose. That wouldn't do, I'm afraid.' In other words, he insisted she should always be in the house whenever he should choose to call. 'What do you want to study for, anyway?'

'I took some lessons when I was sixteen or seventeen, but had to stop before I'd gone very far—and it seems a pity not to have something useful like that to do on the days you don't come.'

'In that case, you'd better get a teacher to come and give you lessons here.'

'That would cost rather more, of course . . .'

'Like having a doctor come, eh?' Yamaji laughed. 'You'll have to find somebody who doesn't live too far away, then. But whoever it is, he's not to be here when I come, remember.'

'I'll try and find someone who can come in the morning.'

Another time, at the suggestion of a friendly neighbour, she had wanted to take up wax print dyeing—not as a pastime, in this case; if her friend would help her, she thought, even as a amateur she might be able eventually to earn something by it.

'You'd spoil those smooth white hands of yours, which would be a pity—they're one of your strong points. I won't have you touching me with chapped hands and nails stuffed with bits of chemicals.'

Fortunately for himself, Yamaji had no idea of the real motive behind her proposal. Anything she could earn, no matter how little, would help to lighten the burden of having to depend on him so completely, and so give her back some semblance of self-respect. He agreed to her having a teacher come to the house to give her lessons in tea-ceremony and flower-arrangement, on the condition that he himself was always to have first claim on her time. The teacher she had gone to when she was still at school had told her she had some talent for both tea and flowers, which may have been merely politeness, but it was enough to make her dream of being able some day to support herself and her mother; and after less than three years she succeeded in qualifying as a teacher of flower-arrangement herself.

Tomoko always told Yamaji in advance when the anniversary of her father's death was due, hoping that he would take the hint and stay away on that day, at least.

'I'd like to burn a stick or two of incense for him myself now and then—I knew him pretty well, after all,' he would say. She could not tell him outright not to come. Yet to have him sit next to her in front of her father's memorial tablet would be unbearable, a defilement beyond redemption. . . . So far, however, the respect he had expressed for her father's memory had never gone beyond words, and he had left her alone on the anniversary.

She always asked a priest of the Takada branch of the sect to officiate. From early afternoon they would sit listening to him reading the sutras, she and her mother, with Shoko on her lap. Shoko would change to her granny's lap when she got tired of Tomoko's, but she showed no sign of wanting to go outside and play. For Tomoko, the day meant a rediscovery of her real self. But it was also, ironically, the one day above all others when she felt her dead father's spirit watching her and all she did, with eyes that could not be avoided and that missed nothing, making her all the more vividly conscious of her degradation. On that day she could no longer pretend she had been forced to sacrifice herself for the sake of her mother and Shoko. She could have found other ways of supporting them, she heard her father saying, and knew it was true. What she was tempted to think of as "sacrifice" had been merely the easiest way out. Tomoko knew now the full extent of her own weakness and self-deception. But weakness and self-deception were all she had been capable of. . . . She despised and hated herself for what she had done, yet no amount of self-disgust could alter the fact of her defilement. Yamaji treated her as a toy still. She lacked the courage to defy him openly, or even to run away from him—her own hand dragged her into the depths; if Yamaji was cruel to the toy he amused himself with, wasn't it what she deserved? Hell was now, Tomoko thought. It was the literal truth; and this hell was half of her own making—this was no story of the torments endured by innocence.

—Father!—

The priest was still intoning. A stick of incense burnt itself out; her mother moved quietly to the altar and lit a new one. The smoke rose as before.—In all these five torturing years, why have I never tried to escape? Why have I let myself get used to it, almost as if it made me happy? I can't understand. . . . I hate it, every day is a new torture, yet still I can't break free. Tell me, father, why I am always afraid. . . . I'm full of contradictions, I know. I don't love him. If I did, there'd still be some hope for me. But I don't, I can't—yet without the money he brings. . . . Supposing I got a job outside, or found some work I could do at home, I could only earn a fraction of what he gives me. I want too much—I know what money means—in spite of the agony he leaves me in when he goes; as if I'd been struck down, kicked. . . . I'm no more to him than a girl off the streets. The moment the car stops outside, I'm terrified—yet I'm always waiting for him, or is it for the money, I don't know any longer. Father! how can I know which it is? Tell me—I can't hide anything from you. . . . I'm not cold . . . a woman, too, has desires she can't fight against, however hard she tries. . . . The worst time of all is the moment he leaves . . . if only I could cry or tell him I was jealous or how cruel he was, it might be easier to bear, but he made that impossible, right from the beginning. . . . I'm forbidden to act as a woman must act—and if I disobey, what will happen to the money? I'm so afraid . . . so selfish, father . . . I can't bear it. . . .

There was a photograph of her father beside the memorial tablet. Tomoko had told him all there was to tell; she was comforted now to feel the searching eyes upon her still.

The sutra came to an end. Leaving her mother to entertain the priest, Tomoko went to the kitchen. She looked fresh and cheerful as she prepared the special vegetarian meal, an altogether different being from the woman Yamaji treated with such casual cruelty. Shoko kept dancing round her in delight at seeing her so busy and apparently so happy, but stopped now and again to stare at her, as if she was wondering what had made her mother change so suddenly.

Tomoko's mother did all the ordinary cooking for the family, as Yamaji disliked Tomoko herself having anything to do with the kitchen. One day her mother seemed rather poorly, and went to bed. She did not get up the next day or the next, saying she felt feverish; but there was no obvious sign of serious illness, and Tomoko did not think much about it. On the fourth day she did not move when she was called. Tomoko shook her, and found she was already dead.

Acute meningitis, the doctor said. Tomoko could not believe it, death had been so sudden. Yamaji's secretary came and made all the necessary arrangements. The funeral was very quiet, as the friends they had kept up with were so few. Yamaji came in his car, and left immediately the ceremony was over. At her father's funeral he had hovered around her as if he had been a member of the family; but this time, to judge from his behaviour, they might have been complete strangers.

Three days later the secretary came again. Yamaji had sent him to say that he wished her to move to Tan'ami within the next few weeks. He was already looking for a house, and she was to tell the secretary of any preferences or special wishes she might have.

Tomoko was too surprised to be able to give any answer. Mr Yamaji, the secretary went on, also wished her to hire a maid immediately. The secretary himself would be responsible for finding a suitable girl.

A few days later the secretary appeared again, bringing the maid with him—a big, strong girl called Sumi, just out of elementary school. She'll be a handful till she's trained, thought Tomoko; but she was also relieved the girl was little more than a child. Shoko took to her at once. Sumi, for her part, was young enough to find it easier to talk to Shoko than to her mother; and in any case she was used to small children, having three younger sisters of her own.

Yamaji did not visit Tomoko again till after the twenty-first day. The moment she heard the car stop, Tomoko asked Sumi to take Shoko out to the park at once. The abruptness of the request bewildered Sumi, who was shelling peas; but her mistress was insistent, and wondering what the hurry could be about, she emptied the peas into a basket and got up.

Just as she and Shoko were ready to leave, Yamaji opened the door.

'*O-kaeri nasaimase*!' Tomoko knelt to welcome him.

'She's grown since I saw her last, eh?' said Yamaji with his hand on Shoko's head. Sumi had never seen Yamaji before. Vaguely aware that there was something odd in the way her mistress greeted him, but still without any idea why she was being sent to the park, she took Shoko by the hand and went out.

'Thank you for all you did when my mother died . . .' said Tomoko, bowing again. Yamaji pointed with a jerk of his chin to the open shrine, where a candle was still burning.

'You'd better shut that now.'

15

Soshu looked out into the garden. The room in which he was sitting was one of two tucked away at the back of the house, between the inner courtyard and the garden. They were the quietest rooms in all the temple buildings, and were only used for guests. Except for an occasional airing on a fine day, they were kept shuttered. On this particular day Shoju had taken advantage of the sunshine to open them up; and soon after, as if the rooms had been specially prepared for her, Tsuruko Yamashiro came with a letter from Ifukube, asking to see Soshu.

There was nothing he could say to her, Soshu thought. He had known that this was so the moment her visit was announced, before he met her. The sight of her weeping in front of him merely made him more painfully aware of his helplessness. She sat bent forward with her face in her hands, the sobs escaping through her fingers. From the shoulders down, she appeared composed; all the misery and resentment that tortured her whole body were concentrated in her face alone.

Let her weep for a while, and she'll calm down of her own accord, thought Soshu. But he was thinking of how a child tires itself with crying, not wanting to face the fact that for a grown-up weeping only intensifies the distress that caused it. It was a woman of thirty-eight, a widow with a child, who was weeping, not a teen-age girl who had suffered nothing but the shattering of a romantic dream. Tsuruko wept for the loss of what for her had fulfilled as real, as vital a need as the daily appetite for food, something without which life seemed literally impossible.

Soshu was depressed. It was painful to watch the sun shining on the fresh green leaves in the garden, to feel the trees quickening with the thrill of early summer.

The sobbing opposite him continued. Now and again he was

aware of sounds in the corridor that led from the guest-room to the living-room; someone tiptoe-ing up to the door to listen. Soshu knew it was Mineyo.

After a while Tsuruko looked up. Soshu met her gaze.

'What is there—so—impossible—in what I ask from him?' The words came in spasms. Tears had dissolved the powder round her eyes and made conspicuous a blotchy mass of freckles under them. The face was stripped of its mask of youth, distorted, shapeless with weeping.

'I've tried my best not to be a trouble or a burden to him . . . I've done everything I could.' Tsuruko could not understand Ifukube's aversion to her. Nervously straightening and refolding her damp, crumpled handkerchief, she dabbed her eyes.

'He was the only real friend I had—and why should that make him turn against me? I can keep myself, without any help from him, I've never asked for money, or a house; and I've never thought of trying to be any kind of a rival to his wife—so why does he hate me? It doesn't make sense. . . .'

Her voice was quite steady now, but fresh tears had gathered under her eyelids, and were running down her cheeks. She wiped her eyes again.

'I'm afraid the fact he means so much to you is just a misfortune, one of life's blows you will have to accept.' The words were on Soshu's lips; but he could not bring himself to utter them. There could be little hope of getting her to take such a dispassionate, realistic view of what she had experienced. For Ifukube, the affair had been no more than a passing diversion—enjoyable enough at first, when there was the thrill of arousing and inflaming her passion, of watching each stage of her growing infatuation for himself—but such pleasure could not last. He felt no responsibility for having awakened her love, the sincerity of which was now merely annoying; nor was he disposed to allow himself to suffer because of it. He would pick all the pleasure he could out of love and throw the rest away, telling himself the woman's passion was her own affair, not his.

'Why should he want to give me up, when I've never done anything to deserve it? I waited patiently when he didn't come for a month or two months—even when he stayed away for half a year, I didn't write him any letters, or try to telephone. I lived only for the days we met . . . though each time I never knew how long it would be till he came again. How can I have been a burden to him? If it was because I'd annoyed him in some way or tried to make use of him, it would be different; I could understand his turning against me then—but all I've done is be faithful. I've lived only to give myself to him. . . .'

Tsuruko's words cut deep into Soshu's heart. But they were not hers alone; behind her voice he seemed to be hearing Mineyo's also, echoing every accusing phrase. An unbearable sense of unreality overcame him, as he sat upright and outwardly calm, to all appearances listening with priestly sympathy. How he envied Ifukube his egoism. If you found you didn't like the woman any more, that was that. You broke with her out of sheer brazen selfishness—no need to give reasons, or to pay any attention to her feelings. It was enough to tell her in so many words, as children do, that you hated her.

But the woman could not help searching for a reason. Dwelling always on how faithful she had been, and growing more and more distracted with weeping, Tsuruko demanded to know what she had done to offend him—the fact that she could find nothing to accuse herself of making his cruelty so much the harder to bear. In the same way Mineyo, when Soshu refused her, would break down and plead their love of the past twenty years, as if time had made their relationship absolute, unconditional.

—No, I can't imitate Ifukube. He takes her like a—like an animal in the mating season. . . . I can't degrade a woman as he does.

Tsuruko sat upright.

'He came to see you specially to ask you about me, didn't he?'

'He asked me to try and persuade you to accept his position—and I told him I could not undertake to do so.'

'Why didn't he tell me himself?'

This was a fresh source of pain and resentment. Ifukube, according to his own story, had told her repeatedly at the inn that he could have nothing further to do with her. Evidently his words had made no impression on her then; and it was from the shock of hearing the truth from Soshu that she had broken down at the beginning of their interview.

'As far as you are concerned—' Soshu stopped. He, of all people, was not in a position to give her advice. 'It's going to be painful for both of you, I'm afraid. You're very upset, I can see—and Mr Ifukube will have a guilty conscience to face whenever he thinks of you. . . .'

'Do you really think all he wanted was just to amuse himself for a while, nothing more?'

To amuse himself—to awake the sleeping fire in her, and then toss her aside, to recover alone as best she could. A woman all but drowning, clutching at the boat that could save her, only to have her hand cut off at the wrist . . . a punishment for trusting too soon? In the moment of trust, of safety achieved, the axe fell, leaving her to drown now in a deeper sea.

'I'm sorry . . . but there's really nothing more I can say—in spite of these robes—' Soshu said in a low voice, 'except one thing. To lose your trust in others is frightening, a cancer—don't let it grow in you. . . .'

'How *can* I trust anybody, after this. . . .'

Soshu nodded slowly. 'Life is going to be much harder for you now, I know. But you must try and bear it, all the same.'

Tsuruko smiled slightly at the emptiness of the words. But it was of himself that Soshu had been thinking, rather than of her; pleading with himself not to yield in his daily struggle to avoid Mineyo.

'Yes, Father . . . but I can't give him up just like that—not without seeing him. . . . You *must* let me see him once more, Father—'

'It will only give you more pain.'

'If I see him I shall know exactly how *hard* it is to trust a man—and how futile and meaningless life is! I'll have to look at things differently now—and I want to find out for myself just how much of a fool I was to trust him for so long!'

So she was in revolt already against her own faithfulness. Soshu stared at her as if seeing her for the first time. Perhaps she had not meant it—had spoken only out of sudden anger or spite? Tears for Ifukube's callous betrayal of her faithfulnes, and now, out of the same elemental passion, a denunciation of herself for having been faithful. Soshu shivered; it might have been Mineyo's reproaches he was listening to.

At the sound of a footstep behind him, he turned away from her for a moment. Shoju was kneeling at the edge of the verandah that gave on to the garden, looking as if he had a message to give. Soshu glanced out across the garden, at the afternoon sun gleaming on the pond, and nodded to Shoju. He still had two regular visits to make that day.

As he was taking Tsuruko along the corridor to the hall, Mineyo suddenly emerged from a room just in front of them. A quick glance at Tsuruko, and she disappeared in the direction of the temple.

After showing Tsuruko out by the side door, Soshu was going to the sanctuary, but stopped at the main door to watch her on her way across the compound. In her walk there was no sign of the passionate, distracted figure of a few moments before. She moved briskly, the picture of an ordinary, sensible woman of her age. Yet emotionally she was racked with pain, Soshu knew, though he was the only one who had any idea of this. Others would judge from her appearance that she was entirely normal—which was natural; she gave one the feeling some other vital force was at work in her life besides mere passion. There was nothing very remarkable about that; it was rather Soshu's intense awareness of her condition that was unusual.

Mineyo was standing by him as he changed into his travelling-robe.

'Where are you going today?'

'The Hoshinas, and the Izutas. I shall go to the Izutas first, I think.'

'Haven't the Hoshinas anywhere in mind yet for that girl of theirs, the one that was widowed?'

'I haven't heard anything about it,' replied Soshu quietly.

'She's so pretty, too. . . .' Soshu saw the trap she was laying, and made no answer.

Tanemi Hoshina, a pale-complexioned girl of twenty-eight, was a good deal taller than the average, and had grown stouter after her marriage. She always wore Japanese dress, though western clothes would probably have suited her better; her figure made it impossible for her to wear a kimono in the traditional way. Now that it was fashionable for a girl to be tall, she did not need to stoop and pretend to be smaller than she was, as tall girls used to. On the contrary, she carried herself as if she wanted to show off her exceptional height and build; letting her figure distort the smooth lines of the kimono, so that her big body appeared almost massive. Her husband had died before they had had any children.

They had been talking in the family shrine-room one day, after the sutra-readings were finished.

'We've had one or two offers for another marriage, but the girl has such notions about the family she wants to marry into, we don't know what to do with her,' said Mrs Hoshina, smiling.

'Might one ask what sort of "notions" they are?'

'Perhaps it's because her first husband died like that, I don't know—but anyway she says she'd prefer someone connected with a temple this time, if there's any temple family that's likely to be interested.'

'A temple family?' Smiling, Soshu glanced at Tanemi. She looked serious enough, as if she really meant what she had told her parents about marrying into a temple family. It was pleasant to sit next to her, he thought. She was certainly large, but her very size seemed to give her an aura of cheerful kindliness and physical well-being.

'You know all the temples, Father—you couldn't suggest somewhere, I suppose?' She was not really serious, judging by the smiles from the rest of the family.

'I'll bear it in mind, anyway. But'—looking at Tanemi—'life in a temple has its disadvantages, you know; one isn't so free as in an ordinary house.'

'I suppose so,' Mrs Hoshina answered for her daughter. 'One imagines temple people have a much easier time than the rest of us, with the parish supporting them always; but they have troubles of their own, I suppose.'

A protruding lower lip gave Tanemi's face a childish look, in spite of her size and her twenty-eight years. 'You look like a Kansai Kabuki actor dressed up as a priest, Father!' she had said to him once.

'I . . . like a Kansai Kabuki actor?'

'Yes—you're not in the Kanto style, you see. . . .'

'And what might that mean?' She laughed, but would not explain. Neither Soshu nor the rest of the family understood the point of the comparison, which was absurd enough: Tanemi had meant that in appearance Soshu was the perfect type of Kabuki actor, not for the part of swashbuckling villain in a melodrama, but for the lead in a romantic play. He reminded her of the great Ganjiro.

Soshu reported none of these conversations to Mineyo. The mere mention of Mrs Mimori's suggestion that she should come to Butsouji for lessons in tea-ceremony had been enough to make her forbid it absolutely.

'Don't you know you're a busy man? You can't waste your time on people like her—as if a temple was a place for people to come and practise their hobbies, indeed! And that's not all, either,'—with eyes smouldering now—'what does she really want to come here for, anyway? A woman can read another woman's motives, as clear as daylight. . . . A lot of women have got their eye on you; you're so innocent, you never see it—they can't deceive me, though . . . none of them!'

In fact, the constant tension of the relationship with Mineyo had so exhausted Soshu emotionally that he was incapable of responding to any interest shown in him by other women. With a sickening awareness of her hold on him, he set out to visit the Izuta family.

The Izutas were farmers. The garden in front of the house was trodden hard and smooth like black concrete; it served as a drying-ground for vegetables and cereals. The house itself was open, but none of the family seemed to be about.

'*Konnichi wa*!' Not expecting any reply to his greeting, Soshu stepped up on to the high wooden floor of the verandah. No sound came from inside. In the living-room the shrine was open, fresh flowers on the altar. Soshu knew where the candles and incense were kept, and soon had everything ready.

As he sat down to begin intoning, he was aware of someone else in the room. A little girl of about seven was standing behind him.

'Are Mummy and Daddy about?'

She nodded.

'Where—in the fields?'

Another, more vigorous nod.

Soshu looked out across the garden at the paddy-fields to the left of the barn. The rape was fully grown, and past its best flowering. White butterflies hovered among the drooping blossoms. There wouldn't be any work there now, Soshu thought; they must be in one of the dry fields. He shook the tiny sutra-bell. The little girl remained standing behind him for a while, then lost interest and disappeared.

The offering had been left on the altar by the flower vase, for Soshu to take. It was wrapped in plain white paper, without the usual inscription. The Izutas had expected Soshu would come while they were at work in the fields; and for them work was a greater necessity than being present for the sutras. Their absence did not imply any lack of respect for the monthly service—it was merely a custom, which their ancestors, who knew the importance of work, would understand. After changing the flowers on the altar, they had gone to the fields that morning comforted by the knowledge that the priest from Butsuoji would come and read the sutras before the family shrine while they were away.

As usual, Soshu finished the service with an extract from the Senshuji Commentaries, the passage he always read for the benefit of the living members of the family, who would normally be sitting directly behind him. Before beginning, he turned and sat at an angle to the altar, just as if the family were there to listen. This last reading ended, Soshu put out the candles. Next he took up the offering, holding it up in both hands and bowing towards the shrine. Finally, changing his stole, he closed the doors of the shrine, bowed once more in front of it, and stepped down into the garden, leaving the house to its silence. '*Arigato*!' Looking back at the empty room, Soshu spoke softly—greeting not the living but the dead; the unseen presences that now watched the priest of Butsuoji leave their home.

The little girl was nowhere to be seen, and Soshu went on his way.

It was not uncommon for him to find everybody out when he paid these monthly visits, especially among the farming families, every member of which, in the busy season, had to work all day in the fields. But they would never think of postponing or of cancelling the visit. Nor was there any need to go to the temple each month and arrange a date for the priest to come; the date was fixed, and Soshu knew almost by heart when he was due to go where. Even in a shopkeeper's house there would rarely be anyone to sit with him before the shrine, if the shop was busy.

His way of reading the scriptures never varied, whether any

of the family were there to listen or not. If they had no time to listen, there would be no point in sending for a priest, one might think — the reading of the sutras is supposed to be an expression of thanksgiving to Buddha, but it could not be said that the parishioners of Butsuoji felt any renewed sense of gratitude to Him on this particular day. They kept up the custom of the monthly visit from the priest for the same reeasons that they would repeat the *nenbutsu* invocation—because it was something their parents had done before them, and because everybody else did it. It was part of their inheritance, which they accepted and continued with a vague sense of piety. When they were specially busy in the fields there was nothing for it but to leave the priest to perform the whole rite alone. They had not lost all feelings of reverence or thankfulness; though but half-consciously held, the inherited attitudes were still strong enough to give them a certain serenity.

'*Gomen kudasai*! I've come from the temple. . . .' Soshu opened the front door of the Hoshinas' house.

'*Hai*!' answered a young voice. A door slid back, and Tanemi knelt before him, fair-complexioned and youthful—yet there was something oddly formidable about her, too, on account of her unusual size. She looked intently at the visitor. After showing Soshu to the room where the family shrine was kept, Tanemi went to the kitchen. Returning a moment or two later, she sat down by her mother and began to pour tea, the little tea-pot all but disappearing between her two big hands. Both hands were trembling.

'What on earth can be the matter with me?' she exclaimed—hardly polite in front of Soshu.

'What is it, dear?' asked her mother.

'I don't know—my hands won't stay steady . . . there's no reason why they should tremble like this. . . .' The trembling grew worse, like an attack of fever; the spout of the tea-pot clicked against the cup on the tray.

'Pour the tea for me, will you, mother?'

'What's the matter? Try and relax—'

'I can't . . . they won't stop shaking. . . .'

Letting her mother take the tea-pot, Tanemi pressed her hands down on her knees, then crossed them on her chest, then gripped her elbows. 'Must be a chill, I suppose.'

'I expect that's it—you look rather flushed.' Unperturbed, Mrs Hoshina poured out the tea.

'I always get these attacks when I've a cold coming on.'

'Better take some medicine, dear.'

Holding her face in her hands, Tanemi stared at Soshu. Her eyes certainly did look feverish—nothing else could have made them shine with such unnatural brilliance.

'I'm so sorry—please forgive me . . .' she said, bowing.

'Not at all—you'd better be careful, though, if you're feverish,' replied Soshu.

The fit of trembling, however, was not the result of a chill, but an involuntary physical expression, so sudden that she could not control it, of emotional tension. No one was aware of this but Tanemi herself. She had been counting the days till this visit from Soshu, but until this moment had never imagined that his presence would affect her so violently.

All night she had been thinking of him. It was she who had cleaned and polished the shrine and arranged the flowers that morning, tasks which were usually left to her mother. Her mind was obsessed with a picture of Soshu, an image of her own creation to which she could talk without reserve and which told her in reply only what she wanted to hear; in her day-dreams, the priest of Butsuoji acted always as she desired. These imaginings were painful for Tanemi. As a woman who had already known marriage, her dreams were shot through with the awareness of a harder reality. Soshu was her ideal; but her dreams were not the fantasies of an inexperienced girl.

'You'd be surprised how carefully Tanemi looks after the shrine, now that she's got this idea of marrying a priest. Her father's so pleased about it,' said Mrs Hoshina. Of her daughter's real feelings, and of the crude sensual longings that lay behind Tanemi's new respect for the family shrine, she had no idea.

But when Soshu was sitting before her in the shrine-room, Tanemi was compelled to realize that in fact she meant nothing to him. The discovery was a violent shock. She was too upset to be able to control herself by thinking rationally about the gap between her image of Soshu and the man as he now appeared to her; and it was this sudden tension that had produced the fever-like fit of trembling.

Soshu turned to face the shrine. Tanemi did not regain control of herself till some minutes after the service had started. She closed her eyes, but saw him before her still—not the man of whose physical presence her senses were aware, but the Soshu of her mind's image. . . . Smiling, he let her embrace him. . . .

She opened her eyes. The shoulders that had been hers to fondle a moment ago were there before her, but different somehow, unfamiliar. She knew nothing about Soshu, Tanemi realised for the second time. She pressed her hands down on her knees.

'You *have* got a chill, dear,' her mother said softly.

'No—it's all right now.'

'You'd better take a dose of that medicine, all the same—just to make sure.'

Tanemi understood nothing of the sutra, but Soshu's voice was delightful. Its modulations affected her like an aphrodisiac, playing subtly not only on her ears but on every secret nerve of her body. She listened in a trance.

When he reached the *Shoshinge,* her mother joined in the chanting. Tanemi knew the scripture, and could chant it when she had the text before her; but she sat silent with her eyes shut, unwilling to miss any of the beauty of Soshu's voice by adding to it her own.

Finally came the Pure Land Hymns. Tanemi loved the deep-felt solemnity of Soshu's intoning of these hymns from the Commentaries. The words themselves were easy to follow; and they somehow gave her the illusion of a tender dialogue between Soshu and herself. She listened intently, with closed eyes. After the service was over, Soshu turned to face them, and Tanemi, no longer trembling, poured out fresh tea.

'And how is your cold now?' he asked, sipping at his tea.

'How *can* you—' Tanemi nearly exclaimed, but stopped herself in time, smiled, and lowered her eyes.

16

It was dusk when Soshu returned to Butsuoji. He went straight to the temple hall to read the evening service. Mineyo had finished the service at the house shrine when he came back from the hall, and a moment later Shoju came to tell him the bath was ready.

The smell of burning rape-husks pervaded the bathroom, the smell of the open country and of sunny fields, bringing back childhood memories.

Someone entered the little changing-room. 'Father Soshu . . .' It was Shoju. Soshu could see his faithful, stooping figure shadowed through the clouded glass of the door.

'Mrs Tachi called earlier this evening. Mr Tachi would like to come this evening to borrow a book, if it's convenient. I took the liberty of saying I thought you would be at home this evening.'

'That's all right—I've no more visits to make tonight.'

'I wasn't sure whether I'd done right or not. . . .'

'I lent him two volumes of the *Doctrine, Works, Faith and Attainment* some time ago—I expect he's finished them and wants the third. It's remarkable how keen and interested he is, in spite of being at work all day.'

The *Doctrine, Works, Faith and Attainment* contains the whole of Shinran's thought. Tachi had borrowed an annotated edition of the volumes on Doctrine and Works; no doubt he wanted to go on now to the volume dealing with Paradise and Incarnation. A priest or specialist in religion would read the books as a matter of course, but for a layman it was another matter, and Tachi's interest in the work was the measure of how different he was from the ordinary Buddhist. Soshu had long felt inferior to Tachi, and never more so than now; he had begun to be afraid of him. In a mind so convinced of materialism as Tachi's, how could there be any room for spiritual ideas like those of Buddhism? Shinran had never depended on the abstract ideas of Buddhist philosophy. All through his life he believed man was made to call on Buddha and awaken to Him. By this single act of awakening to Buddha, a man would know the meaning of his life, and where and when he would die. Soshu remembered a verse from the Shozomatsu-wasan: 'Even those who cannot read may have true faith; but every word of him who boasts of his learning is vain.' Shinran had not offered an intellectual explanation of human destiny; instead, he had penetrated to the ultimate source of life itself, and had been overwhelmed with awe at the majesty of what he found there. That the Buddha-Vow should dwell in men who were yet in bondage to the flesh—he wept in gratitude for such boundless mercy, so far beyond all human understanding. Knowing himself to be no saint but an ordinary sinful man, he had experienced in his own person the saving compassion of Amida, and with deep thankfulness had accepted the Vow, sinner as he was. This was a natural stage in all our lives, he believed. 'When a man feels in his heart a desire to call upon the name of Buddha,' this is the first motion in him of the divine mercy. All men have within them both a Buddha-nature, and that which is its enemy—the arrogant human intellect. When in times of danger we call on the name of Buddha, what makes us utter that involuntary cry, Shinran believed, is none other than the grace of Amida working within us. At such a time we have only to repeat that call, in simple faith; all questioning, all reasoning is vain.

Soshu wanted to find out how much of this teaching Tachi could understand and accept. In the meantime, he could not rid himself of the feeling that Tachi and himself were on opposite sides.

Someone else had come into the changing-room. Through the glass he could make out the untying of a sash, the slipping of a kimono from smooth shoulders. Mineyo seemed not to realise that he was in the bathroom.

Hurriedly he climbed out of the bath. As the water was splashing against the sides of the tub, the door opened and Mineyo came in, naked.

'I'll wash your back, shall I?'

'No, thanks, I've finished.'

Seeming not to hear, she put the bath-stool beside him for him to sit on, and began ladling water from the bath into the little wooden bucket.

'I can do it myself.'

Mineyo was standing in front of him. To argue with her would mean their continuing to face each other's nakedness. Soshu knew he must turn his eyes away. She had planned it like this—childish, absurd, he thought. But obstinacy on his part would be equally foolish; he did not want a noisy quarrel in the bathroom. To avoid such a scene, the only thing to do was to let her have her way.

'It wouldn't make things easier if anybody saw us like this . . .'

'It wouldn't matter if they did—everybody knows about us, anyway,' said Mineyo sharply. Soshu sat on the stool. She rubbed his back with a soapy flannel, one hand on his shoulder. Her breathing grew heavier. Soshu pitied her for the passion that had driven her to try to restore their broken intimacy in this way; the motive was too transparent. He did not try to answer her.

Mineyo went on unhurriedly rubbing his back and pouring water down it from the bucket, obviously expecting some reaction from him which would enable her to approach him in the old way. Soshu closed his eyes.

'You never told me anything about this Mrs Komiyama, did you?' No doubt she had not intended to make any such remark, with its bitter overtones; but the silence was too much for her, and it came out of its own accord. Soshu did not answer.

'She came here today with her little girl, to ask you to read the anniversary service for her mother. She's pretty, isn't she?'

Soshu still did not answer.

'Haven't you anything to say about a woman as pretty as that? Or is it just because she's so pretty, that you don't want to talk about her—not to *me*, anyway. . . .'

'That's nonsense.'

'Do you think I can't read your heart by now?' The bitterness was in her words only; she had not stopped washing his shoulders and back.

'What do you expect me to say?'

'You're attracted to her already—'

'Only in your imagination! Doesn't it ever occur to you how childish it is to invent accusations like that, when there isn't the slightest bit of evidence for them?'

'Evidence! As if it wasn't obvious from the way she kept insisting it was *you* she particularly wanted to take the service—'

'Wouldn't anyone rather have me than Shoju, since I'm the priest? Your suspicions are ridiculous. . . .'

Soshu stood up and drew back the glass door.

'Have you finished already?'

'And don't try it again, forcing yourself on me in the bathroom like this . . . it's going too far—'

'Soshu!' She caught at his elbow, but it was still wet, and her hand slipped.

'You always have your bath with Ryokun—he'll be wondering what's happened.'

'Soshu!'

On the verge of tears, she streched out both hands towards him. Far from feeling ashamed of her nakedness, Mineyo seemed to intend it as a confession of her weakness and need, that would draw him to her in pity and thus enable their intimacy to be restored.

Unmoved, Soshu watched her as he dried himself. In spite of her age, her skin was still beautiful, her body perfectly proportioned; but now her beauty aroused in him only unpleasant memories—though even this was only the result of his own selfishness.

Among his parishioners there was a couple with one child who for three years now had been living separate lives under the same roof. The wife had several times come to Soshu to complain about her husband, saying she could not endure the sight of him any longer. They ate in separate rooms, the son with his mother. When she told him she needed money for their food, he had taken to eating out in meal-ticket restaurants for most meals, making do at other times with bread and butter and cheese or jam in his own room. He refused to let the floor-matting in his room be turned, saying it was unnecessary and a waste of time. Once she wanted to buy a new overcoat for the boy, and had suggested they should go shares in paying for it; but he retorted that that too was unnecessary, and a waste of money. Even the *miso*[1] which a friend sometimes sent him he would not let his son touch. So they lived, like enemies, but hating each other worse than enemies—with the deep hatred, born of a too intimate knowledge of each other, that makes reconciliation impossible, and in comparison with which hatred of a mere enemy is superficial.

'Ryokun!' Soshu called. A boy's voice answered from the distance. 'Hurry up—Granny's waiting to give you your bath!' Stillness returned to the bathroom, absorbing the voices of love and hate, of anger and pain.

Soshu sat opposite Yosuke Tachi in the room where the precious *nenbutsu* scroll was hanging—it was said to have been written by Rennyo for the faithful in the northern provinces. In one corner was a movable *tokonoma* with a painting of a seagull, so old that all the colours had faded, leaving the bird itself unrecognisable; only the parts drawn in black ink still stood out clearly.

'Don't feel you have to sit up straight all the time—I'm used to it, of course, but it must be uncomfortable for you.'

'Thanks—I'll make myself comfortable, then.'

The shoji were closed, but through the glass panels at the bottom the soft red of the garden azaleas could still be seen, braving the surrounding darkness.

1 A paste made of beans and fermented rice, much used in Japanese cookery.

'I've kept them longer than I should have, I'm afraid,' said Tachi, producing from his kimono the first and second of the three volumes of the annotated edition of Shinran's *Doctrine, Works, Faith and Attainment*. They were wrapped in neat book-covers he had made himself; Tachi was particular in such things. Soshu took out the third volume, 'Faith and Attainment'. 'There's still this volume. I wouldn't be in a hurry, though. It's just as well to take one's time over a book like this.'

Shoju brought in the tea.

'The explanations are detailed enough, as you might expect in an edition of this kind—but the trouble is, even the explanations are a bit difficult for a poor layman like me,' said Tachi, smiling ruefully.

'They're too learned, I suppose.' Soshu was pleased at Tachi's frank admission. 'I couldn't claim to understand everything in the book myself, or that I have grasped the whole of St Shinran's religious thought. I read and interpret it in my own way as best I can, that's all.'

'Well, that's comforting. I can say the same about these two volumes—at least I've read them right through and got what I could out of them.'

'The saint read the whole of the Sutra of Eternal Life, apparently, when he was studying on Mount Hiei. You can see from the mass of notes he wrote in the text how earnestly he himself thought about its teachings—passionately would be a better word. Have you read the Gutokusho?'

'No, not yet.'

'You would understand the *Doctrine, Works, Faith and Attainment* much better, I think if you read that first. Let's see . . . suppose I suggest some more books for you to read. . . . First the *Jinen Honi,* then the *Shosokusho,* then the *Mattosho,* and finally the *Tannisho*—I'll lend you them one by one, in that order. You'll be able to see how St Shinran arrived at his unique, original interpretation of the Sutra of Eternal Life.'

Shutting his eyes, Soshu recalled a verse from the Sutra.

'In one place, for instance, the Sutra says, according to the usual reading, "When the people shall hear the Holy Name of Buddha and think on Him with true piety, He will show himself in mercy to their faithful hearts. He who wishes to be reborn in the Land Beyond shall attain Paradise, and pass beyond the world of change." But Shinran takes the same words as meaning "when the people have but one sincere thought of Him, He will shew unto them His mercy, ever-faithful." '

'I don't suppose there's too much anyone like me can get out of the *Doctrine, Works, Faith and Attainment,* even when he's read the whole of it; but still, there's a lot of things I'd like to ask you, Father.' Tachi began to fill a pipe. 'I was brought up in a religious atmosphere all right. Both my parents were very pious and strict. I had to learn by heart the *Monrui*, the *Shoshinge* and the Pure Land hymns; but it was only parroting what they taught me—there was never any question of thinking for myself about what the scriptures meant, or applying them to my own life. I was copying what mother and father did, that's all. I always had a vague feeling of awe, though, in front of the shrine at home, ever since I was small. Then when I grew up and had to go to work in the porcelain factory because we were so poor, I forgot all about Buddhism and didn't give a thought to it for years. A passion for social science took hold of me then.'

Soshu merely nodded, not wanting to interrupt.

'You know what I mean by "social science", no doubt.' Tachi had spent several short periods in prison, Soshu remembered.

'Marxism still rejects religion, you see, even if churches have now been recognised in the Soviet Union. When I was in prison, though—it's the way these things happen, I suppose—I found myself beginning to believe that there really might be such a thing as religious truth. I never told my wife about this; but when I came out she soon noticed how interested I was in the shrine all of a sudden. She certainly was surprised, and then relieved, I think, to see me so religious for a change.' The faint ironic smile with which he spoke these last words gave way suddenly to a look of intense concentration. He turned his face away from Soshu. 'Marx says in his critique of Hegel, "Religious misery is in one mouth the expression of real misery, and in another is a protest against real misery. Religion is the moan of the oppressed creature, the sentiment of a heartless world, as it is the spirit of spiritless conditions. It is the opium of the people. The abolition of religion, as the illusory happiness of the people, is the demand for their real happiness. The demand to abandon the illusions about their condition is a demand to abandon a condition which requires illusions. The criticism of religion therefore contains potentially the criticism of the Vale of Tears whose aureole is religion." There was a time when I believed every word of it.'

He had been speaking mechanically, as if repeating a lesson learnt by heart, and when he finished, his eyes seemed to light up again. Yet his expression as he looked at Soshu was still intensely serious, with a depth of feeling he did not show at the Butsuoji parishioners' meetings. Half-afraid, Soshu wondered what he would say next.

The house was quiet now. Shoju had gone home to his cottage on the hill, and Ryokun was asleep.

'Gods, Buddha-spirits, and what have you—they're all the same, products of human consciousness.' Such directness shocked Soshu, but he let Tachi continue. 'Man made the gods in his own image. That's why they look like men and have so many human qualities,' he went on, looking almost angry. 'All that about God creating the world and everything in it—it's mystical nonsense, as far as I'm concerned, and I don't believe a word of it.'

Soshu managed a smile.

'That's an elementary question, I know—not the sort of thing I should trouble you with, Father. But we shan't get anywhere if I don't make my position clear at the start.' Tachi smiled slightly, too—though the subject was hardly anything to smile about, nor did he consciously intend any irony. 'Man made the gods in his own image—not the other way about,' he repeated.

'It's natural, I suppose, for a Communist to want to reject anything that smacks of the irrational, or "mystical nonsense", as you call it.'

'I'm a hundred per cent materialist still—I believe emotion and consciousness and spirit are products of matter, and matter alone.'

'But what about the "religious truth" you were talking of a moment ago?'

'It's the product of consciousness,' Tachi said with finality, as if he were knocking religion down like a ninepin, 'and consciousness is simply the functioning of matter in the form of the human body.'

'And what's the connection between this religious truth and the social doctrines you believe in?'

'None—none whatever.'

'Then what about "Man shall not live by bread alone" and the high ideal of man that that implies?'

'When I talk of religious truth, what's happening is that I'm being conscious of my consciousness—making my mind take a look at itself, if you like. Forget about Shinran for a moment—it's all very well for people who already have faith to start right away on him and his teaching, but for unbelievers, if you don't begin by getting clear what religious truth is all about, none of his doctrines will mean a thing, no matter how profound and wonderful they may be.'

'I quite agree—go on.'

Tachi paused for a moment to order the thoughts that kept flooding into his mind. He had stopped smoking.

'There's no telling how far human knowledge is going. We've got the hydrogen bomb, and even space travel is within reach now. All this is just consciousness developed to a very high level. As science has advanced, so knowledge has covered more fields and got more and more exact; which means that we are in a position to deal more and more effectively with our environment—with the whole external world, that is. But religious truth has nothing to do with this outer world—so it isn't of the slightest use.'

Soshu listened intently.

'Religious truth is concerned only with our consciousness, not with our knowledge of the external world. A being capable of consciousness is conscious of himself—consciousness becoming self-conscious, you might call it—and that's where religious truth begins to operate.'

'Consciousness becoming self-conscious . . .?'

'Tell me, Father, can you see your own eyes?'

'My own—?'

'Of course you can, if you look in a mirror. But what you see then is only what the mirror is capable of reflecting. Your eyes can see everything in the outer world, but not themselves. But religious truth is consciousness directed inwards, not at the outer world the eyes can see—consciousness operating on itself, in fact. It's a different kind of activity from the ordinary working of consciousness which makes us aware of physical objects and experiences. Or am I talking nonsense?'

Soshu shook his head, painfully aware how much less clear and logical his own grasp of what is meant by religious truth was than Tachi's. He had been born and brought up in a temple family, had graduated from a Buddhist college and become a priest himself, without ever rebelling seriously against what he had been taught. Nowadays, he heard, sceptism and doubt were common among students in the Buddhist colleges; but his own religious development had been uneventful, almost unconscious—he had followed the beaten track, no more.

'If religious truth has to do with the self-consciousness of consciousness, as I think it does, it obviously depends on consciousness working in a very special way, and can't be measured by the ordinary workings of the mind, because it's outside them altogether. That's the most fundamental thing about it. When we start thinking about prayer to God or Buddha with our ordinary mental processes, we get tied up in doubts and inconsistencies. Even talk about doing away with idols and images is absurd when you come to think of it —images make it possible for consciousness to operate *inwardly* in the way I spoke of, and to use the processes of ordinary consciousness to condemn them or do away with them is to destroy the basis of religion. . . . I don't have any use for these "new religions", and the material benefits some of them make such a noise about. They don't know what religion is. Religious truth and scientific truth are quite different—they deal with different worlds, religion with the inner world and science with the outer. People say, what about psychology then; but psychology treats the mind as science treats an object—the method is the same. The mind it talks about is not the mind alive, any more than the reflection of an eye in a mirror is the real eye itself. It's a mind objectified, solidified—dead.'

'Shinran says in the Ichimaikishomon, "A man shall cast aside learning, and all show of wisdom, and become as the nuns that have entered the Way,"' recited Soshu, half to himself. 'And again in the Yuishinsho, "He who longs for the Pure Land must no longer strive to seem wise or virtuous; let him harbour no secret thoughts, and make no show of piety." He was saying the same thing as you, I think—that religious experience can't be even begin to be assessed by ordinary mental processes.'

'I don't think he meant that a man with a brilliant intellect couldn't be saved. He was simply warning us not to think of spiritual things in physical terms. The first thing is to realise that as far as insight into religious truth is concerned, ordinary knowledge and ordinary intellectual processes are not of the slightest use.'

'Ordinary knowledge' meant the reflection of external phenomena in the mind, phenomena being the object and mind the subject; relativity as between subject and object was an inevitable condition of such knowledge. Religious knowledge could only be reached by the mind contemplating itself, a form of activity transcending the subject-object opposition. Tachi held religious truth arrived at in this way to be absolute and unconditional.

'All secular knowledge is not merely unnecessary, it's a positive hindrance to religious faith—that's the real point, I think. Shinran didn't talk about the difference between religious and scientific truth, or about a creature with consciousness being conscious of itself, or about the self-consciousness of mind—he used simpler words in his teaching. But his simple words aren't simple any longer, in fact; they're meaningless to ordinary modern people. Nowadays you have to explain the teaching by using Kantian phrases and talking about "something fundamentally different from all phenomena," "something that by its nature belongs to a world totally other than that of phenomena in the ordinary sense of the term," "something unattainable by the intellect, existing only in a world beyond the visible and to be illuminated by faith alone"—people won't listen now unless you use this sort of language.' As if afraid his ideas might seem too metaphysical for a Marxist, Tachi went on, 'These two processes, you see, the understanding of scientific truth and the understanding of religious truth—we know now that both are functions of the human mind.' Which was perfectly true, Soshu told himself. 'And our mental processes are merely the functioning of highly developed brain cells which form part of the higher animal organism we call man.'

Tachi spoke forcefully and with an impressive air of certainty. He might have been preaching to his fellow-workers, thought Soshu, remembering the union meetings that were often held in his house; there was an argumentative note in his voice which it never had when he talked to Soshu after the monthly service.

'So I don't need any invisible "other world", even if I do admit there is such a thing as religious truth. The second coming of Christ, the Western Paradise, and all the rest of those mystical ideas —to me they mean just nothing.'

Soshu remembered a verse from the Jinen Honi: 'It is not the will or choice of the seeker, but the holy power of Amida, that causes us to have faith in the prayer with which we call upon His Name, and seeks to turn us to Himself. This working of His mercy, I have learned, is called Jinen. The meaning of the Vow is that Amida has promised to lead us to supreme Buddhahood. This final Buddha-hood or Nirvana is Being without form; and that is why it is called Jinen. When we describe it as having form, then it is no longer the supreme state that we are speaking of. It was Amida, I have heard, who first taught us that Nirvana is without form. . . .'

Paradise is described in the vaguest terms, such as 'the land which is real and yet not real', which 'exists and yet does not exist', and so on. What was important is not whether or not it existed, thought Soshu, but whether one could or could not reach it. Where true faith was, there was Paradise already; where faith was lacking, Paradise could never be. The question was, did one believe in Paradise or not? Paradise, it was said, was in the peace that comes from faith in Buddha and in the calling on his name. It was invisible to the eye of reason, but could be known, the preachers said, by an instinct that lay hidden behind man's faculty of reasoning. If one asked who first became consciously aware of this instinct, the answer the preachers gave was—Amida; and it was through his Original Vow that all men learn of its presence in themselves. Such was the teaching; but nowadays people responded more readily to a rational explanation such as Tachi's.

'This is really where my problem begins,' said Tachi with a smile, relaxed again now. 'I've worked for the Union all these years, and can't remember ever having done anything I'd want to apologize for, as far as the Union's concerned anyway. When it comes to really personal problems, though, what you might call the spiritual side of me, I suppose—it's another story, and not a pleasant one. I've never liked to play second fiddle—always wanted to be at the top; and if I'm Chairman of the Union, it's not just pure disinterested zeal, but conceit, too. I'm twice as conceited as the next man, and more. I managed to hide it from other people, somehow, but a man can't fool himself. There was a time when I talked a lot about a life of unselfish service. It was only talk—self-deception, as I soon found out. Prison taught me something, and I'm grateful.'

'By "something", do you mean spiritual peace, or salvation?'

'Yes. At first I thought I'd go mad when they locked me up, from the loneliness. The *nenbutsu* was almost part of me, of course, I'd been so used to hearing and repeating it since I was a baby; but I never had any real faith. Then it happened, in prison. Suddenly, without thinking, I found myself repeating 'Namu Amida Butsu' ... In that moment I knew I had a Buddha-nature. It was Mind becoming conscious of itself—'

'Tell me, do you think salvation is really possible?'

'I wanted to ask *you* that question, Father.'

'But I don't know ... I don't know ...' As he spoke the words, Soshu seemed to hear a drumming in his ears, as of lust and greed and all sin transmuted into sound—the cry of a wounded beast on a moor. ... He would hear it for ever ... now it was the dull roaring of the sea, a sea of evil in which he was condemned to drown, beyond all forgiveness.

'What assurance can there be of salvation ...' His voice was sad.

Tachi's expression showed that he was moved. 'You are honest, Father ...' he said.

'I know all we have to do is to forget self and trust Him for everything—but I—I've a long way to go yet before I get that far ... I haven't thought deeply enough about Shinran's teaching.'

Mineyo and the maid must have gone to bed while they were talking. Silence filled the house.

Tachi stood in the porch, holding the new book he had borrowed, and apologized for having stayed so late. There was no sign of the maid O-Sugi, who invariably appeared when a visitor came or went.

'Come again whenever you're free. I've learnt a lot tonight.'

'As if you could learn anything from me!—it's me that needs to learn from you. I've got a whole lot of doubts I want to ask you about.'

'Thanks to what you said this evening, I think I've begun to understand you a little,' said Soshu, with a frankness that was new between them.

'People begin to get suspicious when a man in my position shows signs of being religious—I realised that quite a while ago. So I felt I ought to explain.' Smiling at his last remark, as if it were a joke, Tachi pushed back the wooden door.

If O-Sugi was asleep, Soshu had to do the locking-up himself. All the house was deep in silence now, as Butsuoji had been for every night for ten, for fifty years. His clogs clattering as he walked across the stone floor of the porch to lock the doors, he listened to

Tachi crossing the compound. A moment later Tachi reached the gate; Soshu heard the little night-door swing to.

He tidied the room where they had been talking, and took the tray with the tea-things back to the parlour, his footsteps echoing in the stillness. Then he went to his own room—and started involuntarily as he slid back the door.

Mineyo was waiting for him. He could tell from the way she was sitting that she must have been waiting there all the evening.

'Still up?'

Her eyes looked at him accusingly. Soshu remembered what had happened earlier that evening; he was afraid she was going to make another such scene. Trying to look as though he had forgotten their encounter in the bathroom, he sat down quietly opposite her.

'Don't you feel just the least bit ashamed,—Father?' said Mineyo, fiercely sarcastic.

'Ashamed?' Soshu did not understand.

'When you were with that Tachi—I heard everything you said. . .'

Soshu went over his conversation with Tachi, wondering whether he had said anything to repent of; but he could think of nothing.

'What do you think you are priest of Butsuoji for?'

Soshu stared at her. Mineyo as a self-appointed spokesman for the congregation—this was something new for her, or at least a side of her he had never seen before.

Taking advantage of his surprise, Mineyo renewed her attack.

'What do you think you are going to say to the parishioners? Or doesn't it matter if a man who's supposed to be a priest starts telling everybody how little he himself believes? Isn't it a priest's job to help other people in their doubts? As if there could be any hope for them when their own priest hasn't any convictions! How could you say such things and not be ashamed? I was so upset, sitting here listening. . . .'

Soshu smiled. 'Do you mean I should do nothing but repeat what Shinran said?'

'You ought to know your duty by now—or what was the point of all that study in Kyoto, and all the years you've spent here as priest?'

'I can't speak of what I don't feel.'

'How is it you manage to preach, then?'

'I'm a very poor preacher—and I hate doing it, anyway.'

'But even so, you *do* preach . . .'

It was the custom for him to speak after the annual memorial services for the dead which the parishioners would ask him to conduct in their homes. Sitting in the middle of a roomful of relatives and neighbours who would gather for the occasion, his back to the family shrine, the priest was always expected to give an edifying message. Soshu hated it, but it was a professional duty he could not escape. Rather than preach himself, he would have preferred to listen to others; he knew his own faith was too meagre for him to be able to set any kind of example, and was ashamed of the ease with which he wore the mask of religion.

There were Buddhist preachers who were widely known and as popular as *naniwa-bushi* reciters. Some of them came now and then to preach at Butsuoji. Masters of gesture and of every trick of eloquence and emotional chanting, they could fascinate their simple hearers and draw them up little by little to a state of exaltation. Soshu listened to them sometimes; but their performance was hardly something he could imitate. It was not so much exposition of Shinran's teaching as an impressive display of a certain kind of acting technique. The listeners appeared to understand and to be convinced—but once outside the hall, everything was forgotten except the brilliance of the performance. The very fact of their coming to the temple at all meant that they were psychologically prepared for the sermon before it began, and the period of waiting for the preacher to appear made them even more receptive. Not one of the congregation had the smallest intention of doubting or criticising what he was about to hear; all had come prepared and eager to enjoy an orgy of religious emotion. By sheer eloquence the preacher would fulfil their expectations.

Not that the exaltation they experienced at Butsuoji was unreal, or that they were merely the victims of a clever deception. Nor was there anything wrong in what they themselves longed for. The question was how far their real need was met, especially at Butsuoji. The mood in which the parishioners came to the temple was a special 'Butsuoji' mood, which they could only feel in the peculiar atmosphere of the temple, and which was soon forgotten when they left it. Or not forgotten, perhaps, so much as dispelled by the totally different atmosphere at home. Gradually, and without being aware of it, Butsuoji people had come to treat their temple as a 'special' place, in a category altogether different from the houses in which they lived. They had deluded themselves into thinking that religion was merely an affair of the temple, forgetting that its place is either in ordinary daily life or nowhere. This was the unquestioned assumption behind all their dealings with Butsuoji.

As a result of this attitude to the temple and to himself, Soshu was always conscious of a feeling of isolation from reality. He was treated as if he had no concern whatever with the ordinary lives the parishioners lived, and was expected, as the 'priest from Butsuoji', to be a different sort of human being from the layman, a professional specialist in religion. Years of such pressure, and the force of habit, had made him conform outwardly to this popular idea of what a priest should be.

'It's hard to believe a man who's supposed to be a priest could talk so openly about his own weakness—and to one of his own parishioners, of all people!'

It was lack of 'professional confidence' that Mineyo was accusing him of.

'I was born in a temple family, I went to a Buddhist college, and I've been priest of Butsuoji for nearly twenty years. . . . I can do everything a priest has to do well enough. But all that's nothing but show.' He looked depressed and lonely now. 'Reading the sutras over the dying whenever they send for me, holding funerals and periodical memorial services—that's all I'm expected to do, apart from arranging the regular temple events and keeping in touch with the central temple. But is that really enough? Mightn't I just as well have been a doctor's son, who started out as a doctor when he left medical school twenty years ago and has been practising quietly ever since? A doctor's duty ends there—but doesn't a priest have any duty besides officiating at funerals and temple functions? It's hard to understand what a priest's life is really for. . . .'

'What on earth are you talking about? Have you gone mad, or something?'

'Priests of our sect are allowed to eat meat, and to marry, thanks to Shinran. He was determined that being a priest shouldn't prevent a man from sharing the life that everybody else lives. He suffered a long while before people would accept this idea—one mustn't forget that. Even a priest is a man, he taught, and Pure Land priests nowadays take it for granted they should lead normal lives—it never occurs to us to wonder whether meat-eating and marriage are right or not. I've thought too little about what Shinran went through. Not that I have to endure the same *kind* of ordeal he faced—but he did suffer, and so must I, in my own way. . . . But what I am doing now—I'm not suffering . . . far from it, I'm sinning, as I have done all these years, to my shame. . . . I don't know how I can preach to the Butsuoji people. But if the time comes when I can preach a *real* sermon. . . .'

Soshu shut his eyes, breathing jerkily as if in physical pain from the intensity of his conflicting feelings. He was imagining a scene in the temple hall: a meeting of all the parishioners—there would be others there, too, who did not belong to the temple—and himself speaking to them, confessing. . . . From the shrine behind him, Amida looked down upon him as he told the crowd the long story of his sin with Mineyo, begun before he was made priest, in his student days in Kyoto. He kept back nothing, even explaining how his wife Renko had been driven to leave home in despair. From the preacher's platform, looking out across the congregation, he confessed to them he was not fit to preach, was unworthy of his priesthood. If he did make up his mind to confess, he would have to leave Butsuoji, of course; his whole life would be changed in a moment. Such a decision would mean ignoring the consequences for Mineyo—and what would happen to Ryokun?

He could not bring himself to do it yet. Not because he was selfishly worried about his own security, nor even out of concern for Ryokun's or Mineyo's future. He merely lacked the courage—not only courage to face the world, but the courage to confront the reality of his own situation, the need to gouge out of his own nature the weakness that made him so easy-going and willing to compromise, that for twenty years had prevented him from speaking out. That his relationship with Mineyo and the reasons for Renko's flight were no secret to most of the Butsuoji parishioners, and to a good many other people besides, Soshu knew. But it was not courage that enabled him to continue sinning year after year, in apparent defiance of all opinion.

Every kind of family and personal trouble could be found among the two hundred families that belonged to Butsuoji. Compared with many of them, with Ifukube's scheming to get rid of a woman he was tired of, for example, Soshu's sin was probably regarded as not so serious. The inner life of the temple family, which should have been an model of purity to others, was in fact the most ugly and sordid; but they had learnt to preserve at least the appearance of purity.

'I told Tachi frankly what I felt, because he asked me, that's all.'

'You went too far!' You didn't think who you were talking to.' Mineyo spoke with a force and intensity of which Soshu felt himself to be incapable.

'Suppose Tachi starts telling everybody what you said to him!'

'He won't. He's not that sort of man.'

'No one thanks a doctor for giving him an injection if he keeps on saying he doesn't know whether it'll do any good or not. The patient has to feel he can trust him. You're a kind of doctor, aren't you? A priest his people don't trust isn't fit to be a priest.'

'I envy Tachi . . .'

'You ought to be ashamed of yourself!'

'He found himself repeating *nenbutsu*, he told me, when he was in prison and nearly desperate with loneliness. It was the same *nenbutsu* I recite . . . and yet so different! When I say it, it's a priest's prayer. It's true that sometimes, when I'm upset, I repeat it without thinking—but even then there's something 'professional' about it, which is what Shinran so often warned against.'

'There isn't the slightest difference between Tachi's praying and yours.'

'How do you know?'

'Aren't we told that Amida will have mercy on all that call on his Name, and keep faithful watch over them for ever? Shinran spent his life saying practically nothing else.' Mineyo's tone was accusing; like a creditor demanding payment of an debt. Soshu saw her in a new light, realizing that she understood nothing of what he was thinking. Shinran had come to the point where he felt himself to be so hardened and steeped in sin that he was beyond even the hope of being saved—but it was this very despair of self that proved to be the beginning of his salvation. Soshu wanted to say that he had realised how far from complete his own self-despair had been. The moment he became convinced beyond all doubt that for him there would be no salvation, then and only then would the way to salvation open. But he was still a long way from such certainty.

'You'd better think a bit more in future about what you say in company—and be specially careful with people like Tachi. There are things that can be said, and things that can't be said; what will people think of Butsuoji if it gets about that the priest, of all people, doesn't have any real religion?'

Even as she scolded him, Mineyo was longing for a renewal of their former intimacy. If Soshu had made the smallest advance, she would have given herself to him at once; the angry reproaches were merely another expression of the old passion.

He could not believe her when she spoke as if she herself had faith in salvation through Amida. If she did have any faith, it was probably only the veneer one acquires automatically by spending years in a temple household. She could talk like a priest, but only because she happened to live in Butsuoji—if she had belonged to a lay family, she would never have come by such religious knowledge as she appeared to possess. Even now, her knowledge consisted only of words and phrases she had picked up from Soshu. In her case it was something very different from religion that controlled her life and led her into suffering; something utterly remote from the process —dominating his life and making him suffer, too—that was working itself out in Soshu.

He remembered one of Shinran's farewell poems:

> Now that my years are fulfilled, I must return to the Pure Land of Peace; but again and again my spirit shall revisit the world, as the waves fall without ceasing on the shores of Waka-no-ura. If a man finds joy alone, he shall know then that another is with him; if two rejoice together, a third shall ever be with them—I, Shinran, their companion unseen!

If he was honest, Soshu had to admit that he rarely felt the unseen presence of Shinran. And if he did feel it, it was because he had decided he ought to feel it. Intellectually he had accepted the view that the gracious eyes of Amida looked in eternal calm upon all human fears and passions and conflicts, and knew, or thought he knew, that "the Merciful One lightens our path for ever"; but he was unable to go beyond such intellectual acceptance to a direct experience of the truth. When he recited the *nenbutsu* he was still struggling with his lack of faith.

17

The hot days continued. Cycling through the paddy fields, Soshu saw the jagged holes where the parched soil had cracked as if in pain. The streams were dry; even the river behind the temple was down to its bed, and eels could be picked up alive as they moved sluggishly in the gaps between the rough stone blocks with which the bank was lined.

The water-wheel in the little rice-mill was silent. The miller had installed an electric machine for pounding rice now, but the old wheel was still used whenever there was enough water to drive it. The family belonged to the Butsuoji congregation.

Ryokun and a friend were walking barefoot along the uneven bed of the river, overturning the big stones to find the eels hiding underneath.

'There's lot of eels in the big tunnel near the mill—and carp and catfish, too!'

'Have you been inside?' Ryokun asked.

'It's pitch-dark . . . Tatsu went the whole length, all the way to Shinkawa. I got frightened, though, after about fifty yards and came back.'

The conduit, an underground tunnel, not quite tall enough for Ryokun to stand up in, ran for about five hundred yards from the mill. When the river was full the water raced through it after leaving the mill, until it joined the river again at Shinkawa.

'Let's go and see!'

'I don't want to, it's too dark . . .'

'It's not dangerous—'

'Suppose the water starts flowing? We'd be drowned.'

'There won't be any water—it's dried up.'

'We don't know what it's like in the middle—nobody would hear if we cried.'

'Coward!' Ryokun was determined to see what the inside of the conduit was like.

'I don't want to . . .'

'If you're afraid, I'll go alone.'

'If you go, I'll go, too!' They were near the mill now.

'Let's not tell anybody we're going!' There would be trouble if they were found out. Ryokun's companion was pale, and Ryokun himself was excited at the adventure. They were going into a cave, a quarter of a mile or more of darkness; the conduit was very old—it was built of clay—and they had no idea what they would find on the way. If it should start to crumble over their heads, they would be buried alive. Nobody would hear their screams.

Ryokun stood at the mouth of the conduit and peered inside. It seemed to breathe a cold dark air; a feeling of life itself being sucked away into the darkness made the boy shiver. Guarding the entrance, which was walled off from the river proper, was the wooden water-wheel, rotting in places and black as iron with age and use. Ryokun gave it a push; it creaked slowly round, like an old man's pulse.

'Are we really going in . . .?' His friend asked in a small voice.

'Of course we are!' Ryokun answered. He would not give up the thrill of finding out what the tunnel was like inside.

'Let's get somebody else to come with us . . .'

'No, if several of us go, there'll be that much less to take home—we can get all the fish ourselves if we go alone.'

Ryokun stepped into the conduit. A vague fear made him shiver again. I'm a coward, too, he thought; but it was only a natural reaction to the beginning of the adventure. A few steps farther in, out of the darkness came a mysterious noise, a cold metallic, subterranean echo.

In one of the Tan'ami temples there was a 'mystery tunnel', as Ryokun and the other boys called it. This was a long underground passage, directly underneath the temple hall. When you went down the entrance steps, you found yourself in complete darkness, so that you had to feel your way along. At one point a key projected from the wall; you had to find this and touch it—if you couldn't find it at all, it was supposed to be a sign you were not fit to go to the Pure Land, while if you reached the other end of the passage without touching it once, you were sure to be unlucky. Ryokun had gone through this 'tunnel' three times with a friend, and had found the key each time. It guaranteed that you would go to Paradise. Ryokun never gave a thought to Paradise; but he loved the thrill of groping his way along the polished wooden walls and sliding along the floor that blindly shuffling feet had rubbed so smooth, till it, too, seemed polished. The key was underneath the temple shrine. But even when you knew that, the darkness made it easy to lose your sense of direction. Most people kept their eyes shut when they were in the tunnel, presumably from a vague feeling that they were no use anyway in such darkness, and trusted entirely to their hands and feet. The darkness represented illusion—the world of everyday; he who could touch the key would be blessed in being able to find his way through the dark paths of life, relying only on the guidance of Buddha. Ryokun, after paying the small admission fee without which no one could enter, would creep slowly along the tunnel, giving himself up to a mixture of fear and excitement and just managing to keep a hold on himself till he reached the far end. In those moments he felt he knew how the blind and deaf must suffer. The key was about on a level with his face. There would be a strange grating sound when his groping hands happened to touch it.

'Found it!' he would cry in the darkness.

'Where, Ryokun? Where?' His friend's voice was breathless, crushed with fear.

'Here!'—clasping the key in both hands and shaking it.

'Where—where?'

The grating of the key was his only guide, though in the darkness even sounds seemed at first to come from no particular direction.

But the waterless conduit was a very different matter from the wooden tunnel. Sand and stones, fragments of china, rotten wood, bucket handles and old tins covered the floor, which had never been meant for human feet. Ryokun had come ten yards or so, stooping all the time; it was too low to walk upright. Perhaps because the level of the conduit was lower than that of the river, it still held some water, though the river itself was completely dry. It went under the mill first, then under some houses, then under the river, coming out beyond the elementary school.

'Nobu!'

'Ryokun!'

The voices echoed through the darkness. Half-crouching, Ryokun felt his way forward with one hand on each sloping wall. The water around his feet was ice-cold, and there was no sign of it ending. He began to wish they had stayed in the sunshine.

'Nobu!'

'Ryokun!'

Echoing off the water, the two cries were louder than before and touched with panic. Ryokun did not know what he was treading on. His feet kept slipping, and his hands on the smooth, damp walls.

'Nobu!'

He had no idea how far they had come. Fishes began to leap round his feet, carp and catfish and eels. The big catch he had meant to take home was forgotten; his only thought now was to keep on walking to escape from the darkness. Invisible fish he disturbed brushed against his arms as well as his feet—he knew they must be fish from the cold slimy touch. He could do nothing to keep them off; they would have slid through his fingers the moment he started trying to catch them. The darkness grew more terrifying every moment, an unseen enemy pursuing the boys.

'Nobu!'

'Ryokun!'

By calling to each other they managed somehow to keep themselves from panic. Ryokun was wet all over from the fish—they seemed to resent the invasion of their refuge, and thrashed about blindly in the shallow water whenever a foot came near. There was no end to them; the boys could have scooped them up as easily as picking the catch out of a fishing-boat's net.

'Nobu! There's a huge one!' Ryokun had wanted to say, but he was too terrified to do more than cry out. How much longer would it be so horribly dark. . . . He knew the conduit ended at Shinkawa, but that must be a terribly long way still, and walking bent forward all the time was so tiring.

'Ryokun!' His friend was nearly crying. It was his fault—it was he who had dared Nobu into coming. Ryokun's heart was racing. They would die without anybody knowing—the water would come rushing down from the river and drown them instantly . . . invisibly . . . If he had to die, he wished it could be where someone would find him.

'Nobu!' he called again, involuntarily. Darkness swallowed the echoes. Gradually he lost all sensation, his hands moving mechanically along the walls, his feet no longer searching for obstacles before each step. Often the rounded floor made him slip and fall. Cut off from the light, helpless, unable even to protect themselves against the fishes, the boys grew desperate.

'Mother!' Ryokun cried out—thinking he had only called his friend's name again.

'Mother!' Not a cry for the mother he had known and who had abandoned him; only an instinctive expression of misery and loneliness and fear. Ryokun did not think of his father or grandmother, or of Shoju. Suddenly a huge fish lashed his face; a monster, it seemed to him, the lord and guardian of the darkness.

'Ryokun!'

'Mother!'

If only they could get through safely to Shinkawa, he would never come near the conduit again. How far had they come, he wondered. They had never dreamt there would be so many fish. Probably the conduit never dried up completely, even when drought emptied every stream above ground. Apart from the continuous weird sighing of the underground air, the only noise was the splashing of angry fishes and the boys' wading feet. Years afterwards, in moments of despair, Ryokun would live through this horror again.

'Mother!' Again the instinctive cry—'mother' was only a name for some unknown rescuer, some power beyond his conscious imagining; the invisible One to whom all men turn for relief when suffering becomes unbearable, who hears our cry out of the darkness and stretches his merciful hand towards us when we are left helpless and alone with the fear of death. Awareness of the nameless power he called 'mother' flooded Ryokun's mind. He supposed he would die soon—fall into some hidden airless pit, and thresh the water in a brief feeble struggle until death put an end to his agony. 'Mother! Mother!' The cry was unspoken now, though Ryokun himself did not realise he had stopped crying aloud. Innumerable thoughts and half-remembered scenes seemed to swirl round him.

'Shinkawa!' his companion shouted. Although he was in front, Ryokun had not noticed the point of light in the distance. He had been walking with his eyes shut, and now the gleam from the tunnel's mouth was almost painful, he was so used to the darkness.

'Shinkawa!'

'We've done it!'

Their shouts echoing down the tunnel, the two boys splashed through the water now with furious energy. Gradually the darkness lifted.

At last they emerged into the real world, and stood for a while in the concrete mouth of the tunnel, drinking in the bright air. Neither of them spoke.

Ryokun climbed to ground level and looked back. A parched river with a little stone bridge, a few farmer's sheds, some clumps of bamboo, and beyond them the two-storeyed school building, which stood directly over the conduit; nothing had changed. It was hard to realise that underneath the quiet fields was hidden the terror they had come through.

They looked at each other, soaked from head to foot.

'Lots of fish, weren't there?'

'Mm.'

They could not talk about the tunnel for a while yet, and walked off in silence, wanting only to get as far away from it as possible. When they finally separated, Ryokun only said:

'Don't let's tell anybody.'

He wanted to keep their adventure a secret for ever, so he would never have to recall the tunnel and its horrors.

'Mm.' His friend nodded.

18

Most of the parishioners who lived in the Niizu-cho Section were farmers, many of them quite well-to-do and therefore important to Butsuoji. Every autumn, in the slack time after the harvest, group services were held in their houses. There were more than thirty families altogether, and the series of services, repeated in each home, took up two whole days from early in the morning till late at night. With the weeding of the rice-fields completed, the farmers could afford a brief rest.

One member of each of the thirty families would come to each service. For Soshu, though most of the time he had only to read the scriptures, these two days were particularly exhausting, because he was repeating the identical service again and again—this being one of the occasions when Shoju could not take his place. In the morning he would read the Amida Sutra, then the Shoshinge, and in the afternoon and evening, the Monruige. The last two he would intone slowly, so that the farmers sitting in rows behind him could join in. The final hymns, especially the Jodo-wasan, the Koso, and the Shozomatsu, had to be repeated very slowly in perfect unison; it was explicitly forbidden to hurry over them. Year after year for generations the farmers of Niizu-cho had held these services, on the same two days each autumn.

The houses whose turn it was for the midday and evening services would provide the priest with lunch and supper, the order being changed every year. In the evening, after Soshu had read the last service for the day and given a short sermon, he and the farmers would all sit down to a meal together, which the wives had spent all day in the kitchen preparing.

The first day of services for this year had just finished. Soshu took off his stole. He was sitting with his back to the house shrine, his shoulders bent with weariness. After the long day, even to speak was an effort. He could not let himself appear aloof or unsociable, however. No matter what the occasion, he must always hide his feelings from these people, on whom his livelihood depended. The thick damask cushion on which he was sitting made it look as if he was a specially honoured guest—but it was not because of any real authority or influence that they had given it to him, he thought, silently watching the rows of faces.

Rice-wine was brought from the kitchen. The annual services gave the farmers a good excuse to enjoy their *sake,* and they made the most of it, drinking out of tea-bowls instead of the usual tiny *sake*-cups. Savouring the wine in his tired throat, Soshu watched their hands, knotty, hardened to the soil, the skin leathery like the soles of their feet. The meal their wives cooked was the same every year.

At first they hesitated to speak to him directly, but tongues loosened as the *sake* began to take effect.

'What about those people in Kiyota-cho that just joined Butsuoji, Father?'

'Mrs Komiyama, do you mean?' said Soshu, putting his half-emptied *sake*-cup on the table.

'That's it—Mrs Komiyama . . .'

With a sudden surge of feeling, Soshu remembered Tomoko's face.

'I've done the collecting there since way back. Didn't realise for a long while new people had moved in, though.'

For generations the farmers of Niizu-cho had collected the night-soil from Kiyota-cho. In the absence of any sewerage system, this was the only way the town houses could dispose of it. The younger men disliked going to Kiyota-cho for this purpose. It was the geisha quarter of Tan'ami, and to some of the houses and their girls the young farmers themselves were regular visitors. Dragging the long bucket-filled carts behind them, they would make their "collecting" rounds of the restaurants and tea-houses very early in the morning, their heads wrapped in towels, because they didn't want their faces to be seen. Among the night-soil they ladled into the buckets was their own; and they hated the girls to see them doing such work. Gradually Kiyota-cho came to be left to the older men.

'Komiyama—what sort of a family is there? Seems to be all women.'

'She never had any connection with Tan'ami before, I think; but she joined our temple as soon as she moved here.'

He could not speak of her connection with Mosuke Yamaji. It was best to keep quiet even about the fact that he had introduced her to Butsuoji, unless he himself chose to let it be known. Nor was Soshu certain that Yamaji was keeping her, though in fact, of course, his suspicions were perfectly correct. And Yamaji's brother, an elder, was sitting with them now. Tanned a dark, earthy red from one year's end to the next, he was utterly unlike the corpulent Mosuke; and it was common knowledge that the relations between them were less than brotherly.

'Must be some money somewhere, if she can stay at home all day and still afford to keep a maid. . . .'

The speaker had evidently made up his mind about how Mrs Komiyama supported herself. It went without saying that any woman who lived in Kiyota-cho must either be connected with the geisha-houses or else be someone's mistress—such was the neighbourhood's reputation. There was even an alley known as 'Concubine Street'.

Soshu's *sake* tasted bitter now. It was painful to hear Tomoko discussed in such a gathering.

'That's Mrs Komiyama you're talking about? She's pretty enough, isn't she?' said somebody else, who had been carrying on another conversation up till then. He was one of the elders, who were always the first to get to know any new members, since they went round calling on all the parishioners whenever a special service was to be held at Butsuoji.

'What does she do?'

'Nothing . . .'

'How much does she give to the temple?'

'A lot—you'd be surprised how much. She's one of the exceptions—most people in town don't take much interest in the temple nowadays. Salvation really means something to her.'

Soshu tried to appear unconcerned; but he could not help putting himself in her place and imagining what she would feel if she heard them speaking of her. His cheeks stiffened.

'She's got one child.'

'Has she now? I didn't see any children.'

'Somebody's taking care of her all right. Doing nothing like that all day, and living in that style. . . .'

'Must be, I suppose.'

Soshu's uneasiness grew. He closed his eyes, trying to breathe more steadily.

It was the custom at these meetings for the parishioners to unburden themselves of whatever had been on their minds during the preceding months. Coming together like this gave them confidence; alone, deprived of the support of the group, these good people were too diffident to speak even of their hopes. Soshu felt like a prisoner in court. How utterly dependent Butsuoji was on its parishioners, he thought. Sitting in the seat of privilege, on the thick silk cushion, only intensified his wretchedness.

'Something must be done about Butsuoji, anyway—and the sooner the better . . . isn't that so, Father?' said one of them, the remark setting off a general conversation on the subject. Soshu could evade their questions no longer. He had been expecting something of the kind—the thought had made the silk cushion a bed of thorns—and now it had happened. Every eye was fixed on him.

In the dock . . . his conduct dragged from obscurity to come before its judges. They could know nothing of his repentance, of his struggle to end his sin. For them the mere fact that he and Mineyo were living together in the temple house was enough; they had no idea of any conflict between them, and even if Soshu were to tell them, they would only take it as an attempt at self-justification. Soshu bent his head, as if in silent admission of his guilt. He was pale still, in spite of the *sake* he had drunk.

'Whenever we go to Butsuoji, the old lady's so stuck-up, it doesn't feel like *our* temple any longer.'

'She'll hardly even speak to any of us, come to that.'

'And no one ever thinks of the old priest. He belongs to Butsuoji, after all, she ought to treat him better. He's so good-natured, he never complains, however hard she works him.'

'How old is she, anyway?'

'A year younger than our Granny at home—that'd make her fifty-three.'

'Fifty-three? I'd've said forty-three, more like!'

Appreciative laughter greeted the sarcasm. Soshu could not raise his eyes.

'The scent she leaves behind her—the place reeks of it! As if she were a girl in her teens. It wouldn't be so bad if there really was a young woman in the house. . . .'

The women laughed again.

'She doesn't like us because we stink of honey-buckets, that's what it is. After all, Father—' one of them was determined to force Soshu to look them in the face—'the lady who looks after the temple house must be somebody who's accepted by the rest of us, mustn't she? You'd soon know the difference by the way the contributions'd go up. We don't want a lady who thinks of nothing but clothes, but someone who'll have a smile and a welcome for us when we go to the temple. If she's not friendly . . .'

Soshu could only nod.

'And then it's awkward for us if you're always going to be single, Father—'

'That's true, sure enough! And it must be difficult for you too, Father, in all sorts of ways.'

There were murmurs of agreement from the whole company.

'Then there's that poor little Ryokun.'

'Don't forget about Shoju when you marry again, Father! It's only him and Ryokun that have the old Butsuoji blood in their veins now. All of us here should think more about him and his position.'

'We'll have to ask the new lady to see he's treated properly.'

'We all know what we think—but what about Father Soshu himself? Isn't the first thing to find out whether he's willing to marry again or not?'

'How about it, Father? Everybody is hoping you'll marry again, and the sooner the better.'

Soshu had no special idea of remarrying, nor had he made up his mind to live the rest of his life alone. Before that question could be decided, he had first to solve a greater problem. There was cruel suffering to be borne and inflicted before he could think of letting them arrange a second marriage.

'It wasn't any one individual who arranged your coming to Butsuoji, Father—all of us had a hand in it; and we're still in duty bound to be of any service we can.'

Soshu felt his eyelids burn. They loved him—which made him suffer the more. They knew Renko had been driven out of Butsuoji, but hated only Mineyo for it, not himself. They knew he was a good man, as well as a pitifully weak one—a butterfly trapped in a spider's web, and beating its wings in vain. Most of those who sympathized with him were farmers; the townspeople were less well disposed, or perhaps it would be fairer to say they took a more objective view of what went on at the temple. Both partners in an affair of that kind seemed to them equally responsible, so they criticized Soshu no less than Mineyo. But all the parishioners alike had their misgivings about Soshu's continuing indefinitely to live with Mineyo. It seemed so strange, knowing him. Was he so completely under her spell that his will was literally paralysed—as a frog is paralyzed by the snake's stare before it strikes?

'As far as marrying again is concerned, won't you leave everything to us to arrange, Father?'

Soshu started. He looked at the speaker, swallowing to hide his feelings.

'We shouldn't do anything that would distress you.'

Even if he was to marry, it would be the parishioners who would be taking care of all the arrangements—in any case, the temple family was in no position to undertake anything of that sort by itself. Soshu could guess what lay behind that "leave everything to us": Mineyo was to be dealt with before a marriage could take place. Perhaps they would insist on her going to live elsewhere. It would be impossible for her to defy any such decision, since she was so entirely dependent on them for her livelihood. But if she *was* forced to leave Butsuoji, it was hardly likely she would go quietly, and when the parishioners said they were still bound to 'be of any service they could' to Soshu, they no doubt meant they were prepared for whatever trouble she might stir up before she finally went.

It would be easy to leave it all to them. They would cut away the hidden abscess of lust that had poisoned Butsuoji for twenty years, while he himself had only to watch. She would weep, she would scream; never, even in dreams, could she have foreseen anything like this—that she herself should be driven from Butsuoji, as she had driven her own daughter. Perhaps she might set fire to the house in a fit of passion . . . they would drag her screaming away, while he stood by and watched. The poison gone, he would marry again; exchange vows with some woman he did not know, and spend the rest of his life with her. Leave it to the parishioners—that was the surest way, besides being what they themselves most wanted. They were so anxious for a new lady who would quickly get used to temple life, and who would care for Ryokun and be kind to Shoju. They would be satisfied if he went on visiting them as usual, as if nothing special had happened. The final passing of the cloud that hung over the temple would mean as much to them as a happy ending to any crisis of their own. Mineyo's pleading sounded in Soshu's ears, only to be stifled by the pitiless hands of these good men and women—in the name of devotion to their temple. For they would have no difficulty in justifying to themselves another expulsion from the temple household, in giving it a suitably religious explanation, as a vindication of moral justice on Mineyo for her sin. They would not hear her cries; that was reserved for Soshu alone. He could not stop his ears—or even if they stopped them for him, waking or sleeping his spirit would still be listening to her agony.

—But why should I alone be privileged, immune?—

Soshu was walking home, his stole and sutra-books in the little basket he carried for the purpose. There were few street-lamps in Niizu-cho, but the winding road shone white under a brilliant moon. Houses crouched dark on either side.

The frogs croaked incessantly. Niizu-cho was on the outskirts of Tan'ami; paddy-fields bordered it to the east and south. Avoiding the main street, where the trucks were still running. Soshu kept to the narrow lanes he knew so well. They were deserted, and the houses all asleep. Only the clop of his clogs on the moonlit road disturbed its stillness.

He was grateful to the parishioners for the goodwill they showed him. Yet his very popularity was a kind of reaction from the dislike which Mineyo inspired, and therefore undeserved. Soshu felt guilty towards her still.

—How *can* I stand idly by if she is forced to leave Butsuoji— when the fault is as much mine as hers?—

But then there was Ryokun. . . . Soshu realised that he himself deserved to be punished if anyone did; but still he could not bring himself to accept the agony such punishment would entail. To leave everything to the parishioners would be to put all the blame on to Mineyo, and that he could not endure either. Invariably weak and hesitant in his dealings with others, in assessing his own conduct Soshu was inflexible to the point of tormenting himself, so that the conflict within him was continual; yet all his struggles with his conscience could not justify the record of twenty years, because even the bitterest remorse belonged to a different world from that of actual conduct, and one could not cancel the other out. The passion of twenty years was still a reality. It could not be obliterated, as one strikes out a phrase in a manuscript; he would carry it with him to the grave—and even when he was dead, it would still remain in the memories of those who survived him. What he and Mineyo had done would outlive both of them, to haunt Ryokun. An obsession would grow upon the boy, that lust had fouled the blood of the Getsudos . . . and whose was the sin but his? Soshu walked with bent head.

Someone was approaching from the opposite direction, evidently wearing straw sandals, for the footsteps were noiseless. '*Konbanwa*!' The figure spoke in greeting as they passed. Looking up in surprise, Soshu returned the salutation. It was the wife of one of his parishioners. The sandals were thick, home-made.

He entered Butsuoji by the back gate, which had been left unfastened, and locked it after him. Out of the silence of the compound rose the temple, black against the moonlit sky. As he passed the main hall he stopped and stood for some minutes with his hands joined in prayer, yet without any very clear idea of what he was praying about or for. The Buddha saw through all he did, had watched him in every action of those twenty years. Without reproaching, without hating, without despising, steadfastly the Holy One had gazed upon him. There were eyes from which nothing could be hid, that could read every secret of the heart, before which every aspect of Soshu's life was laid bare. His priest's robes gave him an outward dignity; but how much of the disciple was there about the man who wore them? He was tainted, unclean . . . And in his struggle to rise above the lust to which he had played the slave for so long, still the Buddha was watching him, intently . . .

He opened the door of the house, and at once heard feet hurrying towards him, as if she had been waiting for the moment.

'*O-kaeri nasai*! You must be tired, it's so late.' Mineyo took from him the little cane basket, which he used on daytime visits in preference to a cloth wrapper, because it did not make the hand sweat.

'You can take your bath right away. The water's just right—I tried it a moment ago.'

Mineyo helped him off with his robe, and he entered the bath, his body surrendering suddenly to the sense of well-being the contact with the steaming water gave. He realised how tired he was.

'Is it hot enough, Father?'

It was O-Sugi, waiting outside the fuel-hole.

'Put another bundle in, would you?'

Although there were no chinks in the wooden wall, a strong smell of rape-seed husks permeated the bathroom as soon as O-Sugi began to push them through the narrow hole into the fire. They crackled and caught fire immediately, burning up in a few seconds, so that she was kept busy refilling the furnace.

Someone entered the changing-room. Soshu stiffened. A moment later the footsteps withdrew. Mineyo had brought him fresh underclothes to put on after the bath.

She had opened the sliding windows and shutters along the verandah, and brought a cushion for him. Fresh from the bath, he sat down. Even in the hottest weather, he would never take off his robe, or sit cross-legged as other people do when they relax; and he had corns from always sitting upright—the skin on the instep of each foot had grown dark and as hard as the sole.

Mineyo sat by his side fanning him.

'It'll soon be time for the Honzan elections. Are you going to refuse to stand again?' She was speaking of the elections for the Council of the central temple of their sect. The organization of this temple, Senshuji, resembles that of the Government and Diet. The rules are strict. Besides the Council, there are the Executive Board, the Administration Office, the Committee on Doctrine, and the General and Delegate Assemblies of Laymen, each having its part in the enactment, administration, and enforcement of the general regulations of the sect, and together forming a miniature state. Soshu had the right to vote in elections for the council, as does any priest over twenty who has lived for at least six months in a designated temple, branch temple or preaching-house, an electoral register being compiled shortly before each election takes place. Any priest of over twenty-five who has spent a year or more in a designated temple is eligible for nomination—with the exception of 'persons physically or mentally incapable, bankrupts, persons undergoing terms of imprisonment, under probation or having been under probation within a period of one year prior to the election, and persons in arrear with contributions to the central temple'; such people also being deprived of the right to vote. Members of the Council are elected from small electoral districts, of which Tan'ami and the branch temples surrounding it form one, contributing two representatives. Elections are conducted in the usual way: a candidate is required to submit his candidature and a deposit of five thousand yen to the General Affairs Office of the sect during the period beginning with the official announcement of the election and ending fifteen days before the election itself. There are 'election campaigns', and a rule limiting each candidate to one 'campaign manager'. Voting and the counting of votes are governed by regulations similar to those obtaining in political elections, with a right of appeal and penalties for misuse of the ballot. The candidates in any constituency can only be officially elected if together they poll more than one-fifth of the total valid votes. Service on the Council is for a three-year term.

Soshu had no desire to be a candidate.

'The last two elections everybody wanted you to stand, but you wouldn't accept. Are you going to refuse again?'

'That sort of thing doesn't appeal to me.'

'Some priests are so anxious to get on the Council, they run their own campaign.'

Mineyo's make-up was lighter than usual, but still a faint fragrance hung in the air. She sat at ease in a gaily-coloured bathrobe.

'Some of the parishioners wish you would be more active in that sort of way—for the honour of Butsuoji.'

'I'm not the right person.'

'You haven't the slightest ambition, have you?' Mineyo smiled. 'Refusing to stand when there isn't even any need for a campaign—they'd elect you without your saying a word.'

There were among the parishioners some who were anxious for Butsuoji to be given a higher rank. The colour of the priest's robes varies according to the rank of his temple, which also determines where he sits when the priests meet in general assembly; and a natural warmth of feeling for their own priest made the congregation of Butsuoji eager for Soshu to occupy as high a position as possible. When the memorial services for St Shinran were held at Butsuoji, the seating of the priests coming from other Takada temples of the same sect was also determined by the status of their temples, in order to emphasize the dignity and solemnity of the occasion—though in this case, of course, the priest of Butsuoji would take the seat of honour, irrespective of status. Priests are classified into nine ranks; all wear robes of coarse silk, but coloured according to rank—lilac for the first three ranks, dark brown for the fourth and fifth, a lighter brown for the sixth and seventh, and pale green for the last two. For all these robes the parishioners pay. In effect, the rank itself depends on how much money the parishioners contribute to the central temple, for even Senshuji has not been able to escape the evils of large-scale organized Buddhism—in fact, it is the possession of such a huge temple that has compelled the Takada branch of the Pure Land Sect to have so many rules and to standardize even the colours of priestly robes in different classes. St Shinran, the founder, wore only the simplest black. Nor did he ever seek the refuge of a temple. Even when he was over ninety, he still had no real home. Yet his teachings spread throughout the eastern provinces, taking deep root among the people; they had nothing to do with temples, large or small. To the end of his life he strove consistently to avoid dependence on outward forms.

Soshu turned his face away; she kept looking at him. A breath of wind drifted into the house. Gradually, with the feelings she could not control, Mineyo's breathing grew less even. Sensing the change in her, Soshu's whole body turned rigid.

19

Tomoko got out of bed in a much more cheerful mood than usual. In the fresh morning breeze, she felt younger and eager, with a sudden resurgence of faith in life. Folding the kimono she had worn until the previous day, she put it away in the cupboard, and took out a new one of deep blue, which she had not yet worn. She had a sash which she had intended to go with it, but now she changed her mind and chose another.

The flowers she had bought the day before for her altar vase were still in the wash-basin. After washing her face and hands carefully, Tomoko started to clean the tiny, toylike shrine, dusting its gilt and lacquer surfaces with a feather-brush. Not that it needed any attention this morning, for it was always being dusted and polished; but she could not feel at ease till she had gone over it again. She did not think of anything in particular while she was dusting. Yet the cleaning of the shrine had never seemed to her a mere duty. It was something one chose to do, an act of service. Nor did this attitude derive from any feeling that her youth was past and should give way to more 'elderly' habits of thought. On the contrary, a youthful colour rose in her cheeks when she knelt before the shrine; it was a moment, not of conventional piety, but of joy, of sheer delight in being alive. For the first time in her life, she knew what it was to hope. Then, without any warning, the very fact that she was aware of hope without any experience to base it on terrified her. In an instant she was torn between opposite, but equally powerful, emotions. The blood drained from her cheeks. Yet she could not stop cleaning; her sense of expectancy had not vanished, after all—it was stronger than ever; only her fear grew equally intense, as if answering hope's challenge. Calmly the tiny Buddha of the shrine looked down upon the conflict.

With the approach of this particular day each month, Tomoko

grew tense and nervous, only to be paralyzed with disappointment after it had gone. For this day she lived; though when it came, nothing happened, it was no different from any other day. Yet she clung to hope still, and again began to look forward. She came to expect the impossible, imagining it not as a remotely beautiful dream, but with the realism which the experience of a woman of thirty-two had taught her. The audacity of these imaginings made her blush sometimes. It was not as if she were a teen-age girl, she told herself, with misty longings for stars and violets in a wood. Nor did she ever think of making any advances of her own, or even imagine any such advances being made to her; she only waited for the moment when her experience would assert itself in a natural, frank expression of tenderness. There was no need for Soshu to say anything. His hand, perhaps, might rest for a moment on her lap, she would lay hers upon it, their hands would clasp—that was all she asked. But each month when Soshu came to read the scriptures, an invisible barrier rose between them, of which both were conscious, and to which both had now grown accustomed. Tomoko had not the courage to break it down. That was only for the dreams that made her blush for her imagined boldness; in reality she was too timid to take the slightest initiative. The same was true of Soshu.

'Mummy, can I go to the sea with Sumi?' Shoko asked her mother again at breakfast. For two or three days she had been full of the proposed expedition.

'If you promise you'll stay close to Sumi—'

'I promise!'

'Don't you worry, Mrs Komiyama—it'll be all right.'

It was ironic that Shoko should choose to go to the beach on the day of Soshu's visit, making it seem as if Tomoko had deliberately sent her daughter and maid away for the occasion. She had had no such intention, but was as agitated over the coincidence as if it had been a secret plan.

'Be extra thorough with your cleaning, won't you, Sumi—the priest will be calling today.' Sumi had been reminded of this already on the previous day. Tomoko sat at her dressing table, while Sumi cleaned the upstairs room, then came down to sprinkle water on the earthen passage and outside the front door.

'Isn't it time for lunch, Mummy?' Shoko could hardly wait for the afternoon. Her mother, too, was waiting just as impatiently at first. But Tomoko grew less eager as the morning passed, every hour making her more certain of another disappointment. Extreme hope becomes unbearable, and in time creates its own opposite, with which it struggles until the victim of the conflict is utterly exhausted and indifferent. It is not because he is submissive by nature, or has a philosophical temperament, that a man decides he can hope no longer.

Eventually Shoko and Sumi went out, Shoko clutching a little basket filled with fruit and cakes. There was no wind. Tomoko thought of the sea, brilliant under the cloudless sky, and of the hot, shimmering air of the beach. A moment later she had forgotten Shoko and her friends.

A candle was already burning on the shrine, and on the floor-matting before it, Soshu's cushion awaited him. Tomoko walked up and down the room. Soshu would arrive, she would bring him straight to the room where the shrine was kept, then go to prepare tea. The house was so silent today, he would be sure to notice it. They would be alone together—she must make him aware of what that might mean; if only he would feel the significance of this meeting, some word or act would naturally follow. What he was to say or do, she could not define to herself. He was a man, after all, like Mosuke Yamaji—though they seemed to her so utterly different. But when he was actually before her, every thought of trying to influence him would vanish. Suppressing all her own feelings, she faced him as if he were no different from any other visitor; serving tea, making conversation, listening to the sutras, serving tea again as custom demanded, and finally showing him out, without allowing a hint of emotion to appear in her face. Inwardly she suffered torments of frustration, the pain of which she could deaden only by forcing herself into a mood of numb despair. The months went by, and each time the same process was repeated.

Sitting down by the shrine, Tomoko smiled bitterly. She had tried to keep her hopes from running away with her, but without success. Soshu knew nothing of her feelings; all her visions of how their relationship might develop were only the creations of her imagination. Yamaji had told her what people were saying about the priest of Butsuoji. At first the story of the expulsion of his wife and of his intimacy with her mother had aroused no more interest in her than any other local scandal might have done. Later on she had gathered from what Yamaji said that the mother-in-law was the real villain in the case, and that up to a point Soshu was to be pitied; but she still felt that he had been needlessly weak and was as much to blame as Mineyo. As time went on, she came to hear about him from others besides Yamaji. His gentle personality had made him surprisingly popular, and most of the parishioners took his part. As she came to realise that this man was suffering because a genuine goodness as well as weakness of character prevented him from breaking with Mineyo, Tomoko began to be interested in him, though still with little more than the curiosity evoked by such an unusual 'case'. Then she met him at the gate of Butsuoji, after she had visited the temple for the first time. He had looked somehow different from the conventional image of a temple priest, but just how, she could not precisely define. There was no 'religious' air about him. He had been a priest for many years, of course, but still the role did not seem entirely natural. She had an idea he was not perfectly at home in his robes; perhaps even now he would be more at ease in ordinary Japanese or western dress. No, he did not look the priest, she thought. The fact that he wore his hair like a layman intensified the impression. Give him a black felt hat, a black jacket, and a brief-case, and he would make a perfect university lecturer. It was strange that twenty years as a priest had failed even to make him look like one—but after all there must be men like that, Tomoko supposed, even among priests.

Soshu began to visit her house to read the scriptures. He came twice, three times. As she sat and talked with him, her earlier impressions gave way to another. Gradually she forgot he was the central figure in a sordid story. It did not occur to her that what she felt while he was reading the service was love; but she realised her growing disgust at her relationship with Yamaji must have something to do with the priest—if Shoju had come instead, sheer force of habit would have made her continue to receive Yamaji as before. Only a more powerful force can dam the current of such habitual reactions, and once that force begins to operate, it can have dangerous results.

Again Tomoko began to walk up and down the room. It was almost time for Soshu to call—not that he had fixed any definite hour for his visits, but he always came at about the same time. Tomoko stopped; a sudden shock ran through her body as if she had been struck, obliterating the mood of pleasant anticipation. Supposing Yamaji were to come today. . . . He came whenever he felt inclined, not on any particular day. She had to be ready for him always.

—Not today . . . please, not today! . . .

Not only because this was the day for the service of remembrance of her ancestors, though this was half the reason. She could not bear to lose the sense of expectancy she had felt all the morning, giving her new life as she waited to welcome Soshu.

—But perhaps Yamaji *will* come today of all days . . . that's how things happen . . .

It was nearly time. She was not ready for Yamajji—and even began to feel doubt about her longing for Soshu. It was so awkward that Sumi had gone out. Left alone in the house, what would she do if Yamaji and Soshu both came . . .

Did Fate torture her like this for its own amusement?—If only Soshu would come first, then at least . . .

There was a grating sound from the outer door. Tomoko held her breath; she could not tell whether it was Yamaji or Soshu. She went out to the porch, trying to prepare herself to greet either appropriately.

'Where's the maid?'

It was Yamaji—as she had feared. Nobody, nothing was on her side, then; not even chance. Yamaji went upstairs in his usual hurry.

For a moment Tomoko was tempted to give way to the violence of her feelings. She picked up his shoes, but could not bring herself to put them away in the *geta-bako*.[1] A pair of man's shoes—they would be the first thing Soshu would see when he came, but she did not care: he probably knew all about Yamaji, anyway. Leaving them with the toes pointing to the door, ready for Yamaji to put on, she slowly followed him upstairs.

Yamaji had thrown his coat into a corner and pulled down the wooden shutter, exclaiming several times how hot it was. In fact the window faced east, and the sun was no longer shining directly through it; he only wanted to prevent any of the neighbours from seeing into the room. Sweat glued his shirt to his massive, fleshy back. Tomoko went downstairs to fetch a towel. If Soshu came now . . . but why hadn't she known it was Yamaji at first—when no one but he ever opened the door with such a clatter? She was so much more agitated now, Tomoko realized, than when he usually came.

Two lines of moxa marks, six on each side, ran down Yamaji's back, a little swelling surrounding each of the white shrunken patches of skin where the moxa had been applied. Tomoko wiped off the sweat. He had taken off his trousers now.

'Black or white is best for you, I suppose, but that blue you're wearing now suits you well, too. You can't wear soft shades though —only strong colours.'

Snatching the towel from her while she was still drying his back, Yamaji wiped the sweat from his face and armpits, then threw it into the *tokonoma*. His hairy brutish hand grabbed Tomoko by the wrist.

'No time to lay the bed—it's too hot anyway!' Without giving her a chance to answer, he swung her down on the floor, and then, upon her upturned face—like a waterfall, flashed across her mind, with a massive, irresistible force . . .

'Someone's at the door!' A spasm shook Tomoko's body.

'The maid, I suppose?'

'I suppose so . . .'

[1] Cupboard for shoes and clogs—including those of visitors—in the porch of a Japanese house.

'Somebody's talking—doesn't sound like the maid.'

'Perhaps it's the priest . . .'

'Hm, today's the day he comes, is it? It would be today, curse him!'

Twice they heard Soshu's *'Konnichi wa'* at the door. No one answered. Tomoko lay as if dead; but her body, at least, was still conscious. Nothing but disasters today, one after the other.

'He'll come in and get on with his sutras without your saying anything. He's used to it—people are often too busy to attend to him.'

Her hopes of the morning destroyed so mercilessly, nothing was left for Tomoko but to suffer in secret, hating life for the wound that had torn her body and heart in two.

Even Yamaji seemed embarrassed, as he heard Soshu enter the house and go to the shrine-room. The candle Tomoko had lit was burning still. In a moment, when he had put on his stole, he would begin to read. Yamaji and Tomoko kept perfectly still—till the sutra-bell rang, faint, as if it were some distance away, but quite distinct. Tomoko listened to Soshu intoning; with her hand resting on the floor-matting, she could hear perfectly. His voice sounded exactly as it always did. He must have seen the shoes, which were proof the house was not empty. She was afraid even to breathe.

'The shrine's directly underneath, isn't it?' Her eyes stared back at him uncomprehendingly.

'Does it worry you?' Tomoko shook her head with a sudden access of courage—she knew Yamaji wanted her to say 'yes'; that would make his pleasure so much the keener. He took special pride in having a woman in a room over a Buddhist shrine, as an act of brazen impiety, the special flavour of which he could only rarely taste. Such deliberate, conscious sinning gave him intense pleasure, for he had long since learnt to suppress any signs of repentance or fear in himself—unlike Tomoko.

The intoning continued. It was impossible to conceal the fact of their presence upstairs; Yamaji would have had to keep as quiet as herself if they were not to give themselves away, and that he was no longer inclined to do.

Both hands covering her face, Tomoko lay prostrate and limp. Yamaji picked up the towel he had thrown away a few moments before, wiped his face and back, and began to dress. He looked down at her motionless body with a smile, as if to enjoy to the full a spectacle he might not have the luck to see again. She was breathing fitfully, as if in pain.

'Must be going now.'

Tomoko did not move. There was nothing urgent in his voice now; even a hint of pity.

'Stay as you are—you can hardly go down now. . . . Stay up here, and he'll show himself out when he's finished.'

Tomoko did not reply, and Yamaji went downstairs. The rooms were so arranged that he would not meet Soshu between the foot of the staircase and the front door. As he was putting on his shoes, he stopped for a moment to listen to the sutra; then opened the door with deliberate slowness, to show he was not running away from anybody, and disappeared into the street.

Still Tomoko lay on the floor upstairs, half-unconscious, yet with her feet neatly together, and the blue kimono thrown across her body, as if it were the only remaining protector she could claim. Her face covered still, she listened to the sutra.

The bell rang a second time, for the beginning of the Monruige. Though this time there was no one sitting behind him, Soshu's manner of reading was the same as always, a gentle rhythmical intoning. Tomoko did not get up.

Suddenly she realised he was beginning the last reading, from the Senshuji Commentaries. Forcing herself up with both arms to a sitting position, she looked at her legs, flung out before her. She shook her head; her face was covered with sweat. What looked like the natural exhaustion of a consummated passion was for Tomoko the aftermath of an agony of remorse and fear, which did not die with the completion of the act, as they did with Yamaji, but were alive still and would live on into the future.

Abruptly she stood up, and to prevent herself from falling, clung suddenly to the sliding door, so that it clattered in its groove. Then in short, jerky movements she began to go downstairs—but stopped after two or three steps.

Soshu extinguished the candle, shut the doors of the shrine, bowed once in reverence before it, and stood up. Leaving the empty room precisely as if someone were there to see him out, he stepped down into the passage—and turned round, realising that somebody was standing on the staircase. Tomoko was staring at him; he hardly recognized her.

'You were at home, then—I didn't know . . .' Soshu lied. The wild disorder of her luxuriant mass of hair, hitherto always tied behind her neck with such care that not a single strand was out of place, gave her a grotesque look. She was white-faced.

Soshu spoke gently, but with a troubled air. 'You'll find everything put away where it belongs, I think—'

'Don't go, Father! Don't go—not yet!'

With the sudden, agitated movement that accompanied her words, her dishevelled hair fell in worse confusion about her neck and shoulders. Noticing at the same moment that her kimono was half-open, she tucked it hurriedly into her sash, then came down the stairs towards him, and stepped straight down into the passage, without stopping to put on her clogs.

'Father, you can't . . . you mustn't go . . . please . . .' The words carried a feverish urgency.

'Mrs Komiyama, what's the matter? your clogs—?'

Tomoko still had not realised she had forgotten them. 'Come back to the shrine-room . . . please, come back, Father!'

Yielding to the desperation in her voice, Soshu stepped up on to the corridor. Tomoko watched him from the passage; not trusting herself to speak or move till she saw him enter the shrine-room.

Soshu sat down on the cushion by the shrine, as though for him that was the only permissible place. Unsteadily, as if on the verge of collapse, Tomoko knelt opposite him and bowed, her hair tumbling over her shoulders on to the floor.

'What is it, Mrs Komiyama?'

Tomoko looked up at him reproachfully.

'Don't look at me so calmly, as if you didn't know—' Soshu was reaching for his little cane basket. '—when you *do* know, Father, you *must* know everything!'

'If you would tell me what it is I'm supposed to know . . .'

The wild impulse she could no longer control forced her to speak of what habit and fear had kept secret.

'How could you *not* know what—what I was doing upstairs—what Yamaji and I . . . while you were reading the scriptures . . .' She stared at him, her eyes flaming still with anger and reproach. Soshu remembered how he had shuddered at another such look, in Mineyo's eyes. Yet in the eyes before him now there was nothing hard or impure—rather something he could pity. But perhaps it was only because he was not personally involved.

'Every house in the parish has its own ways, of course . . . but all I'm concerned with is the services they ask me to hold.'

'Listen, Father! I can't refuse him. . . . I hate him, I hate him—yet I have to obey him. . . . I heard you come, but he wouldn't let me go—it amuses him to see me upset. He never wants me, only my body, that's all he pays me for. He thinks only of getting all the pleasure he can for his money—even when he can hear you reading the scriptures. . . .'

'It was an unfortunate chance, that's all—please don't worry about it. I'm sorry to have caused you extra distress, of course; but it hasn't embarrassed me, I assure you.'

'Father, isn't it part of your work to listen to your parishioners when they're in trouble?'

'It is—and a great many things they come to me about. But whether a man like me can help them at all is another matter. . . .'

'Everybody has his own weak point—is that what you mean, Father?'

'Precisely—and what is there about you and Mr Yamaji that—'

'Father! do you think I should be content with this kind of misery? Is it wrong to be tortured with the longing for something better—for happiness, even, or at least for a life I wouldn't need to be ashamed of?'

'You're very upset today, Mrs Komiyama . . .'

'I couldn't tell you all this if I wasn't.' Tomoko looked at her kimono. The collar was rucked out of shape, and the band of her sash twisted, with one end of the bustle projecting.

'I ought to be ashamed to let you see me like this—but it gives me courage somehow; I—I couldn't have spoken to you otherwise, it's gone on too long . . .'

'You're young still. You might have seemed reserved, perhaps, and rather lonely sometimes; but I've always thought of you as so happy, so—untouched.'

'Look at me, Father, the real Tomoko! Despise me, I don't care. A typical back-street prostitute, if you like—but one who's terrified every time the man who keeps her comes!'

'Don't make it worse for yourself. I know now how feel—it's very hard—'

Tomoko was the kind of woman he had imagined her to be, thought Soshu. He felt drawn to her, responding to the weakness in her that was so like his own.

'Why don't you send Shoju to read the monthly service?' Her tone was formal, polite; but the abruptness of the question prevented Soshu from answering immediately.

'Because you want to make somebody who's new to the temple feel at home—is that why you always come yourself?'

It was futile to try and deceive her; her eyes would see through a lie the moment it was uttered.

'My mother asked me the same question . . .' he said openly, realising now that it was not merely a sympathetic listener that she wanted; now that she had broken the barrier between them, he would have to answer her question, whatever the cost.

'Why don't you change that kimono, or arrange it? It doesn't make it any easier to talk, if you don't mind my saying so, and I—'

'If you will stop play-acting, Father . . .' Tomoko stood up as she spoke.

Soshu bowed; the mere gesture seemed a confession. Tomoko went into the next room, without closing the sliding door and opened a drawer in a wardrobe.

Before adjusting her kimono, she turned away from Soshu, and sat down to put on her *tabi*. Fate had taken over, thought Soshu;

he could only drift now on the racing flood. But that this was how the blow should come—and on this day of all days!

In a few quick movements, Tomoko had put on another kimono, recovering some of her composure with the change. Kneeling in front of the mirror to tidy her hair, she gave a little cry of surprise and shame as she saw the state it was in.

Soshu sat with bowed head. The bitter sense of defeat had faded; he felt now only an inward peace, as if at Tomoko's bidding all the fears that had imprisoned him till that day had vanished, and he was free, a dream achieved.

Tomoko unravelled and combed her hair, fastened most of it behind and arranged the rest in a ring, the curls slipping into place naturally, for this was how she always wore it. Finally she powdered her cheeks.

'So you've suffered, too—I didn't know you disliked Yamaji so much.'

She sat down opposite him, dressed now in a white patterned kimono, with a dark red sash. Soshu was relieved; this was the Tomoko he had known.

'Now you must listen to my confession,' he said and closed his eyes for a moment. What he was going to tell her would determine her attitude toward him once and for all.

'All the parishioners know what has been going on at Butsuoji, and even some people who have no connection with the temple at all. I know what people say about me. I forced my wife to leave me—her mother may have been behind it, but the responsibility is mine. I knew that well enough—but still I didn't give up the affair with her mother. There's a devil in me, if ever there was in anyone, and a vicious one at that; but a man can't change in a day what he's done for nearly twenty years. I couldn't face a head-on collision with her, and I hadn't the strength to break with her completely after so long—so I went on sinning out of sheer habit, knowing all the time how wrong it was. And then unexpectedly, a new strength I'd never known before seemed to grow in me; and since then I've been able to keep away from her. So there's been a change at Butsuoji . . . but it's a change nobody knows about, not even Shoju or the maid, though they've probably wondered why she's been getting so much more irritable in the last few months. There've been scenes . . . I've fought against the mad passion she still clings to, and the hatred that's grown out of it. It won't be long now before it comes to a head in one way or another; but there's no peace yet. I'm afraid to go home, afraid of Butsuoji. . . . And all this, not because of anything anyone has said. . . . Mineyo tries every kind of trick to find out why I'm so changed. I couldn't make out myself why I suddenly seemed so different, where the sudden courage came from, after all those years I'd dragged myself through the mire. But the answer was simple enough—it came from you.' Soshu spoke the last words with an awkward, desperate sincerity.

'What did I say . . .?'

'It was nothing you said. The relation between us is that of parishioner and priest, no more; that's what we have been till now, and that's what we shall continue to be. It's best that way. I've watched you each time I've come. In the three or four months since I started coming regularly for the services, you've taught me how to begin life again—that's what it comes to, anyway. Having somebody like you for a parishioner started me thinking—made me feel there might be a way out after all. Not that you said anything; but somehow chastity came to seem desirable, worth suffering for. It was a complete change for me—the first real revolution in thinking and feeling I've had in nearly forty years—all my life. And a living woman taught me, not the Shinran whose teachings I've been so strict about; can you imagine the humiliation, for a priest? But at least it gave me the courage to break the hold Mineyo had on me. She's made more trouble since than I'd thought possible; but that only makes me long for chastity the more. Perhaps I shouldn't have told you this secret of mine—perhaps I shouldn't have told anybody. I never dreamt I'd find myself talking about it to you, of all people. This confession will only give you needless worry, I'm afraid—and I shall suffer for it myself, in another way . . .'

'Father—'

'The parishioners are urging me to marry again. They want to persuade Mineyo to 'retire' somewhere away from Butsuoji, apparently—a polite way of getting rid of her for good.'

'Father!'

'It's bound to happen before long. But I can't let her be driven out, as if she alone were responsible. If anyone should be made to go, it is I . . .'

'Father!' Tomoko's voice grew more urgent.

'I'm grateful to you—it was your joining Butsuoji that was the turning-point. If I've been able to pick up a few fragments of self-respect since then, it's due to you.'

'Father!' Tomoko was struggling to hold back a rush of feelings from pouring themselves out in words; her eyes were hollow with suffering.

'It's a terrible confession to have to make,' Soshu went on calmly as before,—'the priest a worse sinner than any of his flock! These twenty years have been one long round of lust, repentance—madness grown into a habit; ever since I was a student. It wouldn't have been so bad if I'd come to my senses when my wife was turned out.

She gave up hope of her mother and husband ever changing, and married again, quite happily, I believe. She was wiser than I.'

'Father—'

'I knew you were dependent on Yamaji; but that isn't any business of mine. All that matters to me is that you should never give up being a member of the Butsuoji congregation. I don't hope for anything more—as if I had any right to . . . You showed me the way, that's all. How can I preach any more, after all that's happened? Preaching is an agony now—each time I have to do it, it seems to drain a bit more life out of me.'

'Do you—will you ever marry again, as they want you to?'

'It's you I love—'

'I, too . . .'

'You asked me why I came to your house myself, instead of sending Shoju. I wanted your encouragement, the strength I knew you could give me.'

'I'm sorry . . . you must have gone home sad.'

'If I did, it makes me happy now to be able to admit it; I thought it would have to remain a secret, all my life. But you have your own life—'

'Don't marry again, Father!'

A smile flitted across Soshu's face. 'There are bridges enough to be crossed before I can even think of it.'

'Don't marry again!'

'I shall suffer all the more for having told you all this,' again with a twisted smile of self-pity. 'I'm glad you know my secret, though. Your knowing gives me courage, too. I love you, you see—but that's only . . . I shan't always be such a waverer. Maybe I shall even have dreams one day. I'm such a coward; I can't fight her alone, so I made you help me. The price of breaking with her has to be a new weakness, it seems. I am closer to Shinran, through what I feel for you; he is with me now.' Wherever a man suffered, Shinran was always at his side. That the suffering was the result of lust made no difference; the pain itself was a way to approach him.

'Father!'

Tears stood in Soshu's eyes. Tomoko trembled more violently; her longing for him no longer counted the cost.

'There will be a new pain for me, too,' she said, more slowly now, 'whenever he comes; a new pain, and sharper than before . . .'

The front door slid back with a clatter.

'Mummy!'

A wave of fresh, sea-scented air followed Shoko and Sumi into the house.

'We have a guest, Shoko dear.'

Shoko knelt on the floor-matting and bowed. Then she began

pouring out all the news of what she'd seen and done at the beach. Tomoko gave her all her attention. The moment the girl had come in, she was a mother again, without a trace of her earlier agitation. Soshu was bewildered by the sudden transformation, as if the woman he had been talking to a few seconds earlier had suddenly disappeared. She listened intently, nodding at each incident or description, as Shoko chattered on. Soshu took up his basket.

'Must you go now? Can't you stay for a cup of tea?'

When they had both made such confessions . . . and with their words still sounding in each other's ears—or had even the echo died already? To Soshu's embarrassment, for he himself was incapable of such an abrupt change of expression, Tomoko's transformation was instantaneous and complete; as far as she was concerned, his confession had ended with the last word he had spoken.

She followed him, however, when he stepped out into the passage, and bowed. For a moment their eyes met; they were priest and parishioner no longer.

'I shall keep a diary—' A tap was running in the kitchen as Tomoko spoke, so that no one but Soshu could hear her. 'I'll put down everything,' she went on hurriedly, 'how lonely it is here, and the horrible things that happen sometimes . . . will you read it?'

'I'll take it home when I come for the service.'

'I want so much to talk to you—even if it's only in a diary.'

The tap was still running as Soshu left. The way home from Tomoko's house was familiar enough, but he walked now with a new vigour, each step bouyant and purposeful.

An elderly woman, one of the elders' wives, was just leaving Butsuoji as he returned. They would be coming to the temple next day, she told him, to polish the oil lamps. It was not long now till the autumn services in memory of St Shinran, and every year at this time ten or more of the women would come and spend a whole day polishing the brass of the lamps and the Five Ornaments in the temple hall. Soshu never had to remind them; they fixed a day among themselves, and came to tell him when it would be.

Mineyo stood in the doorway of the Lute Room while he took off his robe.

'You're very late today. What did you find to talk about at Mrs Komiyama's?' The question was natural, for he had been gone nearly three times as long as one such visit usually took; but it appalled and frightened him nevertheless, the bitter cynicism in her voice seeming to probe directly into his secret, and at the same time to hint at a coming convulsion in both their lives.

'I called somewhere else on the way home.'

'The Mimori woman, I suppose. I guessed as much. Going to Kiyota-cho gives you a convenient excuse to stop by, and give her a lesson in tea-ceremony.'

Soshu had in fact done this two or three times already.

'She'll be glad she didn't arrange to come here for lessons!'

To avoid further conversation, Soshu went to the library, where the night-shutters had not yet been put up. The glass sliding doors were open on the two sides looking out into the courtyard and temple garden, and the scent of the trees drifted through the room on the cool evening air. This was the only room in the house where one could sit without sweating even in midsummer; faces looked pale there, in comparison with the other rooms.

'Ryokun! What are you up to?'

Ryokun was crouching perfectly still at the edge of the pond. With a look of intense seriousness on his childish face which made Soshu smile, he signalled to his father not to make any noise, then crept stealthily up towards the verandah.

'Snake!' he whispered, pointing towards the pond. Soshu strained his eyes; he could just make out what looked like part of a withered branch lying on the motionless water.

'I've been waiting for him to show his head . . . ' Most of the snake was under water. 'He's bound to come up soon—he can't stay under much longer.'

'And you're going to stay watching till he moves? You'll need some patience—see which can last out longer, eh?'

Afraid the snake might have heard their voices, Ryokun crept back to the edge of the pond. Soshu watched him, with a sorrowful pity for the motherless boy.

20

Standing on the riverbank behind the school, Ryokun stared at the sheet of water that stretched away almost as far as he could see. The three stone steps where he and his friends would wash their feet when the river was running at its normal level were under water. Where the flood had come from, he did not know. River, dykes, paddy-fields, the patchwork of ridges and raised paths connecting field with field—every landmark up to the edge of Heron's Forest had disappeared, except for a few fowl-houses sticking up here and there like tiny islands. The hens would be huddling on their perches, unable to move. Driven by a powerful current, the waters swirled past where Ryokun stood. The flood was the immediate result of heavy rain that had fallen in the mountains for several days on end, after the long period of brilliant weather. It happened regularly every two or three years, and was not serious enough to damage the banks of rivers of any size. The farmers were unmoved; they seemed to know by instinct when the water would recede.

'Nobu!' Ryokun called to his friend. 'The tunnel'll be full now!' Nobu had been his companion in the underground adventure. The conduit ran directly under where they were standing—Ryokun thought of the floodwater surging through it, and shivered, imagining himself trapped inside. In fact, it was only rarely dry; what had frightened him now was a sudden realisation that except for a few days in the hottest part of the summer there was a sizeable stream flowing through it all the year round. On one of those days of drought he and Nobu had crept through it—like thieves, he thought; he had felt somehow guilty ever since, as if their penetration of its secret had been a crime which was sure to be found out sooner or later. They had never spoken about the conduit to anyone else. The adventure was something they could have boasted about to their classmates, but to talk of it would mean reliving its terrors, and that was something neither of them could face.

'Let's swim!' said Ryokun. His friend grinned approval. Visions of how exciting it would be to swim on the floodwaters helped to drive out unpleasant memories of the conduit, both ends of which were under water in any case—at the mill, the water-wheel was racing madly, but it was upstream from where they were standing, and unless they deliberately swam near the mill there was no danger of their being sucked into the tunnel. Only a few ears of rice had managed to push themselves above the water in places. Even the willow trees along the dykes looked as if they were struggling to hold on to the flooded soil in a desperate attempt to prevent themselves from being carried away. Though all landmarks had vanished, Ryokun knew exactly where the river and the dykes and the little stone bridges were.

The boys undressed, hid their clothes and canvas shoes in a corner of the covered way leading back to the school buildings, and dashed down to the flood, Ryokun aiming for the point where the river came closest. With hands raised, he jumped straight in, not trying to dive as he used to do in the swimming-bath. For an instant his feet touched the river-bed, and then the current swept him away. A splash he heard but did not see told him that Nobu had followed him in. Ryokun tried to stand; but his feet were carried away again the moment he pushed them down. Rolling over and over, now on his face now on his side, he drifted rapidly downstream, forgetting everything but the thrill of smooth, effortless movement, of swimming without having to trouble about strokes. Then something began to tickle his stomach. He tried to stop again, and after kicking vainly for five or six yards, finally managed to do so. His feet sank deep into the soft mud of a paddy-field. Unawares, he had been carried over the river-bank on to the farmland, and it was the rice plants that tickled him as he floated over them, innumerable feathery spears hidden under the water's surface, bending to the current. Ryokun drifted on again, pawing the water with a dog-stroke, his body seeming to float on a mass of waving rice-ears. Nobu was swimming, too. Both tried to stand at the same moment, and screamed with delight as the current bore them down. Ryokun clutched at any rice-plants that brushed past him on the surface—they came away in his hand. Most of the plants escaped uprooting in this way, for they went bent low under the water, as if intent on clinging with all the strength of their slender roots to the muddy soil; but many were torn out by the boys as they kicked and splashed. No farmer noticed them. On and on they floated, shouting to each other now and then, beyond the school wall, downriver between the banks again, past the fig-trees that rustled slightly in the lazy wind, dipping their huge leaves in the moving water; over the little wooden footbridge the farmers used. Ryokun remembered the position of the bridge exactly. A little further, behind a farmer's house, the thicker vegetation, and a cluster of tall trees standing on an island in the middle of the river, gave him the feeling of drifting through a forest. Snakes six or seven feet long lived in the undergrowth round the trees: once he had seen one hanging from a branch. They, too, would be frightened by the flood, he supposed.

From time to time he trailed his feet along the river-bottom as a kind of rudder, or kicked down into the mud, making it look as though he were churning himself through the water instead of drifting. They were clear of the wood now. Ryokun floated over a stone bridge with only an inch or two to spare. The river was growing wider; before long they would pass the end of the conduit. A few willows to their right suggested vaguely the line of the river bank. Ahead, the great expanse of water gradually narrowed to the width of the river, both banks of which were lined with concrete from the beginning of the town area, giving it a stateliness it had not possessed in its wanderings through the fields. If they drifted that far, stopping would be out of the question—and the sea was little more than a mile further down. The adventure would have to end where the houses began. Delight in the swift, effortless floating faded as they realized what lay ahead if they did not stop soon and haul themselves out of the flood.

Ryokun was frightened. The current was much stronger now—it had been powerful enough behind the school and over the fields, but not so as to prevent him using his limbs; he had been able to dig his feet into the mud and hold himself against the flow without great effort. Below the mouth of the conduit, however, the flood turned into a raging torrent, sweeping away everything in its path with a violence that would crush instantly any mere human attempt to stand against it. Twisting his head round in the water, Ryokun saw a black head close behind him. Nobu, too, was drifting helplessly, no longer capable of struggling against the current, or even of shouting, a floating symbol of despair. The change had come in a moment, as the current swept them into the danger area. Ryokun himself was too frightened now to speak. They would be out of their depth in the deeper water of the town section of the river; and with the water running at its present speed, dog-stroke or any other stroke would be futile. How stupid they'd been to let the delight of riding the current crowd out any thought of danger. . . . Ryokun tried to cry for help, but his voice would not come—and all the time the current was getting faster and faster. He was too frightened now even to kick down at the river-bed. There was nobody in sight anywhere. None of the farmers wanted to come out merely to watch the damage the flood was doing, any more than anybody would want to take a walk now along the submerged paths and ridges, so that both paddy-fields and river were deserted.

Ryokun and his friend were floating in the middle of the river, between the two rows of half-drowned willow-trees. The augmented river current swept them on with a speed and violence of its own, different from the leisurely movement of the floodwaters over the fields, as if propelled by some secret spring of energy hidden below the muddied surface. Noiselessly, constantly forming tiny eddies, it rushed towards the town. Ryokun was desperate. They should have turned back at the stone bridge, which would have been easy, if they had not been too excited even to think of it. Ryokun tried to catch at the willows that passed on either side, waving slightly in the swirling water and trailing their branches forlornly on the surface, but the current was irresistible; no matter how he tried, it was impossible to move his arms more than a few inches. Then he tried for the bottom again with his feet, but again the speed of the current took all the force out of his kicking, and in any case the river bed was too deep now for him to reach. In the midst of his terror, the futility of his attempts reminded him of frogs he had seen trying to cross the river. They would swim for all they were worth, drifting downstream all the time, but never giving up. Eventually they would tire, their movements growing more feeble and the current would seem to give them a sudden push as if it had been waiting for that moment—then they would make a last spurt, only to give up the struggle a moment later, after a few weary strokes, and let the river carry them where it would. Ryokun might have been such a frog. Exhausted, his hands and feet jerked convulsively. It was certain they would be drowned if they were carried right into the town area. The river was deeper and the current stronger there than anywhere upstream and now, with the added impetus of the floodwater from the mountains, it was racing to the sea with startling speed.

Something like a branch bumped against his hand. It was a rotten willow-stump. He had not seen it, but had been clutching feverishly at the water in a frantic attempt to find something to hold on to, and now his hand closed round it instinctively, his whole body swerving out at right angles to the current, so that for the first time he felt its full impact. Instantly he was tossed out of the main stream on to the bank, like a leaf in a sudden breath of wind. The bank was under water, but at least he was out of danger. Nobu had caught hold of him around the chest the moment he himself caught at the stump, so he grabbed at the branches of a nearby tree, afraid the stump would come away. Neither of them spoke. Even though they had managed to escape the terrible central current, they were still surrounded by water flowing steadily in the same direction as the river and converging upon it. For a moment they stood quite still, as if to make sure that they really had escaped. In Ryokun's mind, the silent movement of the flood around him took on a terrifying roar.

After a while the two boys began to wade across the paddy-fields. The fields formed the inside of a loop in the river, and were bounded on one side by a farm on some raised ground overlooking the bank a little way upstream, which had the effect of slowing down the flood. Ryokun tried to follow the raised paths. The water came only up to his thighs, so it was possible to walk, though he kept stumbling and slipping back into the paddy, finding it hard to keep a foothold on the muddy ridges. After some minutes he and Nobu managed to reach the dry fields behind the farmhouse. Nobu's lips were blue.

'Couldn't have stood that much longer.'

'Mm.'

Without another word, the two naked boys cut across the fields, ran past another farm, and crawled through the bamboo fence surrounding the school grounds. The school was deserted. They dressed quickly, not troubling to dry their dripping hair. Ryokun put on his shoes, looking back once more at the scores of submerged paddy-fields. No one in his senses would swim out there today. He thought of the river, hidden now under the wide sheet of water, but keeping always to its course; and understood how it came to flow so much faster than the leisurely roll of the floodwater across the fields.

'See you tomorrow.'

''Bye.'

Ryokun ran out of the school grounds and through the temple gate, wanting to get away from the scene of their adventure. Shoju was working in the compound.

'What's happened, Ryokun? Your head's all wet,' he called out.

Mineyo caught him as he slipped into the washroom. 'Been swimming, have you? Do you know how pale you are—and those lips! Look at your hands!' The palms were white and swollen. Ryokun rubbed them together.

'What you mean by going swimming in that flood, when I've told you I don't know how many times even paddling in the river is dangerous? Suppose you got carried away, what would happen then?' Ryokun was hurt. For him the terror of being carried away by the current was not imaginary, but something he and he alone had experienced, and he resented her speaking so lightly of what she knew nothing about. He felt like telling her of their adventure in the tunnel—it would probably make her faint with horror.

Mineyo finished rubbing his head and started to change his clothes.

'I shall tell your father!' It was not an empty threat, Ryokun knew; but his father would merely warn him gently not to do it again. In any case he had learnt now for himself how dangerous the flood could be.

Just then he saw one of the elders' wives pass along the corridor between the house and temple, carrying a big kettle. Escaping from his grandmother, he ran along the covered way from the washroom, turned into the corridor and jumped up the steps into the temple hall.

'Hallo, Ryokun!'

'Where've you been, Ryokun? We haven't seen you all morning.'

'Have you finished all your homework, Ryokun? My grandson hasn't done a single page—he'll have a rush to get through it before school starts!'

Nine or ten of the elders' wives were sitting round four new straw mats, polishing the brass vases, censers and crane-shaped candlestands. They had unscrewed the holders from the mouth of each crane, and the brass tortoise on which its feet rested. Only one of each of the three brass ornaments would be placed on the table in front of the shrine during most of the year, but others normally kept in store were produced as the special autumn services in commemoration of St Shinran approached. The hanging lamps, so heavy with their brass shades and under-plates that it was all Ryokun could do to lift one with both hands, were scattered about the floor awaiting their turn to be cleaned. The work was not easy. To get rid of the verdigris, the women rubbed the lamps with a mixture of cleaning powder and old tea-leaves, dried in the sun. Stripped of their coating of rust, the brass surfaces shone brilliantly. Ryokun loved to watch the women, rubbing away at the tortoise-heads and the lamps and the little brass stands for the daily rice-offerings, talking all the while, hour after hour—the cleaning and polishing took from early morning till late at night. He looked at the sanctuary, emptied of its brass ornaments. With a feeling he was doing something rather daring, he stepped inside, walked reverently up to the shrine, and looked up at the eyes of the Buddha. They stared back at him, shining brilliantly out of the face of age-blackened bronze, frightened him with their steady, penetrating gaze. Behind him, the women talked without ceasing. Ryokun stood still, facing the Buddha.

'The Lord Buddha watches over you always, Ryokun,' his father had once told him. 'No matter whether you're happy or sad, or afraid about something, He never leaves you, even when you're asleep.' So the Buddha must know about their going through the conduit. He must have been watching when he ran up the tree-trunk in Heron's Forest and nearly cried with excitement and the pain of longing for his mother; and when they were drifting on the flood. Before those eyes he could not lie.

'Why doesn't He ever speak to me, then, if He sees everything I do?'

'The Lord Buddha does not speak in the way that you and I dc, Ryokun. Only your heart can hear His voice.' But this had only puzzled him the more. How could one hear anything except with his ears?

'You will understand soon' was all his father had said. When that 'soon' would be, Ryokun had no idea. He would sit like his father in front of the statue, and as he gazed up at it, insensibly its sculptured outlines would fade and somehow transmute themselves into an abstraction, an indefinable spirit which seemed to flow of its own volition into his mind and heart. The statue was very old, of the Kamakura period. Perhaps it was only an illusion, his own obscure notion of the Lord Buddha taking shape in the blackened statue before him. Exactly what it was he experienced during these moments he did not understand, apart from a strong feeling of awe and fear.

'Someone said they thought they saw Renko in Tan'ami the other day—wonder if it really was her.'

'I heard she'd been seen.'

'She could hardly come to the temple, anyway.'

'She'd hardly want to, I dare say, considering the way she left it.'

'Maybe she came to see the boy.'

'She didn't have another child, did she?'

'That's what they say, though whether it's true or not I don't know. The man has a child, though—just born when she met him; she's bringing him up, it seems.'

'All the same, she'd want to see her own again.'

'Of course she would—it's natural.'

The speaker glanced at Ryokun. He was sitting reverently before the sanctuary, just as he would have to do one day when he succeeded his father as priest. All the women turned to look at him; then nodded to each other before going on with their polishing. Facing the solemn gaze of the Lord Buddha, Ryokun did not move.

21

The autumn services in commemoration of St Shinran were the most spectacular event of the year at Butsuoji, as at Senshuji and all the other temples of the sect. Many preparations had to be made before the services began. The yellow and purple curtains were hung up again at the head of the temple steps and in front of the porch of the house, and rows of paper lanterns set up in the courtyard, the whole compound taking on a festival air. Ryokun always enjoyed those services. With a feeling of excited anticipation he would stare up at the purple curtain which hung low over the door of the house, darkening the hall inside, and at the ornaments and decorations in the temple itself. The shrine was resplendent with the newly-polished Five Ornaments and oil-lamps; the gilded pillars seemed to shine for the occasion with a mysterious brilliancy. Treading softly on the mats so as to make no noise, Ryokun inspected the shrine and the recess behind it and on either side. Every year he would spend hours staring at the eight scrolls hung in the *tokonoma* of the recess. For most of the year there were only four—one pair consisting only of Chinese characters, the other of a number of portraits of saints, whose names Ryokun did not know—they included the 'Seven Patriarchs' of the Pure Land sect, Ryuju Bosatsu, Tenshin Bosatsu, Unran Daishi, Doshaku Zenji, Zendo Daishi, Genshin Sozu, and Honen Shonin. The scrolls were old and faded, so that it was no longer easy to distinguish the faces. Before the autumn services, however, they were taken down and replaced with eight scrolls depicting the life of Shinran. The first of the many scrolls dealing with events in the saint's life was painted by Joga of Korakuji, with a commentary by Kakunyo, in the 30th year of Einin, only thirty-five years after the saint's death. The Butsuoji scrolls were copied from those preserved at Senshuji, which are generally considered to be the finest extant.

There was no one else in the hall. Ryokun stood looking up at the scrolls, absorbed in the painted scenes; the *tokonoma* shelves above which the scrolls were hung were unusually high, about the level of his chest. The first of the four scenes on the first scroll showed the saint receiving his first tonsure as a Buddhist priest, at Seiren Temple in Awataguchi. Above the painting ran the commentary: 'Inspired by a longing to spread the Law, and aided by the merit of a former existence, at the age of nine he visited the temple of his uncle, the former Chief Abbot Noritsuna, Lord of the third class of the second rank, where he received the tonsure and was given the name of Noriyasu.' Ryokun was fascinated by the details of the scene—ceremonial carriages, the plum blossom, the retainers dragging unwilling oxen, the court pages, the big white tile-covered walls, the figures sitting so straight and stiff, looking as if at any moment they might topple over. Below the first painting was the description of the second: 'In the spring of the first year of Kennin, wishing to withdraw from the world, he visited the saint Honen at the Kissui Temple.' All the figures in this picture were priests. Much of the commentary was too difficult for Ryokun to read; but the sequence of pictures was enough to give him a general idea of the story, and he enjoyed working it out for himself.

Of the saint's birth and childhood nothing is known for certain. Tradition has it that he was born in the village of Hino near Kyoto on the 1st of April in the 3rd year of Shoan, in the reign of the Emperor Takakura, the son of the Lord Fujiwara Arinori, Chief Lord-in-Waiting to the Dowager Empress, and Yoshimitsu, daughter of Minamoto Yoshinobu; and that as a child he was called Matsuwakamaru. But there is no historical evidence for this story, which may have been invented for their own purposes by the priests of the Honganji Temple when they were faced with the necessity, thirty-five years after the saint's death, of compiling an 'official' biography.

No such doubts troubled Ryokun, as he followed the narrative from one picture to the next, the dramatic representation of incidents in the saint's life making them live in his imagination far more than any reading of the archaic script of the commentary could have done. Most of all he was thrilled by the picture of Ben'en, the notorious leader of the mountain hermits of the Hitachi region, attempting to kill the saint on Mt Itajiki. Clad in heavy armour from head to foot, with a halberd in one hand and a bow in the other, and a look of fiendish hatred on his face, the hermit lay in wait for his victim, who was building himself a cell in a field. 'A certain hermit,' the commentary began, 'felt spite against the Law, and harbouring evil in his heart, sought out the saint in the mountain. Many times he lay in wait for him hoping to strike him down on one of his journeys to the solitude of Mt Itajiki; but always he failed of his purpose. Indeed, if we think deeply, it seems no less than a miracle that the saint did not fall into his hands. . . . At last he determined he would visit the saint openly. When he reached his cell, the saint at once came out to meet him. The moment the hermit saw his gracious countenance, all malice vanished from his heart; he wept in sorrowful repentance. Nor did the saint show any trace of fear at his confession of the dark purpose that had filled his mind. Casting away his sword and breaking his bow in two, the hermit straightway abandoned his hermit's robe and cowl, and returning to the fold of the true Law, attained to the salvation for which he longed. . . .'

The scrolls were as exciting as a popular novel in the drama and variety of the events they depicted, so that inability to read the commentaries in no way lessened Ryokun's enjoyment of them. The last picture of all, though, was frightening; it always made him wish he had never looked at the scrolls at all, it was so dark and sad. In the right hand corner, seven or eight priests were carrying a bier on poles, the leader holding a pine-torch above his head. The body of Shinran lay stretched upon the bier. Huge pine-trees and mountain precipices dwarfed the little procession as it made its way to the pyre on the opposite side of the picture, where enormous red tongues of flame leaped forward to meet the bier and its burden. Three more priests, shoulders bared and robes tucked up above their knees, were stirring the fire with long iron poles. In the shadow of a crag nearby four or five other priests stood with linked hands. Ryokun hated them—it struck him there was something brutal, even murderous, in their posture and expression, as if they were gloating over the burning of the body of the saint instead of mourning for him. No less gruesome in this final picture were two other figures, white-hooded after the manner of mountain hermits, who were emerging from the forest on the left of the picture, above the pyre. Finally, half-hidden behind its surrounding fence, there was the open, waiting tomb.

'Hullo, Ryokun! Like those pictures, do you?'

Shoju was standing outside the sanctuary. Ryokun had not heard him enter the hall.

'I'd like Nobu to come and see them.'

'No one outside the priest's family is allowed into the recess.'

'Why are these pictures always brought out for the big services?'

'It's a sign we still remember St Shinran, and are thankful for the salvation he brought us.'

'Then why isn't everybody allowed to look at them?' Ryokun was sorry he had no one with whom to share the pictures, and the thrill of working out the story they told. 'You can't see them properly from outside the recess, they're too small. Even up here I can't see what's in the top ones unless I can stand on tiptoe. There are so many people in them, and they're all crowded together, besides being so small.'

'That's why Father Soshu reads the Godensho at the evening service—so that anybody who wants to can hear about the holy saint.'

Ryokun was satisfied. It occurred to him that the reason he could follow without much difficulty the story the scrolls told, merely by looking at the pictures, was that he had learnt the main events in Shinran's life by hearing his father's periodic readings of the Godensho, the biography of the saint. The text of the Godensho which Soshu used at the evening memorial services was full of difficult phrases from the sutras, but Ryokun could grasp the exciting, novel-like incidents around which it was written.

On the second evening of the services, after the regular sutra-readings, Shoju made the preparations for Soshu's reading of the Godensho. The flickering light from the candles and oil lamps, reflected in the gilded surface of the pillars, the brilliance of the newly-polished brass ornaments, and the slowly drifting wraiths of incense-smoke combined to create a world apart, unique, in which for a few brief moments on this one day of the year, Shoju was the centre of attention. Several hundred pairs of eyes were focussed on him. The preparations were simple. Directly in front of the sanctuary, Shoju placed a small sutra-table, rather higher than the usual one, lit two candles in tall brass stands, one on each side of the table, and laid a small mat, about a yard across, on the wooden floor of the sanctuary. That was all; but the old man moved with a deliberate care and dignity, keyed up by the importance of the occasion. When all was ready, he struck the bell hanging in the corridor behind the sanctuary, slowly at first, then faster and faster, till each sound was barely distinguishable from the next—and then again more slowly, the gradual lengthening of the intervals between each clang of the bell being the sign that Soshu was about to appear.

Entering the hall by the door at the back of the sanctuary, Soshu bowed before the portrait of Shinran, and sat down on the special mat Shoju had prepared for him. He was wearing black canonical robes. A ripple of murmured *nenbutsu* ran from end to end of the hall, which on this one evening of the year was packed to overflowing, worshippers squatting in the surrounding corridor and on the steps. Mrs Hoshina was in the congregation, with the ample figure of her daughter Tanemi at her side; and Mrs Mimori from the Mutsumi-ya. Many came for this special service who did not belong to the temple congregation; and most of the parishioners present were from the farming suburbs rather than the town proper.

Reverently, Soshu lifted the first of the two volumes to his head, then slowly opened it in front of him. At once the *nenbutsu* ceased; the congregation seemed to hold its breath. 'The first volume of the Takada Book of the Life of St Shinran . . .' The words rang out across the silence. Soshu had no need to raise his voice; it carried with perfect clarity to every part of the congregation. Ryokun was sitting on the right, among the elders. He loved his father's voice, and listened to him now with the same rapt expression as the old men around him. Soshu might have been alone in the hall, the whole congregation was so silent. Even among his fellow-priests he was known for the penetrating yet melodious quality of his voice, which came out especially in his reading of the final inflections of each sentence. The last sentence of each chapter of the Godensho was always read in a higher tone than the rest; and now, when they heard Soshu raise his voice slightly as a sign that the first chapter was ending, the congregation responded instinctively with a series of *nenbutsu*. Ryokun did not join in. He would have to wait till he was grown-up, he thought, before the *nenbutsu* would come naturally.

After waiting till the murmuring of the *nenbutsu* had died away, Soshu announced the second chapter. The old people listened with their eyes half-closed, aware only of his voice, but the younger ones gazed at him steadily. His own eyes moved up and down the lines of old, woodblock-printed characters, which after so many years he almost knew by heart. Over the book and desk flickered the light from the two candles. There were fifteen chapters in all in the two volumes, so that he needed to keep his voice resonant for the later chapters. He had never drunk any water during these readings, all through the years. Not that there was any conscious technique to his reading; but his voice rose and fell with a natural flow that was not merely delightful to listen to, but also imparted to his hearers a feeling that in some indefinable way they were being inwardly cleansed. Gently, quietly, it seemed to purge their minds of all that was not pure and healthful and inspiring.

Among the congregation, sitting in the shadow of one of the big pillars, and listening eagerly to every word, was Tomoko Komiyama. She was afraid to open her eyes. When Soshu entered the hall, she had gazed at him for a moment with a peculiar intensity, but no one had noticed anything unusual. Soshu himself gave no sign of agitation. Probably it had not occurred to him that she might be somewhere in the dense crowd of worshippers. She sat with hands tightly clasped, leaning forward slightly; the happiest person in the hall, she thought—and the unhappiest. Suddenly she felt stifled, and then as suddenly numb, as if her nerves had ceased to function.

'. . . must we not admit this glorious truth? If a man say that the mastery of knowledge is equal in efficacy to the gift of grace, he is far astray. When once we have learned the true principle of faith in Paradise, all human striving falls away. St Honen and St Shinran were alike in this, that they achieved faith only through the grace of Amida. . . .' Tomoko listened to the voice that spoke the words, not to their meaning, and opened her eyes only when the murmuring of *nenbutsu* around her marked the end of a chapter.

When he had finished the first volume, Soshu rose and went out. Shoju trimmed the candles; at his touch their weakening flames sprang into new life. Ryokun slipped out of the hall. He ran round to the house in search of his father, and found him drinking tea in the Lute Room. The house was in a bustle tonight, with the elders' wives serving dinner to twelve or thirteen priests in the library—every year a group of priests from other temples of the same sect as Butsuoji would come to assist at the autumn services, and it was the custom to offer them a meal and *sake*. Ryokun was glad to find his father alone; apparently he had forgotten all about his guests.

'It's a big congregation tonight, Ryokun.'

'I know—I was listening, Father.'

'Were you, indeed?' Soshu was surprised. 'Did you understand what I was reading?'

'Not very well. Some of it I did, though.'

Soshu rose. 'You might just as well hear the rest, then. You'll have to read the Godensho yourself some day, after all.'

His voice was clearer, more resonant than ever, as he began the second volume. The elders' wives heard it from across the garden, as they carried dishes to and from the library. Two of them stopped in the corridor to listen.

Mineyo was sitting in the kitchen, giving orders to the women. When two of the elders came in from the temple, she asked them if Soshu had finished reading the Godensho. They nodded. The sermons would start in a few minutes, so after a quick smoke they went back to the hall. Ryokun sat in the porch, looking out across the compound. A few people, who had evidently come only to hear the Godensho readings, were coming down the temple steps on their way home. Several of the big lanterns had gone out; only the light from the hall stood out clearly against the surrounding darkness of the autumn night, the few remaining lanterns making little impression on the gloom. Ryokun felt suddenly lonely and uneasy, wondering at the contrast between the crowded temple, the busy kitchen behind him, and the dark, dead silence of the courtyard.

Someone emerged from the corridor to one side of the porch—a woman. Noticing Ryokun as she crossed the hall, she bowed slightly towards him before passing on. She must be one of the town ladies, thought Ryokun, struck by her kind expression. He did not know Mrs Komiyama.

Soshu had been called into the library to drink *sake*. Some of the priests had already left, and others were preparing to go. One, however, was drunk; he had grabbed hold of one of the elders' wives and was trying to joke with her—it was the priest of Jokaji, on whom *sake* invariably had the same effect. Soshu was forced to stay with him. Meanwhile, the first sermon had begun. It was not until the third was well under way, and Ryokun in bed and fast asleep, that the drunken priest finally went home.

The last sermon was over. Some of the elders' wives were preparing the bedding for the visiting preacher, others were clearing up in the kitchen. They would be the last to leave the temple, though they had had no chance to hear either Soshu's reading of the Godensho or the sermons. The elders had gone home, and Shoju, who slept at Butsuoji during the period of the autumn services, was checking the empty hall, the sanctuary, and the corridors, to make sure nothing had been dropped or left that might start a fire. He picked up the worst of the litter, locked the outer doors, and finally switched off the electric lights.

'Goodnight!' The last of the women to leave called to Shoju on her way out.

'Goodnight, and thanks! We'll see you again tomorrow, I suppose.'

Silence returned to Butsuoji. Soshu lay in bed, breathing with some difficulty after the unaccustomed *sake*. He could feel the blood racing in his veins. Mineyo came in with a glass of water, which she put on the floor-matting by his pillow.

'They always come in crowds to hear you, don't they? Father Soshu's reading of the Godensho is becoming quite a local institution.'

Too tired to feel annoyed, Soshu murmured 'goodnight', and Mineyo left the room. Perhaps because of the *sake*, he fell asleep almost immediately, well content that the services were proving such a success again this year.

Vaguely aware of some discomfort, Soshu stirred, then turned over, but the discomfort persisted, as if there was something in the bed at his side. Unpleasant, whatever it was . . . Suddenly he was terrified. He tried to sit up; it clung to him noiselessly, like some mysterious obscene animal. The *sake,* perhaps . . . that must be why he had not noticed her coming into the bed, when he was normally so sensitive to the slightest sound or movement. Maybe she had interpreted the lack of any reaction from him as a tacit welcome—but it was already too late to think of that. At least he was calm now, in control of himself. He must think calmly how to deal with this body clinging to him; the arms now flung across his waist, mute, trembling symbols of misery and hate, of torment of body and soul, yet with the unnatural strength of passion, in a last, desperate entreaty. To force her away from him, he would have first to break the hold of her arms. It was beyond anything he had ever imagined—several times there had been similar scenes, but she had never driven him to the limit of endurance, as now. She was whispering continuously, as if in delirium, but with her face pressed against his side, so that the words were smothered in the folds of his kimono. Panic overtook him—every moment he lay still, without trying to break away, would seem like surrender. . . . In the darkness he shivered with horror and disgust.

In the midst of his agitation, he remembered Naota Ifukube, whose story was so like his own: Tsuruko creeping into his room and clinging to him in a violent wordless embrace, the supreme expression of her passion. A moment later she might have killed herself, no doubt. She had acted as a woman does when driven close to death—in her torment of shame and despair and bitterness, death would seem painless, in comparison with a final rejection by Ifukube. So it was now with Mineyo. This was her final act, inconceivable in the light of day, the physical paroxysm of an obsession she could no longer bear. Perhaps she too was near to suicide . . . she was moaning, clinging to him as fiercely as ever, probing with all the strength of her stubborn egoism the weakest part of his nature, for which he so despised himself. Ifukube had managed to protect himself without a struggle, merely by lying on his face. To imitate him was unthinkable. When he had listened to him telling of his encounter with Tsuruko that night, he had found it hard to believe that anyone could descend so low. Yet who could tell what a man or a woman might *not* be driven to do, in desperation? Soshu could no longer dismiss Tsuruko's conduct with a glib phrase of disgust or condemnation. No more could he judge Mineyo now. She would be past thinking of shame, aware only of the burning passion; to her diseased imagination, the beating of her pulse, even, would sound as the roar of a consuming fire. . . . Perhaps he should follow Ifukube's example, after all—everything else in their situations corresponded with such exactness. . . .

'Let go! Let go, Mineyo!' He tried to wrench her arms away from his body, but they were not to be dislodged so easily, clinging to him still with a fanatical strength.

'... I'll curse him ... curse him ... kill him ...' The words jutted out amid a stream of delirious mumbling. Soshu shuddered, in anger as much as fear. There was a note of implacable venom in the voice, a visceral obscenity, as of the victim of some evil delusion who worships before a Shinto shrine at midnight and drives nails, cursing rhythmically, into an effigy of his enemy. What was she asking for by clinging to him like this? Probably she had forgotten. The moment had gone when Soshu might have lost the will to resist, for what impelled her now was only the sullen energy of despair. Without much hope of success, Soshu tried to find some way of slipping out of her embrace. Assault with violence, the law might have called Mineyo's action, if she had been the man and he the woman; violence it certainly resembled, if by violence was meant the gaining of one's ends by trampling on another's will. Yet at the same time it was utterly different! With a sudden effort, he tried to jerk her arms from him, straining against her resistance. She had evidently used up nearly all her strength, which was not great, though till this moment the intensity of her passion had given the illusion of an unnatural physical force. He kicked his feet free, twisting his body violently. Her hands fell away; and he tried to stand up, fending her off as she struggled to prevent him. Then the skirt of his kimono tore in her grasp, so that she fell back helpless on the bed. Soshu sprang up, only to stagger against the partition, his legs refusing to bear his weight.

'... curse you ... curse you ... kill ...' The hate-laden words pursuing him through the darkness, Soshu managed to slide back the partition and stepped down panting into the passage. With no clear idea of what he was going to do, he groped for his clogs, and opened the side door of the house, the heavy grating sound momentarily shattering the stillness of the night.

He began to walk quickly across the compound, still with no particular purpose, to where the extinguished lanterns hung in rows on their posts. In front of the hall he stopped and straightened his rumpled kimono, then hurried on, too conscious of his defilement to face the temple. As if of their own volition, his feet led him towards the cemetery. Opening the wicker-gate, he walked down the narrow path between the graves. There was no moon, but he could just make out the tall tombstones, standing erect around him like men and women. A few stars shone feebly; such light as there was came rather from the street-lamps in the distance. Inevitably, as if it had been his conscious objective since leaving the house, Soshu found himself approaching the hereditary tomb of the Getsudo family, in the middle of the cemetery. He sat down on the stone surround, his mind in turmoil. To what lengths of cruelty might a man go, if love once died? Soshu hated himself. He could not bring himself to think of his rejection of her as justifiable 'self-defence'—or, more accurately, he could and did think of it in this way, yet could not help loathing it, even while compelled to admit it was the only thing he could have done. And in another corner of his mind was the memory of Tomoko, urging him to save himself from defilement for *her* sake. He was tortured now by the knowledge that it was because of Tomoko that he had been so brutal. Had he acted out of pure selfishness, then? Confessing to Tomoko had not made him stronger—on the contrary, as far as preserving himself from further sin was concerned, the decision to resist Mineyo's advances had come more easily before the confession, when there was no debilitating mixture of motives. The effect of the encounter with Tomoko had been to weaken him still further morally—a consequence he had never dreamt of. Who would believe him now if he were to talk of chastity being its own reward?

He wondered whether Tsuruko Yamashiro had made a new life for herself after the break with Ifukube. She could always earn a living as a maid at an inn, or as a home-help. But Mineyo could never live on her own . . . Soshu gave way to despair. Not till she died would she leave Butsuoji. No one would be able to make her leave the one place where life held any meaning for her, where she had succeeded in achieving what she had spent the better part of twenty years scheming for—let alone persuade her that the realizing of her desire was the sole reason why she must go.

The cold night air and icy stone of the tomb made him shiver. He looked at the graves around him. They hid the remains of lives of every kind; few, no doubt, of unbroken happiness. The place did not strike him as gruesome, as cemeteries usually do. On the contrary, he felt at peace here as nowhere else. Perhaps among the dead around him there were some who had sinned and suffered like himself. . . . Too weak to take drastic action, he was afraid of the world, afraid of what the parishioners might think and say, afraid for his position as priest, afraid of Ryokun learning the truth about his father. What had the dead done under such a burden? They were listening to his unspoken confession, their eyes fixed on him from their graves. Silently the tall stones clustered about him, like living presences, watching . . . he was glad they were watching him and his thoughts. Then he listened. There was a murmuring, a rustling of voices; the stones were speaking. He turned to where the voices sounded clearest, to the graves that lay directly behind the temple, their massive, moss-covered stones commemorating the dead of the eras of Kanreki and Meiwa, two centuries earlier; to the corner where those who had left no relative to mourn them were buried. Humbly he listened to their whispered reproaches. Only a bigot would deny that stones could speak! Each with its own voice, they stood before him, men in the guise of tombs, clothed in night. Listening, he grew calmer. He could hear each separate voice in the murmured harmony, yet clearly understand none—but it was of him they were whispering. Not whispering only; he felt them moving too, some standing about him as if to protect him, others in the distance, moving . . .

Perhaps Mineyo would kill him, he thought. A woman of her temperament was perfectly capable of putting her curses and threats into effect. Murder . . . he knew now that *he* could never bring himself to kill; but with Mineyo, perhaps it was her karma. If one thought back over her life, her killing him now would be quite in character. She had already murdered a daughter—and he was her fellow-murderer. . . . Because of the sin they had shared, he still could not hate her. So it would always be, until he died—as if death would change anything! And now, when fate was grinding him inexorably down, he found himself in love with another woman. Was he incapable of learning, he wondered—destined to be for ever at war with himself, even in misery?

Around him stood the tombstones, silently intent, missing nothing of his inward soliloquy, yet still withdrawn, impalpable, beyond the confines of waking consciousness. Now again they seemed to speak, interrupting his reflections. Motionless, head bent, he listened. What was he to do? 'Forget Tomoko!' he seemed to hear a voice say in the rustling of the shadow. 'It is your love for her that has made you suffer.' 'Take Ryokun with you and leave Butsuoji!' came another; and another, 'You want to break with her in secret, as you began . . . impossible . . . make confession before all the congregation, let them punish you!'; and another, 'The parishioners know the truth, it is only that they do not speak of it openly; they are waiting for their priest to confess. . . .' Voices through the darkness, echoes of his thoughts, persecuting him—as if the moral energy driving him to a final crisis was in reality no part of his own nature, but an external force with its own independent life. Again he bowed his head and listened. The voices attacked him, reviled him, grew excited and confused; clearer than ever he heard them in the profound unbroken silence that hung over the cemetery. Footsteps, even, sounded near him, as of the living . . . the murmuring did not cease.

'Father!'

The voice calling him was clear. Soshu turned. One of the stones had spoken. . . .

'Father!'

A man was standing among the tombs. Gravel crunched under his feet.

'Is anything the matter, Father?'

Soshu sighed.

'I woke up when I heard the house door open—and then there were footsteps that sounded like yours. I didn't hear the gate, so I knew you must be in the compound somewhere. Then I found the cemetery open. . . . Has anything happened, Father?' Shoju waited, indistinguishable among the tombstones.

'I'm so ashamed. . . .' Coming to himself suddenly, Soshu stood up.

The old priest closed the wicker-gate after him as he followed Soshu out of the cemetery. In front of the temple, where the pale yellow curtain hung limp in the night air, Soshu stopped and bowed. He was grateful to Shoju for not asking any more questions. The old man would know, of course. Shoju . . . he had never once complained at the treatment he received from Mineyo, degrading him to a menial. In the *Doctrine, Works, Faith and Attainment* Shinran had quoted a saying from the Sutra of Eternal Life: 'Every man, if he once find the light, shall leap for joy; in him shall a pure heart be born.' In his own way, Shoju must have found the light of which the scripture spoke. 'Light' meant 'faith', of course . . . Soshu's shame deepened.

'I shall go into the temple. I would rather be alone,' he said as they entered the house. The old man bowed without replying.

He walked along the corridor, hearing the clatter of the front door behind him as Shoju shut up the house for the second time, and without turning on the lights, entered the great hall. It was not now as he knew it at other times. Packed to overflowing only a few hours before, it had been given a rough cleaning after the worshippers had gone home; but the smell of the crowd, its warmth, the hum of its voices remained. From force of habit Soshu was about to enter the sanctuary, when he remembered he was still in his sleeping clothes, as he had been in the cemetery. He sat down in the dark some distance from the shrine, like an ordinary worshipper, and bowed with clasped hands. At once, as if they had been waiting for such a moment of release, *nenbutsu* began to pour from his lips. He was torn, divided, imprisoned in karma; struggling feverishly to escape from the hell of one sordid passion, dragging himself down with another—and in that new hell what promise of delight still tempted! The chance meeting with Tomoko had been a rebirth, a glimpse of harmony, of fragrance—and to it, after all, he owed the sudden access of courage with which he had been able to face Mineyo. He has listened to her confession, and she to his;

from the bond thus formed between them had sprung the hope of new life on which he now depended. He continued to murmur *nenbutsu.*

If his suffering had its origin in self-centred desire, so did his joy. He could still dream of a future with Tomoko—what were such visions but the longings of a naked selfishness? The eyes of the Buddha were upon him, piercing his soul.

Soon after he went back to bed, the first light of dawn appeared; but he slept on. Back in her own room, Mineyo had cried herself to sleep, like a frustrated child. She knew Soshu, and someone she guessed must be Shoju, had come back into the house, but had not heard him entering his room.

The morning brought the third day of the memorial services. Ryokun grumbled at having to get out of bed, and received his regular scolding from Mineyo. At breakfast, Mineyo's attitude was no different from usual. Soshu could not look her in the face; it was impossible to believe in the genuineness of her matter-of-fact air—as if nothing whatever had happened—yet equally impossible to guess what she might be plotting. Two of the elders' wives came early, to wait on the visiting preacher. A little later, when the preacher had finished his breakfast, the elders would begin to appear. Shoju climbed the bell-tower to toll the morning bell.

'What a good thing it'll be if we have another big crowd again today,' said Mineyo. What mental sleight-of-hand enabled her to suppress the memory of their encounter, Soshu wondered. Behind the pretence of normality her frenzied passion remained, to which murder would be as nothing.

22

Smilingly, entering into her daughter's excitement at the prospect of tomorrow's picnic, Tomoko watched Shoko empty the rucksack she herself had packed so neatly, and re-pack everything to her own liking.

'You'll really be all right, Shoko darling?'

'Don't make Sumi come, Mummy—there's no need. Everybody's going alone, except for one or two whose Mummies wanted to come.'

'Their Mummies are going because they're worried, I know. I wonder if it's safe to let you go alone. Teacher will look after you—but Mummy can't help worrying.'

Shoko would not listen to her mother's talk of sending Sumi in her place. Tomoko felt the risk. She had never let Shoko go on an outing like this alone, and would be fretting every minute till she came home. The best thing would have been for her to go herself, of course; but it was impossible for her to leave the house. And the maid was only a girl of sixteen. However, if she once started worrying, she would never stop—there was nothing for it but to trust Shoko and her urge to be independent. It was comforting in a way, in spite of her anxiety, to see Shoko insisting so stubbornly that she would be perfectly safe alone—the little girl revealing already a glimpse of the grown-up.

'All right, then—Sumi shall come home when she's taken you to the school and asked the teacher to look after you.'

Shoko walked up and down the room with the rucksack on her back. 'How light it is!' she cried. Fruit, sweets, water-bottle, plastic cup, handkerchief and toilet-paper had gone in, but there was something she had forgotten.

'There'll be your lunch-box as well, don't forget, and tea to go in the bottle. It'll be twice as heavy then.'

Shoko couldn't imagine what twice as heavy would be like. 'Sumi, Sumi!' she called out, wanting to show off how easily she could carry the rucksack. Already for two or three days she had been full of the thrill of the coming picnic, an artless joy that even the day itself could hardly bring.

'You'll be tired out before you start, if you keep on prancing about like that!' She would go to bed that night more excited than ever, no doubt, with her clothes and rucksack ready by her pillow. Her own heart aching, Tomoko watched the little girl's happiness.

The front door clattered open. Rucksack on her back, Shoko stopped dead, staring at her mother. Tomoko's expression altered; she had recognised the sound. Shoko stood before her with the frightened look of a child dragged abruptly by a rough adult hand from its child's world. Sensing the change in her, Tomoko grew paler still. No voice came from the porch, but from the sound of shoes being slipped off it was clear the visitor was not waiting to be shown in.

'*O-kaeri-nasaimase*!' they heard the maid say. Tomoko stood up.

'*O-kaeri-nasaimase*!' Kneeling, she greeted Yamaji. After a glance at Shoko, who was still standing in the middle of the room with the rucksack on her back, he went upstairs without a word. Shoko's face had lost its childish expression. The whole house seemed different—but not because of the sudden change in the girl, which was merely the reaction to the change in her mother.

Tomoko slowly climbed the stairs after Yamaji. The descent into hell . . . It was always like this, the bitterness of forcing herself to follow him to the room upstairs; no matter how many times the act was repeated, she had never ceased to revolt against it inwardly. Yet she had to go. Tomoko looked back at her daughter, so suddenly and brutally robbed of the delightful happiness of a moment ago, every trace of which had vanished; the little figure was changed out of recognition. A spasm of pain caught at her breast. Even if Shoko was too young to understand everything, she must have some notion of what was happening in her home. Not that anybody said anything to her; but she must have seen for herself by now. Tomoko was filled with pity for her daughter. And one of the cruel hands that had torn away the child's happiness had been her own . . . Time would not heal the wound her young spirit had suffered. Each step slower than the last, as if her body were turning into a dead weight her feet could no longer bear, Tomoko mounted the stairs.

Sitting cross-legged on the floor, Yamaji stared greedily at her body—as though he were licking it, savouring once again her peculiar charm: the paleness that suited her better than any colour, the gentle, submissive style of her hair, and her soft skin, smooth and fine-grained, like the peel of an apple.

'You haven't put up any notice outside about your being a teacher.'

'I've ordered one. But I'm still not sure whether I'd be any good as a teacher.'

'Timidity won't help, anyway. I was going to send you some pupils as soon as you put the signboard up.'

Sumi brought in tea. There was no sound from downstairs.

'Where's Shoko?' Tomoko asked the maid in a low voice.

'She's gone to the park.'

To disappear when Yamaji came had become a habit with Shoko, from the days when her grandmother was alive and used to hurry her out of the house to avoid meeting him. Tomoko could not bear it. Unconsciously, even her own daughter abetted her, though in fact such 'help' was the cruellest form of disobedience to her real wishes. Yamaji would never understand so subtle a source of pain.

'I won't have you teaching tea-ceremony, though. It'd be humiliating—make me look mean, as I've said before; as if you had to do it because the man who kept you didn't give you enough to live on.'

'That's not why I—'

'I know, I know. I'm talking about the effect it would have on me, not about why you want to do it.'

Yamaji stretched out both his hands to her, like a parent wanting to soothe a child after a trivial misunderstanding. To Tomoko, sitting opposite him, the distance between them was infinite, a distance of her own making; yet she could not refuse those hands . . . She turned away, ashamed. The movement suggested a delicacy, a modest unwillingness even now to hide her shame in his arms: but it concealed the bitterest inward struggle. If Yamaji was stupid enough to see in it the playful repulse of a lover—but the mistake was already made, she saw, and his desire aroused. Without looking at him, Tomoko edged closer, while her heart struggled to escape. Still she could not bring herself to come within his reach . . . her heart cried out—life itself revolted within her, abandoning her body, making impossible the last movement of surrender . . . like a toy train stopped a few inches from its destination by a broken spring. Her limbs were lifeless, an inert mass for which she was no longer concerned or responsible.

Yamaji pulled her easily towards him, smiling as he always did at her shyness. In the very lifelessness of her body, emptied of purpose or feeling of any kind, Tomoko kept her last defence, against him and against her own accusing conscience. Yamaji's behaviour never varied. There was nothing to a woman but appetite, he seemed to think; he never noticed her eyes change colour, and took the complex expression with which she would greet him as no more than the reflection of a crude instinct. He was hopelessly blind and insensitive. Tomoko hid her suffering as best she could, while he had his will of every outward part of her, of her soft scented skin and slender body.

The bitterness was twofold. For what prospect was there that she would ever be free of him, or able to earn her living, with Shoko to look after? Very few jobs would be open to a woman of her years, without any special knowledge or skill, and with a child on her hands. Teaching tea-ceremony wouldn't bring in enough to live on. She thought of the Tan'ami Labour Exchange, and of the advertisement columns in the women's magazines she had gone through so carefully. There was nothing she could do, apparently, except help in a restaurant or a geisha-house; and even if she succeeded in finding work as a maid, it would mean giving up Shoko. Tomoko was struck by her own utter helplessness, which made it seem like a miracle that she had managed to live all her life so far without a single weapon to protect herself. All her life, in fact, she had depended on men—it was men that had enabled her to exist at all; and if she had eventually married it was only because she was forced to, out of sheer lack of qualification to be anything else than a housewife. Her situation was something like a wife's even now, with her body at a man's disposal to trample on whenever he wanted to—though she hardly had the right to think of it as 'trampling', since it was only what she could expect in her position, and there was no other way she and Shoko could live. Yamaji's treatment of her was like the perverse delight one gets from muddying a clear pool. With a woman like Tomoko, especially, a touch of cruelty doubled his pleasure. Tomoko struggled desperately not to lose all control, but her body would not respond; she surrendered impersonally to the orgasm it forced upon her, as if the act were another's. Yet this obscenity *was* her act . . . she lay helpless, in utter despair.

'Open your eyes!' Yamaji ordered, breathing heavily.

Tomoko opened her eyes slightly, but instantly shut them again.

'Open your eyes, I tell you—they're beautiful, I want to look at them. Open up!'

Tomoko opened and shut her eyes two or three times, in an agony of fear that their colour would give her away. Shutting her eyes was her way of hiding from herself; she could not lie open-eyed and pretend to stare calmly up at the knot-holes in the wooden ceiling, as if it did not matter that her eyes showed her heart was elsewhere.

'Open them! You spoil all your beauty by keeping them shut. They're so tender, and passionate, too—you don't know how passionate . . . I've never known a woman with such beautiful eyes; so cloudy, so soft. Open!'

To watch the murder of her body—Yamaji having his way with

her, like a boy taunting a puppy? Tomoko was worn out. Somewhere at the back of her throat she seemed to feel herself screaming . . . If only she could have held firmly to the thought that this was the price of living, for Shoko and herself, the pain might have been less; but she was incapable of a man's casual, profit-and-loss attitude, which would see in her conduct with Yamaji a business transaction all the more to her advantage because it involved no love. To love a man, or to be tormented by him—Tomoko could imagine only these two kinds of relationship, both of which demanded emotional involvement, and to think of herself as responding only to violence, mechanically and without sincerity, brought more relief than any attempt at love could have done.

'It's odd, the way you keep those eyes shut tight as a clam now—you never used to, until a while ago. Don't tell me you're getting embarrassed—at this time of day!'

Tomoko's struggle to turn into illusion the reality her body was enduring failed. To visualize Soshu now behind her closed eyes would have demanded a shamelessness she did not possess—though the moment Yamaji left she would be overwhelmed with an agony of longing for the priest of Butsuoji. And now, the bitterness of having done once more that which could never be undone . . . Quivering, Tomoko asked Soshu's forgiveness.

'The elders have started making a fuss,' said Yamaji suddenly as he sat up. Tomoko's hands dropped from her dishevelled hair. She turned away. A faint trace of colour showed in her cheeks. The mole at the bottom of her neck gleamed slightly, as if the skin were damp.

'I've only done what's best for the temple, but those elders have got it into their heads it's all for my personal benefit.'

'What is the trouble about?'

'The cemetery, of course.'

Tomoko did not understand. Probably it was something Soshu knew nothing about, for he had never mentioned the cemetery to her.

'I'll fetch the tea,' she said. Down in the kitchen, she saw with a stab of shame and fear that Sumi had put out the cups and made the tea; she had only to carry the tray upstairs . . . The sixteen-year old maid knew everything, even the moment when Yamaji would be ready for tea.

'The cemetery on the hill, where that old fellow Shoju lives, is going to be developed as part of the town sooner or later anyway, so the obvious thing to do is to find a good spot somewhere else and move the whole cemetery before the Council buys up the land compulsorily. The elders may know all there is to know about paddy-fields, but in matters like this they're stupid and suspicious—don't listen to a word I say, though it's only the barest common sense.'

His own brother, who was one of the elders, Yamaji regarded as one of the chief obstructionists. 'I've heard from a company that would like to buy the land on the hill. It's just the kind of offer we want. Butsuoji will have to enlarge its cemetery sooner or later anyway—there's no more room behind the temple, and not much on the hill, either. The Council's planning people are talking about combining all the temple cemeteries in Tan'ami into one.'

'Where would the Butsuoji cemetery move to?'

'It's not decided yet. I'm suggesting some land at the foot of Shoko Hill, though.' Shoko Hill was five miles from Tan'ami. No bus or tram line ran in that direction. There was a fine panoramic view of the town from the top, which made it a favourable place for primary school excursions and picnics like the one Tomoko's little girl was going on next day. Yamaji owned some land nearby. 'If the town were to designate the land out there as the site for a new combined cemetery, the road would be properly surfaced and a bus service put on. That'd double the price of land in no time.

'It's a pleasant area, with nice views, ideal for a communal cemetery. If Butsuoji takes the initiative and moves its own cemetery out there, it'll be doing a lot for the town plan as a whole. But there are plenty of people still with ridiculous feudal ideas about it being sacrilege for the cemetery where all their ancestors are buried to be moved. They won't be allowed to hold up progress in Tan'ami for ever, though.'

'Does the site of the present cemetery belong to Butsuoji?'

'Yes, the temple's owned it for generations.'

'I wonder what the priest thinks . . .?'

'What he thinks is neither here nor there. It's the parishioners who decide questions like this, and I'm their chief representative and spokesman. Anything I say is accepted automatically—I don't allow any disagreement. I don't know how much money I've poured into Butsuoji, without ever complaining about the assessment, either; I've always paid whatever the elders suggested. If there's any special expense the temple has to meet, more than half of it comes out of my pocket—it wouldn't be able to carry on without me. Selling the land on the hill will bring in a nice little sum in cash, and the priest can use it in any way he wants, to help him find a new wife, if he likes. The woman he marries will be glad enough, no doubt, if he isn't altogether penniless.'

Tomoko swallowed, struggling not to let the shock his words had given her affect her outward calm. His plan was more likely to be realised than any hopes of hers. Her hopes—they were no more than a dream, a prayer that in the nature of things could never be granted: Yamaji's plan was a business-like scheme for pushing up the price of land—for making money. As for Soshu's remarriage—the parishioners would decide everything; he would only have to accept what they arranged. She grew pale again, feelings surging within her that she could not control.

'If this business doesn't go ahead smoothly, I'm quite prepared to give up my connection with Butsuoji altogether—which would set them thinking all right: it would be next to impossible to run the temple without me. I've got a grip on Butsuoji just where it's weakest, you see. For all the authority he has, the priest might just as well not be there at all. If I wanted to, I could make him starve. No, I won't allow anyone to upset my plan . . .'

23

Soshu's uneasiness subsided for a while as he sat facing the shrine in Yamaji's house. Not from any sense that now, at least, he was fulfilling his duty as a priest, but because it was only when he was reciting the scriptures that he could really feel secure and at peace. Once again he could escape into the calm world of the sutras.

He was relieved that nobody came to listen. The shrine-room was in the middle of the house, flanked by two Japanese-style guest-rooms, each with its own *tokonoma.* There were many more rooms than Yamaji needed for his small family, with the consequence that the house always seemed deserted.

The shrine itself had been changed twice. Originally it had been a very small and simple affair, with vases and lamps and candles equally unpretentious. When Yamaji's social position began to improve, he put in a bigger one, about three feet wide; and this in turn was replaced by a magnificent gold-painted one of the most expensive type, six feet wide, with an elaborate wooden statue of Amida instead of the cheap print of some years before.

Yamaji was out, apparently. Soshu's melodious voice flowed uninterrupted through the still rooms. Soundlessly, Yamaji's wife, a tall, thin woman, entered the shrine-room and sat down behind the priest, without, however, clasping her hands or showing any other sign of a reverent attitude. She seemed to have come merely out of a vague sense that if she put in one brief appearance while the sutras were being read, no more was required of her. But she loved Soshu's voice, too. There was still a faint air of the gay world about this woman—she was not 'a wife married in penury', as the saying goes. Yamaji's first wife, whom he had divorced when he began to prosper, was a farmer's daughter, from another family that belonged to Butsuoji. Slow of speech, with a peasant's thick hands and feet, and hair burnt brown by the sun, there was nothing she could do but work. They had had no children. As Yamaji's position improved, he began to find such a wife a drawback, and so divorced her, on the ground that he could not take her into company. Though the divorce was arranged solely to suit Yamaji's convenience, the money she received from him by way of solatium was less than a fifth of what people said. A year later, however, she married again, a farmer this time, and became the mother of five children. Even now, she still worked like an ox in the fields every day. For all anybody knew, she had completely forgotten that she had once been married to Yamaji, who was now president of a securities company. His second wife was the daughter of an innkeeper.

Soshu sensed her presence behind him. These visits to Yamaji's house were always painful, especially when Yamaji himself chose to sit behind him instead of his wife, reading his thoughts, as surely he did . . . Since his confession to Tomoko, the duty of reading the sutras at Yamaji's had become an ordeal, of which he was as terrified as a soldier ordered to cross into enemy territory. He could no longer look Yamaji in the face—as if he himself were guilty of some crime. If only he could bring himself to hate Yamaji, he could face him with more courage; but that was impossible. Yamaji was the official representative of the whole body of parishioners, the most important member of the congregation; important in the sense that not even the smallest temple business could be put through without consulting him. So Soshu was forced to be obsequious—his livelihood depended on it.

In former days, no doubt, Buddhist priests worked hard to win new converts to their faith; but such times are long since past, and nowadays all their efforts are devoted to keeping the loyalty of the parishioners whose families have worshipped at their particular temple for generations. To maintain the present membership is the utmost they can do, any attempt to proselytize being out of the question. With the popularity of the 'new religions', two or three new sects had established branches in Tan'ami. Buddhist priests could hardly be indifferent when these sects, which made much of worldly benefits in their teaching, began to attract converts; but they pretended to be unaware of what was going on, out of a feeling that any attempt to compete for members would be unseemly. Butsuoji was no more immune than other temples to the danger represented by the new doctrines, and little could be done to prevent parishioners from succumbing to their lure. The problem was a serious one, complicated by the fact that since the war religion had come to be regarded as a purely individual concern.

The readings finished, Soshu took off his stole. A maid brought tea. As he was drinking, Yamaji's wife came in again, this time to thank him.

'*Gokuro-sama desu*!'[1] She held out a tray with the temple-offering. Mechanically, Soshu picked up the envelope and placed it on top of the folded stole.

'My husband is waiting in the reception-room.'

Soshu started. So he had been waiting for him all the time, without taking the trouble to join in the prayers . . . Yamaji's wife got up to take him to her husband. Soshu knew the way to the western-style reception-room. He wrapped his stole and the offering in a *furoshiki*,[2] put them in his bag, and followed her, trembling slightly. After showing him round the corner in the long corridor, Mrs Yamaji bowed and withdrew to another room, leaving him to walk the rest of the way alone.

It could only be about *her*—and he was so unprepared, how could he begin to explain. . . Normally the thought of Tomoko refreshed and encouraged him, imparting a new, more cheerful rhythm to his life; but now her image was a source of fear. He was already pale and breathing rapidly, a criminal giving himself away before he was accused. . .

He had never touched her, not even her hand—there had been no opportunity, nor had he sought to make one. She sat perfectly still behind him when he intoned; that was all, and that was enough. When the sutra readings were over they would talk for a few minutes, but the maid was always in the house, and they had to be careful to avoid saying anything they would not want to be overheard. Sometimes Soshu would look into her eyes for moments together, as if straining to reach behind them, and she into his; but they made no attempt to approach more closely, sitting always in the formal position opposite each other and preserving the same cruel distance between them in the words they spoke. Inwardly they both chafed against this distance: outwardly, it was a constraint they could not escape, unless Soshu were to behave with a freedom of which he was incapable.

Yamaji, in Japanese dress, with his short, bulging legs stretched out in front of him, was smoking a cigar.

'Sit down here, will you?' he said, without taking the cigar from his mouth, so that his teeth showed—most of them gold-filled, and all unusually prominent. In Soshu's presence he seemed doubly conscious of his position as chief representative of the parishioners. Sitting in the chair before him, Soshu felt himself cringing already. Around the room were examples of Yamaji's muddled but expensive tastes: a white porcelain jar, a western-style and a Japanese-style painting side by side, above the mantlepiece a big portrait of

1 'Thank you for your trouble.' Much used on occasions of this kind, this phrase is frequently—as here—the merest formality.

2 A cloth wrapper.

himself; a *fuji-musume* doll in a glass case, a stone Buddha-head with its ears broken off, a big new clock, a life-size bronze nude in one corner, and opposite to it a statute of the Buddhist guardian deity Tamonten, with the left arm missing; a Chinese desk and chair, a sofa with bright yellow cushions.

'You know, you really must show a little sense of responsibility, Father—'

So he knew? Soshu swallowed, his body contracting with fear at the shock of Yamaji's words. Priest one moment, sinner and criminal the next—but it wasn't a crime, a voice within him retorted bitterly—a voice not his own, surely? Of course it was a crime; she belonged to Yamaji, he had tried to rob Yamaji of his property. . . what was criminal if that was not?

Tomoko had poured out her story—how she had never loved Yamaji, but had been forced to accept dependence on him after her husband's death as the only way to support her mother and Shoko and herself. Trembling, she had told him with what a rush of sympathy she had read somewhere of a woman who had sold herself only to avoid suicide.

Soshu trembled in his turn, at his own cowardice; he was thinking how he could talk his way out of the crisis Yamaji had dragged him into. He would deny there was anything whatever between Tomoko Komiyama and himself, he would say he had never touched her—but that was *all* he could say. . . At once he loathed and despised himself for fabricating such evasions. No longer understanding his own vacillating emotions, wanting to cry out in self-disgust, he struggled for control. Yamaji had begun again:

'Any new development at Butsuoji has to have the support of the parishioners, of course—but for the priest to leave everything to them, without so much as expressing an opinion—that's really too much. What *is* your opinion, Father? The parishioners can't make out what this silence of yours means.'

Soshu drew a long breath. In spirit he clasped his hands before her, asking her to forgive him. A moment later, and his own unclean feet would have been trampling upon her—no, they had half-defiled her already; and the act had left its mark on him. So that was how much he loved himself—he was ready enough to sacrifice her if he could save himself by doing so. . . Now he had sinned against her as well as Yamaji.

'Are you really happy to let things go on as they are, Father?'

'No,' replied Soshu weakly.

'I should think not. That would be taking too little account of the parishioners altogether.'

'But still, I—'

'That sort of attitude won't do, Father! It's your great fault, all this shilly-shallying and refusal to make up your mind properly one way or the other and have done with it. What makes it worse is that people come to a man in your position with all sorts of problems—but with things as they are now, it won't be long before no one'll think your advice worth asking any more; it's too obvious you don't practise what you preach. Some of the parishioners are pretty fed up, Father, I can tell you. Their families have belonged to our temple for generations, and if they're extra particular about a priest who came to Butsuoji from outside, of course that's only to be expected.'

'It's my sin that's the cause of it all. . .'

'Well, yes, I think it is.' The parishioners knew about Mineyo; but Yamaji did not mention her name. 'You've suffered a good deal on that account, I've no doubt—you're not the sort of man who can go sinning brazenly without ever letting it worry him. But just to say you've suffered, it's been on your conscience and all that—that won't do, either. For you yourself, your guilty conscience may be enough. But there's Butsuoji, too, you know; the temple's got to be kept going. You're forgetting your responsibility.'

'I came from outside, as you said, and the moment I lose the confidence of the parishioners, it will be wrong for me to stay. Several times I've wondered if it wouldn't be best to make a real break and leave Butsuoji altogether.'

'That wouldn't solve anyone's problems but your own, would it, Father? How would the temple manage without a priest? If that's the kind of solution your conscience suggests, it's a very selfish kind of a conscience. Even suffering can be egotistic. How long is it since Renko left Butsuoji? And the shameless way you've acted all this time, as if you knew nothing whatever about why she went and what happened to her afterwards! That's shocked a lot of Butsuoji people. Egoism again, I suppose—you don't feel you have to care about other people so long as you're torturing yourself inside. Mind, I only say this because I have the temple so much at heart, and because nobody else has the courage to open his mouth. Butsuoji belongs to all the parishioners—the temple comes first with them, and the priest second.'

No one knew of the struggle he faced every night—in fact, they were imagining the exact opposite. That he had the right to confront their suspicions, to attempt to vindicate himself by putting his own side of the case, Soshu had all but forgotten. By temperament he was incapable of vigour in his own defence. But now he was being forced to say or do something of the kind . . . why? Because of his responsibility for the good order and peace of the temple community? Did a responsibility to the community involve, by some law, the betrayal of himself, the individual? To speak out in protest was not in his character. Yet Yamaji's insinuations, harsher than ever before, hurt Soshu all the more because of the guilt he already felt. At the parishioners' meeting Yamaji attended there was always an air of condescension about the way he addressed Soshu—the successful company president addressing a junior; but his arrogance tonight was new. The only possible inference, it seemed to Soshu, was that Yamaji now had something definite against him—he must have suspected something in connection with Tomoko.

'It's no longer simply a question of whether you are to marry again or not, Father. I'm only putting to you what the parishioners think, don't forget! Your whole attitude and outlook are being talked about now. Who is he to preach to us Buddhists, they say—look at the kind of life he's leading himself: does he think he's going on like that for ever? You can't ignore the rest of the world in the way you're doing, Father. But you seem to think you can, and it's this attitude of yours that's the trouble. The parishioners wonder what it is you're really after. And so long as they've got this on their minds, no amount of intoning sutras in that famous voice of yours will have any effect.'

Soshu sat white-faced, beaten, the skin twitching at his temples. Yamaji stared at him, keeping perfectly still, as if listening contemptuously to the broken rhythm of his pulse. Soshu could not look up. His feet were trembling.

'And by the way, something else. I'm particularly anxious to get your agreement in that matter of the cemetery.'

Yamaji spoke casually, as if this was merely an after-thought. Soshu looked at him. He had intended to bring up this question himself, only up till now Yamaji had given him no chance. He had heard from a number of the parishioners recently who were concerned about the future of the cemetery.

'I'm one of those who believe in giving our temple every possible support. If that land on the hill is disposed of, it will bring in a pretty sizeable sum, you know.'

'How far has the talk about selling the land gone?' A feeble enough question. Soshu had not yet recovered from the shock of what had gone before, but at least this new problem Yamaji had chosen to raise was more than a purely personal one, and he felt that as far as the cemetery was concerned Butsuoji really did depend on him.

'That's as much as to say you've heard something already, I suppose. It would be ridiculous to hold up the sale. A first-rate buyer has turned up for a piece of land the temple will have to give up sooner or later. If we wait till the Council makes a compulsory purchase order, it'll be giving it away—so now's the moment to sell, when we have a good offer. Here again it's what's best for

Butsuoji—otherwise, of course, I wouldn't suggest it.'

'Is the land on the hill included in the area the town is planning to take over, though? I heard the development was going to be in the other direction, out towards Hamairo.'

'I'm afraid you're a mere child, Father, where property deals are concerned. It's wiser to leave that sort of thing to a business-man like me. One comes across priests nowadays who go in for the stock market, I know, but not at Butsuoji, fortunately: that's one of your good points. No, I have the interest of the temple at heart just as much as you yourself have, and it's hardly likely there'd be anything wrong in something I'm doing solely for the good of Butsuoji.'

'But the parishioners will certainly be distressed if the cemetery is moved. There might be serious trouble, I'm afraid—they believe the spirits of their ancestors are sleeping there, and that means more to them than any monetary considerations.'

'There it is again, this flabbiness of yours; and I tell you it won't do. You can't expect to get unanimous agreement in a big deal like this. There's bound to be opposition, of course, but if we keep putting off a decision just because some people disagree with it, we shall have the Council taking over the land before we know where we are, and without asking us, either. No—a few of us with really strong views have to take the majority along. We won't be popular at first, but as time goes on it'll be obvious to everybody how much the temple has benefited. What I'm asking from you, Father, is that you should be firmer, show a little more strength of character . . . situations like this one are the only chance one ever gets to correct the weaknesses one was born with. I'll give you any little help I can. As far as concern for the welfare of the temple and its people is concerned, there's no difference between us. If you will take the initiative and say the cemetery land must be sold, that's half the battle won already; and my support will help. After all, the final authority rests with you, as the official representative of Butsuoji—the parishioners may talk a lot, but legally they're only parishioners and nothing else.'

So he was being presented with a unique opportunity to turn himself all at once into a strong, decisive character! A less pleasant view would be that Yamaji's strictures on his weakness were part of a wily scheme—a bitter personal attack followed deliberately by something almost like flattery; hitting him first where it was most painful, then taking advantage of the shock to destroy any independent will he had left. No doubt a man in Yamaji's position used these tactics often enough. Soshu had never met them before. All his life, he felt, he would be in Yamaji's power; his relationship with Tomoko had made this inevitable.

'If we do decide to sell the land on the hill, who do you think would buy it?'

'Asano Chemical Industries. They have made a definite offer.' Soshu had no idea what kind of company this was. 'All we need is your seal, and the deal can go through right away. With me representing the parishioners, there's not much chance of Butsuoji suffering by it. Opposition on sentimental grounds there will be, I daresay —we must resign ourselves to that.'

'It's an extremely serious matter, though, as far as I'm concerned. I can't decide alone.'

'Faint-hearted again, Father! You still don't seem to realise—'

'At least I must talk to the elders first . . .'

'Oh, very well; there's no harm in that, I suppose—it'll only be for form's sake. I'm still the chief representative of the parishioners, and if that's not given due weight, I won't answer for the consequences.'

'I understand that, of course.'

'There's such a thing as losing face, you know, for Mosuke Yamaji as for anyone else.'

The decisive stroke, thought Soshu. To offend Yamaji was unthinkable: the money offerings he gave the temple were higher than those of all the rest of the congregation put together.

24

Soshu rode slowly down the street on his bicycle, an embodiment of perplexity and fear. A brisk walker could have overtaken him: he seemed to be pedalling unconsciously, drifting, like a slack wind in summer. Yamaji's words were still echoing in his mind, with all their implications. The talk of selling the cemetery land on the hill was obviously a threat. This was the first time any parishioner had confronted him openly with his intimacy with Mineyo, and though he had long realised something of the kind was bound to happen sooner or later, still he had not been prepared—as if until that moment he had been pretending to himself, as well as to the parishioners, that there was nothing to hide. And even if he was not conscious of ever having tried to deceive either himself or others, his conduct undeniably made it look as though he had.

So all the agony he had been through on account of Mineyo was in vain. It had been merely a long process of self-torture, culminating in the most miserable self-pity. It was his own self he had denied, his own self he had tormented, his own self, Soshu Getsudo, that he had contemplated with such pity; within himself, alone and isolated, he had weighed and judged his sin with Mineyo. How different was his own awareness of that sin from the account of it anyone else would give. . . Soshu shuddered. All his suffering had been misdirected, useless. The tortured introspection, the attempt to judge his transgression in his own puny strength: all this was folly. Dully, Soshu pedalled on. A car nearly ran him down—intent on the silent dialogue with himself, he never heard the warning horn. He gripped the handlebars more firmly. Without thinking, he found himself murmuring a passage from the Gutoku Hitan Jukkai:

> Outwardly, what man is there may not appear pious and steadfast?

Within, he is the slave of evil passions, a creature of deceit and cunning.
How can I rid myself of my sinful nature? Treacherous is my heart, as a serpent;
Even my good deeds are folly: evil poisons them all.

Stubborn, shameless, unrepentant is my soul, ever impure—
Yet the whole world is filled with Amida's mercy, through his saving word!

I, who am without compassion or charity, how can I look for mercy,
How cross the raging sea, but by the boat of Amida's Vow?

My soul is deceitful, treacherous as a serpent; myself, in my own strength, I cannot save.
If I put not my trust in Amida, I am lost for ever, sin's slave irredeemable!

Passers-by turned to look at him. With fixed, unseeing gaze, as if the victim of some obsession, he pedalled slowly on, still reciting the lines of Shinran's hymn; his voice as he began the last verse was a despairing echo of the helplessness the words made him feel, like the cry of a panic-stricken child. He had thought he could save himself. . . the horror, the folly of his arrogance! If only the bicycle would carry him to his death now. . . By rejecting Mineyo, he had thought he could save himself—had thought he was 'right' to reject her: but that, he saw now, was mere selfishness. Refusing her only made her more wretched. If his life was to be transformed, hers must be too; there could be no redemption for him apart from her, no callous standing back to watch as she alone floundered in the mire. Yamaji's insinuations were too well justified for him to be able to resent the directness with which they had been made. Shame struck at him more keenly than ever before. That he, whose profession it was to expound the religion of Shinran to others, should have been the first to betray the Master's teaching. . . For all his familiarity with Shinran's works, all of which he had read, his knowledge of them went no deeper than the characters in which they were written. Misery overwhelmed him, deadening every other feeling, leaving only a sense of utter emptiness, and a strange awareness of the mechanical movements of his body on the bicycle.

A swishing sound as another cyclist brushed past him brought Soshu back to reality. Spiritlessly, he looked at the pedestrians he was overtaking, forgetting them the instant they passed out of his gaze. A woman's back caught his eye: there was a curious listlessness about her walk—Renko! He was past her now, but breathless with the shock of realisation. She was dressed in kimono, a typical

Japanese wife in her early thirties. He did not remember the kimono, nor had he ever taken any special notice of how she looked from behind, but there was no doubt it was her: the line of her shoulders, her hair, her walk—all were instantly recognisable.

He had no wish to stop as he passed her, still less to speak to her; the thought terrified him. As if afraid she would call out, he pedalled on, leaving her further and further behind, not daring even to look back; thinking only of escape, yet knowing he must not seem to pedal too fast.

—In Tokyo some priests do their visiting by bicycle.—Why such a trivial thought should flash across his mind at this particular moment, when he was so weighed down with wretchedness, he did not know. He felt her gazing after him. There were other cyclists about, but a priest in his robes riding a bicycle was a rare enough sight, even in the busier quarter of Tan'ami, to make people look. Perhaps Renko had stopped, and was staring after him in amazement. . . but he had not the courage to turn and look, so great was his horror of being confronted openly with his sin. If they were to meet face to face, he could no longer pretend.

Soshu wondered what she was doing in Tan'ami. Butsuoji lay straight ahead, in the direction in which she was walking. He had heard of her remarriage, and of the step-child she was looking after; and had told himself her life would be happier now. But what right had he to hope for happiness for her? All that remained to him now was to ask her forgiveness. Others might pray for her happiness in her new marriage: to him, that was forbidden. To escape from her, Soshu turned into a side street, but felt no lessening of his misery; in his heart her gaze still pursued him. Perhaps she's come to see Ryokun, he thought. He knew she met him in the janitor's room at the school, though he had no idea how often these meetings took place. He himself visited the little four-mat room from time to time; there was a small shrine in it before which he would sit piously reading the sutras, with an innocent air, as if it had never crossed his mind that Renko might have wept in that same tiny room, hugging the son he had taken from her—had torn from her, it would be truer to say—he who could sit there now and intone the holy words. . .

> Stubborn, shameless, unrepentant is my soil, ever impure—
> Yet the whole world is filled with Amida's mercy, through his saving word!
> I, who am without compassion or charity, how can I look for mercy?
> . . . .
> My soul is deceitful, treacherous as a serpent; myself, in my own strength, I cannot save.
> . . . . I am lost for ever, sin's slave irredeemable!

With bowed head, as if trying to hide his face from passers-by, Soshu pedalled on. To judge from his expression, he might have been weeping—as he would have been, had there been nobody to see or hear, in terror at the pitiless aptness of Shinran's words to his own condition.—See your mother, Ryokun, let her stay with you when she comes! was all he had the right to say.

The bicycle entered the great gate of the temple. Dismounting, Soshu walked across the deserted compound. The tidy, newly-swept courtyard brought the old priest to mind, and set him pondering again what Yamaji had said about the cemetery on the hill. For a long while he stood with bent head before the temple hall, as if praying for forgiveness.

'There's your father, look! Wait till he hears about it!' An angry voice greeted him from an inner room as he slid back the door of the house. He heard the quick patter of Mineyo's feet on the mats as she hurried to the hall.

'You must give Ryokun a good scolding!' said Mineyo after greeting him and taking his bag. 'He's been so naughty, I don't know what to do with him. He's vicious—he does it all to spite me. I can't stand it any longer!' She half-dragged him to one of the inner rooms. 'Look at that!' she said, pointing upwards. The name Ryokun Getsudo had been written in Indian ink in big clumsy characters on the square panels of the ceiling, the complicated characters for '-do' and '-kun' taking up nearly two panels each.

'Ryokun did that, did he?'

'He did. In a fit of temper at being told off for something else—the spiteful child!' Mineyo was incensed against the little boy.

'Did he bring a chair from somewhere?'

'No—he got up on the chest of drawers.' The chest of drawers was just high enough for Ryokun to be able to touch the ceiling if he stood on top of it. Soshu smiled. The boy would have written the characters with his head back, staring up at the ceiling. Probably the ink had dripped from the brush on to his face and shoulders. Soshu found it hard to imagine the workings of the little boy's mind, that had made him think of defacing the ceiling as a kind of retaliation for Mineyo's scolding. The writing had surely not been planned; perhaps there had just happened to be a brush and inkstone in the room, and they had given him the idea. Soshu gave him lessons with the brush occasionally, as he was not studying calligraphy at school. Presumably he had jumped up on to the chest of drawers in a burst of childish anger, furious to have his revenge on his grandmother. But if scrawling with a brush like that was his idea of revenge, why should he have chosen the ceiling, when it would have been so much easier anywhere else? Suddenly Soshu understood. The ceiling must have tempted him just because the idea was so absurd; it was the last place in the world anybody would think of decorating with calligraphy. One character to each panel. . . a grown-up would dismiss any such ridiculous notion the moment it occurred to him, supposing it ever did, but for a child the temptation was too strong.

'It won't come off, either. The whole ceiling's spoilt!'

'That boy will write a fine hand one day. Those characters are surprisingly well drawn, considering he must have been half bent over backwards when he wrote them.'

'There you go again—it's because you're always saying things like that that he's got so spoilt! He'll turn into a real delinquent one of these days, I shouldn't be surprised, and there'll be no doing anything with him then.'

If anything of the kind did happen, the boy's environment would be to blame, thought Soshu. Neither Mineyo nor he himself was in any position to guide him, to prevent the warping of his character. Sooner or later he would find out their secret; and then, no doubt, he would hate both father and grandmother. Already Soshu seemed to hear him telling of his horror at the discovery. For discovery was inevitable; such was his destiny. No less than Shinran himself, he was 'lost, sin's slave irredeemable.'

'What was it you scolded him for in the first place?'

'He wanted to be one of the lion-dancers—of all the ridiculous ideas! Apart from anything else, it would be awkward for the parishioners. Do you think they could just look on quietly, watching the son of their priest making a fool of himself like that?'

'The young people who do the lion-dance nearly all belong to Butsuoji, don't they?'

'Yes, but it'd be impossible to train them properly if Ryokun were with them. They only learn the dance because the older ones keep shouting at them when they make mistakes—and they could hardly shout at Ryokun, could they? It's the young parishioners who would suffer.'

'One can understand his wanting to join in, I must say.'

'Your saying such things only makes it worse. If those practices they have by the temple gate are going to be a temptation to the boy, we ought to stop them altogether, and no mistake about it!'

In preparation for the local festival, which was due in a few days' time, rehearsals of the lion-dance were now being held every evening, just outside the great gate of Butsuoji, on an improvised floor of straw mats. The music of the accompanying flutes and drums echoed round the temple and beyond till nearly midnight, keeping the neighbourhood households awake and rousing in them excited anticipation of the festival itself. Soshu had noticed Ryokun playing with a *sasara* of the kind used in the lion-dance. This *sasara* is one of the instruments used in former times by the players of primitive *dengaku* music. It consists of a thick piece of bamboo about seventeen inches long, split into slivers for most of its length, but with just enough of it left untouched for the hand to hold it by, so that it resembles a whisk, or a bunch of very thin chopsticks tied together. As he dances, the dancer waves his *sasara* and draws it along a notched stick of hardwood, producing a shrill '*sara - - shari-shari*! sara-shari-shari!' each time the movement is repeated. One of the parishioners must have given Ryokun an old *sasara*; Soshu had heard the '*shari-shari*' as the boy practised with it in the house. The dance of the kind performed at the Butsuoji festival is a variety of the court dance called *bugaku,* a development of a dance-form invented in China in the time of Tai-tsung, and has less in common with the crude lion-dances that street musicians give from house to house in big cities than with the elegant, classical dances with orchestral accompaniment which form part of No plays. Two young dancers are enclosed in a cloth lion, the striped portion of which represents the main part of his body. One has his feet in the lion's front paws and wears the lion's head, a massive affair weighing between forty and fifty pounds; the other, bending forward and keeping his hands on either side of his head, acts as the lion's body, swelling out his cloth 'skin' and making it move from side to side in harmony with the movements of the head. A great deal of practice is needed. Both dancers have to follow the music of the drum and flute; and for the one who takes the hindlegs this is especially difficult—not only can he not see, but he is sweating profusely most of the time and is liable to be knocked off his balance now and then by sudden movements of his partner's back and buttocks. The dance represents a lion at play. Always following the flute and drum accompaniment, which can be played in any one of six or seven different styles, at one moment it suggests dignity, at another irresistible power, at another quietness and repose, at yet another, sudden, swift action. In the first part, called *ranjo,* the lion is asleep, and a third young man, who is really the leader of the three, dances in front of him in a leaping, carefree style, making as much noise as possible with his *sasara*. His dance follows a strict pattern of six or seven stages or steps.

The musicians and dancers who gave the dance at Butsuoji were young men who normally worked in the fields every day, members of the farming families which collected the nightsoil from the houses in the town. Every year they repeated the performance, managing the instruments with great skill and carefully preserving the traditional form of the dance, though they had no score to go by.

Soshu could imagine very vividly Ryokun's longing to join them. To dance around the sleeping lion, deliberately provoking him with the rasping *shari-shari* of the *sasara*. . . The noise would first wake, then gradually excite him; he would bite at the dancer, the dancer would leap aside, then provoke him again and again in a series of ever more tantalizing approaches, flute and drum sounding all the while.

'It's taking too grown-up a view to blame him for wanting to dance. For the boy himself it's no more than a dream, and an innocent one at that.'

'Nonsense—how can you say such a thing!' Mineyo was convinced Ryokun's interest in the dance was a calamity. Soshu watched the plump face, that looked so much younger than its years, that tried so hard to keep alive the embers of its beauty. 'A priest's son should sit quietly among the grown-ups at occasions like this, and not draw attention to himself.'

So Ryokun was not to be allowed to have his wish. The world denied his childish dreams. Would the boy ever realise the existence of these barriers, Soshu wondered—the barriers which he himself would never forget, which surround all who live in a temple, thwarting every individual will?

Ryokun did not appear at supper. Children had begun to gather outside Butsuoji even before the old priest shut the great gate; and it was children, by the sound of it, who were now beating the drums, impatient for the festival to begin.

'Call Ryokun in, will you, Shoju?' said Mineyo. The old priest went out to the gate, but among the crowd of nearly twenty children there was no sign of Ryokun.

'O-Sugi, find Ryokun and bring him here!'

O-Sugi left the room, and supper began.

'You *must* be stricter with him—he'll grow up so spoilt otherwise!

Soshu only nodded.

A good while later, when it was already dark, the old priest found Ryokun and brought him home.

'Where've you been, Ryokun?'

The boy's face wore an embarrassed, oddly grown-up expression. The old priest answered for him.

'He was playing in front of the gate.'

'I wonder how it was you and O-Sugi didn't find him there at first, then?'

Ryokun sat down by Shoju, and picked up his chopsticks. Still the strange grown-up air clung to him, as if he were carrying within him some secret too big for his childish body.

'Scold him, Father! He made that mess on the ceiling, don't forget—and it won't come off, either!'

Soshu and Ryokun looked each other in the face. Soshu's eyes were mild. He had guessed the secret: the deep feelings aroused in the boy by the meeting with his mother. Those feelings had not turned into hate for his father and grandmother, then; not yet. . .

Soshu sighed.

25

Lessons were being held as usual, but Ryokun scarcely heard what the teacher was saying. Excitement filled the classroom; it was not only Ryokun's attention that kept wandering to the drums in the distance—in imagination, the whole class was out there already, and for the teacher to insist on concentration now would have been cruel. The drums were too tempting.

The afternoon would be a school holiday, however. The Tan'ami festival lasted for three days. The first day was taken up with local celebrations in each neighbourhood; on the second, festival floats paraded through the streets all day in each of the four districts of north, south, east and west into which Tan'ami was divided for the occasion. Finally, on the third and last day, all the floats from each neighbourhood were assembled and dedicated at Tan'ami Shrine in the centre of the town. On the second and third days all schools were closed, and three hundred thousand or more people would pour into Tan'ami from the surrounding areas to watch the fun.

Screaming with excitement, Ryokun and his friends burst out of the classroom and raced for home, school and lessons forgotten in the longing to enter into the festival atmosphere. As he ran, Ryokun thought with envy of his friend who lived in the neighbourhood adjoining Butsuoji. Each neighbourhood had its own traditional way of celebrating; and in the one he was thinking of, it had been the custom for generations to enact the 'Grand Hunting Party at the Foot of Mount Fuji'. A boy of about Ryokun's age would take the part of Yoritomo Minamoto. Dressed in period hunting costume, he and his retainers would parade up and down the neighbourhood streets on horseback, accompanied by their mothers and sisters—looking so different in their make-up, medieval costumes and imposing hats that Ryokun could hardly recognize even boys he knew well. Nobu, his special friend, took the part of Shiro Jinta every year. Jinta, the warrior who came charging down the hill astride a giant wild boar, finally killing him while sitting with his back to the boar's tusks, was a hero to the boys. At the festival he appeared as a handsome young boy, trying to look very grown-up and brave; not at all like the Nobu who had crept through the conduit with Ryokun. Out in front of Yoritomo and his retinue of famous samurai, heading the whole parade, went the animals; wild boar, monkeys, deer and hares, rushing in all directions to escape the hunt. All were boys, wearing elaborate masks. They loved the parade, as did the boys who watched; it was a true popular festival, and filled them with heroic, colourful dreams. Charging about madly among the other animals was the giant boar, an enormous cloth beast nearly eighteen feet long, slung over the heads and shoulders of two young men; these being replaced every now and then by a fresh pair from among the groups of hefty youths who escorted the monster on both sides, ready to shove it violently back into the middle of the road whenever it missed its direction.

The four floats for Ryokun's neighbourhood had been prepared and were waiting outside the great gate of the temple, ready for the procession. The first carried a large imitation cherry tree; the other three bore lifesize figures—first a young man, then a venerable old gentleman, holding a brush and a strip of poetry paper—these two dressed in the style of the nobles of former times—and finally a girl in ceremonial Chinese robes. Only the cherry-tree float had wheels. Each of the others was carried by a team of four bearers, richly dressed and wearing special sandals. The doll-like figures were enclosed in boxes open on one side, like the feretories on a Buddhist altar; from the top of each box hung a large bell, which every movement of the float would set clanging. In Ryokun's neighbourhood the children could only watch; they were strictly forbidden to join in the festival themselves. Perhaps that was partly why the custom of performing the lion-dance had grown up in this particular district—but even that was restricted, as far as the actual dancing was concerned, to a very small number of youths.

The Kiyota-cho float was a huge contraption of three storeys, on top of which a puppet representing Urashima was made to dance, a group of costumed young men on the second level providing the music. Crowds flocked to see it all through the festival. Every part of the town except Ryokun's had its own float, as elaborate and original as possible, and all the excitement that went with it; Ryokun wondered why there was nothing spectacular like that in his own neighbourhood. He was too young to realise that the reason was economic: the neighbourhood was such a small one that the money collected did not permit anything so grand. And float or no float, Ryokun was thrilled with the whole festival.

The year before, on the second day, he had happened to meet the 'Grand Hunt' on its way home after parading through the south district. Yoritomo, still on his horse, was tearful; his thighs were hurting. Nobu—Jinta the bold, with a sword dangling from his hunting-belt—looked tired out, and was holding his mother's hand as he walked. Some of the warriors were being carried on their mothers' backs.

'Nobu!' Ryokun called to his friend; but Nobu hardly had the strength to look around. Deer and monkeys and hares were dragging along behind, exhausted. They had taken off their masks and were carrying them wearily, in both hands in front of them, or under one arm, all the excitement of the morning gone. Even Ryokun could see they had had more than enough.

Traditionally, the first performance of the lion-dance was given at the house of the priest of Butsuoji. After he had come back from school and finished his lunch, Ryokun watched Shoju open up the hall in readiness for the dancers. The big drum was brought into the compound. The two young men who would dance the lion—head-and-front legs in a kimono and white divided skirt, with white Japanese socks and a white headband, trunk-and-hindlegs with only a white cotton vest over his skirt, took up the traditional position for the beginning of the dance. Ryokun sat directly in front of the lion, between Mineyo and his father. Soshu was robed in white, like the dancers.

A piercing note from the flute gave the signal for the start of the *ranjo,* the solo dance. Ryokun watched spellbound. He had forgotten already how furious, almost hysterical Mineyo had been with him over his practising with the *sasara* and the writing on the ceiling, and had lost almost none of his longing to join in the dance himself. In a red mask with an enormous nose, green and white striped leggings and hand-coverings, and a three-cornered tapering hat, the solo dancer danced and shook his *sasara* in front of the sleeping lion. Ryokun held his breath.

The big drum sounded; the lion began to stir, dimly resenting this disturbance of his sleep. Only his head moved at first. Soshu turned to look at Ryokun; he saw the cruelty of making him give up his longing for the dance, of the grown-up attempt to destroy a child's dream. Suddenly he was conscious, as he had not been before, of the watching crowd. What were they thinking of this family picture, Mineyo and himself and the boy cosily settled between them? Shame overwhelmed him—the 'family picture' was hypocrisy personified, hypocrisy 'stubborn, shameless, unrepentant' . . . so it must seem in the world's eyes. No one could know of his spiritual struggle: outwardly he was still the brazen priest, the hypocrite of Butsuoji—

and sitting here now in the seat of honour . . . Quietly Soshu got up and left.

Back in the Lute Room, he wrapped up the money for the dancers, and sat waiting for the dance to end. The temple performance over, the spectators withdrew all at once, like a receding tide, leaving the dancers and musicians to go round giving a shortened version of the dance at each house in the neighbourhood. Ryokun sat in the porch, watching the little troupe till they had disappeared through the great gate.

Mineyo was standing behind him.

'That was the dance you wanted to do, wasn't it—the one where he wakes up the lion? You don't realize what hard work it is—sometimes it makes the boy ill, and he has to go to bed as soon as the festival's over. And the dance itself is so difficult, anyway, nobody's stupid enough to want to do it just for fun,' she said with an air of finality, as if to drive home the impossibility of his ever having such nonsensical ideas again.

I don't care if I do get ill, said Ryokun to himself, tasting the joys of revenge—of the knowledge of a secret he had shared neither with his granny nor with anybody else. At festival time Mineyo always gave him some pocket-money. When Renko had come the other day, she had given him some, too; and of this Mineyo knew nothing. His mother had come on purpose, he imagined, to give him spending-money for the festival. And he had sensed something strange about her at this last meeting in the janitor's room at school. He had always remembered her scent, but now it seemed different; her new life in a world he did not know had left its mark, changing her in some subtle way he could not understand.

'You'll come again, Mummy?' he had said simply when they parted. These irregular, unexpected meetings did not move him specially, for he never doubted she could come and see him whenever she wanted to. Why should he?

'Next time I'll bring some of those *kintsuba* cakes!'

'I won't tell anyone you've been.' He loved the secrecy.

'One thing Mummy's been anxious about, Ryokun. . . people have been saying there's going to be a new Mummy at the temple soon. It'll be wonderful if she's kind and gentle and takes good care of you, though.'

'I don't know, Mummy. . .'

'Perhaps it was only a silly rumour.'

This was the secret he had kept from his granny and his father, from Shoju, and even from O-Sugi, the maid: a momentous secret, too big for the small breast that held it.

Ryokun left Butsuoji and walked by himself to Tan'ami Shrine, determined to put his extra pocket-money to good use. Every year during the festival a circus troupe performed in the shrine compound. Today was the third and last day of the celebrations.

'It's the day for Mrs Komiyama's service today—shall I go?' the old priest asked Soshu.

'I'll go myself.'

'She'll have forgotten about it, I shouldn't wonder, with the excitement of the festival, and the crowds and everything.'

'No, I don't think she'd forget.'

'She's only just round the corner from the shrine, so she'll probably have visitors.'

'Maybe. I'm expected, though; it wouldn't do to let her down,' said Soshu, painfully conscious of the insincerity of his replies. 'To change the usual arrangement just because of the festival might be even more trouble.'

Mineyo appeared just as he was leaving.

'Mrs Komiyama, is it?'

Soshu nodded.

'She's very thoughtless, I must say. Nobody expects the priest to go visiting during the festival—it's practically impossible to get on the bus, apart from anything else. She should have sent to ask you to come another day.'

'I'll come back if it turns out to be inconvenient.'

'Shoju might just as well take your place today. You're too conscientious, Father!'

Again the shame. . . the monthly service was the merest pretext, an excuse to see her, hear the voice he was starved of, meeting her only once in a whole month. Her presence touched a new source of energy within him, releasing an endless, bright stream of unfamiliar thoughts, and even in the midst of his recognition that the ultimate origin of such feelings was in mere selfish desire, the sense of clarity and freshness remained, like the wiping clean of a clouded mirror. Brought into relation with Tomoko, the vaguest notions took on crystal clarity; every hope he had or could imagine was centred now on her.

As he had expected, the bus was jampacked, the sleeves of his travelling-robe nearly getting torn in the jostling crowd. The priest in his robes looked otherworldly and out of place in the throng of tired holidaymakers, celebrants of a very worldly festival. Kiyotacho, usually so peaceful, with that special calm that hangs over the geisha quarter of a town in the daytime, was all bustle today, the street of the willow-trees in particular being packed from end to end with promenading residents and visitors; as if the whole district had mistaken the sunlight hours for the night, during which alone, on every other day of the year, it came to life. The narrow street where Tomoko lived was as crowded as the rest.

Tomoko appeared immediately he opened the door, as if she had been expecting him. She seemed to have given special attention to her make-up, and to the details of her kimono, no doubt on account of the festival.

'I wasn't sure whether it was convenient for you today?'

'I was expecting you all the morning.'

Soshu went through to the shrine-room. No sound came from any other part of the house. Tomoko began to make the tea herself.

'Shoko wanted to go out and play, so I sent her to the park with the maid.'

'Children will never stay quietly at home if there's something more exciting to do. But don't you have any visitors for the festival?'

'No—this is one of the occasions when it is a relief to have no relatives.'

Yamaji had been on the first day of the festival. It would be four or five days before he came again, so for the moment Tomoko had nothing to fear.

'I think of you every day, Father,' she said, looking at him, 'and then at night, the moment I go to bed, all of a sudden the shame comes back, unbearably—'

'I'm so grateful I can see you once a month. What would have happened if we hadn't been able to meet like this, I can't imagine.'

'I should have gone mad!' On Tomoko's lips the melodramatic words did not sound exaggerated; the experience behind them was too bitter. Soshu caught in them the desperate, charged passion of one forced to live every day at the limit of endurance.

Outside, a constant stream of festival sightseers filled the narrowest street. Their meeting might have been a secret rendezvous, deliberately arranged to escape being seen. Looking into Tomoko's eyes, that were bright with tenderness and a hint of tears, Soshu felt the darkness lift within him, a purification. . . For a while her gaze met and merged with his: then suddenly she trembled, unable to bear the tension.

'The humiliation. . . it's so much worse now,' she murmured.

She meant Yamaji, Soshu knew. He closed his eyes, conscious of his helplessness, and remembering uneasily Yamaji's scarcely veiled threats in connection with the cemetery.

'Perhaps we should begin the service?' Bowing, Soshu turned to face the shrine. While he was putting on his stole, Tomoko knelt by him to light the candles. From the faint perfume that surrounded him, he caught an awareness of her very being, of her thirty years of womanhood distilled into an atmosphere as distinct as the scent of her skin. His senses quickened.

The altar prepared, she sat beside him and bowed formally,

placing her hands on the *tatami* in front of her. Soshu was struck by the beauty of her fingers.

The sutra-readings came to an end without interruption.

'Do you have any more services this afternoon?'

'No, yours is the only one today.'

'That's wonderful!'

Soshu laughed at the girlish exclamation.

'I cooked some of the special festival dishes—I suppose you'll be having them at Butsuoji anyway, but I wanted to make something for you myself.'

'It'll be a joy to eat it.'

While she was busy in the kitchen, Soshu took off his stole and black outer robe. The 'festival dishes' were of the kind known as *shojin-ochi,* the first non-vegetarian dishes eaten after a period of abstinence. In Tan'ami people usually serve *oshizushi,* flattened rice. The rounded, hand-rolled riceballs of *Tokyo-zushi* have been growing more popular recently, but *oshizushi* is still the best for home-cooking. Rice is packed into a small wooden box previously lined with an aspidistra leaf, and covered with pieces of *shigure* clam, lobster or eel. The whole is flattened with a wooden lid, left overnight, and then cut up into slabs for serving. Vinegar-flavoured *sushi-rice* flattened in this way is particularly delicious.

'I love a white robe. It gives one such a feeling of innocence,' Tomoko said as she arranged the slabs of *oshizushi* on two small plates.

'I suppose that means I ought to feel innocent every day of my life, since I scarcely ever wear anything else.' Soshu took her remark lightly, with a smile; she could hardly have intended the ironic implication.

'We are alone now, Father.'

'Have you been writing the diary you promised?'

'I started; but it got too painful. . .'

'I keep a diary in my heart. Somebody would be sure to find it if I wrote everything down.'

'How do you like the *sushi*?'

'Delicious!'

'I made it thinking of you, and hoping you'd stay to eat it. It's plain enough, I know, but at least it keeps you here a little longer.'

And he had never embraced her, never even touched her hand! His priest's robe made him shrink from any such thought. Yet he was thankful that it was so.

'Did you hear anything from Mr Yamaji?' Soshu found himself saying in spite of himself.

A shadow crossed Tomoko's face.

'About the cemetery, I mean?'

The words hit her like so many blows. She remembered what Yamaji had told her about his meeting with Soshu: 'I sent for the priest and gave him a bit of a talking-to. Scared him all right—more than I need have done, I daresay. There'll have to be a parishioners' meeting, of course; but he'll support me, and help to bring the parishioners round.'

'He did say something about it. I don't know about the cemetery—men understand these things better—but the thought of his threats, and all the other suffering it may mean for you—I can't bear it!'

'I was thinking of you when he began to hint at what might happen if I didn't fall in with his plans. That made it all the more painful.'

'For me, too. . .'

'Whatever happens, I won't, I can't give you up—no matter what he threatens me with,' said Soshu with sudden determination, the hand that held the little *sushi-plate* trembling.

Tomoko's eyes filled with tears. Clenching both hands, she drove the nails into her palms, trying to deaden with pain her longing to throw herself on his knees. The festival dishes lay between them, an impassable barrier. She fought with the impulse—now beyond the power of any polite answers to deflect—to seize the hands placed with formal correctness on his lap.

'I only live for your visits—the moment you leave is agony; all kinds of absurd, fantastic thoughts come flooding over me. . . because it's so hopeless, I suppose. And you are hurt, Father, because of me. . . . you have to suffer now—it's this I can't bear—and you'll go on suffering unless I can find some other way to live.'

'I've learnt for the first time what love is. . . It's as lonely as a desert, living at Butsuoji; but even that doesn't terrify me now, as it used to.'

'Please give me courage, Father!' Tomoko's tone was stiff, almost formal. Inevitably, if she could have flung herself forward and embraced him, her feelings would have found a more natural expression. But the barrier between them remained, holding even words in check; she was too timid to push it aside, too guileless to think of rising and going past it to reach him, too full of fear and shame to make the slightest move. With Yamaji, desire had only to be aroused for him to act, surrendering to naked instinct; but Soshu was as ignorant, as powerless, as Tomoko herself. The man of thirty-nine and the woman of thirty-two sat opposite each other like awkward children, embarrassment forcing both to speak in the same formal, halting manner.

'Yamaji is driving me mad. . . I hate him, I hate him!'

Soshu nodded slowly, his love bringing him to a truer realisation of what she must suffer. He began to hate Yamaji himself.

'I'm so afraid of him, too—the fear itself is agony, burning inside me. . . after he's gone, my face must look like a devil's for a while. I didn't feel it so much till I met you, Father. No I'm afraid of myself, even—I never dreamt how violently I could hate anyone. . .'

'I remember how quietly you took my confession. You listened so calmly, as if it were a business talk we were having. Love has united us already. But my dreams won't stop there. . . what will happen if love grows too strong for us—if we can't be content with love at a distance? I'm afraid. . . I've had no experience of love. I'm a man of thirty-nine. Thinking of the future makes me sad sometimes—suppose I were driven one day to act as a man and nothing else, a male animal like other men—'

'Give me courage, Father!'

'When I sit here looking at you, I have a strange illusion I've known you for longer than I can remember, a familiar, intimate feeling, as one has when one glances casually at one's own body.' Soshu smiled faintly. 'And yet in reality you are far away, a woman of whom I know nothing; and there's no peace between strangers, only uncertainty and suspense. I long to know everything now. . . I'm ashamed of the thoughts that come to me. . . a priest wrapped up in his white robe. . . At first I was hardly aware of your body. It never occurred to me to think of that side of your relationship with Yamaji. But since I've known something of your feelings, it's that that's tortured me more than anything else. It makes me hate myself, a priest—'

'Give me courage, Father!'

'You spoke of Yamaji driving you mad. But do you think the priest is so different? He's an ordinary man, like Yamaji—'

'No! I know the man I've chosen. I'm not young, either—long past dreams; I know what I want from life now.'

Soshu looked at his watch. Tomoko shook her head and shoulders, like a peevish child.

'That was a delicious meal—and it's been wonderful to have so much time with you, all the more so because I didn't expect to today. I'd better be going now.'

'Shoko's not back yet. . .'

'After I've been here I can think of nothing else for two or three days; then gradually everything begins to seem hopeless and frustrating again. We couldn't be cut off more completely: you're here every day, and I can't visit you or write. Then the day for your service comes round again, and I'm so happy I don't know what to do with myself. You need hope, and so do I; there's no difference between us.'

'Life's no longer empty when you're here, Father. For a day I have a will of my own, and can act on it. But only on this day.

Every other day I've no freedom, nothing to help me live through the month—except memories of you, which makes me lonelier still. . . I don't know how much longer I can bear this kind of existence, or how much longer I can go on hiding from Yamaji what I really feel about him; it's gambling with life—'

There was a clatter from the front door, and the sound of voices. Shoko and the maid had returned.

'Mummy!'

Soshu straightened his back, thought it was hardly necessary, as he had not once relaxed his correct, formal posture. Tomoko made a similar, scarcely perceptible movement.

'Hallo, Shoko darling!' Tomoko half rose, then sat down again as her daughter came into the room. Shoko knelt and bowed to Soshu. She was surprised to see him in his white under-robe, and her face took on a serious, grown-up look.

'Did you enjoy yourself, darling?'

Shoko nodded. Then she jumped up and followed the maid, who had gone to the kitchen after bowing to Tomoko from the corridor. Soshu began to put on the outer robe he used for all except special occasions.

'Must you go?'

'Yes. . . I feel so much freer now.'

'It's the same freedom you bring me, Father,' said Tomoko in a low voice. As Soshu got up to go, so did she. From the kitchen came the sound of running water.

Tomoko stood without moving, as if waiting for something.

'There's no peace except when I'm with you,' said Soshu as he passed her.

'If only I could give you peace always. . .'

Soshu stopped for a moment, and murmured, as if to himself:

'I'm afraid. . . of love run wild. . . of myself. . .'

As he slipped on his priest's clogs, with their white leather thongs, Tomoko knelt, ready to bow her visitor out. He turned; their eyes met. In the kitchen Shoko was chattering happily to the maid.

26

Soshu had gone out earlier in the evening to visit a parishioner. On such occasions the old priest would wait till he came back before going home to his cottage on the hill. A dim light burned in the *tamari,* the room used by the elders when they had business at the temple. It was an enormous room; the big porcelain brazier in the middle looked insignificant in contrast with the empty space all round. A sunken fireplace and a tea-cabinet occupied one corner, a movable *tokonoma* the corner opposite. The old priest sat with both hands on the brazier and his head bent over it. In fact it was not cold enough for any kind of fire, but the mere fact that the brazier happened to have been put there made him huddle over it instinctively, as if winter had come already.

All was quiet in temple and house. From time to time the buildings trembled slightly, as a truck passed by along the new highway. What Shoju was thinking, or even whether he was still awake, would have been impossible to tell. Voices could be heard now and then from Mineyo's room, but the old man leaning over the brazier did not react; life itself might have quietly abandoned him, leaving only a motionless, insubstantial form behind. It was perfectly possible Shoju would die like this, life merging so imperceptibly into death that one might tap him casually on the shoulder, only to find that he was dead already.

'. . . When was the Kamakura Period?' Ryokun asked his granny, with whom he slept. He was wide awake still. Mineyo's scent filled the room; she had just finished her evening toilet after her bath.

'A long, long time ago—seven or eight hundred years.'

'That's why it's so black, then. . .' Ryokun had been wondering why the statue of Amida in the temple—every inch of it, head, body and feet—was so dark, contrasting strangely with the gold paint and glittering brass ornaments of the sanctuary.

'Has it really been in our temple all that time?'

'Butsuoji is a very, very old temple. You'll be the seventeenth hereditary priest, Ryokun.'

'Is the temple as old as Amida, then?'

'It's been rebuilt several times. The hall is the oldest part now—it goes back a hundred and forty years, I suppose. The house is quite new. Haven't they told you at school about houses, and how long they last?'

'We don't learn things like that.'

'In this district fifty or sixty years is old for a house. After that most houses either have to be repaired from top to bottom, or else rebuilt altogether.'

Ryokun had seen some of the farmers who belonged to Butsuoji rebuilding their houses, but he found it hard to imagine a house having a 'life' of its own, which had an end as well as a beginning.

'Do houses live as long as people?' he asked, without having any clear idea of how long people lived, either.

'A wicked man tried to steal the holy Amida from Butsuoji once. Buddha punished him, though: all his muscles went stiff suddenly, and he couldn't move.'

Ryokun caught his breath, thrilled at the miraculous punishment.

'It happened a long time ago, when grandmother was young.'

'Did he really steal it? What was he going to do with it—sell it? Is it made of gold? Did he really want to sell it, do you think?'

'Well, it's Kamakura work, so it would have fetched a good deal as an antique, I suppose. But men can't do such wicked things—Buddha is always watching.'

Ryokun coiled up inside the bed, still cold in spite of the thick *futon*. He was determined to hear the story to the end, but it frightened him all the same. Even with Mineyo sitting by the bed, he could not stop shivering.

'Tell me about it!'

'It happened very early one morning. Grandmother went out to open the gate—'

'Where was Shoju?'

'Shoju was still asleep.'

'What about Father?'

'Your father wasn't here. It happened before he came to Butsuoji.'

Then it must have been before I was born, thought Ryokun, though without finding much comfort in the fact.

Mineyo told him the story. It was still twilight when she had gone out. On her way across the compound she noticed a man, a stranger, sitting on the stone steps in front of the great hall. The moment he saw her he tried to get up and run away, but he seemed unable to move, as if some enormous weight were holding him down. Then he groaned, kicking and waving his arms helplessly. There was something fastened to his back, Mineyo saw, which prevented him from getting to his feet.

'What's the matter?' she called out. Till this moment it had not occurred to Mineyo that the man might be a thief; he must be one of the tramps, she thought, who sometimes slept on the verandah-like platform surrounding the great hall.

'Forgive me!' he cried, his face twisted with fear; though his arms and legs still moved jerkily, it had dawned on him that he was literally powerless to stand up.

'What's happened?'

'Forgive a poor man! I've sinned, and He has punished me. . . help me, lady! I can't get up— can't move!'

'What's that you've got on your back?'

'The holy Amida. . .'

'*The holy Amida*!'

'The statue—I stole it from the hall—'

The object he was carrying was wrapped in a big cotton *furoshiki*.

'Do you mean to say it's the Butsuoji Amida you've got bundled up in that cloth?'

'I've sinned—He's punishing me now! I can't walk! It's the weight—the terrible weight pressing down on me, I can't move! Help me, lady!'

He must have been a thief of more than usual boldness, to think of stealing a temple image. As he struggled to get up, the cloth he had tied under his chin by way of a disguise came loose, revealing ugly, evil-looking features.

'Where do you come from?'

'Shirahashi Village, lady.'

'That's where Togenji Temple is, isn't it?'

'Yes, lady.'

'What's your name?'

'Denbei Hisai.'

'How old are you?'

'Fifty-three.'

'We know the Togenji priest, you know—he'll soon find out for us if you've been telling the truth or not.'

'I'm not lying, lady.'

'The idea of such a thing—what sacrilege! Namu Amida Butsu, Namu Amida Butsu. . . How could you think of anything so outrageous! You needn't be surprised if you can't move off those steps —you can be thankful He's so merciful, or He might have blinded you! If you're crippled for the rest of your life, it's only what you deserve.'

Mineyo lifted the load from his back, repeating the *nenbutsu* as she did so. A little over two feet high, the image was of Amida in the *tenjo-tengi* posture, seated, with one hand pointing to heaven and the other to the earth. As she held it in her arms, still reciting *nenbutsu,* the thief found himself once more able to move. He bowed to her at once, touching the broad stone step with his forehead.

'He found me out. . . I'll never do anything like it again. Forgive me lady! His punishing me has made me see how wicked I've been. When I couldn't stand up, even, I felt how terrible sin was—I'd never felt like that before. Let me go, lady!'

'Let this be a lesson to you to turn over a new leaf. The Lord Buddha will be watching you—He will know whether you mend your ways or not.'

'I'll change them, lady. . . never knew it was so terrible. . . I'll repent all right. . . terrible, terrible. . .'

Mineyo let him go. Hurriedly folding up the dirty cloth he had tied round his head and clenching it in one hand, he slunk out of the temple gate.

Ryokun was thrilled, partly because Mineyo told the story so well. It was her own experience she was recounting, after all. He had often had the feeling, looking up at the blackened image of Amida in the shrine feretory, that he could never escape that steady, piercing gaze. A Buddha with eyes like that could turn a thief's legs to stone. . . Ryokun never dreamt that his grandmother had invented the whole story.

'Did the man actually belong to Togenji Temple?'

'We didn't enquire—that would have been going too far. When a man repents of his sins, it's a sin not to leave him alone to repent in peace.'

Ryokun listened, spellbound. Mineyo pulled the bedclothes up to his neck and patted him gently.

'It's late now, Ryokun; time for sleep.'

Her story of how she had forgiven the wicked thief and let him go filled the boy with wonder. He buried his face in the bedclothes, but beneath them he was wide awake still, his little mind busy with what he had heard. Sleep was far away.

Mineyo shut her eyes, thinking it would help him to doze off. The fact that her story was not true did not trouble her. She often told it to the young people of Butsuoji, and grew more skilful with each retelling. Gradually she had come to believe that something of the kind had actually happened long ago, in her young days—even if not precisely as she described it now. That she had filled a little boy's mind with a lingering sense of terror did not cross her mind; if she thought at all about the effect of the story on him, it was only to congratulate herself on having sown the seeds of faith in her grandson at such an early age. Shinran, the saint to whom Butsuoji owed its existence, would have nothing to do with the kind of faith that is based on miracles; but of the meaning of his teaching Mineyo was ignorant. 'Don't give the boy wrong ideas,' Soshu would no doubt have told her indignantly, if he had known. 'St Shinran would never have worked a miracle, even on a thief. He didn't believe in miracles. It'll be a tragedy if Ryokun once gets the idea that that's what religion is about. Think how the saint himself suffered—it was Zenran's mistaken ideas about miracles that made Shinran disown his own son.' It was not anything in Zenran's conduct or morals that had led his father to disown his eldest son; nor was the tension that had arisen between them on account of Zenran's dislike of his stepmother responsible. The cause of the breach was rather the weakness of Zenran's faith, his failure to understand his father's teaching. He hinted to other believers that his father had entrusted him with the knowledge of a secret Way to Paradise. This 'Way' turned out to consist of exorcisms, incantations and the like, such as were practised by other sects, and the believers began to waver. Shinran must have suffered agonies at this betrayal of his religion by his favourite son; but the shock seems to have deepened his own faith. The Tannisho says: 'According to Shinran, there can be no faith but by accepting the word of the Holy One that if a man but recites the *nenbutsu,* he shall be saved by the grace of Amida.' The kind of faith the writer was attempting to describe in this passage was obviously both passionate and profound—so much so, indeed, that to some it may seem merely blind, or arrogant, even, in the demands it made; while others might interpret it as a confession of weakness, unworthy of the founder of the True Pure Land Sect. The Tannisho is an account of Shinran's doctrines compiled after his death by Yuien, one of his disciples, who was disturbed to find so many people failing to understand the Master's teaching correctly. Yuien was one of Shinran's companions in his lifetime. It is hard to say, however, whether he has transmitted the teachings without distortion; there can be no guarantee that he did not unconsciously include some of his own views or feelings in his account of the Master's sayings, even though he himself may have firmly believed he was merely a faithful reporter. The Tannisho is regarded by the True Pure Land Sect as one of the official sources of its doctrines, but one cannot help having some doubts, seeing that the book was not written by Shinran himself. The Master's teachings were beyond his son, whose talk of incantations and prayers and promises of a secret Way to Paradise were a cloak for his own uncertainties. If it is doubtful whether Shinran's disciple Yuien understood him perfectly, in spite of their close association, Zenran's difficulties seem easier to understand. At all events, the Master's beliefs made him disown his son.

No one at Butsuoji was particularly startled if footsteps were heard in the middle of the night.

'I heard someone walking across from the hall last night,' Mineyo had told Soshu once at breakfast.

'Did you? I was so tired I didn't notice.'

Ryokun shivered. He wondered how they could be so casual. Grandmother had heard footsteps walking along the pitch-dark corridor, towards the house—this was something as gruesome as any ghost-story, yet they talked of it as if it happened every day.

Soon after Ryokun had gone to school, one of the parishioners came hurrying to the temple to report that the old lady next door had died in the night. The old priest fetched from the *tokonoma* in the recess at the back of the hall the long, narrow box containing a pale yellow curtain and the prayer scroll for the dead, and gave it to the messenger. Soshu left at once to read the sutras at the bedside of the dead parishioner, after which the preparations for the funeral would begin. The footsteps in the night had been those of the dead lady, come to report her death to Butsuoji.

'You'll understand one day, when you're bigger,' his father had said, as if he wanted to put off explaining till Ryokun was grown-up. Or would he understand by himself when he was older, he wondered. Would these things happen to *him* then—the mysterious, ghostly experiences granny had? What did being 'grown-up' mean? Would he be suddenly grown-up when he was ordained and became the next priest of Butsuoji?

Since then, he had been scared to go down the unlit corridor to the lavatory when he woke in the middle of the night. A temple was different from an ordinary house; in the darkness it seemed to swarm with ghosts—not the ghosts of foxes or badgers, that appear in so many old tales, but of real people, of Butsuoji people they knew well, though that did not make them any the less terrifying to Ryokun. To get to the lavatory from the room where he and Mineyo slept, he had to find his way round the corner where the corridor turned, and then run about twenty yards, all in absolute darkness. Even if he ran with his eyes shut tight, he would still know if some white shape confronted him—spirits have other ways of making themselves known. When he was bigger, he supposed, he wouldn't be afraid of ghosts any more. He wished it did not take so long to grow up.

It was only Mineyo who talked of apparitions and weird happenings in the night. Ryokun had never once heard his father mention such things. Grandmother seemed to like telling ghost stories.

One night there was a great crash, apparently from somewhere near the main shrine in the temple hall, which was more than a hundred yards from Mineyo's room in the house. She woke up instantly. Judging from the noise, the two hanging lamps in front of the sanctuary had slipped off their hooks and fallen on the wooden floor. The strange thing was that no other sound followed the big crash. If it was really the lamps that had fallen, one would have expected to hear a clatter lasting several seconds as the different parts of each lamp rolled about the floor and collided with each other—the lotus-shaped holders, the bowls, the fastening clips, and the lids, which were all of brass: but there was nothing of the kind. And the crash itself seemed louder than any ordinary temple lamps would have made, which added to the mystery.

'There was a noise from the hall last night—the sanctuary lamps falling, I think,' said Mineyo as soon as they all met for breakfast. 'Somebody must have died, of course; but that's not the usual way they let us know.'

Soshu showed no more surprise than on the previous occasion. Later in the morning the death of a parishioner was reported. 'We knew already,' said Mineyo to the relative who had come for the curtain and the prayer-scroll. 'Someone came to the hall, just after two this morning.' The relative seemed awe-struck at the mysterious coincidence. 'It was just then that he died . . . he must have come to the temple himself.'

Here was a world of which the living could know nothing. Neither Mineyo nor the parishioners doubted the connection between the death and the noise in the temple hall; on the contrary, they accepted the 'coincidence' with gratitude for what they took to be an authentic revelation of the existence of that other world. The idea that the noise might have been an hallucination never crossed their minds. A hallucination—in reality it was no more than that. Much of a temple's business is with death; an aura of death, so to speak, surrounds a priest and his profession. Mineyo was so steeped in the life and atmosphere of the temple that the hallucinations to which her temperament and physiological condition made her liable inevitably became associated in her mind with the mystery of death. Hence the 'sounds' she heard and Soshu did not; 'faith' was not involved.

Mineyo was especially fond of telling meetings of young parishioners about something that had happened soon after she first came to Butsuoji as a bride. She had woken in the middle of the night, for no apparent reason. Silence filled the house, an all-pervading, oppressive presence. It was late autumn; dense foliage still covered the trees in the courtyard and the two gardens, cutting off the sunlight from most of the rooms. The house was damp, and the air in the long corridors almost cold, though no breeze was blowing.

Mineyo caught the sound of footsteps in the corridor; a leisurely, easy tread, for all the world like someone strolling in his own house—it was not a thief, assuredly. Through the utter stillness of the night, she could even hear the rustle of clothes. As far as she could judge, the nocturnal walker seemed to be a man, tall, thin, and erect. Little by little the uncanny sounds grew louder. Mineyo shuddered. It was still hours till dawn. She had often heard sandal-shod feet walking in the earthen passage leading to the kitchen; but the passage was at the other end of the house, so far away that the noises had never really frightened her. That night, however, it was different. The corridor connecting with the temple led directly past where she lay, following two sides of her room, with a right-angle bend at the corner. As soon as she heard the sound, she recognised it as coming not from the passage but from the temple corridor.

The steps continued, as if the walker were unaware of the presence of the sleeping priest and his wife. They passed behind the family shrine-room. Mineyo remembered the door dividing the three-foot wide corridor into two sections. The footsteps would be halted there, she thought with relief, though still unable to keep herself from trembling. The family scarcely used the door; it was always kept shut, and served as a kind of dividing-wall. The mysterious walker would not open it, surely . . . but if the door did open, at least she would hear the latch creaking, and that would be enough to prove the intruder was no ghost but a burglar—either of which was terrible enough; but there are different kinds of terror. . . Suddenly, as these thoughts were flashing across her mind, the measured tread and the rustle of the kimono stopped. Mineyo breathed again—but only for a second. The footsteps began again, after a silence just long enough to allow for the opening and shutting of the door. There was a new sound—the kimono swishing against the wall of the corridor, she was sure. . . and now against the wall of her own. . . behind the *tokonoma*. In a moment the footsteps would reach the bend in the corridor.

Mineyo wanted desperately to cry out. Her husband, the priest, was sleeping at her side. Still, with calm, even tread, the unseen figure walked on, tall and gaunt. When he came to the corner, he would pass by her pillow—she had laid the bed to face east that night; the paper sliding-doors which separated the room from the corridor were not six feet from her pillow. She could neither scream nor move. The steps turned the corner, came nearer and nearer. . . the night air grew suddenly thin, she could hardly breathe, let alone cry out. The feet were wearing *tabi*. A sleeve brushed lightly against the paper-doors, as if by accident. . .

The corridor widened to about six feet at the corner of Mineyo's room. At the far end was a double door, now shut, which gave on to the verandah of the big room where the elders held their meetings. Mineyo heard a dull sound, as of a foot meeting an unseen obstacle; but she remained taut with terror, telling herself the steps would never cross into the meeting-room—which would have meant opening the big double door, and pushing back the paper-door of the room itself. Silence fell again. Sliding screens formed the only partition between the meeting-room and that where Mineyo and her husband slept. Still the death-like silence, as if time itself had stopped. . . it would drive her mad, she would scream. . . And then—a quiet swishing against the screens. . . For an instant the shock froze her, then her whole body was trembling. It was the screens—she knew from the distinctive sound—not the wall of the corridor or the tightly-stretched panels of the paper-doors. The footsteps had entered the meeting-room—they had stopped just long enough for the walker to open the door—and now she could hear the faint creaking of the mats under his tread. From the meeting-room, they had passed into the little room where the priest's robes were kept, and then into the family shrine-room, till she could hear them no more.

Mineyo breathed freely once more. Feeling now that there was no point in waking her husband, she finally managed to doze off again, and slept the rest of the night.

Next morning, when she told the priest of the mysterious visitor, he showed no great surprise. 'Inugai's dead, I shouldn't wonder,' he said. The head of the Inugai family was in hospital, Mineyo knew, and she had heard that he was dying. He was one of the most influential of the Butsuoji parishioners. 'I'll call and see. I've some visiting to do in Minami-cho, anyway.'

The usual air of bustle was absent that morning from the sea-food shop the Inugais kept. The family took the priest straight to the shrine-room, as if they had been expecting him. Candles were burning on the shrine. Inugai was dead, they told him. The body was still at the hospital.

When the priest had finished reading the scripture for the dead, the new head of the family came back to the shrine-room to thank him.

'What time did you get my message, Father?'

The family had been in confusion all the morning. The priest's coming so soon had astonished the young man, for he himself had despatched a messenger to Butsuoji to report the death only a little while before.

'My wife heard some strange sounds in the night, about three o'clock. I thought perhaps it might be Mr Inugai, so I decided to call and make sure.'

'It must have been Father himself—he died at twenty past three. . .'

Mineyo was very proud of this story. It had never occurred to her that everything she had heard might have been an illusion, the product of the recollection, tucked away at the back of her mind, that the old man was dying, coupled with the effect on her of the atmosphere of Butsuoji in the small hours of the night: she trusted her own memory too much ever to wonder whether it might not have been responsible.

'There are strange things about a Buddhist temple. Even tramps know that. They don't like sleeping in a Shinto shrine, they say, because it's so lonely—but with a Buddhist temple it's different; it always seems alive, somehow, and they can hear voices all through the night, lots of them. I don't suppose I'd ever have had these experiences myself if I'd married a layman, but I certainly have heard queer things since coming to Butsuoji. That crash when the two lamps fell, for instance. When I went to the hall next morning they were hanging from the ceiling again; everything was just as it should be. The dead man went to all that trouble to let us know. . .'

Soshu would never say directly whether or not he accepted her stories as having any truth in them—she had lived at Butsuoji so much longer than himself. Sometimes, so as not to interrupt a conversation, he would appear to believe her, but all the while he would be thinking how easily a 'professional' Buddhist could fall a victim to hallucinations if he were not constantly on his guard. With true religion such experiences had nothing to do. The fact that she alone could hear the mysterious sounds flattered Mineyo's vanity, and struck her as a convincing proof of the depth of her own faith. No rational explanations could have changed the mental habits of fifty years. All Soshu could do was to try to prevent Ryokun from coming under her influence.

Yosuke Tachi dropped in late that evening.

'The head of one of the new religions says that miracles always go with real religion, and that it's miracles that make religion spread. How's that for reaction?' he said, as if it were a joke.

'Fortunately for us, St Shinran rejected every kind of miracle—incantations, faith-healing and the rest. He wasn't interested in magic.'

Insects were humming in the garden of the inner courtyard.

'No—Pure Land people don't pray to the Three Monkey Stone, anyway. I came across some rather interesting statistics the other day, in a report on religion in farming villages. Not that the statisticians had been looking for anything special—it just came out in the figures. Farming does best, apparently, wherever the Pure Land Sect is strongest. And it's not as if Shinran invented some wonderful new method of farming, either. What do you make of that, Father?'

Most of the Butsuoji parishioners were farmers, almost all of whom had owned and worked their own land for generations; but the suggestion of a correlation between religion and the quality of farming was new to Soshu.

'I suppose it must have something to do with the Pure Land doctrines being so rational. And then Shinran was more concerned all the time with *this* world than with any life after death—that seems to me, incidentally, an obvious difference between his teaching and Honen's.'[1]

O-Sugi entered the room noiselessly, carrying two white teacups on a heavy, round try. The tea was of poor quality, without the slightest aroma; the tray, worn with nearly thirty years of use, looked like an antique.

'Shinran was certainly a disciple of Honen; but however much he respected his master—and he did respect him all his life—I can't help thinking he really rejected Honen's teaching. My interpretation may be too extreme, I suppose; but it seems to me he took Honen's ideas so much further that he was really breaking new ground altogether—so new that his final achievement would have been impossible in Honen's lifetime.' Soshu closed his eyes for a few moments. 'Of course, Honen had wanted to find some way of harmonizing the idea of salvation by one's own unaided efforts with that of salvation by grace,' he went on, opening his eyes and looking Yosuke Tachi in the face. 'He longed to give up every thought of trying to save himself, so that he could have absolute faith in the grace of Amida's Holy Vow. But is it really possible for a man to give up all self-striving? Theorizing apart, none of us could live a day without this activity of the self. We feel we ought to give it up, get rid of it altogether, but in practice we can't. Shinran insisted we couldn't save ourselves, just as Honen did. We may not be able to get rid of the selves working inside us, but we can and do know how powerless they are. Shinran believed the attempt to get rid of self was itself as much an activity of the self as any of its more obvious manifestations—in which he was certainly correct. Then the real meaning of salvation by faith struck him. It means a man must take this struggling self, this ego so divisive, so conscious of its own identity, and surrender it just as it is—surrender his whole personality, in other words—to the mercy of the Holy Vow. That was something even Honen had never been able to do. Shinran's great achievement was to show that there needn't be any inconsistency between the ideas of self-salvation and salvation by grace.'

'Believing in absolute, unconditional salvation by "grace" means

1 St Honen (1130-1212), founder of the original Pure Land Sect, of which the True Pure Land Sect founded by his disciple Shinran was an offshoot.

throwing oneself on Amida's mercy exactly as one is, I take it—with all one's passions, with the self that imagines all the time there *is* such a thing as self-salvation, and lives accordingly—is incapable of living in any other way, in fact?'

'Yes, but Amida's salvation doesn't depend on whether we believe in it or not; it was determined long ago. All we have to do, according to Shinran, is to realise that we are saved already.'

'It sounds simple enough, till you think about it. "One has only to realise one is already upheld by Amida's boundless compassion", they say, but how to realize it—that's the problem; it doesn't just come naturally.'

'It means waking up to the truth that our lives as we actually live them, our ordinary day-to-day lives are in fact being lived under Amida's direction all the time. It means realising that each of us is one with his Buddha-spirit. It's true that this realisation is still an act of the self; but it does enable a man to avoid the big pitfalls in life. It gives him security, a feeling that life itself is trustworthy. All this is easy to talk about, of course. The mind has to take a big leap to get that far, though, and I find it terribly difficult. Daisetsu Suzuki says there's a touch of Zen about Shinran.'

A few moments earlier, a rasping sound, made by two big stones grating against each other with a slow heavy rhythm like that of a waterwheel, had broken in upon the stillness of the house. Soshu was silent for a while. The grinding noise continued. Suddenly Tachi looked up, as if he had just noticed it.

'It seems only the other day the festival ended, and now it's nearly New Year already.'

Soshu recognized the sound. Somewhere at the back of the house, O-Sugi was turning the hand-mill in which she ground *mochi*-flour a few days before the New Year holiday. The old mill had been used every year for forty years or more. It consisted of two stones, an upper and a lower, each about four inches thick, the upper one encased in a bamboo hoop with a turning handle. In the middle of the upper stone was a tiny hole, into which, for each revolution of the stone made by his right hand resting on the handle, the *mochi*-grinder would poke a few grains of rice with his left. The rice would be heaped up around the hole, and the grinder needed deft fingers: if too many grains were pushed into the hole at once, the stone would skid round ineffectively—five or six grains for each revolution were all the little mill could take if the upper stone was to engage with the lower and grind the rice into fine flour by its own weight. Ryokun loved pushing the heavy stone round, but he would get tired after turning it two or three times by himself, and had to content himself with putting his hand on top of O-Sugi's—much to her delight.

'Look how easily it goes when you help me, Ryokun! You're such a strong boy—it doesn't feel heavy any more,' she would say. Gradually the newly-ground flour piled up around the mill. They could just as well have made their *mochi*-cakes with ordinary corn-flour; but the old custom of grinding rice died hard. The monotonous sound of the turning millstones fascinated Ryokun like an old, sad fairy-tale. He could not imagine New Year without it.

'By the way, Father, the parishioners are beginning to get a bit impatient,' said Tachi, changing the subject.

'What about?'

'About a new lady for Butsuoji. Gossiping for ever about Mrs Renko and how she ran away won't get us anywhere, they're saying —besides, she's found herself a new home now.'

Tomoko's face rose before Soshu. . . Forlorn, suffering.

'They appreciate your not being in a hurry, of course, but there's a limit, even so. . . It's not as if there weren't any candidates. Two hundred families in the congregation, after all, and they've all been thinking about it.'

Soshu lowered his eyes. With Tomoko at his side, he was hearing destiny give judgement. . .

'If it turns out there's someone suitable among the temple families, hadn't you better take her? Besides, it'll be a lot easier, I should think, if it's someone who knows Butsuoji well already.'

'Is there anyone in the congregation who really fancies temple life? The housekeeping's a headache—it's nothing like running a layman's home.'

'The Hoshinas have a young widowed daughter. . .'

Tanemi: with her ample figure, her rosy cheeks, whose natural colour was as bright as any rouge, her protruding lower lip.

'She must be about five feet four, I suppose. But you know her, of course? Weighs about ten stone, perhaps. I've only seen her in western dress. She looks healthy, anyway, and it takes a healthy woman to run a temple household. Not that they've asked me to speak to you—but one can't help noticing her, and it would make such a difference if someone like her were to take Mrs Renko's place. She's a lively, cheerful girl, they say, and would get on very well with Ryokun, I shouldn't wonder.'

'She deserves to find somewhere better than Butsuoji. She's so young still—no one would take her for a widow.'

'She happened to be standing just in front of me once during the festival—at the Tan'ami Shrine, I think it was. I was surprised to see how big she is—one's used to girls being taller nowadays than they used to be, but she's something special. Her ankles are a bit on the thick side, maybe,' said Tachi with a smile, 'but I suppose she'd topple over otherwise. You wouldn't call her plain, though; and she has a fine white complexion, not like most Japanese. Quite impressive-looking, really.'

Soshu had never seen her in western dress. He recalled how she looked in kimono: faintly formidable because of her height, unusual for a Japanese girl, but not unpleasantly so. Sitting opposite him, she had seemed to find her size embarrassing. Her voice was surprisingly soft and musical.

'I haven't heard her say so herself, but it seems she positively wants her next husband to be a priest, if she does marry again. If that's true, what more could you want? It would be easier to arrange than you think—the Hoshinas are an old Tan'ami family, just right for Butsuoji. She's been married once already, that's the only thing.'

'That's no objection as far as Butsuoji's concerned—besides, there's Ryokun to think of, so it might even be an advantage. Just to hear about the Butsuoji household would put most women off altogether, I imagine.'

'Which is all the more reason for choosing someone from among the parishioners. The Hoshinas know just how things are already. Why not have someone sound them out right after the New Year holiday, if you think she's a good choice?'

'Maybe. . . but I'm afraid I'm not really thinking of marrying again just yet.'

'But it doesn't concern you alone, Father—the parishioners are insisting.'

Tomoko and himself—what were they, thought Soshu, but a pair of hunted animals cowering futilely under a pine-tree, in a last vain attempt to escape the eyes they knew would find them?

27

It was the evening for making the New Year rice-cakes—an exciting time for Ryokun, for it was the only evening in the year when he was allowed to stay up late. According to custom, a sturdy couple belonging to the congregation had been asked in to pound the steamed *mochi,* and an old wooden mortar stood ready in the least cluttered area of the earthen-floored kitchen. Ryokun darted about the room, now standing in front of the stove, now holding his hand in the column of steam rising from the four wooden pans of rice, set one above the other, now stroking the smooth surface of the pestle, now straining to lift it up to test its weight. Mineyo, sitting by a porcelain brazier in the elders' room, was directing operations, while Shoju looked after the stove. The paper sliding-doors dividing the kitchen from the elders' room had been taken down, and the wooden doors of the kitchen cupboards lay face downwards on the floor, covered with the white powdered rice in which the finished cakes would later be rolled.

'Evening.' Another parishioner, one of the elders, entered the kitchen. 'Come to pound the rice, eh?' he said, glancing at the couple, who were sitting smoking Japanese pipes, waiting till the rice on the stove was done. After thanking them, he stepped up into the elders' room, greeted Mineyo and sat chatting with her for a while. Soon, however, Mineyo left. The elder sat on alone at the brazier, as if waiting for the pounding of the rice to begin, yet with no apparent interest in the group in the kitchen. Ryokun wondered uneasily what he had come for. Some business he seemed to have; and there was an air of expectancy about the way he sat, his hands resting lightly on the edge of the brazier.

The woman who had been waiting with her husband took the first of the four pans, and with a quick, vigorous movement turned its contents—a mixture of *mochigome* and ordinary rice, now perfectly steamed and holding together in a compact cylinder from the shape of the pan—into the mortar. Sprinkling water on the thin bamboo strainer that still clung to the rice, she peeled it off: her husband moistened his pestle and began to poke at the white glutinous mass. After it had been pounded, the mixture is known as *tagane*, because of the ordinary rice it contains in addition to *mochi* proper. A cheerful sound, strong and rhythmical, filled the kitchen and echoed through the house. Ryokun sat gazing now at the pounder, now at his wife. He was fascinated by the look of concentration on the woman's face as she turned the rice with a quick, deft thrust of her hands between each descent of the big club-like pestle. The pounder's assistant had to be specially alert; if the two did not work together in a single continuous rhythm, the *mochi* would turn out uneven, not to mention the danger of the woman's hands getting crushed instead of the *mochi*,—or of the pestle coming down on her head if the pounder's hands slipped. But the couple kept perfect time, the man making the earthen floor tremble with each thud of his pestle. The mortar's walls gleamed with a dark sheen; they were skin-smooth after thirty years of use, and no longer seemed made of wood.

Ryokun glanced towards the elders' room. Five or six parishioners were sitting there now; he had not noticed them come in. Mineyo was nowhere to be seen, nor was his father. Tonight was a special night—the night they made *mochi;* but why the visitors? Come to that, O-Sugi wasn't in her usual place, either. Instead of waiting to take the pounded *mochi* when it was ready and rolling it in the rice-powder on the upturned boards, as she did every year, she was busy getting teacups down from the cupboard and carrying them to the temple hall on a big tray; then she came back to fetch charcoal. Shoju had left his post at the stove to help her. A few of the parishioners put some live coals in a small porcelain brazier and carried it off to the hall.

Ryokun wanted to ask the *mochi*-woman if there was some special meeting on, but it was impossible to interrupt. She and her husband seemed to have nothing to do with the meeting, whatever it was. Ryokun waited. Already they had filled and emptied the mortar five or six times. Soon it would be time for them to taste the *mochi* they were making. Everything else was ready—soybean flour, the curd made from fresh-boiled red beans, and a bowl of grated radish flavoured with soy sauce, to go with the *sake*. The first cakes to be made were the big round *kagami-mochi* that were used as temple-offerings, one for each of the images worshipped at Butsuoji—specially big ones for Amida and Shinran, and one more, not so big, for the house-shrine. Picking up lumps of *mochi* from the mortar, the woman dropped them on the upturned cupboard doors and rolled them with both hands in the rice-flour, at the same time rounding them under her fingers, like a child playing with clay. One after another the finished cakes left her skilled fingers, just firm enough to retain the prescribed mirror-like shape she had given them. Her husband had pounded the *mochi* so well, the lumps looked smooth and glossy as she took them from the mortar. *Mochi* pounded so thoroughly may have a few wrinkles on the outside, simply because it is so glutinous; but it won't crack after hardening, no matter how long it is left—not like city *mochi*, which splits right through almost as soon as it's finished, spitting out hard grains of rice that were not properly pounded when the *mochi* was made.

The woman pulled a big piece of *mochi*, fresh from the mortar, into two halves. Dipping her hands alternately into a wooden water-bucket—the *mochi* was still hot enough to scald—she pinched smaller pieces off the big one, dropping them into the bean-curd, the soybean flour, and the bowl of grated radish. The *mochi* expanded into soft, shapeless lumps in the curd, but the radish made it shrink. Even *mochi* feels the sharp taste of our giant white radish.

'There now, Ryokun—you've waited long enough! Eat as much as you can.' She gave him a piece of *mochi* rolled in soybean flour. Ryokun could hardly wait. He ate up all the *mochi* on the plate, then started on a bowl of curd with lumps of *mochi* floating in it. A moment later he looked round in the direction of the elders' room, meaning to call his grandmother; but there was no one there now. The whole house was quiet, he realised suddenly. Silence, the massive silence that filled the big house day in, day out had returned. He had been too busy eating to notice it before. The *mochi*-pounders had each finished a single small bowl of *mochi* and radish, but had no appetite for more; they sat smoking in silence. O-Sugi had begun to eat a bowl of curd. This year, however, even she seemed to be less interested than usual in the *mochi*-making. Perhaps she too was wondering about the meeting of parishioners in the temple hall.

'The old lady likes the radish best, doesn't she?' said the woman to her husband.

'Mm,' was his only reply. He did not trouble himself with wondering why Mineyo had left the elders' room.

'O-Sugi! Don't forget to keep some for Father Soshu.'

'He likes them in soybean flour. The flavour doesn't keep, though, if you don't eat them right after the pounding.'

'Eat up, Shoju! There's lots more yet.'

But like O-Sugi, Shoju could not feel the usual excitement of the *mochi* season. Something else was on his mind. It was odd, too, that Mineyo had not stayed till the *mochi* was ready . . . O-Sugi took two plates of *mochi* and radish to Mineyo's room, and found her sitting by a portable footwarmer. She too seemed uneasy about what was going on in the hall.

The doors of the hall, and of the shrine inside, had been shut, and the lights switched on. Some forty parishioners had come for the meeting. All of them had entered the hall from the house, when Ryokun was still too intent on the *mochi*-pounding to notice their arrival. Soshu sat in the middle of the hall, facing them. Yet he seemed of little significance tonight; the real centre of attention was the figure at his side—Mosuke Yamaji. Yamaji's elder brother was there, as were Yosuke Tachi and Mr Hoshina, Tanemi's father. All the elders had come; but there was not a single woman present. Mr Kashimura, the most senior of all the members of the Butsuoji congregation, had been unable to attend in person, but had sent his secretary. Outside the great gate, Yamaji's car stood waiting.

Soshu sat in silence with his eyes lowered, scarcely seeming to breathe.

'I am the official representative of Butsuoji congregation, for the time being, anyway, and since I was appointed I've never allowed myself to forget the duty this lays upon me. I've been concerned for a long time now that Butsuoji owns so little in the way of property. What property, after all, does our temple possess that's worth the name?' Yamaji was saying. There was an undertone of conscious power in his manner which even those sitting at the back could catch, though he did not raise his voice. His brother listened in silence, with bent head. Men change, it seems, according to the environment life brings them. Mosuke Yamaji's upbringing in a farming household had been exactly the same as that of his brother. Yet now everything about him was different, down to the colour of his skin and the gloss on his hair; everything about him pointed to the class he now belonged to, the comfort in which he lived. There was an aggressive confidence in the way he sat, as though he felt it would be child's play to drive the forty men before him in any way he wanted without himself ever having to yield a step. Through the closed doors, incessantly, came the dull, regular thud of the *mochi*-pounding in the house kitchen.

'There's the bit of land on the hill that's used for the cemetery, that's all. What I'm after when I talk about property is that that land, such as it is, should be put to use, made to earn something. There's no question of selling any of the land in the temple compound, of course. We've got nothing but that land on the hill, which at the moment is not much better than nothing at all. I want our temple to own something, even if it's not much. That's my only wish.'

No one spoke.

'The Asano Chemical Works have been looking for some land near Tan'ami, as it happens. A chance in a thousand, obviously. So I had a word with the president of the company. And the next thing is, I'm had up in front of you tonight for exceeding my authority.' He looked round deliberately at his audience—at all but Soshu, whom he ignored completely. 'But what chance do you suppose there is of taking advantage of an opportunity like this if I have to stop and consult the parishioners at every step? Especially when it's about something ticklish like a cemetery—there'd be all kinds of sentimental red herrings brought up, and nobody would ever get anywhere. That's as plain as daylight, surely. I've had a clear conscience all along—thought only of what was good for Butsuoji, and nothing else. Once start bringing sentiment into business, and as often as not you end up by losing even what you had to start with.'

'They say the price of land round Shoko Hill has gone up suddenly. Don't know if it's true or not—' said a voice from the back, addressing nobody in particular.

'I heard that, too.'

'There's talk of a bus service out there starting soon, and of widening the road.'

'Shoko Hill belongs to Mr Yamaji, doesn't it?' said someone.

'It belongs to me,' replied Yamaji, not in the least put out.

'Some say that's to be the site for a new communal cemetery for the whole town. Any truth in that?'

'Don't know anything about it.'

'I heard it was you that was leading the campaign for a communal cemetery, Mr Yamaji,' said another.

'I don't know anything about it, I tell you. But a communal cemetery is quite a possibility, I suppose. In Nagano City they had to take over some of the cemetery land when the roads were widened. There was nowhere to put the gravestones that had to be dug up, so the town started a communal cemetery. It's no good wailing about hereditary graves when proper roads have to be built.'

'We are not absolutely against selling the land on the hill.' The voice, speaking with a calm deliberation that checked the questioners around him, was that of Yosuke Tachi. Starting, Yamaji turned towards him. Tachi was the one man out of the forty who he knew could give him trouble. 'What disturbs us is that we had to hear the story from town gossip, when we should have had a proper report from you. The way you went about it was mistaken—that's what we say.'

Soshu watched Tachi apprehensively. He had been prepared for some kind of exchange between the two—but not for Tachi to call Yamaji's conduct 'mistaken' to his face, and in public. It wasn't so surprising, though, when you remembered the sort of person Tachi was.

Yamaji smiled sardonically. 'It's a hard job being parishioners' representative. You'd have done the same, Mr Tachi, if you'd been in my position. As a matter of fact, speaking frankly, I never expected unanimous support. If you go on trying to get unanimity, it's only talk, talk, talk and never any clear-cut decision. In a way, I despise unanimity—that's one lesson experience has taught me. Maybe I have exceeded my authority; but one day Butsuoji people will be glad I did—when they see the advantages it'll bring. You can't expect people who can't see in front of their noses to appreciate results in advance. A man who can look ahead has to be ready to act, and act quickly, without worrying too much about what's within his authority and what's not. In business or anywhere else, the rule's the same—if you want to get anything done, you can't hang about waiting till every single person concerned says yes. One man's got to make the decision.'

Tachi shook his head slowly. 'The parishioners object to what you've done because they can read your secret. If this 'decision' of yours is for the good of our temple—well, that's fine. No arguments about that. But your private interests are mixed up with this cemetery business. All of us can see that, and that's what I mean when I say you acted unwisely.'

'Private interests, indeed! That's a vulgar insinuation, Mr Tachi.'

'If you like—but the fact that all of us who've come here tonight believe it makes it a perfectly legitimate opinion. It won't do to ignore it.'

'If my personal interest is involved, it's because my profession makes something of the kind inevitable. The Asano Works made me some small acknowledgement, of course, in return for my letting them know that something might be done about the land—it's the custom in business, and there's nothing unnatural about it.'

'It sounds a bit like the old fanatical patriotism, but when it comes to serving our temple, we believe in "selfless service"—'

'Our positions are different.'

'That's exactly the attitude we object to. You should have brought the whole matter before the parishioners before taking any action—even if they were likely to bring up the sentimental arguments you spoke of, and you couldn't get a unanimous vote. That's the right way to go about it, and that's what we wanted you to do.'

'I am the parishioners' representative.'

'That's just it—you are the parishioners' *representative*: a representative can't ignore the people he represents.'

'Father Soshu approves.'

Soshu swallowed, his breath cold. 'I'm not opposed to what you have done. It will be an excellent thing for Butsuoji to have some solid financial resources, and in any case there will be several special expenses we shall have to meet soon for which we shall need ready money. But what will happen to the gravestones when the land is sold?'

'They'll have to be moved as quickly as possible.'

'Where to? The temple cemetery is full, you know.'

'I'm negotiating with the authorities for a suitable place.'

'Is it to be the land at the bottom of Shoko Hill? Who will pay for the removal?'

'If they decide on a communal cemetery, the town will make a grant.'

'That's all right, then—so long as the gravestones aren't left high and dry,' said Tachi calmly, but evidently with no intention of letting Yamaji escape so easily. 'Everybody says it's you that's behind the plan for the communal cemetery. With you being the president of a securities company, it must be easy for you to see what will happen—the town is bound to carry out your proposal sooner or later. You're the one who can see ahead.'

'I'm a busy man, Tachi—I haven't time to listen to compliments,' replied Yamaji, fidgeting suddenly as if he were really in a hurry.

'That's not all there is to be said, though. We haven't got anywhere yet.'

'You approve what I've done—now what more do you want?'

'It wasn't just to hear about your plans again that we asked a busy man like you to come here specially tonight. You are a parishioner of Butsuoji, and so are we. As parishioners, we are equal. But you say you've done this, and you've done that, and the rest of us must be properly grateful and accept your actions without any murmuring. This kind of talk makes us object all the more. You want to get a communal cemetery laid out at Shoko Hill, as one of your business deals. All right. But the rest of us don't work for your company, you know.'

'Apparently you object to my being the parishioners' representative.'

'Certainly not. Next to Mr Kashimura, you're the most important and valued member of the Butsuoji congregation.'

'I run a securities company. It's true I can't lift a finger without my interests being affected one way or the other; but my business being what it is, that's inevitable—as I think everybody here realises.'

'Very well then—you can't object to our asking a few more questions. How much have you sold the land on the hill for? We'd like to see the figures, all of us—Father Soshu's no more than a child in matters like this. The figures, in black and white, not just a vague statement—and not the figures the sale was registered for, either—including the fee the Asano Company paid you personally. Then we want to know how much you'll make if they do build a new cemetery at Shoko Hill. You've made up your mind to get our cemetery moved to Shoko Hill, I daresay, so that the Council will be as good as forced to choose that site and nowhere else for the communal cemetery. But you'll have to show us a guarantee that the removal expenses will be met—'

'I won't have anyone meddling in my business! I haven't done anything wrong, and I'm not doing anything wrong now.'

'Business, you said?' Tachi leaned towards Yamaji, looking him in the face. 'That's what we don't like, you see. It's not only ourselves; the dead will suffer too if the cemetery is at the mercy of one man's business ambitions. We wanted to hear some kind of explanation from you before anything was decided—what it was you were planning, how much Butsuoji would stand to gain by the sale, and so on. Or failing that, at least a word of apology for having acted on your own.'

Yamaji glanced at Tachi, but did not answer immediately. The silence continued. For a moment Yamaji's face worked furiously, then broke into a bitter smile.

'I was a farmer's son. Now I'm a company president. I've come that far because I've had the strength and the drive to get on. You all knew me as a farmer's boy, and you don't like the farm boy turning into a business man, I can see. That's the trouble. If that's how you all feel, I shall have nothing more to do with Butsuoji from now on.'

A hush fell over the hall, Soshu was stupefied Those last words of Yamaji were what he had feared. He felt crushed, more bitterly aware than ever before of his own helplessness. A priest, charged with the spiritual care of his parishioners—one confrontation with material reality, and his priesthood was as nothing. What had he given Yamaji in all the years he had known? Not one particle of faith, it was obvious. Otherwise how could he talk so easily about leaving Butsuoji, when his family had belonged to the temple for generations? There was nothing he, Soshu, could do to stop him; for what authority did he have to rebuke him for the threat his words implied? The 'religious' authority, which his priesthood conferred on him, was a mockery: even the law, with its declaration of the freedom of religion, might be said to be on Yamaji's side.

The parishioners' reactions were confused. Evidently they had expected Yamaji to play this last trump card. Yamaji had made all his money himself, he was an upstart, to put it bluntly, whom they all remembered as a boy on his father's farm, and it was true they vaguely resented his climbing to his present position; but these were personal feelings, not to be expressed in public. If Yamaji's sudden counter-attack was not necessarily a success, neither was it altogether without effect. He had put his finger on something they all shared: a predisposition, conscious or otherwise, to suspect his motives in everything he did. To Yamaji himself, with his brazen readiness to point in open conversation to other people's half-conscious, buried feelings, such insinuation was natural.

'It's an old trick for people of your class, boy—this trying to make position and money talk. But it's the priest of Butsuoji you're bullying now—not your company union!' The skin on Tachi's lean cheeks twitched suddenly as he called Yamaji 'boy'. He had taken on Yamaji alone. Yamaji glowered at him savagely, forgetting his elder brother was present.

'I've told you frankly what I feel. I have freedom too, you know—religion is an individual matter; the law takes care of that. If I make up my mind, there's nobody on earth can interfere.' In answer to Tachi's directness, Yamaji's language grew more abrupt. 'Up till now, as parishioners' representative, I've done what I could for the good of Butsuoji. I've paid the contributions the elders saw fit to assess me for without a murmur. I've done more than my duty—and what has Butsuoji ever given me in return?'

Soshu bent his head. They were still pounding *mochi* in the house; he could hear the sad, monotonous thud of the pestle. It exasperated as well as saddened him, that peaceful, regular sound that seemed deliberately to ignore this crisis whose outcome could mean so much to Butsuoji. The parishioners huddled together, those nearest the brazier holding their hands over the burning charcoal, others sticking them in their trouser-pockets or in the folds of their kimono. The hall was icy: the floor was raised high above the ground, and the cold December air seeped up through the boarding and mats.

'It is an honour to be chosen parishioners' representative.' Tachi spoke calmly, with an undertone of confidence, quietly ignoring the wealth and social position of his opponent. The rest of the parishioners at the meeting were delighted at his firmness—till they remembered with embarrassment that he was a Communist, which complicated their feelings.

'Honour, indeed! A dog can have the job for all I care!'

'You'll have to take that back—a slip of the tongue, no doubt,' said Tachi, a faint smile on his lips. 'That's not the kind of expression a company president should use. The parishioners' representatives aren't appointed by the priest, but by the unanimous vote of the two hundred households that make up the congregation. And you're not the only representative: Mr Kashimura was elected to the same post—that you'd like a dog to have . . . You've insulted him, and all two hundred of us. If you dislike being representative so much, you're entitled to your feelings, but there's no call to foist your vulgarity on the rest of us. A temple depends for its existence on the faith of all its members. A man doesn't give a few hundred thousand yen to a temple in order to get so much back in return. You're demanding special treatment because of the contributions you've made to Butsuoji—you want us to put up a monument in your honour, I suppose!'

Yamaji's fat, fleshy face turned crimson. Clenching his fists, he rapped his knees, as if what he had heard were more than he could bear; anger flooded up in his throat, but could find no words. Even he realised that he couldn't help himself, that he was showing them his ugliest side. This was nothing like the Mosuke Yamaji most people knew; but in front of these men who had known him since he was a child, the mask fell away, and they saw again the boy in his teens, clever, unruly, determined. Yamaji cursed himself, knowing the stupidity of offending them. It had been a mistake to try and establish his ascendancy over the parishioners as a group, browbeating them as he had done with the timid Soshu.

Soshu looked up and faced the meeting. 'I am largely to blame for what has happened, and I wish to apologize to you all now. I should have gone to Mr Yamaji for confirmation the moment the rumours about the sale of the land started.' During the exchanges between Yamaji and Tachi the parishioners had sat with bent heads, as if by agreement. They all looked up as Soshu spoke. 'It was only because I failed in my duty that the elders had to ask me to call this meeting. I myself should have summoned a meeting earlier. I have learnt tonight how concerned you all are for the good of our temple—it has been a wonderful and humbling experience. Butsuoji can trace its history back through twenty generations; and I apologize humbly to you and to your ancestors for my part in allowing this difference to appear among us.'

The moment he finished Yamaji spoke again. 'Father Soshu approves of what I've done. He understands what I was really trying to do for the temple,' he said with an air of finality, as if there was now no more to be said. The great hall was silent once more.

'I am here as Mr Kashimura's representative,' began Kashimura's secretary suddenly. 'If this affair were to be talked about it might start all kinds of rumours about what goes on at Butsuoji. From what we've heard tonight, I understand nobody objects to the actual sale of the cemetery land to the Asano Chemical Works; and in any case it would be too much to ask Mr Yamaji to lay himself open to a charge of breach of contract by cancelling the sale. Father Soshu seems to be of the same opinion. I would like to propose, therefore, that as parishioners we acknowledge with gratitude Mr Yamaji's efforts on behalf of our temple. . .'

It would be foolish to let the quarrel develop. A peacemaker had appeared, and the worst seemed to be over. No one was against the sale of the land as such—it did not mean a major upheaval of the kind that occurs when people's homes have to be demolished to make way for longer runways at an aerodrome, or something of that kind. And the idea of a communal cemetery was not new; most people realised that something of the sort was necessary. A feeling of relief spread among the parishioners.

'If no one disagrees, then . . .?' said Kashimura's secretary, straightening up and looking round the meeting. Seeing no dissenting face, he turned to Soshu, bending his head slightly as a warning hint. 'We would like to thank everybody for sparing time to come this evening, when we are all so busy preparing for the New Year. I now propose that the meeting should accept the report Mr Yamaji has given us with regard to the sale of the cemetery land on the hill.'

Soshu looked at the faces round him. No one spoke; there was no clear knowing whether they were for or against the proposal. But such was the custom at these meetings: silence was taken for approval. Raising himself on his knees, Tachi looked round at his fellow-parishioners.

'No objection, anyone?' After a final check, Kashimura's secretary turned once again to Soshu. 'The proposal is carried, then.'

Soshu bowed slowly, as if exhausted; and remained with his head bent and his hands on the mat before him. He was deeply moved. Times have changed, he thought. In the old days no one would have dreamed of challenging the word of a parishioners' representative. But Yosuke Tachi, by his manner and the words he used—and he was only voicing what they all felt deep down, though they were afraid to speak—had completely disregarded the aura of absolute, feudal authority that still clung to the office.

Mosuke Yamaji rose. Soshu followed suit unconsciously, like a leaf rising in a sudden breath of wind. Yamaji left the hall and walked along the corridor to the door of the house, ignoring Soshu, who came to see him out.

'I'm very sorry for what's happened, Mr Yamaji . . .' said Soshu in a low voice as Yamaji was sitting with his back to him, putting on his shoes.

'I know now what the Butsuoji people think of me—so the evening wasn't entirely wasted,' replied Yamaji.

So he was not prepared to forgive them. . .

'I do hope you will continue as parishioners' representative—'

'I'll have to think it over.'

'But Mr Yamaji—'

'About Mrs Komiyama, by the way', said Yamaji, changing the

subject abruptly. 'The contribution she's been put down for is too much. She's not in business, you know.'

Soshu faltered, in a momentary panic at the mention of Tomoko's name. He wondered if his face had given him away; but fortunately the porch was only dimly lit.

'The elders decide on the contributions. . . They go by the amount of local tax each household pays, I believe.'

'From the way she lives, it looks as if she was well enough off, I daresay. They mustn't judge by appearances, though, or there'll be trouble.'

Without enlarging on his warning, Yamaji left the house and began to walk across the compound to the gate.

Hate him! Soshu told himself; he deserves it . . . But his fear left no room for hate. He watched Yamaji strut past the temple hall. A moment later headlights lit up the road outside the gate. A car door slammed—as if in his face, it seemed to Soshu.

By now the other parishioners were making their way to the porch. Soshu looked for Kashimura's secretary, and bowed him out respectfully. Not that he was at all abrupt in his manner towards the ordinary members of the congregation; but inevitably the priest's attitude towards their most important representative was different—a more ingratiating politeness. The elders stayed behind to carry the brazier, the charcoal-box, and the tea things from the hall back to the house. The *mochi*-pounding had finished. Several plates of *kagami-mochi* had been set out as offerings in the alcove of the elders' room. When Soshu came to thank the elders, he found Tachi sitting at the brazier.

'The snake's not scotched yet,' began Tachi at once, knowing exactly what Soshu was thinking. Soshu sat down. Among his feelings was regret at the way Tachi had provoked Yamaji: there had been no need to go that far. 'Still, he did talk about leaving Butsuoji altogether, as well as giving up the job of representative.'

'If he does leave us, I don't think he'll be able to join any other temple of our sect. All our temples in Tan'ami have an agreement not to accept new parishioners in cases like this.'

'Religion doesn't mean anything to him, anyway.'

'His family have belonged to Butsuoji for so long—'

'He won't think twice about changing his temple, any more than he would about changing an old name-plate on his front gate. I've found out what he's really after.'

Yamaji's brother had gone home. Two or three of the elders stayed on for no apparent purpose, sipping the tea O-Sugi had brought.

'A Nichiren priest has been visiting Yamaji's house lately.'

Soshu was shocked; he had not known this.

'The Nichiren people are on to a good thing nowadays, with their talk about getting rich by prayer and all the rest of it. They've been trying for some time to get hold of Yamaji.'

'Are you sure of that?' The news was another blow for Soshu; one more proof of his own ineffectiveness. He clenched his fingers. The elders seemed surprised, too.

'He must have decided in advance to change to Nichiren if he couldn't get his way over the cemetery—that's why he was so high and mighty tonight; he was asking for trouble, as an excuse to quit Butsuoji. Or even if he hadn't thought that far, I'm sure he'd at least made up his mind not to give way. He can't leave without finding some excuse, if he's got any conscience at all—as I suppose he has, if he's human.'

'Religion is free. There's nothing we can say if he chooses to join the Nichiren Sect.'

'In the cities the "new" religions you read about have been bringing in converts by the thousand since the war. Some of them cool off after a year or two, maybe, but they're fanatical enough while the mood lasts, and that's what gives these religions their strength—compared with them, old sects like ours are as weak as floating duckweed. There's no law against changing one's religion, and the agreement among temples of one sect can't punish a man if he runs after another. If someone says he prefers Nichiren to Shinran, or the founders of the new religions to the saints who lived seven or eight hundred years back, that's his affair. It's going to get harder and harder to keep these old temples going.'

'There's that side of it, of course; but still. . .'

'Pure Land Buddhism could win converts once because of its big temples and preaching orders. But not nowadays. That's the tragedy of temple Buddhism.'

'There's been a lot of support for a real lay Buddhism recently. St Shinran decided he couldn't depend on temples for his religion, after all, and put his faith in the lay believer till the end of his life, in spite of his priest's robe.'

'Anyway, if Yamaji does change his religion, it'll only be to spite Butsuoji— faith will have nothing to do with it. You're bound to get a black sheep now and then in a temple community, even a small one like ours. The trouble is, he dominates the whole place. He's so puffed up with pride in himself and his money, he's afraid of nothing—nothing. . . He's drunk with self-confidence. All that confidence of his would vanish the moment he met someone stronger than himself—but he doesn't know that. . .'

After Tachi and the elders had gone home, the old priest locked the doors. Soshu stood for a moment at the entrance to the kitchen.

'Goodnight, Father.'

'It's late, Shoju—you'd better sleep here tonight.'

The old priest walked noiselessly across the earthen floor. Though the *mochi*-pounding had long since finished, an air of excitement lingered still in the kitchen. He had not eaten any *mochi* while it was freshly-made, Soshu remembered. He caught the faint smell of pliant, sticky rice.

'Will you have some *mochi,* Father?' O-Sugi asked. It's gone rather hard by now, though.'

'Not now, thanks. Ryokun didn't stint himself, I suppose? He was looking forward to the *mochi*-making all day.'

'He ate plenty, radish and all.'

'You'd better go to bed now, O-Sugi. You've worked hard tonight.'

When Soshu went back to the living-room Mineyo was sitting with her elbows on the table, waiting for him.

'You can't say I didn't warn you. I've never liked Yosuke Tachi; and now he's doing his best to drive away the most important parishioner we have. Mr Yamaji is going over to Nichiren.'

'You were listening?'

'It's the first time there's been anything like this since I came to Butsuoji. How can you face our ancestors after this? It's bound to get about before long, and then we'll have people all over Tan'ami laughing at us for being so stupid!'

It was no use trying to explain to her that the real problem was on another, deeper level altogether. 'As weak as floating duckweed' —Soshu still felt the impact of Tachi's words. If the new religions gained ground in Tan'ami, there would be other Yamajis. How could he prevent it? A wall of despair rose before him.

'The way Tachi spoke to Yamaji was disgusting—enough to make anybody furious. I don't know how many times I have told you not to let him meddle in temple affairs! If we can get Yamaji back, we can just as well do without half of the rest of the congregation. The Kashimura family has always provided the senior representative, but that's only tradition—they don't give much to Butsuoji. Empty status, that's all. It's natural the Nichiren priests should have their eye on Mr Yamaji. They'll be building a big new temple with his money one of these days—and we shall be looking on, sucking our thumbs. . . It'll be your fault. Yamaji's so fond of showing off, he's quite capable of letting them do it.'

Soshu saw himself as a priest without a temple, wandering up and down the country with Ryokun at his side; and sadness rose in his throat. Not for himself; but Ryokun—could he take the responsibility of causing such an unheaval in the boy's life? He closed his eyes. The face opposite glared at him, burning with hate and unquenchable passion. A wave of sorrow and despair sank through his body, merging with the hopelessness of his longing for Tomoko.—Yamaji will tell her to resign from the Butsuoji congregation, too. And if she doesn't do as he says, he'll make it impossible for her to live—

Soshu rose.

'Where are you going?'

Soshu wanted solitude. He walked along the corridor towards the temple hall.

28

The first morning of the New Year began without a speck of cloud, as if in celebration of the auspicious day. Yet there was something oppressive about the intense, unvarying blue of a child's painting; without light or shade, like the visionary sky of a child's painting; a few drifting clouds would have made such brilliance more welcome. A fresh wind must have been blowing high up, for the air was dry and bitterly cold. Used as he was to going about the temple barefoot even in winter, the soles of Soshu's feet went numb when he walked on the wooden floor of the sanctuary; it was like walking on blocks of ice. Today he had been sitting in the hall since early morning. It was the custom on the morning of New Year's Day for the parishioners to come and pay their respects to the priest of their temple immediately after calling at their local Shinto shrine. Some would combine their New Year greetings to Soshu with a visit to their family graves. Butsuoji was decorated for the occasion, with yellow curtains hanging above the steps leading into the hall and the compound swept clean. The trees between the hall and the great gate threw faint shadows in the morning light.

Some parishioners came to worship while it was still dark. The hall kept its solemn atmosphere, in spite of the decorations. On the east side stood a table, borrowed from Soshu's study in the house, with the huge brazier from the elders' room, looking insignificant now in the great expanse of the hall. Teacups were laid on the table. Soshu had been sitting there since just after eight.

Even the floor mats were cold. The heat from the brazier was powerless to dispel the chill wintry air that floated through the hall; nor was there any warmth in the bright light of the morning sun, shining through the paper sections of the sliding doors on the east side. Soshu looked at the sanctuary. *Kagami-mochi* offerings been placed before each shrine, and tapers lit. From its narrow recess, Shinran's statue gazed on the restless hearts of men.

Soshu's thoughts went back to the tolling of the temple bell the previous evening. Always, on the last day of the old year, Shoju struck the great bell in the compound a hundred and eight times. Ryokun had fallen asleep before the bell-ringing began, as he did every year. Originally the bell had been tolled both morning and evening, breaking the long winter night with its solemn call to wakefulness and prayer. In Buddhist tradition, the number 108 represents divisions of time—the 12 months, 24 seasons and 72 periods of the Buddhist year; but it has strong associations of a more strictly religious kind, too—the 108 beads of a rosary, for example, or the 108 passions which lead the mind astray. Each of the six roots of perception in man—eye, ear, nose, tongue, body, and discriminating intellect—when confronted with one of the six 'ignoble dusts' of the world—colour, sound, smell, taste, physical contact, and phenomena—may react in any one of six ways: and the thirty-six primary passions thus aroused may be encountered in any of the three worlds of past, present and future, giving a total of one hundred and eight. No man can live without becoming enmeshed in one at least of these passions; that is why man himself is called 'the slave of passion'.

But Soshu's mind did not dwell on this classification of the manifold varieties of human weakness. Listening to the sombre, monotonous note of the bell as the old priest struck it with the great wooden clapper, he was thinking of the crisis facing Butsuoji. For a temple to lose a parishioner of Yamaji's standing to another sect was an extraordinary humiliation, a disgrace that did not happen once in generations. And there was the scandal within the temple walls. . . the decision closing in upon him. . . That decision rested with him alone—whose heart and mind were lost to one of his own congregation. . . Troubles pressed about him. Again and again the great bell urged him to act, as if by its patient muffled tolling it would purge his tortured mind of sin. Yet no decision came, and he had spent the night in agony.

One of the big paper doors slid back, and a parishioner entered the hall. After kneeling in worship before the statue of Amida in the sanctuary he came to Soshu.

'New Year Greetings, Father!'

'Greetings!'

Soshu gave him tea. Some of the parishioners would slip money into the offertory chest when they had finished worshipping; others brought their contributions wrapped in paper, and would leave them behind on the tatami when they got up to go—to be collected by the old priest at the end of the day, for Soshu himself did not touch these offerings. Fifty or sixty parishioners paid this New Year visit to the temple every year. On this one day the farmers among them wore formal kimono, ill-fitting and evidently borrowed; some with cloaks tied high across the chest, like children, some with their kimono carelessly left open at the bottom. Sometimes their sinewy, chapped old arms, smudged here and there with blood, would make a rasping noise as they chafed against the opening of the kimono sleeve. When any of the elders came, they would talk—so interminably that the sight of Soshu and an elder in conversation was enough to send some of the other visitors hurrying home the moment they had finished their worship.

Suddenly the hall was alive with colour. While Soshu was talking to two elders, Mrs Mimori came up the steps with three of her geisha. Entering the hall, they took off their overcoats, their kimonos making a still more dazzling display, and walked towards the sanctuary. Mrs Mimori herself had on a black ceremonial kimono patterned with her family crest, and one of the geisha wore a design of pine-trees appropriate to her age; but the other two girls were much younger, and their kimonos were gay and brightly-coloured, with long, full sleeves. The four of them knelt in a row, in the proper reverent posture, and worshipped. Soshu smiled slightly as he watched them.

A temple, he was thinking, should be a place where people like that can come and go and feel at home. Life as well as death is a temple's business. He imagined one of the young geisha confessing to him in front of the portrait of Shinran, himself in his black canonicals, with the white under-robe showing immaculate at his neck, fingering his rosary as he listened to her pouring out her troubles. He would not need to answer her questions; if he only listened, she would go away healed. . . What made geisha and others like them think of temples as places apart, irrelevant to their lives? The buildings, perhaps? Soshu thought of the many temples that were still using the temporary premises—built in the style of ordinary houses—put up when their old buildings had been destroyed in the bombing. Who could say whether Butsuoji was more fortunate in having survived? If religion was shut up in a temple, it was that much more difficult to communicate to ordinary men and women; while the absence of an imposing, traditional building compelled Buddhism to go out among the people, to become a lay religion—a religion which would make it natural for men and women to meet in fellowship and talk over their spiritual problems in a house no different from any other. Was not this the religion that Shinran had lived?

Mrs Mimori came and sat in front of the big table, leaving the three geisha still kneeling before the sanctuary.

'Greetings, Father!'

'Greetings!'

Next she bowed towards the elders, exchanging New Year greetings with them. In her formal kimono the mistress of the Mutsumi-ya looked three or four years younger, and there was even an indefinable air of piety about her today; but for this also, no doubt, her ceremonial dress was accountable—it made the girls stare at her now and then as if she were a stranger they had never seen before. The two younger ones were gazing at the sanctuary, enjoying the novelty. Mrs Mimori always brought some of her geisha to Butsuoji on New Year's day, but different girls came each year; the older ones hated being escorted to the temple by their mistress, while the younger ones enjoyed it, as a kind of sight-seeing excursion. Mrs Mimori took tea at the table with Soshu, the girls from a separate tray. The scent of make-up floated across the hall. The elders stayed with their arms resting on the edge of the brazier, taking no particular notice of the geisha party.

'I hope you'll be so kind as to go on teaching me this year, Father,' said Mrs Mimori.

'I'm afraid it may be more of an inconvenience to you than anything else, since I can't ever promise a definite day.'

The elders looked from Soshu to Mrs Mimori.

'Any time will be convenient—whenever you are free, Father. If I should happen to be out, which is not very likely, one of the girls will let me know, and I'll come home at once.'

'Really I don't think there's anything more I can teach you—'

'Nonsense, Father! I need a lot more practice if I'm to perform in public.'

Mrs Mimori and her geisha left the hall, walked down the steps and put on their clogs.

'*Ka-san*!' One of the girls who had walked on ahead was calling back to her mistress. To Soshu, her voice embodied, in its shrill and slightly raucous tone, the atmosphere of the Mutsumi-ya.

'What would you be teaching her, Father?'

'Tea-ceremony. She has a magnificent set of tea-things that once belonged to Shinzan Ito. She says it's better to use them for practice than shut them up in a cupboard as antiques. One or two of the bowls are worth a million and a half yen.'

'A million and a half!' echoed the elder; the sum was too big for him to grasp.

Gradually other parishioners began to arrive. Some worshipped after visiting their family graves. Some had arranged beforehand to meet at Butsuoji, and came in groups of three or four. As members of the congregation, they all knew each other and the association with Butsuoji gave them a deeper sense of friendly community than that which derived from the mere fact of their being fellow-citizens of the same not very large town. Soshu was kept busy serving tea. Dishcloth in one hand, he washed and dried each cup as it was emptied and used it again.

Footsteps sounded from the house corridor.

'Daddy—lunch!' It was Ryokun. Soshu was talking to Mrs Hoshina and her daughter; he had not noticed it was time to eat. Still standing, Ryokun bowed awkwardly to Mrs Hoshina.

'How big you've grown, Ryokun!'

'He's got his father's eyes exactly, hasn't he, mother?'

Destiny urging him to a decision. . . ? If he said the word, it was as likely as not this girl would become his second wife. Tachi could not have been making all that up. Tanemi kept looking at Ryokun, with no noticeable reaction on the boy's part—to him she was just another woman, who happened to be rather fat.

If he willed it, this big, fair girl would become a mother to Ryokun. If he willed it, both their lives would be changed for ever—whether for better or worse, he could not know. They faced each other across the table—strangers; a relationship that a single instant of decision would irrevocably transform. Soshu shrank back, afraid.

This was the first time Tanemi had visited Butsuoji on New Year's day. Usually one or other of her parents represented the family. She herself had wanted to come, no doubt; but a sense of guilt and unworthiness was all she aroused in Soshu, and he made no attempt to speak to her. Her beauty was that of perfect health. Half the tainted air of Butsuoji would be dispelled by the mere presence of such radiance. . . Soshu watched the floor mats give under her feet as mother and daughter walked out. This was partly because the mats were old and had lost their springiness; but still the sight gave Soshu a curious pleasure.

After a while the procession of New Year visitors ended, abandoning the great hall once more to its customary silence. Soshu sat on, expectant. Last night he had recalled with painful vividness Tomoko's promise that she would come to greet him at the temple on New Year's day. Fortunately, the elders had all gone home, though even if Tomoko did come they would not be able to talk freely, for fear of the watchful eyes in the house. Soshu longed to meet her, to see and feel her presence. Someone was climbing the steps outside . . . he listened, holding his breath. A paper door slid back, a figure entered noiselessly, evidently under the impression that there was nobody in the hall. It was the widow of the farmer who had died in October, a peasant woman of forty-seven. She had never come to Butsuoji on New Year's day before.

Noticing Soshu, she stopped abruptly. Soshu understood.

'Please feel free to worship,' he said quietly.

Shyly, the woman walked to the centre of the hall and knelt. She would feel more at ease if he left her alone, Soshu thought. With her parents-in-law and her own big family to look after, she would have no leisure to remember her dead husband. Probably it had been difficult enough to find time even for this New Year visit to his grave. She must have been to the cemetery already, and would want to be alone for a while. The solitude of the temple hall would give her a chance to recall the dead, to absorb in the quietness the feeling that now, at least, she could speak to him again. . . She was wearing an ordinary, workaday kimono, Soshu noticed.

Telling her again to stay as long as she wished, he left the hall. Her hands joined in worship, the widow bowed towards the sanctuary and began to recite the *nenbutsu*. With eyes closed, hands drawn in to her breast, her whole body motionless, she gave herself to prayer; as if now for the first time she could be alone with her grief, released from the round of long hard days that scarcely left time even for sleep, free at last to call upon her husband's spirit. Amida and Shinran gazed down upon her, powerless to lighten the lonely woman's burden. Perhaps in her heart she was complaining to him for leaving her so soon, telling of the bitterness of her days; or merely crying out in wordless misery at responsibilities that were too heavy for her to bear. Calmly, Amida and Shinran looked down upon her heart.

When Soshu returned, she was still kneeling, her hands on her breast. Again he left her, this time on tiptoe.

The second time he re-entered the hall, it was empty. She must have gone as she had come, noiselessly opening and shutting the big sliding door. Soshu took his place at the table once again. It was well into the afternoon now; the hall filled with sunshine, filtering through the white paper of the doors and lighting up the polished surfaces of the pillars, shrine and ornaments. The tiny flame of the oil lamp was hardly visible, no longer a flame but a fleck of red suspended motionless in the bright air. Soshu sat upright, his eyes closed. 'Sit at ease, stretch your legs, won't you, Father?' the parishioners would say when they served him some meat or fish delicacy after a period of fasting; but for him, to relax in that way was actually painful—the habit of years had made the stiff, formal posture the most comfortable of all.

A faint sound of footsteps approaching from the house—someone anxious to know what was going on in the hall? A moment later, the steps receded. Mineyo or the old priest, no doubt.

Two voices outside the hall broke the silence—a mother and her daughter. . . Soshu drew a deep breath, thankful he had waited. He wanted to get up to welcome them; but that would be to violate openly the priest-parishioner relationship. He could only sit waiting, unwillingly driving all expression from his face, until she appeared. The door opened. Tomoko glanced in his direction, then turned to close the door, as if she were hardly aware of his presence. Kneeling, she took off her coat and Shoko's, the little girl standing and looking at Soshu with no more than the usual interest she displayed when he visited the house in Kiyota-cho. The coats neatly folded, Tomoko took Shoko by the hand and led her up to the sanctuary. Mother and daughter knelt before Amida. Imitating her mother, Shoko put the palms of her hands together in the attitude of worship, fingertips touching her forehead.

Tomoko was wearing a formal crested kimono, but no cloak, which made her look thinner than usual. Whatever indifference to any other presence her unhurried movements seemed to suggest, she was aware every instant of Soshu's eyes; it was her nature to act when she was alone precisely as she did before others, so that when other people were actually present her awareness of them was not reflected in any difference in her walk or gestures. Overcome by a fresh surge of emotions—fear, a thrill of joy hardly distinguishable from guilt, anticipation, delight at her sudden nearness, a strange sense that it was his own life that he saw kneeling there before him —Soshu felt he could watch her in silence no longer. His excitement mounted—and an unbearable sadness, one extreme yielding suddenly to the other. Tomoko was like an actress, deliberately prolonging the interval between two favourite scenes to tantalize her audience. . .

At last her prayers were over. Turning, she put her hand on Shoko's head.

'Let's greet Father Soshu, shall we?' She rose and faced him, then the two of them knelt in front of the table and bowed.

'Greetings for the New Year!'

Still the stage-play, thought Soshu.

'Have all the parishioners gone home?'

'They've usually gone by this time. You're the last.'

'I'm sorry, Father, if I kept you waiting. . .'

'I was waiting.' The words were lightly spoken, but carried all the meaning he intended. Tomoko's eyes grew tender.

'I called a parishioners' meeting a few nights ago. Something terrible was said—I don't know what its going to lead to, and I've wanted so much to talk to you about it.'

'I've been worried about it, too, I can't tell you how much.'

As if by a shared instinct, neither of them mentioned Yamaji by name.

'We can't discuss it here, though.'

'I don't know how I can wait till I come to your house again.'

'And even then, there's never really time to talk at Kiyota-cho.'

'There are quiet rooms in plenty here, if it wasn't like living in the middle of an enemy camp.' Soshu managed a smile.

'I know.' Then, lowering her voice., 'You must find a way for us to meet—somewhere else. . .'

Soshu remembered that he had never once left Butsuoji on business of his own. It was strange, how he had let himself become so much a part of Butsuoji that the temple was involved in everything he did. Never once had he left its gates without being able to tell those he left behind where he was going and why. Yet when he was not out visiting he had plenty of time on his hands.

'You never go out just for the pleasure of it, do you? A model priest, aren't you, Father?' she said half-mischievously. Smiling, Soshu looked at Shoko. She was still staring at the sanctuary, fascinated by the rich array of ornaments.

'You'll be going to the memorial services at Senshuji Temple?' From the ninth of January—the anniversary of the saint's death—to the fifteenth, special services in commemoration of Shinran are held every year at Senshuji in Isshinden, the head temple of the Takada branch of the True Pure Land Sect. Priests from local temples must attend for one day, partly to take part in the services and partly so that they can pay their New Year respects to the senior temple.

'Will you be?'

'I think so—Mother always used to go at New Year.'

'I'm thinking of going on the tenth.'

'The tenth? About what time?'

'I shall leave in the morning, and come back that evening.'

'But you can leave before the end of the service, can't you?'

Soshu nodded. He was startled for a moment, as well as grateful to her for making the suggestion. He was the one who had to go to Isshinden, after all, and nothing would be easier than for him to arrange a meeting there. She had shown him the way.

'I mustn't stay long—there may be peeping eyes somewhere.' But when Soshu glanced in the direction of the corridor leading to the house, he knew at once they were not being watched: he would have sensed Mineyo's presence had she been hiding there. A few moments later Tomoko called to Shoko, and the two of them went to the door. Soshu was struck by the pure white of her Japanese socks, standing out against the black of her kimono as she knelt to help Shoko on with her coat; the exquisite arrangement of every detail of her appearance, even when seen from behind, suggesting again the figure of an actress on the stage. Turning towards Soshu with a smile, she put on her own coat over her kimono. He watched her as if hypnotised, his life absorbed into hers, a stranger to the big table, the rows of teacups, the great hall itself. . . forlorn now as Tomoko and Shoko disappeared down the steps.

The thought of what lay ahead revived him. Already he was looking forward to the tenth with the excitement of a child, warming once more to the dreams that had passed him by in youth. With slow deliberate movements he poured and sipped at a cup of tea, in an attempt to calm the flurry of expectancy a man of his age should be ashamed to feel.

The old priest appeared at the entrance to the corridor.

'Shall I clear up now, if they've all gone?'

'Please.'

Soshu was about to leave the hall when something stopped him. Turning, he knelt before the sanctuary with bent head—but not to recite the scriptures. With all-discerning eyes, Amida looked upon his thoughts.

—Wasn't it a sin to take the hint she gave? Sin upon sin. . . Forgive me! I cannot forget her—it is she who gives me strength to reject the other. . . or is it cruelty, not strength? I am *using* Tomoko. . . a woman who has transgressed as I have. She has given me life. . . life that cannot last. . . Lord Amida! I, a sinner, even beneath your unchanging, all-merciful eyes, I long for the joys of this world. . .

Without thinking, he recalled a verse from the Tannisho:

> If you had free will you would have no compunction about murdering even a thousand men on being told that by doing so you could obtain rebirth in the Pure Land. But because there is no karmic necessity for you to kill even a single man, you do not commit murder. That is why you do not kill, not because you are good. On the other hand, even though you did not want to kill, you might nevertheless kill hundreds or thousands of people. . .

Karma lay behind every thought, every action in human life. Yet how deep the Karma-caused joy of his love for Tomoko! If it was karma that the woman he loved should be another man's possession, it was karma too that he could find strength to live in the knowledge of that love. 'That is why you do not kill, not because you are good. . .' It was a terrible thing for a leading member of the congregation to be driven out of Butsuoji—yet 'you might nevertheless kill hundreds and thousands of people'; and he himself was deceiving Mosuke Yamaji. . . A despairing sadness underlay even the brightest moment of joy.

Quietly, while Soshu sat before the sanctuary, O-Sugi and the old priest cleared away the table and brazier.

29

Sitting in the hall of the great Senshuji Temple at Isshinden, Tomoko was thinking of her mother. Most of the worshippers around her were of her mother's generation, as it happened, though she did not need any such reminder. Her eyes closed, listening to the chanting of the priests, she could not help reliving past visits to Senshuji. Her impression of the huge temple had been exactly the same three, five, ten years ago: the dark sanctuary, its gloom like that of a dense forest, accentuated by the surrounding daylight, with depths the eye could not penetrate; the rows of priests from subordinate temples sitting on either side of the shrine within the sanctuary, their choral chanting filling the hall; the tiny, flickering lights of countless lamps and candles. The priests, she thought, looked like unruly children crawling on the sanctuary floor, they were so dwarfed by the vastness of the hall and the exceptionally high roof. Yet the chanting of the sutras in unison was impressive, suggesting a great demonstration of the dignity and majesty of the Takada branch of the True Pure Land Sect. But what chance was there here to approach the one who mattered above all—St Shinran himself? In such a place as this, there would surely be steps to be climbed, stages to be reached, before he would have a chance to hear the voices of those who called upon him. Had not he himself always been ready to go anywhere in his black robe, his case of books upon his back, and talk in the friendliest way with anybody he met, till the end of his days? He would have hated to be shut up in a great temple like Senshuji. At Butsuoji, Tomoko felt, she could pray more truly, with a deeper sense of his presence. Her mother had insisted on paying this visit to Senshuji every year. Had she really believed her timid yearnings could reach the figure of the saint, hidden in the innermost recess of the sanctuary? Tomoko realised she could no longer share her dead mother's feeling.

Taking from her sash an old-fashioned ladies' watch her mother had given her, she glanced at it, picked up her coat and muffler, and walked between the worshippers to a side door. Her footsteps made no sound on the thick flooring of the corridor, whose ceiling was high as the roof of an ordinary house, making her feel tiny and lost. Senshuji oppressed her with its vastness.

Only half her face showing now from behind the thick muffler and the turned-up collar of her coat, Tomoko made her way across the compound towards the lecture-hall, past the little pond half-hidden in its cluster of pines, which the priestly gardeners had left to grow as nature willed. She would wait among the trees behind the hall, she decided. The rich purple silk of the old Shiozawa kimono she was wearing peeped out from under the hem of her coat.

For nearly twenty minutes she stood waiting. Most of the visitors in the compound were old people, with here and there a young priest hurrying past on temple business, and little groups of five or six worshippers being escorted to the great hall. No one paid any particular attention to the woman waiting under the trees. In some indefinable way the atmosphere of the place differed from that of Tan'ami, even from that of Tan'ami shrines and temples. An air of calm pervaded the compound—the calm of the 'peculiar' the cynic might say, long since left behind by history—like the kimono which the vast majority of visitors had chosen to wear.

Suddenly she caught sight of Soshu, standing in the hall of what looked like the temple library, though today a big sign with the words TEMPLE OFFICE hung over the doorway. Putting on his coat as he stepped down into the porch, he hurried towards her. Together they walked towards the two-storeyed eastern gate.

'I'm sorry—I kept you waiting.'

'Did you find it difficult to get away from the service?'

'I was looking for you, but the crowds are so thick, I couldn't find you anywhere.'

'You were looking for me, and I was looking for you—and in his holy temple. . . St Shinran must have had his eye on the pair of us!'

'I was asking forgiveness all the time I was chanting.'

Soshu noticed the change in Tomoko, though he could not have described it exactly. Perhaps it was the new energy in her manner, springing from her consciousness that today, at least, she was acting of her own will.

Following the dusty, medieval walls of Senshuji, in a few minutes they reached the main street. Tomoko turned and looked back at the gate; with its rooms built into the wall on either side, it reminded her of the entrance to some feudal prince's mansion. In the distance they could see the main gate of the temple, towering even higher.

'It's come true. . . I've wanted so long to walk with you like this, Father.'

Tomoko spoke softly from behind the collar of her coat, but Soshu caught every word. They were walking towards the station of the Kansai Electric Railway, as if on their way home after attending the New Year service. There was no inn worth the name, or place where they could rest, in Isshinden, which was a sleepy town—long streets lined with private houses and usually almost deserted, except during the Senshuji services. They passed the restaurant, at the entrance to a side-street, where Tomoko had been taken for lunch by her mother when she was a child; it was no longer in business.

'I suppose we could meet someone from Butsuoji. I don't think many of our congregation come, though: it's too far.'

'A stranger would take us for some country priest and his wife.'

'Not for a priest and a member of his congregation? No, perhaps not. . .'

But the passers-by would hardly suspect that they were lovers. The place would make the idea improbable, for one thing—the small, out-of-the-way temple town; and then there were Soshu's robes. None of the crowd of Senshuji worshippers would push his curiosity that far, and if any of the Butsuoji parishioners chanced to be visiting Isshinden, very few of them knew Tomoko anyway.

Tomoko said nothing about their immediate destination, nor did Soshu have any idea where they might go.

'What do you think I was doing yesterday evening?' she asked him suddenly.

Soshu himself had lain awake all night, picturing over and over again the coming meeting with Tomoko. In imagination, at least, he was no longer unsure of himself: her will, her feelings were his, to lead wherever he chose. Yet behind this imagined freedom, in the very shadow of the delight it brought him, lingered still the doubt, the fear, the sadness inseparable from the briefest thought of their meeting. Never for a moment did this feeling of constraint leave him. No matter how delightful the visions; when it came to action, in every direction there was a clear point beyond which he could not go—no more free than a monkey on a leash.

Soshu had no answer for her question.

'I was sewing till nearly midnight.'

'You must have been busy.'

She did not say what it was she had been making. An express clattered past; they had reached the station now, and were making their way to the platform for stopping-trains, Soshu having bought two tickets for Tan'ami. There were several passengers in the little waiting-room, so they did not talk. Carrying his rattan basket—a little work of art, with the maker's crest burnt into the inside of the lid, the thick canes from which it was woven gleaming after years of constant use—Soshu walked over to the ticket gate. Now and then, wrapping her collar more closely around her face, Tomoko looked up at him with feelings she could not hide. No more than Soshu did she have any clear idea of how they would spend these hours; she was waiting, it seemed, for some suggestion for him. A train came. Once aboard, they would be carried willy-nilly to Tan'ami—and who might they not meet when they got off the train there. The ticket-collector opened the gate, and they walked out into the January wind that was blowing down the platform. Stretching away below the embankment were paddy-fields ready for seeding in early spring; in the furrows, narrow lines of water gleamed like ice. Soshu stood between Tomoko and the wind, trying to shelter her. So far they had seen no face they knew.

The train was packed. At every station where they stopped, as many passengers got on as got off, and they were gradually pushed further down the car. Soshu found a strap to hold on to, while Tomoko steadied herself by keeping close to him. Finally, after the train had stopped five or six times, her hand sought his, and clasped it; wrist met wrist, arm touched arm, the slight movement carrying all the passion that words could not have expressed. Yet now she was calmly looking out of the window. The touch of his hand gave her real support, and he understood—merely to lean against him each moment the train jolted her off her balance made the frustration unbearable.

When a few moments later the train stopped at one of the larger stations, Tomoko suddenly pushed her way to the door. Soshu followed. They were still about an hour's journey from Tan'ami. Tomoko hurried along the platform without looking round, and joined the crowd converging on the station exit, signalling to the ticket-collector as she passed the gate—with a casual air, implying that she was accustomed to travel in this way—that somebody behind her would produce the ticket. The town was close to the sea, and little drifts of beach-sand had gathered here and there on the path leading from the station. Still not looking round, her face buried deep in her collar, Tomoko hurried on out into the street, her body bent slightly from the waist, as she walked into the strong wind. Soshu followed five or six yards behind. The rows of shops along the sandy street leading up from the sea gave way to scattered weekend and holiday cottages, and in a short while, climbing up a gentle slope to the top of a ridge, they caught the sound of waves.

Tomoko stood with her back to a row of pines twisted by the sea winds. Her face was set.

'I'll ask. . . '

Her words mystified Soshu. The skirt of her purple kimono flapping about her feet in the wind, Tomoko went up to the door of an inn nearby—and he understood: it was she after all and not himself who could be courageous and decisive. She beckoned to him now, after talking with a maid in the porch. He began to walk towards the inn. The place was deserted . . . only the pines, the white strip of beach against a dark blue sea. Nor were there any boats to be seen.

They were shown to an inner room—the only guests, perhaps, for all the inn was silent except for the sound of falling waves. As Tomoko took off her coat, Soshu noticed how well the *haori*—it was of Indian red, splashed with patterns in the Oshima style—suited her figure and character.

'I don't suppose you've ever been anywhere like this, Father?'

'The inn, you mean?'

'I'm ashamed of myself for dragging you here without a word. . . the idea suddenly came—'

'It's I who should apologise. But for me, you'd have no reason to be ashamed.'

The maid returned with a tray of tea and Japanese cakes, which she laid before Tomoko, pretending not to notice her companion in the white robe and travelling cloak. A moment after she had left, they heard a clatter of boards as she covered the bath, and a sudden gush of water. The sliding door opened a few inches: it was the maid again.

'When would you like dinner, madam?' she asked Tomoko.

'Not just yet, I think.'

'Later, then—'

'Please.'

'Is there anything you would like to drink?'

'Bring some *sake,* please.'

'Yes, madam. The bath will be ready in a moment—along the corridor here. The changing-room is next door.'

The Tomoko who treated the maid with such confident ease was a stranger to Soshu.

'I'm the kind of woman who's at home in places like this, you're thinking?'

Soshu started.

'You're disgusted with me?'

'No.'

'I've been taken to this kind of place two or three times—but you won't want to hear about that.'

Soshu was sitting in his usual stiff, formal posture, as though he were visiting a parishioner's home.

'Won't you take a bath?'

'No, I'll wait—'

'But you must! They say "when in Rome, do as the Romans do!" don't they? I've had all kinds of ideas about what we might do today; and one thing is, you have to do as I tell you. . . Take a bath, and the inn will give you one of their kimonos to put on afterwards. Show me the other Father Soshu, the one I haven't seen yet!'

'Are you going to take a bath?'

'When you've finished.' Even this—the bath which every Japanese inn offers its guests as soon as they arrive—Soshu had all but forgotten; in comparison with Tomoko, he knew nothing of the world.

'There's something I want to ask you first. Has Mr Yamaji said anything to you since the meeting I told you about?'

'He's been trying to get me to give up Butsuoji, too.'

'He's already decided to change, then?'

'The Nichiren priest keeps visiting him, I believe. It's all out of spite towards you. He's agreed to give them a big donation, to help towards enlarging their temple; but I don't think he's actually decided to join.'

'Then it's true he has this connection with the Nichiren people. There's nothing we can say about his giving them money, of course. If only he won't leave Butsuoji, though—'

'There'll be trouble if he finds out about us.'

Soshu was silent; there was nothing he could say.

'He was born cruel. . . he loves making the Butsuoji parishioners kowtow to him, and manipulating the temple business the way he wants it. It's power he wants more than anything else. Even to me he's cruel, though I do everything he says and never complain. . . He came here after that meeting, you know—told me he was on his way home from Butsuoji. If you knew what happened that night, Father. . .' Tomoko dropped her clasped hands abruptly on the table in a gesture Soshu did not understand: as if to throw off the burden of remembered pain. 'If I happened to say anything that sounded as though I sided with Butsuoji, I don't know what he'd do to me. It's easy to see it's only your being a priest that stops his jealousy going any further. . . I think he may be suspecting something, you see—he asks me occasionally why the old priest never comes to read the sutras instead of you. He'd be happier if it was Shoju coming every month.'

'One of you I'm bound to loose. . . yet I'm so weak I can't give up seeing you, nor can I let him—'

'He told me once he'd like to "have the pleasure of seeing you weeping". . .'

Soshu trembled.

'I even trembled, you see. Losing a parishioner like Yamaji. . . He said himself it would make Butsuoji the laughing-stock of the town. And how could I face the rest of the congregation?'

'I wonder what he'd say if I refused to leave Butsuoji. If he does go over to Nichiren, I'm sure he'll tell me I must change too.'

'I suppose he will. There's so much more involved than just Butsuoji and me.'

Still fuming as he left the temple, Yamaji had ordered his driver to go straight to Kiyota-cho. Tomoko, flustered by his bursting in upon her at such an unexpected hour, had hurried upstairs with a brazier to supplement the electric stove in warming the unused room. He had come to work off his anger on her, apparently. At once he told her to 'get ready', as if that was all he had come for. In the room downstairs Shoko lay in bed, but not asleep.

'Tonight, anyway, I gave that priest a shock. Not just about the cemetery, either. Told him I'd give up Butsuoji altogether. . . That was a bombshell, if ever there was one!'

Tomoko listened quietly as she lay down on the bed, her expression unchanged.

'It's not so easy nowadays for temples to pick the kind of parishioners they need. The new religions may be booming, but ordinary Buddhism can't get new members any more. They'll be putting their heads together at Butsuoji now, I suppose. . . ; but if they think they can trample on a man whose family has belonged to Butsuoji ever since it was founded, and expect him to carry on as if nothing had happened—they're mistaken. Times have changed, for one thing. Religion is free now, but they're dreaming along in the old way. If they don't wake up, Butsuoji will be losing two parishioners, not one. . .'

Yamaji handled her like a machine he had learnt to manipulate expertly. For a moment she tried to think of Soshu and his love for her. . . till all such feelings quivered into chaos under the hands that touched her, leaving only misery and loathing of a body that was her own, yet ignored her will. Yamaji's practised fingers knew every inch of her flesh, its tenderest secret places; he could force her senses to respond—but not her will. . . she struggled in vain to save her body from surrender.

'The priest keeps on refusing to marry again. Got some women of his own, I shouldn't be surprised.'

'It must be because of his mother.'

'Maybe he's not out of her clutches yet. Mineyo still has some life in her—she never gets any older, so long as there's a youngish man around for her to take care of. Must have drunk an elixir or something.'

Anathema—the body he could break so perfectly to his will. . . Yet he seemed to think her body was her life—

'You've learnt from me the joys of womanhood, eh? You won't admit it, but your body tells me. . . You won't forget me all your life. I've given you what's most worth having—there's not much else a woman needs to be happy.'

Tomoko was silent. A woman isn't an animal, she retorted inwardly: she has feelings, a spirit, even if you choose to ignore them. Yamaji never caught a glimpse of a woman's intense disgust at the sensual pleasure he was so proud of awaking. He himself discarded his normal personality when he came to her; he found it enjoyable, apparently, to play the male animal, leaving behind the company president and the Mr Yamaji of the big house and taking his fill of crude brutality. Or perhaps it was something in Tomoko that drove him to behave as he did—the impression of purity, and the perfect blend in her of yielding weakness with other womanly qualities. Such women seem to draw out the contrary qualities in men, tempting them to positive violence. In his treatment of Tomoko, experimenting, as it were, with his instincts, Yamaji exposed a part of himself he could let no one else suspect.

Tears began to appear in Tomoko's eyes. Turning away, she felt for Soshu's hand and took it in her own.

'I shall leave him. . .'

Soshu did not answer.

'And you, Father—you'll let him go if he decides to leave Butsuoji? You won't keep worrying about him?'

'I can't stop worrying about him, for the temple's sake. But it's you that matters.'

'It's been fate, anyway, as far as we are concerned.'

'At least I've found you—' Soshu's smile was subdued.

'Thank you for finding me!'—in a bantering tone; but she leaned closer, her shoulders bent towards him, Soshu embraced her. The warmth of her response startled him. He glanced down at the black sleeves of his robe.

'I stopped feeling anything for him a long time ago. Ever since I first asked you to come to the house, I've hated him. . .'

Soshu gazed at the lovely fine-grained skin, like distilled water. It had never occurred to him that mere human flesh could be so beautiful, and he could not believe now that this woman could be his. A rush of delightful visions—and with them a goading urge to desecrate such beauty. . .

'I'll leave him first!'

'No, I'll take the first step—'

'No, let me!'

Soshu bent to her upturned lips and kissed her. Timidly her hands slipped round his back; and the storm broke. Her whole body shuddering, she cried out in the uncontrollable passion of their embrace. Tears streamed down her cheeks and Soshu's.

It was some moments later that Soshu heard the breaking of the waves. Then silence, unexpectedly abrupt, till he caught the sound again... and again—at oddly irregular intervals.

Released from his arms, Tomoko sat before the mirror. Soshu stood awkwardly behind her.

'A bath, perhaps—I think I'll take a bath,' the face in the mirror murmured to itself.

'Do—I'll have mine first, then.'

The bathroom was small but clean, with a faint salty tang even in the hot water. Soshu heard someone enter their room two or three times while he was sitting in the bath—the maid, no doubt. Waiting till she had gone, he put on the blue wadded kimono provided by the inn and returned to Tomoko. Hot *sake* stood ready on the table.

'Stranger!' Tomoko smiled at seeing him in kimono instead of his usual robes.

'I feel like one myself.'

'It does make a difference. Not that the kimono doesn't suit you, though. Hm... what might the gentleman's profession be, I wonder?' Tomoko enjoyed not being able to make up her mind what he looked like.

'Always wearing robes made me a hypocrite without my ever noticing it. I should have worn ordinary dress when I went out visiting—sweater and trousers—'

'Half-priest, half-layman?' Tomoko took up the *sake* bottle as she spoke.

'I hardly ever drink.'

'Nor do I. One feels one has to order some, though, in a place like this.'

'We'd better pour it down the sink in the corridor, and pretend we've enjoyed it.'

'Won't you drink just a little, though?'

In a sudden change of mood, Soshu took the cup.

'As our wedding cup—yes...' Bowing to Tomoko, he drank, and offered the cup to her in turn.

'I promise... to be a good and faithful wife.'

Each of them drank three sips from the cup, which was larger than the special cups used in weddings. Feeling they must follow as nearly as possible the traditional wedding custom of drinking alternately from three successive cups, Soshu drank again, and Tomoko after him. But both had filled the cup to the brim, forgetting its size; and when she turned it face down on the table after drinking for the second time, Tomoko was already suffering. Suddenly pale, she complained of pains in her chest, and tried to push down her sash.

'Why didn't you just pretend? You didn't say anything, so I thought it wouldn't harm you.' Soshu suggested she should undo her sash; but the fit of intoxication was so sudden that her fingers fumbled even in trying to untie the cord of her *haori*. He untied it for her, and the haori slipped off her shoulders. Again her fingers shook as she unfastened the bustle of her sash, her breath coming in long painful gasps.

'I shouldn't have let you drink. . . you'd better lie down for a while.' Soshu looked round for something to serve as a pillow. Finding nothing, he opened the screen-door into the next room—and started. It was dark, the shutters had been closed, and two beds laid on the mat floor, filling the whole room. When had the maid got the room ready for the night, he wondered—and did Tomoko know. . . She had untied her sash now, but had no strength to fold it, and was sitting with her shoulders bent, breathing heavily.

'It hurts to breathe.'

'Lie down in here till you feel better.'

Tomoko tried to stand up, tottered, and fell.

'Can you manage?'

'My head's all right—I can't stand, though—'

Finally she managed to get up, half-standing, half-kneeling, revealing beneath the crumpled skirt of her kimono a brilliant underrobe of plum-blossoms on a white ground. Soshu supported her into the next room. At once she collapsed on one of the beds, and lay still, her eyes closed. Sliding the door to, Soshu returned to his cushion at the table. He had no idea what the treatment was for sudden intoxication—whether he should send for wrapped ice to put on her chest, or prop her head up, or. . . he looked at his hands, wondering how he could be so helpless. Again the sound of breaking waves. . . So as not to disturb Tomoko, he tried to be perfectly still; but for his feelings there was no rest. He thought of Ryokun—as she must think of her daughter? If the worst came to the worst, the parishioners might refuse to let him have the boy. He was the only Getsudo left, they might say, and he must stay. And he himself? He would find his way back to the temple where he had been born, he supposed. But they would expel him from the priesthood; he would have to find some job. . . . . Anyway, he must find out what was really in Yamaji's mind, even if he was going to leave Butsuoji—otherwise he would not know what to say to the parishioners. Soshu saw the extent of his own selfishness; however genuine his love, selfishness was at the bottom of his willingness to sacrifice Yamaji so that he could possess Tomoko—for it would be obvious to all except himself which of them meant more to Butsuoji. And then there was Mineyo. . . wasn't he dreaming of abandoning her just to save himself, when he ought to be worrying about how he could take care of her in her old age? Soshu's eyes wandered round the room, as if seeking escape from the mass of contradictions in which his life was centred.

'. . . cruel. . .' Tomoko's voice was indistinct, hardly more than a murmur. '. . . leaving her alone. . .'

Soshu opened the screen-doors. Her eyes were open. He had not heard her take off her kimono—she was lying in one of the beds now, not where she had fallen. Out of a pink and white sleeve an arm stretched towards him.

'I finished sewing this last night. . .'

So that was it—her under-robe. . . Soshu remembered what she had told him when they were walking through Isshinden.

'Everything I was wearing today is new—like the dress for hara-kiri. . . everything, clothes and heart and body. . .'

'Do you feel better?'

'We finished the wedding ceremony, didn't we?'

'Do brides usually get drunk?' laughed Soshu.

'If the wedding ceremony's over, this must be our wedding night. . . .'

The word so hard to speak was spoken. A rich scent—Japanese or foreign?—drifted towards him at each movement of her beautiful under-robe.

'I'm a clumsy stupid fool! You make me ashamed—you, of all people. . . you say the words as if they were yours, but they're not—it is I, in my sin, that made you say them!'

Tomoko hid her face in her sleeve. Her breathing had grown less painful.

They left the inn after supper. Across the dunes came the sound of the breaking waves, louder now in the darkness.

'We'd better not be seen leaving Tan'ami station together. You go on ahead, Father.' She stayed behind when Soshu stepped on the train. As it pulled out of the station, he could still see her face buried once more under the high collar, leaning against an iron pillar on the platform. The loneliness of the figure, with no light near enough to cast a shadow, made him feel her fate as his own: her life too was a tragedy, that was only deepened by their meeting.

'Daddy!' Ryokun came running to the porch. 'Did you bring me a present?'

Soshu took from his basket a bag of red and white cakes bearing the Senshuji crest.

'You took your time, didn't you?' grumbled Mineyo.

'I had another call to make.' The change in himself surprised Soshu. The house, his family, were as they had always been; renewal, if he could call it that, had come to him alone. He hated himself for his ready dissembling, and thought of Tomoko having to suffer in the same way.

'Some of the elders called today. They want to hold another meeting, and came to ask you what day would be convenient.'

'What do they want to talk about? Mr Yamaji again?'

'No, something else, by the looks of it. They wouldn't tell me, though.'

Soshu wondered. If they would not tell Mineyo, it might be that what they wanted to discuss concerned her too closely. Perhaps it was about his marrying again. . .

Abruptly, Tomoko's image faded.

30

Soshu's gaze wandered round the art-objects that filled the room, the statue of Tamonten, its left arm missing, the exquisitely-worked *fuji-musume* doll in its glass case, the vase of pure white porcelain, smooth like a woman's skin, the bronze nude. None of them held his attention. Like a criminal awaiting conviction, he was conscious only of time, of the minutes bearing down upon him. He looked down at the floor, as if to avoid invisible eyes. The big portrait of Yamaji stared at him from the wall.

Yamaji's wife, tall and thin, had come to the door when he called.

'Did my husband send any message? This is not your usual day to call, I believe.' Her tone was brusque.

'I came about some special business—'

'Unfortunately he's not at home today.'

Inwardly Soshu sighed with relief. He had known, of course, that Yamaji was not likely to be at home on an ordinary working day—in fact, that was why he had chosen this time to call: it was not his object to meet Yamaji in person. The house he had to visit; but for the time being, at least, he lacked the courage to look its owner in the face, even if he could manage to avoid, as he still felt he might, the kind of exaggerated obsequiousness that would give his secret away at once.

'I expect you know what I've come about, Mrs Yamaji. A few days ago we had a meeting at the temple, and Mr Yamaji—'

'If that's what it is,' she interrupted, as if this were what she had been waiting for, 'I can speak for my husband. I know exactly how he feels.'

Her hostility was apparent—so much so that Soshu felt there was little more for him to say. The note of intimidation was exactly that of Yamaji himself. In her such arrogance sounded merely childish:

in him, it could mean disaster for the whole Butsuoji community.

A maid showed him into another parlour, where he sat in one of Yamaji's armchairs, awkward and out of place; only before the shrine could he feel wholly at home in a parishioner's house. Mrs Yamaji did not come immediately—perhaps she was phoning Yamaji. He was kept waiting beyond the limits of courtesy.

'My own family belongs to the Zen sect,' she said when she finally came.

This Soshu already knew.

'I've been worried by what I've heard. . . though I couldn't really believe that Mr Yamaji. . .'

'We've talked it over together. It's an odd custom, don't you think, this changing of one's religion? Take me for instance—my family have always been Zen, so naturally I ought to follow in their footsteps; but just because my husband was Pure Land, I had to be Pure Land too.'

'It will be such a terrible blow for Butsuoji if Mr Yamaji leaves us—'

'My husband doesn't think very deeply about religion, you know. Business is his religion, he says, and he thinks about nothing else morning, noon and night.'

'His brother is one of our most faithful parishioners.'

'He doesn't have much to do with his brother; and his brother never comes here. You would hardly know they were brothers.'

'Then what the rumours say is true?'

'My husband hasn't said in so many words what his plans are. He dislikes any kind of fuss or unpleasantness intensely, you know—and a man in his position can't help having a good many enemies. . . He's not the kind of man to compromise, though. There's nothing he enjoys more than a quarrel, and if anyone *does* make trouble for him, he fights it out till he gets his own way. That's his nature, I'm afraid.'

There was to be no formal resignation, then. He would merely stop coming to Butsuoji, and if any of the elders called on him, they would be told he was not at home and turned away. So the connection would lapse. Butsuoji parishioners would no longer feel they could visit him when it became known he was inviting the Nichiren priest to his house and generally behaving as if he had actually joined the Nichiren Sect.

Was this his punishment—prepared for him from the first moment of his love for Tomoko? Soshu glimpsed as if for the first time the terrible meaning of the law of inescapable retribution, to which every thought and deed of man is subject.

The thought of Tomoko was his heart's only resource. By being what she was, she had pointed to a way out of his weakness, to a life of purpose and self-respect. He had struggled, and failed; she was a challenge to a fresh start—and the reason why Butsuoji was now to lose its leading member? If so, he had sinned irredeemably against the dead, the generations who had served the temple in the past, and was an offence to their descendants whom he served as priest. Should he give up Tomoko? Would the disaster never have happened if he had given her up earlier? Even then, supposing there had still been this talk of Yamaji leaving, would he have been able to appeal to him in a friendly, natural way to change his mind, just because his own conscience was clear? Perhaps the affair of the cemetery would have estranged them in any case. Yamaji knew nothing about Tomoko and himself. Yet what he was doing now was cruel enough to have been the perfect act of vengeance, as if he had in fact known everything—strangling the life out of his victim. . . How could he believe all this was merely an ironic coincidence?

His own heart had its trickery. He was two Soshus. One played the role of priest of Butsuoji: he was overwhelmed by the shock of Yamaji's leaving his temple, nor was there anything feigned about this reaction; yet the other—he was overjoyed that Yamaji was cutting his ties with Butsuoji, that he need never see him again . . . Never to meet Yamaji again—the first condition for the fulfilment of his union with Tomoko. . . Bewilderingly, each struggling to exclude the other, the two selves clashed within him.

Gradually, as Tomoko's image lodged more firmly in his mind with each monthly visit, there had developed as part of Soshu's attitude to Yamaji a defiant awareness—it had not yet the clarity of determination—that a final break between them must come. From the beginning he had realised that as far as he himself was concerned he would sooner or later have to choose between them. If only Tomoko had been in the same position as Tanemi, he had sometimes wished—a young widow, living with her parents—how easily a marriage could have been arranged. . .

He sat with bowed head before Yamaji's wife—the priest of Butsuoji.

'My husband said he would let you have the papers in a few days, as soon as he's got them ready,' she said casually, as if she knew every detail of the affair and was therefore hardly interested any longer. 'Papers'—separation money, said Soshu to himself, ironically, recalling the old custom of sending a gift of money as formal token of the breaking of a relationship.

—If he's no longer a parishioner, no more need for the absurd humility, the constraint, the fear—he and I will be equals. . . If he thinks he's taught Butsuoji a lesson by going over to Nichiren, maybe there's a lesson I can teach him—

A spasm of savage anger passed. He raised his head : all Yamaji's wife could see was an expression of hopeless defeat.

'One of the elders came and asked Mr Yamaji to attend another parishioners' meeting,' she said as he stepped down into the porch. 'He won't be going, of course. When was the meeting to be—today, was it? I really don't quite remember—'

Her parting shot. . . The 'of course' stung. It was clever acting to keep that message about the meeting until the last moment, and then to bring it out casually, as if she'd forgotten all about it till then. Yamaji himself, behind every word she spoke.

Soshu rode off on his bicycle. He chose quiet lanes where there was hardly any traffic.

—How would the parishioners react if they found out about Tomoko? They would guess it was not only the disagreement over the sale of the land that made Yamaji leave—and what could he say then? If he tried to explain that there was no connection between his relationship with Tomoko and the trouble over the cemetery, they would never believe him.

His feet revolved mechanically on the pedals.

Yamaji's break with Butsuoji might not free him, after all. If Yamaji came to know about Tomoko, he would find some way of revenge. The parishioners would not necessarily side with their priest. He would be abhorred. . . expelled from his temple. 'We can't have a priest who runs after women reading services in our homes,' they would tell each other.

—Are you going to keep it secret always—your affair with Tomoko? came the voice of his other self.

—That would be impossible. . .

—Then are you ready to face the consequences?

No answer.

—The loss of Yamaji is enough to make your position with the parishioners all but impossible. Mineyo's right there. And on top of that, to get yourself involved with another woman. . . Mineyo will cast the first stone—you're only an adopted son, don't forget. No, you'll be driven out of Butsuoji. . . and *she*. . . she has to let Yamaji keep her as his mistress, because she can't support herself. . . they'll despise you because of her, sneer at you, hate you!'

A middle-aged woman coming from the opposite direction greeted Soshu. She was a member of the Butsuoji congregation, but Soshu did not see her. She turned to stare as he passed.

When he looked up from the road, he was already in Kiyota-cho —his bicycle had brought him of itself to the track by the shallow river lined with willow-trees. He dismounted outside Mrs Komiyama's house, as if he had come for the usual sutra-reading, though in fact he had no such excuse, as it was more than a week till the day for the monthly service at her house. The desire to see her, aroused perhaps by the interview with Yamaji's wife, had grown upon him as he rode through the quiet back-streets. The longing to be with her never left him now, nor the loneliness, of which he was most bitterly conscious late at night and in the early morning when he rose. Gradually the memory of those hours at the inn by the sea faded, leaving in its place unrest and fear.

His hand on the door, Soshu paused, searching vainly for a reason to justify his coming; but his longing was reason enough. In a mood remote from that of the monthly visits, he slid back the door—and stood guiltily silent, in terror at his own audacity. No sound came from the house. Someone must have heard the door, surely? Soshu waited. There was no sign of the maid, nor of Shoko. Nobody at home, then? He looked up towards the upstairs room. He should have called out the moment he opened the door to ask if anyone was in; now it was too late.

Still he waited. The punishment he deserved, to make him despise himself for his shamelessness. . .

A movement from the top of the stairs—someone had heard the clatter of the door, then, and was coming down a little suspiciously, perhaps, wondering why there had been no sound of the visitor's clogs in the porch, of his stepping up on to the mat-covered floor. Suddenly, from the opening through which the steep staircase led up to the room upstairs, he glimpsed the hem of a woman's skirt, slipping hesitantly over the topmost step, then a white foot, pushing it aside. . . no one would go barefoot so early in the year. . . The woman's hands were hidden, feverishly tying her sash behind her back.

'Ah!' Shock stifled her cry. Soshu stared at her, too taken aback to move.

'Father!' Tomoko came down to the foot of the staircase, her hands still behind her back. Her face was pale, as if she'd just woken from sleep; yet there was a light in her eyes, as of tears. She seemed unconscious of the wild disorder of her hair.

'You. . . you met his car—?'

'His car?' repeated Soshu. Then he understood. He shook his head.

'Father!' She could hardly stand; his outstretched arm caught her in the same instant that she flung herself upon him, crushing her face against his shoulder. The body in his arms was shaking.

'I can't bear it any longer. . . I want to die!'

Soshu caught the fragrance he remembered, mingled with the warm scent of her woman's breast.

'I had to see you. . .'

'And I. . . my life. . .' She embraced him convulsively. 'He left me the moment before you came. . . Forgive me! I've no courage to resist when he's here. . . too weak. . .'

'I should never have come today. I've only made you suffer.'

'Hold me! Hold me, so tight I can't breathe! I—I can't feel. . . *make* me feel I'm in your arms!'

Still trembling violently, Tomoko clung to him; struggling desperately to free her body from imprisonment to the will that had forced itself upon it. Only her mind could respond to his embrace; her body was still unaware, her senses drugged with what had gone before.

'I only came to see you—to see your face for a moment—I'll go now. It's such torture not to be able to come.'

'Why aren't you angry with me? I've deceived you, Father—why don't you tell me I've deceived you, instead of pretending?'

Soshu shook his head, not knowing what to reply. He had a right to feel angry; but speak to her in anger he could not.

'Father! What is there left for me if you don't reproach me now—if you won't be angry. . .'

'Don't persecute yourself. I'm as much to blame as you are.'

Unable to stand any longer, Tomoko sank down on her knees, on the narrow strip of raised wooden floor beneath the porch and the corridor—at first she had looked down on Soshu, who was still standing in the porch; now she knelt before him, her arms about his waist. He stroked her dishevelled hair.

'This body is defiled, unclean . . . animal. . . I'd made up my mind to reject him once and for all. When the moment came, I was too weak to say it. . . He does what he likes with me. He tells me I'll never be able to leave him, all my life—after what he's done to me, he says—'

'But it's only your weakness: you are not sinning.'

She buried her face in his robe.

'I've wept at myself for being so weak. . . Why is it so hard to make a new start? I was crying when he left, half-paralyzed . . . then I heard something downstairs . . . the door. . .'

'Shoko or the maid will be coming back soon. They mustn't see us—I'll go now.'

If he opened the door, they could be seen from the road, himself still standing, Tomoko prostrate at his feet. He loosened her arms gently.

'I must go.'

'Father!'

'I'll come again when I can't bear to keep away any longer—without warning, probably, like today. I was on my way home from Yamaji's.'

'—while Yamaji was . . . amusing himself with me. . .'

When he turned back at the gate, she was sitting motionless in the hall, as if paralyzed.

Without hurrying, Soshu took his bicycle and rode off slowly down the road, in the gloom of a deepening sadness. Since their meeting at the inn, Tomoko's burden had grown beyond her power to endure—thanks to himself. But he could feel her arms about him still, in that violent embrace which implied not merely passion but strength of will. In the knowledge of that strength he could rest.

When he got back to Butsuoji it was time for the evening service. Mineyo came hurrying after him as he started towards the temple hall.

'How was it at Mr Yamaji's?'

'I saw his wife. The rumours are true, it seems.'

'Then he won't be coming to the meeting toninght?'

'No.'

'And you accepted that without a murmur, I suppose?'

'I'm not in a position to make him change his mind.'

'There'll be some questions asked about this at the meeting. You're responsible, you know.'

Soshu walked down the corridor to the hall. The old priest had already lit the candles; he had only to sit before the shrine. He bowed his head.

—'If a man attain faith, he will leap for joy, and a Buddha-mind be born within him'. . . If so, how was it that in every action he still rebelled against the Buddha-mind? What was he but a slave to instinct— and worse, forever seeking specious justification for each pull of his wayward senses . . . what faith did those senses acknowledge?

The old priest stared at him, waiting for him to raise his head so that he could strike the gong for the beginning of the service.

That evening, forty parishioners gathered for a second time at Butsuoji. Kashimura sent his secretary, as before. Most of those who came wore Japanese dress. Looking like hunchbacks in their thickly padded kimonos, they huddled in groups of two or three round little charcoal footwarmers. All were looking at Soshu, who sat with head bent and hands upon his knees, unable to face their collective stare. The eyes were pitiless, determined to probe and force from him what he had so far refused to tell.

'We haven't come here tonight to discuss what Mr Yamaji told us at the last meeting.' said someone. 'It's something even more important for Butsuoji and more urgent, too. This meeting wasn't called by Father Soshu, either—we called it ourselves, because the subject is something we parishioners can't let go by default any longer. It's not quite the kind of meeting we usually have.'

Tachi was present, but said nothing. At such meetings he sat behind the others, leaning forward and half-rising when he chose to speak. He understood perfectly what Soshu must be going through—his timid spirit at the mercy of the ring of accusing eyes. Soshu's indecision had annoyed him often enough, but now, from his own very different position, he could see that just because of that weakness the priest was facing deeper suffering than he himself would ever experience: for with the weakness went finer sensitivity, greater susceptibility to pain. Tachi did not like the abrupt way the first speaker had opened the meeting. For most of the parishioners, that was the only way they could bring themselves to speak at all—by getting the whole group on their side in advance; and this too Tachi understood. Even so, that opening . . . as if Soshu was to be interrogated like a criminal. Tachi felt the danger of their surrendering to the herd in whose protection they could pour out, too easily, what none of them would have the courage to say alone. There was a cold brutality in the herd psychology, he knew: they would attack the priest, pursue him, strike at him again and again without mercy till they could force out of him the answers they wanted. The questions might start quietly, but the tempo would soon change, and they would be after him. . . Tachi watched the changing mood of the meeting.

Soshu did not speak or raise his head. The muscles of his face were numb; and he wondered whether it had suddenly grown warmer, that even his skin seemed not to feel the cold air. All he was aware of was a tumult of barely-defined impulses in his own mind, imprisoning a great decision . . . the bitterness of knowing that in his own strength alone he could never speak.

'If Father Soshu will only say it's what he wants, we'll arrange everything, whatever the difficulties.'

—They would make Mineyo go, then—

'Butsuoji matters more than anything to us. Butsuoji, and our priest—'

'We want to know what Father Soshu really means to do. No beating about the bush, either.'

'A priest needs a proper wife.'

'We won't force on you a wife you don't want, Father. Do our best to find someone suitable. But are you willing to marry again? We want you to tell us tonight, yes or no.'

'It's anxiety enough when somebody one hardly knows has to marry again, and comes hunting around here and everywhere for the right woman. All the more so when it's our own priest and temple. Butsuoji means as much to us as our own families—that's why we're so worried: it's natural.'

'Tonight's not the first time we've felt like this. We may have kept our mouths shut before, out of respect for Father Soshu's feelings, but there's a limit—'

'All the parishioners are concerned about Butsuoji. There'll be trouble if you don't take more notice of them, Father.'

'We're here tonight to talk things over in a friendly way. There's no knowing what your mother would feel— we understand that may make it difficult for you to speak out. But that's just it—that's the most important question, and that's got to be settled before everything else if our temple is to be a place where people can come freely without having to worry all the time about what's going on behind the scenes.'

The workings of the human mind are strange. Helpless, unable even to speak under the succession of veiled attacks, at this moment he found himself recalling, with a shock of guilt, Tomoko's embrace of a few hours before. What inner process made the memory so vivid, when it brought him neither courage nor comfort? Outwardly his expression did not change. The hands dropped limply on his knees, the bent head, the figure revealing in every line a tortured mind.

'Maybe Father Soshu doesn't like the idea of him and his mother living apart?'

Wearily, Soshu glanced up at the speaker, neither admitting nor denying the truth of the insinuation. Either answer would have been a relief; silence would only make them distrust him the more—already, he noticed, two or three were shaking their heads. . . They all knew about Mineyo and himself. Not that anyone had the least proof; but no one doubted that the suspicions everybody shared were true. The parishioners had had misgivings about him ever since he came to Butsuoji. For twenty years he had chosen to ignore these unexpressed suspicions—out of mere indifference, it would seem to them: for who among them knew what that sin had cost him?

For a while no one spoke. A harsher gleam appeared in the eyes focussed upon him. For Soshu, the silence was suffocating.

'Obviously we are not going to trample upon Father Soshu's wishes. If he says he's content to let things go on as they are, we'll have to accept that,' said someone sharply. 'We're here to find out what he wants, not to give him orders. Maybe some people won't like what he intends to do—that can't be helped. But a decision there must be, one way or the other; otherwise there'll be no peace of mind for any of us—'

'Most of us know Father Soshu's character, I think. We know there are some things he can't say, however much he'd like to. We didn't call this meeting to persecute you, Father; we hoped the numbers would give you support, and make it easier to speak frankly. . .'

Still Soshu did not reply. His stubborn refusal to speak had begun to exasperate the meeting. To some it seemed dishonest, to others shameless; others were disgusted at his hesitation—spinelessness, some preferred to call it to themselves—or astonished at this revelation of how long their priest could hold out against such questioning. His unwillingness to be candid with the community he served was immoral, some thought, whatever might be said for such reserve in ordinary individual intercourse. Tachi watched him; it goes deep then, he was thinking.

A confused murmuring began. Finding no outlet, the tension that had built up behind the parishioners' questions turned to whispered expression of what till now had only been implied, or left unsaid altogether.

'Father Soshu's a man, like the rest of us,' said one man to his neighbour, not meaning anybody else to hear. 'You can't expect him to change overnight what's gone on for twenty years.'

'The old lady's not that worn out, either—plenty of women of her age marry widowers, come to that.'

'It doesn't matter how hard we try. . . people have their problems, after all. Trying to be helpful, are we? Pushing our noses in where we're not wanted, more likely.'

'He's been used to her ever since he was a boy, as near as makes no difference. You don't turn out a wife of twenty years at five minutes' notice. Maybe we're being too hard on him.'

'But Butsuoji's mixed up in it, that's the trouble. We'd laugh if we heard of this kind of thing happening in any other temple; but Butsuoji is ours, and we're the laughing-stock.'

'A temple may be a public place, but it's like home to us.'

'If it wasn't for the old lady, there'd never have been any trouble.'

'She'll live another twenty years yet! Fifty-four isn't she? Doesn't look much more than forty, when she puts a bit of that powder on.'

'I used to think he could make her go, if he only made up his mind to it. Seems it's not that simple, though.'

'She's not afraid of him—she can twist him round her little finger.'

'Maybe he really loves her.'

'If he does, we can't interfere.'

'He didn't make any fuss when his wife ran away, did he? Must have been Mineyo he wanted all along. Suppose we did make her go and live somewhere else, what good would it do, if he went on visiting her every other day?'

'That's one thing we can't do—force them apart. He can't get free of sin and lust, any more than we can.'

'But it's our temple, not his. The priest has to be trusted; he can't stay any longer than the parishioners want him.'

'Can't he though? How do we know whether we have the right to dismiss him or not?'

'There's no question about that. We can ask them both to go, if it gets that bad.'

'It's no more than they deserve, the pair of them.'

In the darkness of the connecting corridor, Mineyo was standing. Even when the meeting had hardly begun, her nerves were on edge, and now she was straining to catch every word, breathing jerkily from a parched throat, her mouth hanging open. Lines creased her face; suddenly she was old, beyond concealing. What would he tell them? Her life depended on his answer. The way the meeting had gone had caught her unprepared, for she had not troubled to find out in advance what it was the parishioners wanted to discuss. Who had called them together? Parishioners—who were they, after all? The idea of their concerning themselves with her life in this way had never occurred to Mineyo. It wasn't for them to talk about the priest's family affairs—and in any case, she had surely kept the secret as well as it could be kept? She did not think nobody knew; merely that she had succeeded in making it impossible for any of the parishioners to mention the subject. In talking with the elders' wives she never allowed the conversation to come anywhere near it, so the elders should have received no hint, either.

One word from Soshu now, and she would know what he intended. For a moment she was conscious of how utterly she depended on him. But what if he angered them with some clumsy, weak reply? She was ready to defy them all. For her—he was her adopted son, she could not forget—the parishioners' insinuations carried a different significance. She trembled, the blood pounding in her head and chest. The corridor was icily cold, her legs numb.

—They knew nothing! Nothing of Soshu's coldness, how he had come to neglect her. . . There was plenty she could say. They were both guilty—why should she let him get off so easily, just because they were biased in his favour? Anger swept over her; she was ready with a furious, indignant outburst, as if she had suddenly seen what the upshot of the meeting would be. Why didn't the parishioners leave them alone—herself and Soshu and Ryokun, and the old priest and the maid? The family lived in reasonable harmony, didn't they? People outside might have their suspicions, but these ties that bound them together, ties these busybodies wouldn't understand—why break them now? The world had heard before of wives fifteen years or so older than their husbands. If Soshu couldn't speak, she would go up into the hall and tell them herself the whole story of their relationship, make them recognize it for what it was. . . Soshu would be only too glad; it would bring him back to her. They would be a perfect couple, if the parishioners would give up interfering. Mineyo remembered Soshu's coldness: her courage broke.

'I hope you'll recognize the goodwill towards yourself and Butsuoji that's brought us here tonight, Father. You must surely realise how important this meeting is, from that point of view alone.'

Mineyo shivered. There was no escape: they might as well deny her the right to live at all, to exist. . . Steps were crossing the compound outside. Latecomers, probably. She heard them enter the porch of the house, kick off their clogs and step over the rows of other people's up on to the wooden floor. Passing on tiptoe down the corridor, they noticed her suddenly in the shadows; looked away, and hurried up the steps into the hall. There were five or six of them. Mineyo made no attempt to speak to them.

—The parishioners would know now that she was listening. But she was still defiant, and felt no urge to leave. Maybe the parishioners had been cross-questioning Soshu all along in the knowledge that she would be eavesdropping; intended every word for her, a last warning.

Sitting in the lighted hall, Soshu had wondered, with mingled sorrow and fear, what would happen if Mineyo found out what the parishioners had said at this meeting. Perhaps—probably—she was listening already. . . He found himself listening with her ears as well as his own, yet with his mind and heart imprisoned in a single concentrated awareness that at last escape was impossible.

—They only know half of my sin!—

He saw a picture scroll unfold before him, the record of his life. Mineyo was there, and Renko, and Tomoko, in brilliant colours; here and there his own figure, pretending to be a good, kind father to his boy. What had forty years brought him but deepening consciousness of his own sin?

'Father Soshu doesn't say anything; but we've told him our side of the picture, anyway. We want Mrs Mineyo to leave, and himself to agree to marry, the parishioners to choose the lady. We want him to make Butsuoji a place we can feel at home in, and be sure of a welcome whenever we come.'

'Butsuoji isn't the private property of the Getsudos. There are two hundred of us, and if Father Soshu has special ties that stop him coming out into the open, now's the time for him to break them, for the sake of all of us.'

Still Soshu did not reply. The silence grew more tense. Outside, moonlight filled the compound. The doors of the lighted hall were closed; across the steps below, in sharp outline, lay the shadow of the overhanging roof. Someone was approaching the temple, walking along the narrow paved strip that bordered the gravel path—the figure was that of a woman, no longer young, her face muffled in the high collar of a winter coat. No parishioners' wives had come to the temple tonight. Perhaps it was the peculiar atmosphere of such meetings that kept them away. The woman evidently had no intention of entering the temple from the house, as the others had done; but she seemed to know of the meeting, and to be determined to find out how it was going, for after a moment's hesitation she tiptoed up the steps leading to the main entrance to the hall. Light showed between the doors. Nervously the woman stepped up on to the weatherbeaten floor of the gallery surrounding the hall. The voices inside were inaudible. Unable to catch what was being said, she hurried up and down, peeping through cracks here and there till she could see where the parishioners were sitting; then stooped to listen. The voices were still indistinct, and she pressed her ear to the chink between two sliding doors.

'There are two or three ladies who'd be very willing to marry into the Getsudo family—and one who's what you might call enthusiastic—'

With the quiet laughter that followed this remark, the tension lessened. The woman did not move. The listening figure hidden in the shadow, its face pressed against the wooden edges of the doors, was that of Tomoko. After listening for several minutes, motionless as a lizard in a cleft of rock, she straightened, turned up the collar of her coat and walked down into the frozen moonlight, bent as if in pain. Without looking round at the house, she crossed the compound and went out at the great gate.

She had not heard of the meeting till early that evening. 'There's to be a meeting at the temple tonight. One of the elders came and asked our lady to go, if she was free,' a servant from the Mutsumiya had told her.

'What are they going to talk about?'

'Something about Father Soshu and his marrying again, I think he said. Mrs Mimori won't be going, though; she's not feeling well.'

Soshu had not mentioned the meeting when he came to her house—perhaps the subject was too painful. Tomoko had no intention of going herself. As it grew later however, she found it unbearable to sit quietly at home—she knew, or believed she knew, what Soshu's feelings were: but what did they count for, she kept asking herself, when the temple and the whole of its congregation were involved? Without telling the maid, she had slipped out. Now she was returning, bent and slow, by the same road. Every escape was cut off. She could see Soshu now as she saw herself, like an animal half-paralyzed with fear, but still groping wildly for ways to freedom that did not exist.

She had not heard him speak. For her, at least, his stubborn silence had been welcome, a proof of his devotion to her: or so she chose to interpret it. The moonlight traced her shadow on the road.

—It was she who was to blame! What courage could he find in her drifting acceptance of her life? If only she was strong enough to break with Yamaji, wouldn't that be half the battle won for Soshu too?

She hated herself for shrinking from the least change, for her readiness to compromise, her passivity, her dishonesty. If her decision was really made, she ought to be able to drop the whole of the past there and then, and the start of a life without the burden of shame and self-accusation would of itself surely bring new courage —what meaning would there be in such a rebirth if it did not? But the reality was not so simple. 'You've learnt from me the joys of being a woman. . . you'll never be able to forget what I've taught you—and that means you'll never leave me, never!' Yamaji had said. If man were entirely animal, it might be true; but she could not believe it. Yamaji himself could and did. It was grotesque, his inability to realize that she too might have a mind, or to recognize that she could be anything but mere body, to be visited solely for the animal in her: proof that the animal was all he was capable of himself. Between a man and a woman he could imagine no other tie. On recent visits—he came twice a week as a rule, leaving his car at the corner where the road to Tomoko's house turned off the main street—he had been neither passionate nor cold, as if she were merely an item in a routine he was repeating from force of habit. How she spent her time apart from the few moments they were together in the upstairs room did not interest him, and in those other hours and days she could feel herself to be alive, an individual woman with her own right to exist; but Yamaji's visits could not be pushed back into a corner of her mind. Her mind and body preserved their innocence under the mechanical love-making, but were drawn by his caresses into involuntary surrender, even while she was despising them—and despairing of herself. . . the spell was irresistible. Physical ecstasy and self-loathing combined to mock her, coexisting in the single body which could yet distinguish so sharply between emotion and sensation.

—Hadn't that evening at the inn given her courage? It had reawakened a once fastidious instinct for purity, perhaps stirred her out of her easy-going acceptance; yet—humiliatingly—the inner strength she longed for would not come. Material comfort had won after all, she thought. She was simply afraid to face hardship, terrified of losing the money he paid her every month, too timid to risk the leap into an unknown future. If she could bring herself to work as a housekeeper or maid, she could live. But for a woman who kept a maid to turn herself into one overnight—that was not so easy. It would need real courage—like jumping from a cliff, for instance. Tomoko saw through her own selfishness. All her complaints of Yamaji's cruelty, of the misery her sex forced on her amounted only to transparent self-deceit, so many mean attempts to turn her own feelings of guilt at accepting her livelihood from Yamaji into bitterness at him and loathing for herself. Wasn't it true that Yamaji had brought her a kind of fulfilment, in spite of all her revulsion? What would there be left of Soshu's illusions if he should ever find out—if he could know of the subtle change that Yamaji's caresses induced in her? Yet always, the moment Yamaji left, she was prostrate with disgust, bitterly angry with herself—that was true too, as was the longing for another kind of life that Soshu had aroused in her. Two roles she had to play, in each of which she was no less herself than in the other. Not that she had chosen this dual character; it had been forced on her. Yet she had no reason to hate anyone but herself. That was clear to her now.

—No one else was to blame. The evil was of her own making. If she was defiled, it was because she had walked with open eyes into the morass; so no one could rescue her but herself. . . Perhaps it was wrong to lean on Soshu. She could redeem herself. Sin or redemption, both lay with her alone. But when she found herself longing for someone or something outside herself to turn to for support, she would take refuge in old Buddhist ideas of the weakness of woman, of the Five Obstacles that made it impossible for a woman to attain salvation alone.

Gazing down at her shadow, black across the moonlit road, Tomoko walked back to the house in Kiyota-cho. At Butsuoji, O-Sugi and the old priest had begun to clear up after the meeting. Soshu sat at his table in the Lute Room, his eyes closed, the parishioners' voices echoing confusedly through his mind. No matter how often he had told himself something like this was bound to happen, their rebukes had struck him more powerfully when actually spoken than he could have imagined. Vaguely he was aware of O-Sugi's and Shoju's footsteps: they were returning to the house. He sat on, waiting. Waiting for what would not come till the clearing-up was finished and every room in the house and temple quiet again, for one whose cross-examination would be harder to bear than the insinuations of forty parishioners, and from whom there was no escape. The silence was broken again by footsteps from the elders' room.

'Goodnight, Father.' He heard the old priest kneel on the other side of the screen door.

'Goodnight,' Soshu answered in his usual tone. 'Better stay here tonight.'

'Yes, Father.' More footsteps, then silence again. Mineyo's door opened, as if she had been waiting for this moment. She entered the room and sat at the table, at right angles to him. Soshu did not raise his head or open his eyes. Nor did Mineyo speak; too much lay between them for speech—Soshu's youth, her blind infatuation and the fierce, diseased passion it became; his marriage to Renko, the birth of Ryokun, Renko's pursuit of the actor and eventual flight; and now, after twenty years, the ironic final act they had never foreseen, this inescapable confrontation as the bitterest of enemies. . . Mineyo must have overheard all that was said at the meeting, Soshu knew. Both sat in paralyzed silence, as if bound by some unspoken command forbidding any sudden outburst of self-pity or recrimination. Utterly unable to foresee how would Mineyo react, Soshu felt his terror mounting. . . Suddenly her throat trembled. With a half-articulate cry, she buried her face in her hands, her back heaving, weeping violently. . . and painfully, it seemed to Soshu; as though only a fraction of her wretchedness could find release in tears. Her face shaking, she tried to wipe the tears from her cheeks, first with one hand, then with the other. Still Soshu's eyes were closed. The sound of her weeping broke with piercing sharpness on the stillness of the house. It was convulsive, belying her age; as though in the flood of tears she were laying bare for the first time the sensitive essence of her womanhood.

Soshu did not respond. He had not expected this outburst of weeping, but saw now how inevitable it was, the only possible outlet; and it was no use speaking till the storm was over. Ryokun would be asleep by now, he thought. Shoju and O-Sugi, in the little annex, could hardly help hearing. They would know what had happened at the meeting, and the reason for her outburst. Probably they were both lying quietly in bed. The tragedy went too deep for casual, whispered remarks before going to sleep; for twenty years it had determined the very atmosphere of Butsuoji and the lives of all who lived there.

He looked up—in horror at the cold indifference he knew was all that showed in his face. He could feel no attraction in the weeping woman before him. The attempt at youthful chic, the smart permanent wave, were merely disgusting; only the texture of her skin, where it was not too heavily disguised with make-up, gave some idea of her real age. After a while the paroxysm worked itself out. Gradually she grew calmer.

Raising her face from the table, Mineyo caught the edge of her under-kimono betwen two fingers, pulled it out an inch or so, and slowly wiped her eyelids in an elegant, old-fashioned gesture, like a Kabuki actor. Another woman was taking possession of the dishevelled, weeping figure of a few moments before. Soshu watched her. . . another moment, and she would be once more the Mineyo he knew and feared. He thought of the moonlit night outside; of many such nights, in which he would be wandering, homeless. . .

'The mere idea is ridiculous. . . you would never drive me away from Butsuoji, would you?'

The words were more of a rebuke than a question. Mineyo stared at him. In her voice there were no tears, though Soshu noticed her eyelids were still swollen. He did not answer.

'You couldn't, of course . . . it would be the wrong way round, anyway. I've always meant to die in Butsuoji.'

'I couldn't aswer all their questions at the meeting. I didn't say anything—what is there I could say?' Soshu spoke gently.

'Telling me to leave here is telling me to die—there's no difference!'

'The parishioners are kind enough—but I've lost the right to their good will.'

'I won't leave Butsuoji, whatever they say! I've lived here longer than you have—'

'I haven't forgotten I was only adopted.'

'The parishioners think you're the important one, because it suits them that way. They've forgotten it was I who found you and brought you here.'

'There's nothing of the priest about me except the name. Butsuoji doesn't need me—'

'You can't let the parishioners have everything their own way! If they've got that much authority, they ought to think a bit more what's really good for the temple, oughtn't they? Mr Yamaji goes over to Nichiren; they don't lift a finger themselves, and try to make out behind your back that you're to blame. The impudence! Everything has to be as they see fit to decide. The priest's in a weaker position than they are, so they bully him until he gives in and lets them have their way—it is bullying, whatever kind words they wrap it up in. We should starve if their contributions stopped, and they know it. . . They wouldn't dare criticize an ordinary lay family like that, but they can stir up as much trouble as they like in the temple, because the priest can't answer back. They had no business to hold that meeting tonight. . .'

How wide was the gap between her preoccupation and his own, thought Soshu. But to point that out to her would be futile. Even his own wretched self-questionings had been in a sense misguided, he saw now, just because they could never take him beyond the imprisoning bounds of self. How did Mineyo interpret his rejection of her? She hated him for the mere decision on his part to try to rebuild his broken life; for his sudden indifference—how could she appreciate the suffering that indifference cost him? If she knew that Tomoko had influenced his decision, nothing would make her believe he was not simply abandoning her. And was that so false—wasn't he throwing away an old mistress for a new one? It was only in his own intuition of them that his motives were pure; nobody else would believe that, least of all the parishioners. If they thought that the habit of twenty years kept him from ending his sordid relationship with Mineyo even now, there was no way he could show them they were mistaken. Perhaps for Mineyo to go would provide the only vindication of his innocence. Of a selfish innocence; a pretence, it would amount to, that he at least was righteous—after all these years. . . No, he could make no answer to the parishioners. How could he make *her* understand? Hating, tormenting himself, mocking his hypocrisy, hating, tormenting, mocking, longing for release into new life—endlessly the cycle continued, yet always hidden from anyone but himself. Tachi might guess something of what he felt, perhaps; but there was no counting even on him. By its very nature, his ordeal demanded to be shared, made known—or it would be no true ordeal. But he had not the courage. It was not obstinacy that had kept him silent throughout the meeting—though that again they had not understood.

'Suppose I were sent away—what would happen? No one gets expelled from a temple except for a crime; people would say I must have done something so bad that being expelled was the only possible punishment. You'd be left here—and bring in some other woman. . . What sort of justice is that?'

Soshu could not answer.

'I'm not saying what I did wasn't wrong. It was, and I'm sorry for it. But where's the reason that I should be the only one to be punished? Anyone can see that the parishioners are prejudiced. I won't take it quietly, though. If they tell me I've got to go, everything in this house goes with me, kitchen stove and all—I won't leave much behind, I can tell you! Such unfairness—I won't let them!'

Soshu's mind went back to the day long ago when during a visit to his lodgings in Kyoto she had complained of a pain in her stomach. He could see her now, suddenly clutching at his hand as he was nursing her . . . still he could not hate this woman. His sin was not of her making; he could have refused her, and if he had, that would have been the end of their relationship—before it had begun. He alone was to blame.

'You're as guilty as I am, Father; if I'm to suffer, so should you.'

Soshu bowed.

'It's too much altogether, this sudden talk of getting rid of me when for twenty years they've never said a word. If they didn't like me, why didn't they say so earlier?' None of her bitterness was turned against herself. 'If I was younger, I could have made some sort of living, quite a good one, I daresay. But they have to wait until I'm old and can't support myself . . . it's cruel, and I shall tell them so. They're as much to blame as we are. If they are so devoted to their temple, why have they kept their mouths shut until now?'

Soshu placed his hands on the table, and clasped them, as for prayer; but the gesture spoke only of suffering.

'I know why you don't want to have anything to do with me any more. . .' The voice was thick and clinging. 'It's because I'm old. . . That's all it is. You're forty now; I'm fourteen years older—in six years from now I'll be sixty. No, I won't let you say you've never thought of it! You're so high-minded, maybe you've never admitted it to yourself; but it's true all the same, and if you say it's not, you're deceiving yourself. You can't deceive me, though. . . If I were the same age as you, or younger, you wouldn't behave like you do.'

Soshu shook his head very slowly, as if the movement was unconscious. The accusing conscience from which he was never free struggled on the edge of expression. He clenched his hands more tightly . . . but the shadows only deepened. Through the silence he could hear the night trucks rumbling along the new highway.

'Not that I'm so attached to Butsuoji I can't bear to leave it—if I have to go, I'll go. It's the unfairness of it; if they're going to sit in judgement over me, they must do the same with you. You've shared in the crime, haven't you? If they expel the pair of us, there'll still be a chance of our settling somewhere and making some kind of living. It's no good your trying to get parishioners on your side by discarding me. . . You can get a job teaching somewhere, with your college degree. We'll take Ryokun, too. The parishioners will soon find another priest—and Shoju can manage very well till they do.'

Plaintive, spiteful, and optimistic by turns, Mineyo struggled to keep her hold on him. She was already thinking, then, of her life after leaving Butsuoji; that was clear enough, behind the reproaches and angry protestations that she could never be forced to go. If the two attitudes were absurdly inconsistent, to Mineyo, at least, they were meaningful, reflecting what she genuinely felt; but from Soshu's way of thinking both were equally remote. Mineyo was nearing the age when the balanced harmony of mind and body breaks down, and each pulls its own way. If she were to guess at how wide the gulf was between them, thought Soshu, perhaps her reason would go. How could they have drifted so far apart, when for twenty years they had shared the same secret and given up so much for each other, when each should have been the other's support for the rest of their lives? Neither had kept anything back; no partnership in guilt could have been deeper. Yet he knew nothing of this woman.

What had he ever learnt about her—what had he ever given her, over the years? She, of all people, should have felt the reason for the sudden change in his attitude towards her. She should have known intuitively, as no one else could have done, of his growing sense of terror at their sin. But she saw only the difference in their ages. . . Mineyo knew no more of him that he did of her. And now, her mere presence was enough to renew each day his torment of self-accusation. . .

'I always knew Renko would run away. And what about you, Father—you didn't try very hard to stop her, when you realised she wouldn't stay? But then it was only for appearance's sake you married her. You never said so, of course; but I knew it well enough. . .'

Soshu remembered how Mineyo had gloated in her victory. Her beauty had been irresistible; and then the extreme, exquisite pleasure of yielding to such temptation. . . He was overcome with melancholy remorse. Between the two women—Renko, an innocent hardly out of her teens, and Mineyo, the young widow, fourteen years older than himself, but still in her thirties, and sexually at her most attractive—there could have been no comparison. He had let Mineyo teach him. . . it was she, not Renko, who had awakened him to sexual pleasure, and he had no wish to pretend otherwise. Somebody had once said something about a lesson in sex from an older woman being a guarantee of happiness—ironically, he had not recommended spending the rest of your life with the woman who taught you. When he was still young, a sense of fulfilment had made Soshu imagine that Mineyo and himself were perfectly united. But he had only been blinded; there was no understanding between them, and she had never noticed the gradual awakening of conscience within him.

'We laughed at the widow Kushimoto for the way she ran after the preacher. . . I envy her now.'

The little widow still hung about Butsuoji every time the famous preacher came. Soshu had given up hope of persuading her to change her ways. Sitting in the hall, in the shadow of one of the big pillars, she would listen open-mouthed to the visiting preacher's sermon, doting on the mere sound of his voice and never taking in a word of what he said. He paid not the slightest attention to her; but still she would slip into his room in the house when nobody was looking, or stand outside the hole in the hedge, hoping he might speak to her. Mineyo understood her infatuation perfectly.

'It's cruel. . . Mr Ifukube made you tell that woman of his he wouldn't have anything more to do with her. Does a man really hate a woman that much, when he gets tired of her? She was faithful enough. . .' Mineyo's lips curled. The smile was repulsive, the unmasking of a face at once old and obscenely ugly. The skin above her mouth had sagged and lost its rounded softness; the whole profile suggested only spite, and a scheming selfishness. 'But you wouldn't do anything like that, Father. . . you're too frightened, aren't you? Or *do* you have the courage, I wonder—the courage to confess the truth about you and me—before all the congregation?'

With a start of fear he looked up at her—and quickly turned away.

'You won't confess. You can't. . . I know that better than you do yourself!'

Soshu was trembling, tormented afresh by suppressed anger and bitterness and despair.

'The parishioners don't expect you to confess, either. All they want is for you to say you'll leave the decision to them. They're only waiting for you to give the word. First of all they'll get rid of me. . . shut me up in a rented room somewhere and tell me never to set foot in Butsuoji again. Then they'll find you a wife, and you'll marry her. It won't make any difference what you say, or don't say—that's how it'll go, you being what you are. You're clever, aren't you? You know very well it's the easiest way out, leaving everything to them, without ever saying a word about us—'

Soshu smarted under her malevolent stare.

'—but so long as you don't confess, Father, you won't get rid of me, you know.'

The easy certainty in her voice terrified him.

'You can't tell them, and you know it. So we shall never be parted, you and me—never!'

There was mockery as well as assurance in her tone, and exultation in the power she held over him.

'I'm your real wife still, Father, however little you treat me like one. You may hate me, but that won't separate us—I'm still yours!'

Soshu feared her more now than on those nights when she had slipped into his bed and forced herself on him in the darkness without a word. Then at least, by an effort of will, he had been able to escape, but against these taunts he was powerless; they struck at the heart of his weakness, where he could neither defend himself nor pretend indifference.

'If you did confess before the congregation I'd leave you, I promise—you'd have gone too far away from me then. But it won't happen. If there was the faintest likelihood of your doing anything of the sort, you'd have done it at the meeting tonight. But you didn't, and that proves you never will.'

There was a hypnotic quality in her constant harping on his lack of courage, proof of how well she knew his weakness, and of her intention of probing it till he was driven to admit the truth. So far, at least, she understood him. . . Soshu caught her scent, as she moved slightly. Not the scent of her make-up or perfume, but of her woman's body, the scent that hung diffused about her room, as the scent of maleness pervaded his. It had bewitched him once, as an emanation of her sensuality. Now he hated her for it, but with a hate unwilled, and dulled by lingering memories.

'The parishioners know about us, but they won't say so directly, and there's all the difference in the world between knowing and telling us to our faces that they know. It's just the same with you. . . either you let things go on as they are, or you confess—but what's the point in confessing what they know already? They'd only laugh at you for coming out with it now, after all these years. And that wouldn't be all. Confession would mean you've deceived them all for twenty years, pretending you were so saintly. . . You can't do it! And why go out of your way to make things hard for yourself anyway, when there isn't the smallest need to go?'

Soshu was trapped. There was enough truth in what she said to bring home to him more vividly than ever how difficult public confession would be. He shuddered as he thought of the effect it would have on the parishioners. . . The tragedy was reaching out beyond himself and his private fears.

Mineyo got up. He did not move, and she stood looking down at him, smiling.

A moment later her footsteps died away in the gloom of the unlit corridor.

31

Soshu was intoning before the shrine at the Mutsumi-ya, Mrs Mimori and two of her geisha sitting in a reverent attitude behind him.

The girls left when he finished the service, and almost at once the plucking of samisens broke through the silence that had descended on the house since his arrival: an abrupt reminder of the geisha world—like a swift change of scene in a play, hidden from the audience only by a momentary darkening of the stage. With this other world the priest had little to do.

Mrs Mimori began to prepare for ceremonial tea, and Soshu took off his stole, the lapels of his kimono rucking untidily below the neck as he let his shoulders sag, pale and preoccupied with his own troubles.

'May I trouble you now?' said Mrs Mimori when she was ready to begin. Soshu watched her hands as they went through the prescribed movements. A mood of calm, of harmony, filled the room where they were sitting; but upstairs two or three of the girls had started singing to the samisen, and Soshu found himself listening in spite of himself. Quietly Mrs Mimori stirred the powdered tea. She loved these tea lessons: while they lasted, she could so easily distil from the geisha-house atmosphere a delightful private world of serenity.

The geisha were singing the song a second time:

A flower's colour dies
Fragrance is its life
How sad to count
The days of loneliness!
Brief is a Flower's life
'Touch not its fragile blossoms!'
They may point at our love, condemning—
Yet what do temples know of love?

Love turns to pain
Past bearing—let me die!
You call me back, still loving—
Why end our lives in vain?
How strong the karma-bond
Of destined love!

Soshu took one sip from the tea-bowl Mrs Mimori placed on the floor before him. The irony of that song. . . A third time the girls sang the same melody, without thinkng what the words really meant, no doubt; but how exactly they pictured his own suffering!

'What is that song they're singing?' His hands still held the costly tea-bowl. It was an exquisite piece, and had been one of Shinzan Ito's most prized possessions.

Mrs Mimori listened for a moment. ' "Flowers", it's called. It's a new song,' she said, noticing with interest his haggard expression. A man's face appealed to her all the more when it was clouded with sorrow or grief. 'A charming song, really, but the girls sing it so woodenly.' It was one of Monta's, she added—a name Soshu had never heard of, which was hardly surprising, since he knew little about such things. But the song was such a strange echo of his own tortured feelings; and to hear it here, of all places. . .

'What happened at that parishioners' meeting the other day, Father?'

'They gave me a good scolding,' Soshu answered, half-smiling.

'Has any decision been come to, then?'

'No, not yet.'

'Well, there are complications at Butsuoji, of course: it's not so simple as it would be for a layman. But the congregation are worried, certainly.'

'It's not often nowadays, I must say, that people care about their temple so much. A man may belong to a temple one day, and have nothing to do with it the next. It's all "freedom, freedom" now, and a man can do what he likes and believe what he likes, or not believe, as the case may be.'

'Oh come, that may be true of Tokyo, but there are plenty of people here who are still faithful to the religion their families have always belonged to. They're as devoted to their temple as they are to their ancestors, lots of them.'

'It's such a pity a big temple like ours is hardly used at all for most of the year. Not just a pity, either; it's positively wrong. If only I could find some way of serving the congregation better! I shall be asking them all for suggestions when the time comes.'

'What about starting a kindergarten?'

'I've thought of that—or a day nursery perhaps.'

'So many of the parishioners are farmers, it would mean a lot to them to have someone take their children off their hands for a few hours when they're busy in the fields.'

'We used to hold a Sunday School, but had to stop for lack of funds. Our policy was wrong, too; it was too obvious an attempt to proselytize. I want people to come to the temple and use it, not to be preached at, but because they feel it's really theirs. But the authorities won't give us permission to start a nursery unless we're willing to make some alterations to the hall and turn part of the compound into a play area; and a lot of the parishioners are so conservative, that's enough to turn them against the whole idea.'

Soshu asked her formally for a second bowl of tea. Her posture and breathing, as she sat a little behind the iron brazier, hands on her lap, were perfectly controlled; she had mastered all he could teach her, and he could allow himself to savour the moment of tranquillity the ritual had created.

'You would be wiser not to marry again, Father.' Mrs. Mimori smiled as she placed the tea-bowl before him.

'With my son to think about, I can't afford to marry anyone I'm not perfectly sure of,' Soshu answered, merely for the sake of something to say.

'Several of the Butsuoji families have widowed daughters living with them, of course, but you might just as well marry into a family with some disease or deformity as choose one of them. And to be quite frank, they would really rather not have somebody like you, who is quite content as he is and has a happy home already. You must have found things difficult, Father, since your wife left Butsuoji; but in a way the very fact that you've had to suffer like this has made you popular with many of the parishioners. "Popular" may not be the right word, perhaps, but at least they feel closer to you now.'

'Won't it be for their benefit that I marry again, if I do?' said Soshu, smiling wryly.

'You won't have such a hold over them then. It means a lot to them if there's something not quite perfect in your life, some trouble or weakness you have to face, like the rest of us. . .'

What precisely Mrs Mimori's advice meant was obscure—or perhaps the meaning lay in its very obscurity. . .

32

Even Shoko thought it strange when Tomoko started wearing the same kimono day after day. In her half-unconscious, child's way she had sensed the care her mother had taken up till then to change her kimono every day. Nor had she ever seen her carelessly dressed, either at home or when they went out together. Yet it never occurred to her that Tomoko was vain, or what a grown-up would call 'fashionable'. The quick intelligence of a child of eight pictured to her clearly enough what such a woman would be like: endlessly making new kimonos, surrounding herself with clothes, changing several times a day, and thinking of nothing but showing herself off. Her mother wasn't like that, and if she put on something different every day, there must have been some special reason.

'Why are you still wearing that dress, Mummy?' she asked when she came from school one day, staring at Tomoko's kimono. 'You wore it yesterday, and the day before, didn't you?'

'You're very sharp, darling—I didn't think you'd notice.'

'Is it a special one, Mummy?'

'Very special. I like it best of all the dresses I've got.'

It was a Shiozawa kimono of deep purple, set off with a sash of rust-pink. Over it she wore a patterned cloak of Indian red. The kimono shared her secret happiness, her dream of a new life—and would give her courage, she told herself now, to fulfil that dream. When she wore it she heard again the sound of breaking waves, the rustling of pines in the sea-wind; she was no longer degraded. . .

And now, in this kimono, she was waiting for Yamaji. As usual, there was no knowing exactly when he would come; but she was prepared now. Each morning she put on the kimono with a fresh awareness of all that it symbolized, and took it off at night with a renewed determination never to give in to Yamaji again. She had been troubled to know what to wear for that first secret meeting with

Soshu. She wanted him to see her in the clothes that most suited her. But when she tried to choose, it seemed to Tomoko that almost all her clothes were somehow soiled, however spotless they might be: if Yamaji had seen her in a kimono only once, it was defiled. This left very few to choose from. But the feeling of contamination was too strong to be disregarded, and so it was that she was driven back upon the purple Shiozawa kimono. Of this secret of hers Soshu knew nothing, nor would she tell him. The under-robe, of course, was new. In the simple, astringent purity of its pattern—pink plum blossoms on a white ground—lay a suggestion of decision, a challenge. Tomoko had begun to make it herself, long before she promised to meet Soshu at the temple in Isshinden, even before she could have guessed such a meeting might ever be possible. She was not consciously building on what for all she could tell was an empty dream. Yet what delight the long evenings of sewing had given her! Hopes that she could not define, a woman's first faint intuition of new life awaiting fulfilment, returned as the pink and white silk took shape under her hands. Of these feelings Soshu could know nothing; they belonged to the secret world a woman creates for herself alone.

Yamaji had come when Tomoko was wearing this kimono for the fifth day. The clatter at the door was unmistakable, and the maid hurried out from the kitchen. Tomoko held her breath. She did not move as he went upstairs, although until now she had always gone out to greet him in the hall.

'Tomoko! Tomoko!' came an impatient summons from the room above her. She called the maid and told her to prepare tea.

'Tomoko!'

'Take it up yourself, will you, Sumi?'

The maid stared at her open-mouthed for a moment, then went out.

'Tomoko! What are you doing?'

Above her the boards creaked. Yamaji was stamping restlessly up and down, like a caged animal.

Tomoko stood in front of her three-sided mirror. Yamaji had never seen this kimono, only Soshu. . . A noise outside the room—that was Sumi, of course, going upstairs with the tea.

Determined to defy him, she prayed for courage. But her nerves grew tense with fear, through which by some strange process memories rose of the inn by the seashore.

Tomoko had a peculiar way of putting on her sash. She would lean stiffly against a pillar to hold the bustle in position at the back while she adjusted the ends of the sash and tied the fastening band. So she was standing now, her body braced against the corner post of the *tokonoma*. Soshu had asked her if she always did it like that, she remembered—why should she think of it now, of all times?

That was what came of staring so long in the mirror. . . It was a little trick she'd invented, she had told him, when she began to live alone after her mother's death; it hadn't been necessary when there was someone to help her.

Very quietly she went out into the corridor, passing Sumi at the bottom of the stairs. Yamaji was standing at the top.

'Taking your time, aren't you?'

Tomoko looked at him calmly, as if he were far away and of little concern to her. Then she knelt and bowed in a wife's formal greeting to her husband.

'*O-kaeri-nasaimase*!' But the words were dead. . .

'Going out, were you?' Smiling now, Yamaji sat down. Her kimono seemed to have pleased him. There was something striking about her taste, he always thought, and she was so much more refined than his wife, an innkeeper's daughter. He drank his tea with deliberate carelessness, spilling some of it on his coat. Tomoko pretended not to have noticed, though normally she would instantly have wiped the spot clean with her handkerchief. Yamaji did not seem to mind, however, and rubbed the mark with his hand.

'I've told you the kind of woman I wanted you to be, and I can see my words weren't wasted. I'm pleased with you, very pleased. You're what I've made you—Yamaji's creation, you might say.'

To have before him at one moment the purity and refinement of a woman like Tomoko, whom nobody but himself might touch, and an instant later to maul and mutilate such beauty with all the brutality of which he was capable—such was Yamaji's way of satisfying his lust. That was what a woman one kept was for; and that was why he insisted on her taking such care of her appearance. What her reaction to this attitude of his might be he had never troubled to think. It gave him exquisite pleasure to see her lying crushed by the storm he himself had roused, hardly conscious and breathing faintly through half-closed lips; to renew the knowledge that the woman Tomoko was no more than an animal, a female beast, while he chose to make her so.

Yamaji caught at her hand. She did not resist, or if she did, no doubt it was a gesture with which a woman instinctively provokes the storm she knows is coming. But there was a stiffness in her hand he was not used to.

'There's something I should like to talk—'

'Talk can keep for afterwards.'

'No.' With her other hand Tomoko tried to loosen Yamaji's grip, and something of her meaning dawned on him.

'What is it?'

'Let go my hand, please.'

'What's the matter with you? I can hear just as well like this, can't I?'

'Let go my hand, please.' A firmness behind the words made itself felt. Yamaji dropped her hand.

'Sulky, eh?'

Tomoko did not answer.

'Sulking because I don't come often enough? Well, you've some reason, I suppose. Still, I'm a very busy man, you know.'

Tomoko shook her head slightly, struggling to keep herself under control.

'Let's hear what it's all about, then. Quickly now!'

Still kneeling, Tomoko bowed till her forehead touched the floor. Yamaji stared at her.

'The time has come when I ought to thank you—'

'What do you mean, the time has come?'

'—to thank for all you have done for me. It must come to an end, of course—but I am very grateful.'

'Tomoko!' Yamaji was thunderstruck, the more so because her tone implied a strength of will of which she had never, until now, given the least sign. He moved closer to her. 'Are you being serious?'

'Please forgive me for being so selfish.'

'Do you mean you are going to leave me?' said Yamaji disbelievingly. He glared at her, gradually sensing from the unfamiliar seriousness of her expression that something important to himself was involved. Tomoko looked determined enough—as if she expected to suffer, and was prepared. A woman like her wasn't capable of such obstinacy unless she were driven to it. . . Her resistance astonished him all the more. For a moment contradictory feelings distorted his pudgy face; then, abruptly, he laughed. 'So Mr Yamaji has to slink off with his tail between his legs, does he?'

Tomoko's shoulders quivered.

'You take a woman and look after her in every way you can think of—and then she gets up and tells you it's all over, thank you! That's a new one. I must say.'

The words were spoken without anger or bitterness, as if he were telling an amusing story of some friend's discomfiture.

'And you dressed up specially to soften the blow?'

So that was how he took it! thought Tomoko with disgust. Always himself in the centre of the picture, complacently interpreting everything around him to suit his own vanity.

'Who is he? he asked suddenly.

Tomoko raised her eyes, forcing herself to look him in the face. She was paler now.

'Who is he, I said?'

She longed to tell the truth. But Soshu had said nothing yet of when they would take the last decisive step together. That moment would come; but how or when, Tomoko could not know. Till then, at least, she must say nothing that might make Soshu's position even more difficult than it was. But she vowed again and again, that night at the inn, that she would break with Yamaji first, and now she was keeping her word.

'You suddenly announce you've had enough of me. All right—I'm asking you who the other man is. Doesn't that make sense?'

Tomoko did not answer.

'You can't tell, eh?'

'There's no one. . .'

'No one, indeed!' retorted Yamaji incredulously, looking as if he were ready to grab her by the shoulders and shake the truth out of her; like a parent vexed by some childish attempt at deception.

'No one at all, eh? Then why all this talk of deserting me?'

'I've been thinking, it's not right for this kind of thing to go on indefinitely.'

'Is that all?'

'It's on my mind always; there's no peace. . .'

'You mean to tell me that's your only reason?'

'And there's Shoko. She's growing up very fast now. I'm so afraid she'll realise what it is her mother's doing.'

'Now you're trying to make me laugh,' spluttered Yamaji, ignoring the desperate seriousness with which she had spoken. Here was something so ridiculous he could not help laughing, even in the midst of his anger.

'What do you think of that—starting a conscience at your age! Never heard anything so absurd. Or have they suddenly made you president of the local PTA or something?'

The mere mention of Soshu's name would be enough to settle everything. But how violently would Yamaji react—and what revenge would he take?

'Childish nonsense, that's what it is, and it won't do for me, I can tell you. Like the ending of some cheap sugary film. And you thought I'd let you go without a murmur, did you? Perhaps I will, come to that—if you can give me a reason that makes sense! That's why I'm asking who the other man is. What's the point of a woman in your position giving up the man who keeps her, unless she's found someone else? If she has, all right, the first man's in the way; but if not, she *can't* have anything against him. Don't you remember how glad your mother was when I came along? Thanks to me, you've got a comfortable home, money enough to keep yourself and the girl; you can go shopping in the department stores, see films and plays whenever you like—and if you're going to turn round now and say all this is disgusting and wrong, it can only be because you've got some reasons of your own so strong that they'd convince anybody. Miracles and freaks apart, women just don't act any other way.'

Too well aware that she could give no good reason without mentioning Soshu, Tomoko still did not answer.

'And there's no sense in getting worked up about your daughter. She'll have guessed long ago about us—she's quite sharp enough, and anyway your mother as good as told her. No, you won't make me believe it's for her sake. Do you have the courage to give up this life, for one thing? How do you suppose you'll make a living?' Excited by his eloquence in exposing her flimsy excuses, Yamaji grew steadily angrier. 'There's somebody else—and you want to marry him, I suppose.'

As if it were as simple as that, thought Tomoko in a rush of despair.

'If he's serious, and the right sort of man, I don't say I won't let you marry him. I'm not that pig-headed, I hope.' In fact, Yamaji was very far from any thought of letting her go. His lust was roused—she would surrender at once if he chose to use force; but even Yamaji had some notion of keeping up an appearance of consent on Tomoko's part, and wanted to make her say in so many words that she had never really meant to break with him. That wouldn't be difficult—and force could come after, anyway. . .

'If you let it be known you've decided not to depend on me any longer, people will admire you for a while. Do you think you can live on admiration, though? Sentimental dreaming, that's what your fine ideas come to. Women have these notions. Of course I don't say you're wrong, mind you. But the tremendous sacrifice it would mean—it's obvious to me, but you've never seriously thought about it. Even then, I wouldn't object, if I thought you had the smallest chance of standing on your own feet. But you haven't. It's a hundred to one—a hundred to nothing at all—you'd ruin yourself if you tried to go your own way. Wishful thinking won't help you. You've never suffered like the rest of us—if you had, you wouldn't have kept those good looks; you don't find every woman your age with a complexion like that I can tell you! If you've stayed pretty womanly, it's because I've looked after you, given you a comfortable life all these years. I've made you what you are. I'm in your blood, you might say—or you're a work of art I've created, if you like. If you think that somewhere tucked away inside you you've got a "conscience", or whatever you want to call it, that doesn't belong to me, you're mistaken. I don't mind your sulking now and then. In fact I find it attractive. But don't upset me with this sort of talk again; it only shows up how weak and stupid a woman you really are.'

Tears—a woman's way of admitting defeat, thought Yamaji complacently—filled Tomoko's eyes.

'You've never shown any sign of jealousy or grumbled about anything up till now. Something must have been bottled up inside you so long, it finally had to explode. Morbid brooding, that's what it is; and it'll have to stop. What is it you want me to do, eh? What d'you want? Keeping it all to yourself won't do you any good.'

'Please, Mr Yamaji—'

'Still moping? Can't you understand what I'm telling you? All right, go on with your moaning if you must: I shan't listen.' Quite gently, Yamaji picked up her hand. She tried to pull it away; he smiled, enjoying her attempt at resistance, and gradually tightened his fingers over hers. Tomoko's cheeks reddened, her arm straining to free itself.

'Sentimental, schoolgirl nonsense! One doesn't expect it from a woman of your age.'

The struggle could only end one way, but it was taking more effort than Yamaji had anticipated. For a second hesitation flickered; but he was in no mood to stop now, and grew more stubborn.

'You're an obstinate, stupid fool of a woman!'

Tomoko shook her head repeatedly, astonished and elated by the power to resist she had discovered in herself. She could be brave, then, even heroic; no longer the old Tomoko. . . Freeing her hand meant so much—the symbol not so much of her hate for Yamaji as of her longing to break utterly with her other self, the plaything of his lust, the tortured woman who sacrificed her body to him and yet was fulfilled in that very sacrifice. . .

'There's more to you than I thought, I can see now. So much the better! I prefer a woman one can—get one's teeth into, you might say. One gets tired of pretty little dolls after a while. . . Now you begin to excite me—'

'Let me go!'

'Fool! Struggling won't get you anywhere. It's not the first time I've done what I liked with your body . . . you're only living here in luxury because your body's mine to use in whatever way I like. Quite a change from the normal routine. . . but quite as amusing!' His complacency still very little shaken, Yamaji tried to pull her to him. Tomoko slipped out of his arms, and, trembling, backed across the room, wriggling like a caterpillar out of several more attempted embraces and managing to push him away when he grabbed at her waist with one hand. Yamaji was furious.

The Tomoko he had known, it dawned on him, had been merely a body divorced from its owner's will; now this woman's body was alive, repelling even his first approach. . .

'You're going too far altogether, Tomoko!'

'Please forgive me!' Her hair hung loose, dishevelled.

'Stop fooling!' Yamaji's breathing grew more violent. 'What'll you do if I let you go, anyway?'

Tomoko had no answer.

'What about this house?'

She would leave, of course. Lowering her eyes, Tomoko straightened the skirt of her kimono.

'You really want to give all this up—everything?'

What other choice was there? Tomoko looked Mosuke Yamaji steadily in the face, unafraid, though a sudden breath of sadness seemed to chill her throat.

'Suppose I don't let you have your way so easily, though.' Yamaji had stopped trying to embrace her, and was sitting some distance away. 'You're a piece of property I've put a good deal of capital into, and I don't feel like giving you away. I took a fancy to you when your husband died—no, earlier still. I'm fond of you, but there's more to it than that, if you want to know; I'm not in the mood to throw away all the money and trouble I've spent on you all these years.'

'It was hard for me to say what I said: but I can't go back on what I've made up my mind to do—I'd rather die. . .'

'What d'you mean, you'd rather die? Don't exaggerate—that sort of talk belongs only in films and old plays. What's more, it's ridiculous, when you think of it. Where's your life, if not in your body—and doesn't your body owe every pleasure it's capable of knowing to me? Or haven't you got any sense of shame left?'

Tomoko turned away.

'What is it you're after?'

What exactly did he mean? She wanted their relationship to end, of course; but she had made that plain already.

'You don't imagine you'll stay on in this house, do you?'

Tomoko shook her head.

'You've got some notion of where you'll go, I suppose, since you're not exactly a child. What else are you after, besides a place to live?'

Nothing else—only an end to this. . . What did he really mean, Tomoko wondered—refusing to let her go, and in the same breath pressing her to tell him what she would do when she was on her own?

'Your girl will suffer, of course. You say our relationship is bad for her, but that's one-sided. Who's to say the ease and comfort it brings you isn't what she'd choose? There's no knowing how terribly poverty can affect a child's mind; but with all the advantages she has now, she'll get on like a house on fire. You've got to see things from her point of view. If you think she's going to grow up wicked just because of me, that's absurd. And you said you'd rather die than stay here. . . Are you ready now to get out of this house, leaving everything behind,—*everything*, mind you?'

'Yes.'

'Liar! What about the kimonos I've had made for you?'

'I can manage without them.'

'Rubbish. You'd take them all with you.'

'No.'

'D'you mean that?'

Tomoko nodded.

'Someone I know had kept a woman several years, when she found herself another man. He was so angry, he called at her house with a truck one day when she was out, and took away every single thing—the furniture, the sewing machine, her clothes and everything else. He'd paid for them all, and he swore he wasn't going to let her run off with his property. Finally he sold the lot to a dealer for next to nothing and dropped the money in a Salvation Army charity-box.'

Yamaji would even take Shoko's clothes, thought Tomoko. It was easy to see how his mind worked. Few people are original in anything they do; fits of anger or weeping, the passion for revenge, or stinginess with money, all, in the last resort, are imitations of the way someone else has behaved. Yamaji had merely found himself a convenient model—which he would certainly follow if he were to find out about Soshu. Tomoko was no exception, either. Any woman in her position would gladly give up everything, if that was the price of the new life she longed for, and would see herself as something of a tragic figure, too. She herself, it occurred to Tomoko, was acting like the heroine of a film or serial novel: she might have been following the kind of advice given to 'Perplexed' in a newspaper question-and-answer column.

'If you've really made up your mind, all right—I'll know what to do. As it happens, though, I haven't tired of you yet, so I don't feel like turning you over to someone else.'

'Please!'

'That's why I keep telling you I'll have to meet this man you've got mixed up with, whoever he is. But we're only going round in circles and getting nowhere, because you keep hiding the only thing that matters behind all this 'please, Mr Yamaji' and 'forgive me' nonsense. His promises may be a pack of lies, for all you know. Anyway, we'd better forget about all this for the time being. You've told me what you want, but it's not the kind of thing to be settled in five minutes. How many times do I have to tell you—I won't let you go until you can show me some good reason why I should? Once I meet the man, of course, I may feel differently.'

At last, to her relief, Yamaji stood up. She had forced him, then, to recognise that she had a will of her own. Given time, he would surely bring himself to agree to their parting.

When she too rose, following his example, he was standing by the window. Outside was the view she knew so well; row upon row of grey roofs, and in the centre the cluster of tall trees surrounding the Shinto shrine. Yamaji turned round. Tomoko did not move, standing listlessly as if all strength had left her. The lobes of her ears caught his eye: they were very pale, yet plump and unusually prominent for a woman. . . Desire for her returned, inflamed by the new awareness that she would break with him if she could.

Tomoko did not trouble to watch him as he began to move. He crossed behind her; she thought he was heading for the staircase—when his arms caught her from behind in a savage embrace, dragging her roughly to the floor. For a moment she tried to resist. It was useless. Yamaji's strength was overpowering, and he kept her arms pinioned so tightly that she had no chance even to crouch.

'Let me go!'

'Not this time, you spiteful little bitch!' Yamaji spoke softly, his mouth against her ear.

'Let me go. . .!'

'Want to scream do you?' He was laughing now. Tomoko tried once more to wriggle out of his arms, but they were clamped round her immovably, like some great wooden vice; the struggle as ineffectual as the last vain quivering of a butterfly caught in a spider's web. To cry out would be useless. With the secret world of this upper room—whatever might happen there—no third person could have anything to do. . . Tomoko lay still. Yamaji did not loosen his vice-like embrace; he would hold her there, apparently, till she fell limp on the floor. He had not intended this assault. If Tomoko had been sitting opposite him, as she had been earlier, he might have passed her with some casual parting phrase, and gone downstairs. But when she had stood there, her back half turned, for a moment no longer tense against him, her ears had suddenly fascinated him.

Tomoko had stopped struggling when it struck her how absurd she must look, her body bent and twisted in the forced embrace of the arms of a man whose face she could not even see. If they had been only playing, it would have made no difference. But now—the very moment she had told him she would leave him—to be treated like this. . . her 'heroic' determination snapped, leaving only misery. She had made no impression on him; she must start over again, find some other way. Yet passive acceptance of suffering came easier to her than defiance, and of hysterical violence—screaming and clawing and scratching—she knew herself to be incapable.

'You've insulted and humiliated me. But I'm feeling generous, and I'll forgive you.'

Her body sagged against his arms, inert.

'There's precious little you can do now, is there?' Yamaji laughed, rubbing his face against her back. 'And the sooner you realise that, the better. I wasn't taking you seriously when you said you wanted to be on your own.' He was still holding her, swaying slightly with the effort. 'Not because I don't have any feelings about it. I'm too fond of you—that's why I couldn't think of letting you go. I love you, Tomoko, I love you, I tell you!'

Still held in this humiliating, absurd position. . . to hide it from herself, Tomoko covered her face with her hands. For Yamaji there was no absurdity; only a pleasant sensation of relief that his final strategem had been successful. She had never imagined that her fierce, passionate resolve could be so brittle, to be shattered in a moment by a single action of Yamaji's—and one which made her look so ridiculous. . . if he had flown into a rage, it would have been easier.

His arms released her without warning, and she fell prostrate.

'Take a bit of taming, don't you?' Yamaji said. 'No more of this nonsense about leaving me. You couldn't give me up, anyway—you may think you could, but your body knows better.'

Halfway down the stairs he turned and called out to her.

'I'll be going to Beppu in a week or two on business—by plane as far as Fukuoka, and then the train. You said you'd never flown before. I'll take you with me.'

Tomoko listened dully to the voice of the maid politely showing him out. Like a petal idly twisted from its flower, she lay numb and motionless on the floor, aware of nothing but a sense of desolation. The house was silent once more.

Suddenly she turned on her face and broke into a violent spasm of weeping. Nothing was left to her but tears—the last confession of her weakness. . . Every one of Yamaji's taunts had been justified. The kimonos he had given her, for instance; she *did* long to keep them, in spite of all her heroics. What she had said about Shoko was true, certainly, but so were his insinuations. If only she could have defied him to the end. . . The pink and white pattern of her under-robe caught her eye, peeping from her sleeve, Pink plum-blossom on a white ground; their purity was defiled—and with them, Soshu. . . what she could do but weep?

Some time later, the fit of weeping exhausted, Tomoko rearranged her kimono and went downstairs. She sat before the mirror for a moment, and noticed the faint swelling of her eyelids.

'I'm going to the temple for a while,' she called to the maid. Soon she was on the bus, the high collar of her winter coat turned up to hide her face.

No sound disturbed the deep stillness of Butsuoji, from the great gate up through the motionless trees to the bell-tower and temple hall; the air seemed clearer, more transparent than elsewhere. Tomoko went up the steps into the hall. Against the cave-like gloom of the unlit sanctuary, the gilt pillars and the brass of the Three Ornaments gleamed coldly. Clasping her hands, she stood with bowed head. Whatever the mitigating circumstances, it had been of her own choice and will that she had let Yamaji take her. She had no one else to blame for the misery she had endured as his mistress. By the same token, no one but herself could end it. When she had made her promise to Soshu, she had been so confident of herself, imagining she had only to tell him their relationship was at an end for it to be so. She could—and would—act, to cleanse herself: since the meeting with Soshu at Isshinden she had lived on that belief. But the man to whom she had surrendered herself had no reason to feel as she did. She sinned of her own will, it was only by her own will that she could save herself—but in neither case without involving others. There was no resisting a man once he used force; not all her fear and loathing of continued degradation could protect her. But it was no use blaming Yamaji. Only her own weakness had made her capitulate, and, deep down beneath her conscious determination to resist, a readiness to take the easy way. The words of Christ came to her:

> For whatsoever a man soweth, that also he shall reap.

But the power to reap the harvest of her decision was no longer hers. Tomoko pictured Soshu, Soshu as she had often seen him, sitting reverently before this sanctuary. He could not save her. 'That also shall he reap. . .' Even Soshu, of all people, was caught up like herself in this agony. How deep, how far-reaching her karma must be, she thought. Had karma not made her what she was, as the karma they brought with them into the world shaped the character and life of every man and woman? Her relationship with Yamaji, the meetings and growing intimacy with Soshu, and now the longing to free herself from Yamaji for Soshu's sake—all were the work of karma. A verse of the Tripitaka describes it:

> All the deeds men can do in the world
> Are karma.
> All they may call their own
> Is karma.
> This they carry with them

When they leave the world.
This it is that must follow them always
As the shadow follows the light.

And from this she was struggling to escape, torturing herself to achieve the impossible! The struggle itself, perhaps, was a sin; the sooner she gave up the attempt to save herself by her own will, the better. . . The deep, silent calm of Butsuoji surrounded her.

Nor less I deem that there are Powers
Which of themselves our minds impress;
That we can feed this mind of ours
In a wise passiveness.

Think you, 'mid all this might sum
Of things for ever speaking,
That nothing of itself will come,
But we must still be seeking?

wrote Wordsworth. The 'mighty sum of things for ever speaking', the 'Powers' that impress our minds—what are these but the operation of the Infinite Being, the very life of the Universe, upon mortal men and women? Karma it is said, is one such 'Power', deriving from the structure of the universe itself, against which finite human beings are utterly helpless. To claim that Tomoko's present suffering was merely the consequence of her own folly would be far too simple; her life was directed by the invisible 'sum of things'. Can there be any release from one's karma, any cancelling of accumulated evil? Only when a man throws himself upon the mercy of the Infinite Being, abandoning all hope of saving himself, and preparing a way within his heart for One greater than himself, to enter. Though scarcely aware of such concepts as 'finite' and 'infinite', Tomoko was all but ready for this step.

How can I look for mercy,
How cross the raging sea, but by the boat of Amida's Vow?

In such simple words had St Shinran spoken of the Infinite Being. 'The boat of Amida's Vow'. . . Tomoko saw the meaning of the words so easily now, so clearly—proof of an unusually sensitive Buddha-nature, the ability to feel that Other which is beyond the self and yet within it. For this, the many memories her parents had left engraved upon her mind had prepared the way. Thanks to her mother, in particular, she had been used to a religious atmosphere ever since she was a child; and the Buddhist piety of her ancestors

Basis for the affair

took root easily in Tomoko, nourished by the sincere faith of the whole family.

She was now sitting motionless, statue-like, on the cold floor of the hall. Nothing in her nature prompted her, even subconsciously, to attempt to justify herself. Yet she was oppressed by a vague sense of guilt, as her ancestral faith clashed with the way of life she had chosen—out of self-preservation—to lead. At its deepest level, her life was grounded in that faith; yet so long as her conscious mind was preoccupied with her petty human self, struggling for its own survival, there was no way for the merciful, infinite power of Amida to enter her soul. The moment a man casts off all thought of self, that Power reveals itself within him. For Tomoko, that moment was not yet.

—Supposing she had gone away suddenly, she thought, instead of staying to submit to his brutality—mightn't that have been one way out? Not for her. But not because Soshu had not suggested it. How to break with Yamaji concerned no one but herself—Soshu or no Soshu, it was a problem she would have to face sooner or later. As if running away to some other town with Shoko would be simple. . . Shoko's schooling, for instance. Tomoko had read in the paper of a mother who had disappeared like that, with four or five children. Easy enough to say 'how irresponsible! the woman's no better than an animal—simply gave in when life got a bit too hard for her'. But in fact, running away would make life twice as hard. . . Tomoko saw herself threatened with the same dilemma: imagining all the suffering flight would bring, yet knowing as clearly there was no alternative. If she been alone, she could have gone now, with only the kimono she was wearing. But Shoko—she must take all the child's clothes, at least. Yamaji had taunted her with being too fond of her kimonos to leave him. She would miss them, of course—but Shoko's dresses mattered so much more, she couldn't part with *them*. . . so that in the act of turning against Yamaji, she would be clinging to what he had given her, making a mockery of her good intentions, forced to compromise with the vulgar mercenary streak in her woman's nature in spite of all her longing for purity. . .

Steps sounded in the corridor leading to the priest's house. Tomoko had meant to leave unnoticed .The thought of meeting Soshu had not crossed her mind, nor indeed did she want to see him now. But it turned out to be only the old priest, Shoju. Tomoko stood up quickly, as though embarrassed to be seen there.

'You've come to worship?'

'Yes, just to pray for a while.'

Picking up her coat, Tomoko left the hall. The droning of an invisible aeroplane echoed across the dark winter sky, like distant peels of thunder.

33

A bell began to ring just as Renko entered the school by the back gate. The porter was swinging the heavy hand-bell in the covered way connecting the school-buildings, with a hand on one of the roofposts to steady him. The sound brought back so many memories. . . From all over the playground children began filing into the corridors towards their classrooms. Some hung back, rushing up only at the last minute; but little by little the clamour died away, till finally silence returned, and teachers left the common-room to join their classes. Ryokun stood at the head of his class as they waited, lined up in the corridor in double-file—he was a class captain now. Glancing quickly up and down the two lines, their teacher gave the word, and Ryokun led the class into their room.

Renko stood looking across the empty grounds. It seemed only the other day she herself had grown used to the porter's bell—impossible, surely, that it was Ryokun, not herself, who now heard it every day? She saw herself a child still, skipping about the playground. . . Renko turned towards the porter's room. It was old and shabby now. In this one room the porter and his wife—they had no children—had been living for more than thirty years. The priest of Butsuoji came regularly to read the sutras before its tiny family shrine.

'You'll have a cup?' It was cheap *bancha* the porter's wife offered her, with little of tea about it but the colour. Renko sat down. The water in the huge pot on the brazier was nearly boiling; the porter was waiting to fill the kettles, nearly twenty of them, which he would take round to the classrooms when the lunchbell rang.

'Shall I call him right away?' said the porter's wife.

'No, a bit later, if you wouldn't mind. They've only just gone in. When they stop for lunch will do.'

'Master Ryokun goes home for lunch. All the children who live near do.'

'He used to eat with his friends at school—he always loved the lunch-boxes I made for him.' His little ways were changing without her knowledge, Renko realised with a pang. Yet always on these occasions, the moment she arrived at the school she felt at peace, in the certainty now at last she would really see her son. Like a happy child intend on finding excuses to spin out its playtime, she tried to think of ways of prolonging the moments they met face to face. Afterwards, the desire to see him again would revive, growing stronger, till it filled even her dreams—and she had found a way to satisfy the longing when it was no longer to be suppressed.

'I'm sorry to keep troubling his teacher. It's really asking too much—' Ryokun's class-teacher was a member of the Butsuoji congregation.

'You needn't worry, Mrs Renko. Mr Sakakibara knows how things are at the temple. He's glad he can help.'

Renko had arranged with the teacher that he should write to her from time to time asking her to come to Tan'ami, ostensibly to talk over some aspect of Ryokun's schooling which 'it would be more appropriate to discuss with her than the temple family.' Without some such pretext, her husband would not have let her come.

'I don't suppose everything's that easy for you even now, Mrs Renko.'

'The old lady isn't too easy to get on with, it's true—you know how mothers-in-law can be.'

'Everybody's so happy you've been able to settle down again, though.'

'It was hard at first, with some one else's baby to feed all of a sudden; but by now he's forgotten I'm not his real mother, and that makes a lot of difference. The old lady, though—she's a bit difficult, naturally. She really hates my making these visits to Tan'ami. She knows very well I never set foot inside the temple, but for some reason or other she always tries to stop me coming.'

'How old would she be?'

'Seventy-seven.'

'It's the thought of you seeing Ryokun gets her back up, maybe.'

'But what's wrong in my seeing him now and again? It's nothing to do with her.'

'She doesn't like the idea of you having any ties outside her family, least of all with the temple, even indirectly. That's all it is.'

'What with her complaints and my husband not approving either, it's getting quite an ordeal to come here now. And then the teacher has to go out of his way to write. . . I feel so guilty.'

Renko had settled down well enough to her new life in the village, accepted by her husband's relatives and by the villagers in general as an excellent choice for the headman's second wife. If she had to be patient at times with her mother-in-law, so did every bride; and in her case the lady was so old, there was no question of any real quarrel. Gradually, as the memory of her life at Tan'ami faded, she noticed herself slipping into country ways. This did not disturb her: the thought of living quietly on into old age as a headman's wife gave her a kind of serenity, even. But at a deeper level she saw her new life only as a temporary, dream-like state, in which she could never rest, for her heart was elsewhere—with the treasure she was forbidden to possess. She had no home she could visit when she was lonely. Her mother was living—but how could she call her 'mother' now? Soshu was all but forgotten, Butsuoji held no pleasant memories, she hated Mineyo; yet her mother was still her mother, and by now even her hatred had cooled. Time and forgetfulness had saved Renko from her past. All those theatre visits, the secret, hectic meetings with the actor, belonged only to some far-off dream, now that she had established her position as the headman's wife. But Ryokun she could not forget. Her love for him went deeper than memories; it was part of her consciousness, of her very identity.

The porter picked up as many kettles as he could hold and started off to the classrooms, leaving his wife to fill the rest. White steam swirled in a furious dance above the boiling pot before evaporating. Renko looked down at her bag. She had brought some of Ryokun's favourite *kintsuba* cakes, remembering how he loved sweet things—but only the best; he wouldn't touch the soft, sticky candy they sell in cheap cakeshops.

'There's trouble enough at Butsuoji, too. They had a parishioners' meeting the other day about Father Soshu. . . He himself never opened his mouth, they say. What's he really want, I'd like to know?'

'What do they say he's done?'

'They can't just leave things at the temple as they are. . .'

'Was it about his marrying again?'

'That's what they're after, but he won't say a word one way or the other.'

The tainted atmosphere of Butsuoji. . . deep within her, Renko felt its presence still. Running away had brought no purification; her blood was her mother's, her own responsibility inescapable.

'He's bound to marry fairly soon. What will happen to mother then, I wonder?'

'The parishioners say she'll have to go away and live on her own.'

'But she'd still be free to visit the temple, wouldn't she?'

'Not if the parishioners have their way. There'd be no point in her getting out, they say, unless she promised to keep away altogether.'

'Do you think she'd ever agree to that?'

'She's guessed what they're after, anyway, judging by the face she made at some of them when they went to see her the other day.'

'Mother would never dream of leaving Butsuoji. She's always been convinced she would die there.'

The prospect of Mineyo's expulsion from Butsuoji shocked and saddened Renko. That something of the sort might happen had occurred to her occasionally in a vague way, but the reality was a very different matter: there was a limit to her hatred, even of this mother who had driven her from her own home. How would Mineyo manage, forced to live alone? Would she send for her daughter—knowing Mineyo, it was likely enough, out of the monumental selfishness that had once made her scheme to get rid of that same daughter—to come and visit her and keep her company? If the temple was forbidden her, there was no one else she could turn to. And Renko knew she could not refuse. She would have to care for Mineyo, give her the attentions no one else could or would. Once every eight weeks or so, probably, she would be sent for. What would her husband and his mother say? She saw too clearly how difficult things would be.

Mineyo had no one but herself to thank, of course. This was only the punishment she deserved. But she herself would never see it like that. She would spend her days nursing her hatred of Butsuoji, now that there was nothing else to live for. And Ryokun? They would forbid him to see his grandmother, she supposed. It was no good trying to persuade herself she was just a village headman's wife, thought Renko, with the years stretching quietly before her into old age. Her ties with the temple remained unbroken; a curse that would haunt her all her life. Was that her destiny? Sitting in a corner of the porter's room, Renko let her thoughts wander into the future.

—Perhaps she'll get a bunch of old women together and amuse herself preaching to them. . . Renko remembered how cleverly Mineyo could parrot the sermons visiting priests used to give. One thing was certain, wherever she lived she would never stay at home quietly by herself all day. Renko found herself pitying her mother.

The porter had just started off with another set of kettles, this time for the classes in the first grade. In the classrooms children began whispering and fidgeting the moment the kettles arrived—as if they had suddenly realised they were hungry and could not wait any longer. Usually the porter deposited a kettle just inside the door of each room and then went on to the next; but in one room he paused, then went up to the teacher and whispered something.

Ryokun stiffened as the teacher's eye fell on him, reacting instinctively to their unspoken message.

'Getsudo!'

He stood up. A flash of expectancy darted through the small body.

'Go to the porter's room at once.'

Ryokun followed the porter out. The porch at the end of the corridor was a solid mass of shoes, a whole field of them, looking almost indistinguishable from each other; but in no time Ryokun had picked his out and was dashing across the playground.

'I wonder how your mother is?' his grandmother had said half-tearfully two or three nights before, though normally she never spoke of Renko. Ryokun had not mentioned their secret meetings in the school-porter's room even then: keeping the secret gave him a feeling of superiority. The feeling was stronger than ever, now that he was to see her again.

'Mother!' he called out as he burst into the porter's room. She stood waiting for him, her hands outstretched.

'What are you doing every day, Mummy?' Ryokun could not understand what was meant by his mother having 'married again': for him, she was only on a long visit somewhere, and still belonged to Butsuoji. He might have some vague idea of what a 'second marriage' was, but could not connect it with her.

'Oh, I'm busy with all sorts of things.'

'Aren't you coming back to the temple?'

'Not to the temple, no.' Renko's answer was resolute. But a grown-up's determination means nothing to a child, and Ryokun took no particular notice.

'Granny's talking about you.'

'What does she say?' Renko's interest was aroused. She knew the loneliness, the terror her mother would be facing.

'She wonders what you're doing, and says she's angry because you don't write to her.'

Renko smiled bitterly, but not in malice, at the thought of the suffering her mother had at last brought on herself. Mineyo was an unhappy woman, born under an unlucky star. It was as the village headman's wife, a member of a wholly different circle, that Renko thought of Butsuoji—of Soshu, of the parishioners—now; distance lent objectivity even to her understanding of Mineyo. To that extent, at least, she had grown up. All women who marry, of course, go through a period when they feel they belong neither to the old family nor to the new, but are somehow stranded as it were, between the two. So it was now with Renko, and would be for five or ten years, perhaps, until her transformation into a member of the headman's family was complete, and the old ties forgotten. This was how she would have felt when she married Soshu, she supposed, if the marriage had meant her leaving home in the ordinary way.

Ryokun had begun to eat one of her cakes. Blissfully she watched him, forgetting to speak. There was nothing else she could do to make him happy. With Soshu, with her mother even, she could have been objective, impersonal; but not with Ryokun. . . That alone would prevent her from ever becoming truly one of the headman's family.

Supposing she had another child? But her affection for Ryokun would not change; on the contrary, because he had been left almost an orphan and so lonely, she felt she loved him all the more. Ryokun had such big eyes, just like Soshu's. She smiled as he stared at her, eating away at his cake. There was something inexpressible, a deep, hidden sadness, it seemed to Renko, in those eyes. But in fact they were innocent of any such meaning—merely gazing at the face that happened to be opposite; the sorrow she saw there was her own. Tears came to her eyes. The porter's wife poured her a second cup of tea.

'It's nearly lunchtime. You go back to Butsuoji for lunch every day, do you, darling?'

'Mm. I don't like bringing a lunch-box. The rice gets cold.'

'You'd better not eat too much now, or you won't want any lunch. Your granny wouldn't like that.'

'I don't care.'

'She worries so much about your meals, Ryokun, and whether you have a good appetite or not—she'll know at once you've been eating somewhere else.' Yet she loved the eager way he ate what she had brought. Mother and child were alone now—the porter's wife had left the room a moment or two before. For a while they sat in silence, as if the food Ryokun was eating were the only bond between them. Renko longed to talk to him more freely, to find some physical gesture he would accept into which she could pour her love. To bring him something to eat was the only way she knew.

'What would you like Mummy to bring next time, Ryokun?'

'Pineapple!'

'Do you really like pineapple so much? You can get that anywhere nowadays. Never mind—I know all your favourites, darling. I'll find something.'

'Shall I tell granny you've been?'

She might just as well approach Mineyo now through Ryokun, thought Renko. She must be on her guard still, of course; but her mother had surely changed, and at least it was a relief to feel that she herself was no longer the chief enemy.

'There's no need to tell her specially—but don't keep it a secret, either. You'd better not tell your father, though.'

'Father never talks about you.'

'He knows Mummy comes here to see you.'

'Why doesn't he ask me about it, if he knows?'

'No one can stop Mummy and you meeting, darling—no one at all.'

'Is the place where you're staying far, Mummy?'

'You have to take a bus first, and then a train—'

'I want to go!'

'There's a mountain, and a big river with trout in it.'

'I can swim, Mummy! I went out fishing with Sei-chan and caught a catfish—*this* long!'

'The river's dangerous, darling, unless there's a grown-up with you! Didn't granny give you a scolding?'

'I didn't tell her where we'd been.'

The little conversation was trivial enough; but Renko was satisfied. Every word of Ryokun's she would take back with her to the village to remember afterwards: so many tiny reflections of her son's life.

They went on talking, but it seemed only a moment till the porter came back to fetch the big hand-bell.

34

Tomoko was cleaning her family shrine, dusting every corner meticulously. This was one task she would never give the maid, a duty she enjoyed, to be performed with deliberate, loving thoroughness. Facing her on the altar was her mother's memorial tablet. Her mother's spirit was watching her, Tomoko felt: silent but omniscient, knowing the passionate eagerness with which she awaited Soshu's monthly visit the next day. Not that she was ready for his coming. . . she had broken her promise to him; it was brute force that had made her break it, perhaps, but that did not make the promise any the less her own decision, for which she alone was responsible. How could she face him, defiled as she had been in that kimono that he alone had seen. . . involving even him in her sin? Now she was beyond even the hope of redemption.

—Mother must have known the misery a woman inherits with her sex. . . Tomoko hated the body her will could not control, the physical organism that Yamaji had trained to respond to his lightest touch, like the strings of a harp, as accurate and inevitable in its reactions as some finely-built machine. Worst of all, it had betrayed her at the very moment she was struggling for freedom—when her conscious self was withdrawn. . . For Tomoko this was the moment of final crisis, which would decide whether or not she could ever find the way back to self-respect. Death would at least be simple. . . There had been such a confusion of emotions at the time. The shock of his sudden grabbing at her shoulders, forcing her down from behind—like being set on at night in a dark street. . . She had fought to escape, but knowing all the time she must not scream; his male strength biting into her sides till she was all but choking, his breath on her cheek. But she had felt no physical panic, as she would have done if the assault had been by some unknown attacker. A trial of her strength against his, in the knowledge that her life was never threatened—it was that, and no more. Her life *was* threatened, but the threat was for the future; its terror of the mind, not of the body. And because she was not in physical danger, and knew it, her struggle had ended as it had—in a lovers' embrace! As if she had merely been in a particularly bad mood, and had given way to caresses. Tomoko could not forgive herself. Yet it was only her body that had given way. If it had been any other man, she might have resisted longer, even to the point of physical danger; but it was Yamaji, whose touch her senses knew with an intimacy that had sapped her will. Yamaji's fit of violence had passed; he had had his usual way with her passive body. A feeling of sadness overwhelmed her, and faded as quickly. It was scarcely surprising if her physical sensations had been hard to analyze—like harpstrings plucked in a strange chord never heard before. Frustration, self-disgust, and a deep sadness were all she was conscious of now. And her mother knew. . .

Perhaps Yamaji's brutality had been clever in a way. It was also inhuman: the action of a man who utterly ignored her as a person, a spiritual being, and saw even her faculty of physical sensation as his property. By it he had shown himself as animal as he assumed her to be. If he had contented himself with merely showing her how strong he was, the words she had spoken would have remained to encourage her, a step towards a final, unshakeable decision. But not now. . . Yamaji had shattered her will to resist. She could not bear the humiliation of pretending to defy him still, as if nothing 'unusual' had happened. What was left but to admit defeat? He must have realised that mere talk would never make her change her mind, Tomoko supposed, and so had taken deliberate advantage of her physical weakness. Clever of him, if you could call it that. . .

—But she would not give up. At least he knew now. Maybe it had been stupid just to tell him and expect the rest to be easy. To give meaning to her words, to be able to face him on equal terms, she should first have proved she could live alone. It would be all the harder now. There would be months, years perhaps, of hardship, of the sordid contriving she shrank from. But still, he knew—and surely the fact of his knowing would gradually force them apart, till the break came of itself, inevitably?

Her mother's death-name faced her from its tablet on the altar, watching her thoughts. Was it only for her mother's sake she had been able to call up that brave mood of a moment ago, Tomoko found herself wondering uneasily—when in fact it was only wishful thinking?

The front door clattered open. Abruptly, Tomoko stopped her dusting.

'Are you there?'

To her horror, it was Yamaji. Today, at least, Tomoko had thought, she would be left in peace. . . their quarrel had been only yesterday—

'Nobody at home, eh?' the voice repeated sharply, and with a note of arrogance. Sumi had gone to the market, Tomoko remembered.

'Coming!' she called out, as if she had not recognized whose voice it was at the door.

'Where's the maid?' he asked when she appeared in the hall.

'She's out shopping.' Tomoko knelt on the polished floor to receive him. Taking off his shoes, Yamaji went into the living-room, instead of hurrying straight upstairs as he usually did.

'Been cleaning the shrine, I see. Very pious of you,' he said, brusquely offensive. The mood was simulated, Tomoko guessed; a crude attempt to overawe her.

'Finished, have you?'

She nodded.

'Then you'd better shut it.' Yamaji watched her as she closed the doors of the shrine, fascinated by the grace of her kneeling figure. She clasped her hands for a last silent prayer—when thick hands seized her shoulders; she fell back—

'Couldn't sleep a wink last night, thanks to you! I've discovered I'm fonder of you than I thought.'

She lay quietly, half-upright, where his arms held her—or where she had leant against him, surrendering?

'Maybe you haven't always liked the way I've treated you. I've loved you, though, in my own way. I love you now—and I'm going to go on loving you. . .'

So that was why he'd come rushing back so soon—just to tell her that. Strangely, Tomoko felt no urge to struggle. Not out of despair, but in a mood of quiet acceptance of a single defeat, now that the first excitement of her decision had faded.

'The old lady at one of the geisha-houses keeps trying to get me to take one of her girls, but they don't appeal to me. You set the standard, you see. If ever a more attractive woman were to turn up, I tell myself—but none ever will. I'm certain of it. You were born to be loved, Tomoko, though you've never realised it. You could never support yourself; you're not that kind of woman. Not the fussy, domestic kind, either. Marrying that husband of yours and having a child was a mistake; that sort of thing doesn't suit a woman like you.'

Still in his embrace, the thrust of his body against hers merging with the words in a single compelling pressure, Tomoko could hardly pretend not to hear him.

'I wouldn't like to give you up. I wouldn't like it at all. . . I never thought I'd feel like this over a woman, of all things. Now I've told you, confessed, if you like, you'll start getting big ideas, I suppose, but that can't be helped: it's the truth. You must have thought about us a good deal last night, eh? You're still thinking, I shouldn't wonder—like me; I couldn't get you out of my head last night.'

'The maid will be back in a moment—'

'No matter. She'll see my shoes in the porch.'

Tomoko let him caress her face, in an agony of wretchedness that somehow failed to stimulate her paralyzed will. Suddenly his face fell upon hers. Helpless, she submitted to his kisses—only for her body to be overwhelmed in a flood of awakening response.

'A lot of my friends tell me they're in the same sort of position. They're all so busy, they can never relax properly with a woman. Women want to have leisure to talk quietly with the men who love them, and the men know that as well as anybody else. It's not that they don't want to talk, or haven't anything to talk about: they just haven't time. Never having time makes a man *feel* in a rush always; that's why he can't always be thinking about the woman's side of things. They keep their cars waiting outside, just like me. Can't even stay for the woman to make tea, they say. Back to the office the moment they've done what they came for. And what does the woman feel about her man rushing off like that? He feels he's done what he can, just by going to visit her—but she's bound to get a bit disconcerted in time. Anybody can see that: it's natural. But if she starts complaining and making all sorts of difficulties—that's a different matter. Always being in a hurry doesn't mean he doesn't care for her. She begins to feel she's just being used—all right; but there's something to be said on his side as well. One girl I heard about doesn't even see her man out when he's finished—lies on the floor for hours sulking.'

Tomoko managed to hide the twinge of guilt she felt.

'You can say the man's selfish. He takes her just for her sex, ignores her personality, and all the rest of it. But that's not how he feels at all; and that's where the trouble starts. Women dream up all kinds of nonsense, for the simple reason that they've got nothing to do but sit at home all day.'

'It's so—unnatural, living like this. . .'

'Do you really want to throw your life away on housework—a woman like you? Maybe if you'd never been married before—but you have: you know what happens to wives in ordinary marriages. . . Are you so sure you envy them? That sort of life might suit ordinary women, I daresay; but not you.'

Yamaji pulled her head up till it was opposite his own.

'Then there's your daughter. Suppose you were to marry again. What sort of affection would your new husband feel towards a child that wasn't his own—or would he even hate her? It's not likely he'd ever really care for her, but even if he did, how could you be certain he wouldn't change? Loving you doesn't mean he'd love Shoko too, you know. And look how well she's getting on as it is. You say you're worried about her future; that's only because you want to be conventional—but you can't be. . . the rules don't apply to your life now.'

35

There were only twelve or thirteen passengers in the first-class car. One arm resting on her fashionable greyish-purple suitcase, Tomoko sat waiting for the train to leave. Just as the whistle was blowing a man rushed into the car from the door behind her. After looking round for a moment he recognized Tomoko, and was evidently relieved at having found her.

'I was beginning to be afraid you hadn't come,' he said as he sat down opposite her. It was Yamaji's secretary. Smiling, Tomoko apologized. Not that she was in the wrong—her apology was one of those meaningless phrases, as automatic and unconsidered as breathing, that people use to greet each other when they meet.

'If we'd known the first-class car was going to be half-empty, there wouldn't have been all this fuss. Mr Yamaji insisted I should get on one station before, so as to make sure of finding seats in case it was crowded.' Tan'ami has two stations, one on the edge of the town and one in the centre. 'This will be the first time you've been with Mr Yamaji on one of his trips, won't it?'

Tomoko nodded. For years the secretary had been the only one who knew of their relationship.

'I shall be calling at your house once a day till you come back. Mr Yamaji's orders.'

'Thank you. . .' Perhaps if she asked him, Tomoko thought—'Is it true that he's changed over to the Nichiren Sect?'

'It certainly is,' replied the secretary. 'And as a matter of fact, I think he's rather annoyed about all the extra expense it involves, in donations and so on. But he won't change his mind. It's a complete break with the old family religion, he says. An expensive break, though.'

'Then he's no connection with Butsuoji any more?'

'Some of the elders still call now and then. His wife can't be positively rude to them, of course, but it's awkward for her. I don't think she quite knows how to treat them.'

'He keeps telling me to change too.'

'I'm not surprised, now he's got so determined about it. But people can't be forced to change their religion, surely—least of all someone like you, whose family have been Pure Land for generations. I shouldn't worry if I were you.'

Already they were nearing the big buildings of the central station.

'Will there be anybody to see Mr Yamaji off, do you suppose?'

'No.' The secretary shook his head. The reassuring expression on his face struck her like an insult. She was a 'woman of the shadows' —and how appropriate the phrase was!—condemned to a furtive, underground life, with no defence against the barbed judgements of conventional morality.

The train glided slowly to a stop. This time there were a good many passengers waiting to board the first-class car. The secretary gave up the seat opposite Tomoko to Yamaji, and went outside to see them off from the platform.

'Beautiful today, aren't you?' said Yamaji as the train began to move. For a moment Tomoko did not understand.

'That's what comes of seeing you always at home—I never realised how much prettier you look outside. Everybody's staring at you. . . and beginning to envy me, I suppose.'

Yamaji seemed to relish the thought of being envied on her account. None of the seven or eight other women in the car, not even the youngest, had anything like the natural loveliness of her complexion. Not merely that it was finer in texture, more delicate. Young girls are brimming over with the energy and joy of life: it only gives them a cheap, flashy look when they daub on paint indiscriminately, as some do, but shines out in a lovely radiance if the make-up is tasteful and in harmony with their age. Tomoko's beauty was of a wistful kind, her complexion moist and appealing, its classical whiteness shadowed with a hint of melancholy which seemed to soften the clear-cut lines of her eyes and nose and mouth.

'We shan't be in Itazuke before early evening—maybe even later, depending on which plane we catch. The train takes three hours from here to Osaka, and then it's still quite a way out to Itami. Ridiculous, Tan'ami not having an airport.'

Tomoko had brought their lunch with her. Yamaji had told her he did not like the lunch-boxes sold at the station, so she had spent the previous evening making preparations.

'Japanese husbands and wives don't talk much in public—if you see a couple chattering away and laughing, it's ten to one they're just lovers, or may be only just married. I wonder what people think of us?'

Yamaji stared at her again. In her heart there was something he could not see; a dark, silent anguish, lying heavy and immovable, like a stagnant pool. No cry could have given it relief; it was beyond tears, different in kind from the shallow pain of the senses. If she wept, it was unconsciously—like last night, for instance, when she had been startled by the mark of tears on her pillow. . .

'Typical married woman—that's what you are! Every detail perfect.' Yamaji was satisfied. 'If a woman of your age is not married, it goes without saying she's some kind of entertainer or geisha. There's nothing of the geisha about you, though. You're younger than me, of course—that's obvious; but you carry if off so beautifully, nobody would guess you were anything but a perfectly respectable housewife travelling with her husband. I always felt that was how it would be.'

About an hour later the train stopped at a large station.

'These trains with no restaurant car! I'll go and get some tea.'

She should have gone herself, Tomoko felt for a moment; but decided there was no need to worry—Yamaji was even rather pleased with himself, apparently. Perhaps he wanted to show he was capable of doing something for her, now that they were together in public instead of in the house where he kept her.

They began to eat their lunch.

'Quite a few changed their minds when they saw me going to buy the tea, I expect. Must be husband and wife after all, they'll be saying. Most husbands nowadays look after their wives in public, however much they throw their weight about at home.'

There was little else he could find to talk about, and Tomoko had nothing to say, not even when, annoyed at her silence, he took up his paper for the second time. Still without speaking, she watched the hills and fields slipping by. There was no expression, no feeling, in her face, Yamaji complained. But that was her nature, not her fault; not being able to show your feelings did not mean you were incapable of having any. There were people who would never show any weakness in front of others, yet who would break down the moment they were alone. . . Tomoko glanced at Yamaji, buried in his paper. A shock of revulsion at her own dishonesty swept through her. All this pretending with Yamaji, pretending there was no one—how easily it came! Vulgar, selfish, brazen-faced—what would Yamaji not call her if he knew of the storm raging behind the face he had just complained was dull, unemotional! A gentle yielding femininity was all he saw; the reality, a crude, unashamed sensuality, masquerading as its opposite. . . Yamaji could not see himself as he really was. Tomoko could. But even while condemning herself she knew she wanted only to continue as she was, the shameless egotist she despised herself for being—to welcome degradation instead of bearing it as a victim. The memory of the priest's last visit hung still fresh upon her senses. . . Tomoko looked out of the window, wondering at the shameless way she could sit in front of Yamaji and visualize every detail of that day. She had acted then from impulses she did not understand, as if in a trance—or on the verge of madness: panting feverishly, blind desire constricting her throat, her eyes bloodshot. . . Why that hysterical display she had always managed to avoid before—on that particular day? It was not Soshu's first visit since their meeting at the inn. The day before, Yamaji had called while she was cleaning the shrine; the only result of her plea had been to make him more determined than ever not to give her up. So she must forget her dream . . . or at least there could no longer be the same naive freshness of hope, the vivid sense that some transformation in her life was actually possible. Yet Soshu meant no less to her than before. Feelings crowded upon her, confused and dark. Maybe it was her imagination, but Soshu had looked strangely worn, she thought, when he called that day for the monthly service. She had sat behind him as usual as he read the scriptures, letting his voice soothe her tense nerves. But while her senses absorbed the music of the sound, Tomoko's mind was in revolt, forming other, more sensual images. She would like to serve him tea upstairs, she had said when the readings were over; and led the way without waiting for his reply. Something in her tone made refusal impossible. She had not planned the invitation; it was suggested by a sudden physical response to his presence, at the moment he stopped reading. Taking off his stole, Soshu followed her.

'Bring the tea-things upstairs, Sumi,' Tomoko called down to the maid. Soshu sat down in front of the *tokonoma,* upright and formal as always.

'This is a beautiful room. So light, and restful, too.' This was not mere politeness on Soshu's part. It was the only properly furnished part of the house. It would be here that Yamaji came, he remembered—there was no other room where he would be able to relax and feel entirely at ease.

Tomoko took the tea-tray from Sumi at the door.

'I told Yamaji—'

Soshu started, both hands holding poised just below his lips the tea-bowl from which he had just begun to sip. Tomoko smiled—a smile, for matter so serious? Soshu could not guess at the desperation that smile concealed, let alone at its meaning, which was the bitterest self-mockery. . . Edging closer to him, Tomoko put her hands on his knees.

'—and he refused to let me leave him.'

Their kimonos touched. Tomoko looked up into his eyes.

'Did you tell him about me?' Bitterly ashamed that Tomoko had acted first, Soshu cursed the weakness with which he had put off his own decision so many times, day after day, week after futile week.

'No, I managed not to. He kept asking me who the other man was, though.'

Soshu heard her like a criminal who is told his execution has been postponed.

'The time has come, then. . . I'm so angry with myself for being so weak—and so miserable—'

'Tomoko—' Tomoko spoke the name as if it were someone else's, not her own—'Tomoko has deceived you, Father!'

'*Deceived* me?'

'Once I'd said what I did, he ought to have been nothing to me. . . Be angry with me, Father! I am sinful, an evil woman. . . I didn't tell Yamaji about our meeting at the inn by the sea. I just said I wanted him to leave me alone, as if there were no other reason—but I failed. . .'

'How "failed"?'

'How can I make him understand, when he treats me just as he did before—and I let him. . .'

Soshu turned away so that she should not see his face—not knowing her suffering was identical with his own.

'It was his sheer brute strength, I suppose. But afterwards—that was the end of all my fine words: I might just as well have been tempting him. . . I'm not worthy to face you, Father! I'm. . . unclean!'

Leaning sideways, Tomoko pressed against him in a heavy, half-unconscious movement. Her face might lack expression, as she had been told: but when the moment came her whole body spoke for her.

'I too have been thinking—'

'You can't love me now!'

'I forgot too easily there were others involved besides myself. It was wrong to love you, right from the start—all the time I was thinking only of myself. But then I made my confession to you, and that saved me, in a way. I must find my way through now with the courage you gave me. But whether that makes it right to take you with me—I must think again. . .'

'No, Father—the moment I leave this house I can be yours!'

'You found the decision you took was not for you to take alone.

For me, it's not only Mineyo. We both have children, you and I—we'd left them out of our dreams.'

'I won't leave you, Father!'

'If only we had thought more about them earlier, we wouldn't have let things go so far.'

'I don't repent, Father! What we did was right and good, the most wonderful thing that ever happened in my life. You were actually kind, you treated me as a human being. Don't cast me off now—not back into *that*...!'

'I should have kept my love to myself. That would have given me the strength I needed; it was stupid and wrong to hope for anything more. I should be so helpless—how could I give you the life you want? and even supposing you could bear the poverty it would mean, you couldn't make Shoko's life miserable, just for my sake?'

'If her mother lives as a mother should, sooner or later she'll understand.'

'That's wishful thinking, a grown-up's trick to keep one's conscience quiet. Children have a destiny of their own their parents can't interfere with.'

'That's what Yamaji said.'

'Mr Yamaji knows the world better than I do.'

'Nothing will make me leave you, Father!'

'Your telling Mr Yamaji gives me new courage. But the idea was ridiculous in a way—to think he would give up a woman like you just because you asked him to!'

'A man may be able to forget someone he's loved, just by not thinking of her. A woman can't—I can't... I shall never stop loving you, Father.'

'I only make you suffer more—'

'I can bear it! There's a horrible, mercenary selfishness hidden inside me; even I don't know how deep it goes or what it will drive me to. If I wasn't always giving in to this selfishness of mine I couldn't face you like this. I made you a promise—and let the opposite happen... I ought to be on my knees pleading with you to forgive me. Instead—here I am... not even crying.'

'There are tears the eyes don't show.'

'Maybe. I brought you upstairs because I couldn't bear to think of your going. Till now I've been so careful to keep what was clean and pure unstained. But not any more... This is the room where Yamaji plays with his toy. Picture him, Father—and the impudence of the woman who decides to entertain you in the same room, her mind no more chaste than her body... There's no excuse, Father. I'm weak and selfish. I can't part with Yamaji, and I won't part with you. It doesn't make sense, a woman giving herself to two men at the same time—but that's what I'm doing. Maybe because something inside me is broken. . . That's the kind of woman I am, Father. If only I could dream once more of that time by the sea—and then again, and again. . . nothing else is real. . .'

'You're distraught—and because of me—'

'No more distraught than I've been for years now. There's never been any peace, not for a single day. That's why I've always depended so much on Amida, I suppose, just as my mother did. . . I turn to Him all the more when I think how great my karma-burden must have grown since I met you—and talked of a new life, only to go on sinning! I can't help myself any longer; as though there was nothing left of me but karma personified. . .'

'So it is with me.'

'Let me live as I have dreamed, Father!'

'And half your burden is of my making. . .'

Little by little, as if without her knowledge, Tomoko's fingers slipped under his kimono below his neck, where the white edge of his alb peeped out from under the black outer robe.

There in front of her sat Yamaji, eyes shut, newspaper spread out on his lap. She had never had an opportunity to observe him closely before. Even when he was talking, he would never face his hearer directly—and for her part, though normally she would look steadily and directly at whoever she happened to be with, Tomoko avoided Yamaji's eyes, not so much from fear, as from a hidden sense of guilt, as if something within herself that she could not bear to face had taken physical form, appearing before her as Yamaji. It had nothing to do with that kind of aversion with which one turns away sometimes from an unpleasant face seen casually on the street, in an attempt to erase the disagreeable impression. To his face as such, in fact, she would have been indifferent, if it had not reminded her always of the long chaos of her own feelings since her mother's death, the awakened desires, the bouts of conscience ending always in hysteria and futility. There was nothing to disturb her now, she told herself. Yamaji would never suspect what she was thinking or feeling; thanks to his ignorance, she could let her memory linger on each moment of that last meeting with Soshu.

She looked out at the yellowing mountains, their contours changing with bewildering speed as the train hurried past. For a while the track ran parallel with a stream, following the boundary of Nara and Mie Prefectures. There were many tunnels.

A blind passion had overwhelmed her. At first Soshu did not respond: the approach had been hers, the initiative a woman must not take. . . the blood racing through her body as it never did when she submitted, passive and all but indifferent, to Yamaji. Breathing heavily through barely-parted lips, her eyes flushed and burning, Tomoko knew she could act in no other way; and in a corner of her mind the knowledge cast a melancholy shadow.

'I should have stopped seeing you long ago. Parting has been our destiny, ever since we met.'

'I'll never leave you, Father, never.'

'I don't want you to suffer any more—'

'You mean you'll leave me to Yamaji?'

'But for Shoko's sake—'

'If that's what parting means, you'd repent of it afterwards, Father. You'd be unhappier than ever.'

To drift on as they were now, neither as lovers nor as merely priest and parishioner, was impossible. Tomoko was desperate: if for some reason they were compelled to stop meeting as priest and parishioner, she would agree to any way of continuing their relationship, if only she did not have to lose him altogether. But could she stand such a compromise, with the added suffering it would bring? Perhaps she had only spoken of it because she felt she could not: otherwise they would have been 'lovers' long since, though the word were never spoken between them.

'I've made up my mind not to see you again.'

'Father! Then I'll come to the temple. I've planned it already—like the women in foreign novels who find ways of meeting their lovers without upsetting their homes. . . It's not as if Yamaji came here every day—nor you, Father; I wouldn't ask you, anyway. I could manage so nobody would know—'

'I don't think you could, Tomoko. You're not that kind of woman. It couldn't last, and the blow would fall on you first when it came.'

'Father! . . . can't you be my lover?' Tomoko buried her cheeks in his priest's robe, unconscious of her body's instinctive, snake-like writhing as she pressed against him.

'Your lover?' Soshu smiled weakly. Some men, he supposed, would accept such a situation. If they could be content with meeting once or twice a month, the pain of frustration would be over. Would that mean fulfilment? Or was it better they should never meet again?

The wide sleeves of her kimono slid back as she rested her arms on Soshu's shoulders. She was trembling violently, hanging from his neck, and might have fallen had his arm not caught her.

'That's one way, I suppose, if we have the courage, or the audacity. The parishioners are right—Mineyo will have to leave Butsuoji, and sooner or later they'll find another woman for me to marry—or for the temple to marry, you might say; that's what it comes to—and so long as I can get on with her without any more upheavals, they won't worry any more. I could meet you somewhere once or twice a month—'

'Promise you will, Father! I could even bear your remarrying. . . it wouldn't be so different from Yamaji and me, anyway. I could bear anything, then—but not parting.'

Soshu felt the warm, milk-like flavour of her breath on his mouth. Her eyes were so close, the distance between them seemed somehow exaggerated, unnatural. . . he could make out each strand of her eyelashes, of the fringe of hair lying neatly on her forehead, the delicate texture of her skin. . . Suddenly she was in his arms, limp and heavy. A moment later she reached out a hand to straighten the edge of her rumpled skirt over her legs. Below the hem, the soft lines of the white Japanese socks she was wearing looked strikingly beautiful against the floormat, as though she had placed them there deliberately when she fell against Soshu.

'But I can't do it.'

'Father!'

Holding her head against his cheek, he spoke softly, as if talking to himself.

'Why do I have to suffer like this. . . it seems so absurd sometimes. In ancient China, married men used to have mistresses, three or four of them, even, without disrupting anybody's life—and even now a Moslem can keep three women besides his wife. Monogamy is only a custom. Maybe that's what makes our lives miserable, just a custom. . .'

Tomoko said nothing. Now and then her shoulders quivered uncontrollably.

'No, it's not that. When I met you I knew for the first time how unclean I was. Loving you has taught me what suffering means—real suffering: I was unhappy before, but you couldn't call it suffering.'

'You *can't* leave me, Father!'

Soshu kissed her. Yet there was little passion in his lips, and Tomoko knew at once that he was deliberately holding back.

'If it was only a question of our meeting, and nothing else besides, everything would be simple: I could be your lover, and we'd see each other secretly now and then. But I don't want that! If all this suffering were only superficial, that sort of solution might do. But it won't. I've discovered now the kind of pain I didn't know before, the pain that's worth enduring. . . you've taught your priest so much; he's grateful.'

'And what must *I* do? Tell me! I couldn't bear to lose you. . . don't take away the only hope I have, Father!'

'You'd suffer more than ever.'

'I know. I've been through so much already, I can bear it—if you'll give me just a little happiness, Father: the feeling that life is worth living, that's all. . .'

'There are plenty of other women in the same sort of position as you, forced to give up all their scruples and live in a way they hate because it's the only way to keep alive.'

'And some who do it just for the sake of their children—'

'And others who won't: the women who slave away at some menial job for a few hundred yen a day, putting up with every kind of hardship you can think of rather than lose their self-respect.'

'It's terrible how poverty can stunt a child's mind. . .' So Yamaji had said; now the fear was her own.

'Or the mother can sell herself for the child—but even then there's no knowing whether the child will grow up in the way she wanted.'

'I don't know which is right, Father. . .'

'Nor do I.'

She lay against him all the time they were talking, yet in spite of this physical intimacy passion had somehow receded. Soshu's embrace was without ardour; diffident, as if the woman in his arms were the embodiment of some unknowable, yet ominous mystery.

'You don't love me any longer, Father?'

'What do you mean?'

'I suppose the ordeals you and I have to go through must be different. . . I can understand what you say, somehow; but I'm a woman, and I can only think a woman's thoughts.'

'Which is as it should be!' There was life now in the arms that held her limply a moment before. 'This *is* happiness, for me too. It doesn't need any explaining.'

'You're so *cold*, Father!'

'Not cold—only inexperienced. This is the first time—'

'This is all a woman needs, Father—she can bear anything afterwards!'

Soshu smiled. 'You're stronger than I am.'

'A woman can afford to be stronger. She's less complicated.'

Soshu buried his face in hers. . a lost traveller surrendering to the quicksands. Her response was immediate, a sudden, desperate flaring. Gently, supporting her head with one hand, as if he were handling some rare, fragile treasure, he laid her on the *tatami*.

'Mummy!' It was Shoko, back from school, and Tomoko went downstairs to fetch her. Soshu struggled to regain his pretence of calm.

Kneeling on the *tatami* by the door, the little girl bowed to the priest, then was chattering away to her mother. At once and without effort, Tomoko seemed perfectly attuned to the child's mood, and Soshu alone was left the prisoner of their secret. Or maybe in this house pretence had become so habitual. . . Looking at her talking to Shoko, he saw where the centre of her life lay. Not his embrace but the child's company was the source of what faith she could find in life; without it, she would be pitiable . . . deformed.

Tomoko saw him out.

'Till next month, Father! she cried softly. Soshu did not answer. In her face no tension remained, only a faint lingering warmth. For a while she was at peace, her eyes tender in the renewed assurance that he would visit her again.

And Yamaji still knows nothing, Tomoko thought. A secret like that wasn't so difficult to manage, after all. And the pleasure of it, once savoured—how could one give that up? So life had made an actress of her; and a clever one, evidently. Suppose the parishioners did insist on their priest remarrying. She wouldn't let it upset her, she decided; it wasn't as though he'd be marrying for love.

The train steamed into Osaka. As they hurried out of the station and boarded a taxi, Tomoko gave herself up to the bustling mood that afflicts travellers. It was her first visit to Osaka, and she wondered at the time it took to reach the airport on the fringe of the city. The buildings at Itami Air Terminal were smaller than she had expected, but the field itself startled her with its mass of aeroplanes of every shape and size, more than she had ever seen: some about to take off, many more parked in long gleaming rows, others circling overhead, awaiting orders to land. A loudspeaker crackled: the next flight from Tokyo would be an hour and a half late.

'It's no good complaining, however late they are. There'd be no sense in taking off before they're through with the servicing.' Yamaji laughed. 'I've had to wait three hours sometimes—nearly four, once, at Itazuke it was: they wouldn't let her go till the mist cleared. It's quick enough when the weather's good, though—not much more than two hours from Fukuoka all the way to Tokyo.'

After a drink in the tea-room, Tomoko rested on a sofa till the plane from Tokyo had arrived and was ready to take off. No one could have guessed they were not husband and wife. Yamaji was attentive and courteous; on the plane, he gave her the window seat.

'Doesn't anybody worry about the danger?'

'Nonsense—look at that stewardess! Does she look as if she ever thought we'd crash? People notice she never gets flurried, even when the plane runs into an air-pocket and starts bouncing—so they don't either.'

Their plane started to move. Tomoko waited expectantly for the take-off; but they were only taxiing into position at the end of the runway. Then there was another long delay.

'They have to wait for orders.'

Childishly, Tomoko wondered who would bring the 'orders'. A plane that had been circling the airport for some time landed. At last their turn came; no sooner had she realised they were moving again than the plane was racing down the runway, the sudden acceleration jerking her against the seat like some giant, invisible hand pulling at her back. For a brief, confused moment her senses seemed to hold back, struggling to meet this onslaught of speed before surrendering to the numbness it imposed.

'Now we're away,' said Yamaji. Two or three times Tomoko was vaguely conscious of the plane dropping and lifting beneath her; then, against the smooth, steady roar of the engines, awareness returned. The ground was rushing into the distance, dotted with toy houses.

'You're calm, for a first flight!'

Tomoko smiled. She was gazing down at Osaka: its factories and rivers, its dense, jostling mass of homes and great modern business blocks.

'I suppose there'd be nothing left of any of us if we crashed.'

'Why think about crashing—it only makes it more likely.'

'With trains or ships you can't help feeling there's bound to be at least one survivor; but not with aeroplanes. Doesn't that scare people off flying?'

Tomoko had not told Soshu of this air trip she was making with Yamaji, though Shoko and the maid knew all about it, and had been talking of nothing else for days. Again she turned to the window. They were over the Inland Sea now. Here and there she could pick out a boat, white flecks at bow and stern the only indication it was moving. In the fading light the sea was a vast grey board, less beautiful than she had imagined.

'The islands are beautiful. You'll see some more of them soon.

A big island swam into view as Yamaji spoke; she could see the hill sloping to the sea, the houses at its foot, the notched, curving line of the shore, white beaches. It was hard to believe there was life in each of those tiny houses; the endless cycle of joy and suffering. . . A few days ago, Soshu's lover, and now—the docile wife of Mr Yamaji, for all the world knew. How easily it came, the double role she had imagined would be so painful. Tomoko shrank in horror from the weakness hidden within her, sapping every attempt at decision. She saw now how it was that for years Soshu could be sincerely penitent while never ceasing to commit the sin of which he repented; how habit and inertia corrupt a man's soul, and how when you sense the corruption, it has already poisoned your very nature, beyond healing: she thought of people she knew in Tan'ami, whose lives were like that, repeating themselves mechanically in a paralysis of will. Perhaps she herself would soon be little better. . . . Another group of islands drifted out of the clear air, fascinating her with their endless variety of shapes.

Over Butsuoji the clouds still lingered. It was nearly nightfall, too dark already to read in the Lute Room without the electric light. Soshu sat at the big table, writing to an old college friend of his Kyoto days, a priest like himself of the Pure Land Sect. He had inherited the charge of a temple away in northern Honshu, and it was many years since they had been in touch.

Footsteps sounded outside just as he was finishing the letter.

'Father Soshu.' The voice was that of the old priest.

'Yes?' Soshu's reply was barely audible, fainter than the tiny scraping sound of the bamboo letter-case he pushed to one side as he spoke. The old priest entered.

'I've called on all the households you mentioned, Father.'

'Will they be able to come?'

The old priest looked at the younger enquiringly, but was disappointed; Soshu's expression told him nothing. The parishioners had questioned him closely. Why was the priest calling another meeting? To give them his answer to the proposal they'd made at the last one? If that was all, there was no need for a big, formal meeting. There were such people as elders, after all: they could go from house to house passing Soshu's decision on to the congregation, if he found it embarrassing to let everybody know in person. And this was the first time he had ever sent the old priest round with a message, instead of asking the elders—what was in his mind, they wanted to know. The old man could give no answer.

'Has anything happened to him?'

'No; nothing has happened.'

'Perhaps he's quarrelled with the old lady, and that's what's made him decide all of a sudden?'

'I don't know. . .' There was nothing else he could say. He knew that the breach between Soshu and Mineyo had grown more serious, and more recently had sensed a mood of desperation in Mineyo. O-Sugi, the maid, had noticed this too. She and the old priest went about their tasks in house and temple with a subdued air, awaiting uneasily the crisis they were certain was near, though neither could guess what form it would take. Only Ryokun felt nothing, as if his sensibility were different in kind from theirs; the doings of grown-ups seemed to cast no shadow on his child's world, and his days continued as before. The old priest and O-Sugi had once known such self-centred innocence, before the long hard years had made them sensitive to the rhythm of other lives beside their own.

'Mr Kinoshita and Mr Morikami said they wouldn't be free, but all the others will come.'

'I don't like troubling them so soon after the last meeting.'

'You said not to ask the widows, so I didn't call at Mrs Mimori's or Mrs Komiyama's. It's always difficult for the women to get to meetings, anyway.'

Soshu showed no sign of recognition at the mention of Mrs Komiyama. There was a stillness in his expression, as of a mind purged of all bewilderment and distraction, yet missing somehow the deepest certainty. The old priest went back to the kitchen to light the fire for the bath. O-Sugi was squatting in front of the cooking stove, the reflected light of the flames playing across her wrinkled face.

'You'll be wondering about that dog of yours, eh, Shoju?' she said out of the blue. The old priest seemed not to have heard. The bundle of stalks crackled into flame, reddening his face like hers as he bent over the fuel-hole. O-Sugi did not repeat her question, and for a while there was silence.

'Mm. Can't help thinking about him now and again,' Shoju answered at last. Ten days earlier he had left the cottage on the hill and moved to Butsuoji. Although the removal of the cemetery had not yet begun, surveyors for the Asano Chemical Works had already arrived to carry out preliminary work for the factory the company was going to build on the hill. In the daytime there was little to show the tiny windswept cottage was occupied; and the men had taken possession, making a fire during meal-breaks and parking their equipment when they left at night, though so long as the cemetery remained, the house and the land it stood on still belonged to the old priest. Soshu saw he was worried, and told him to move down to the temple. Mineyo said nothing. If the move made anyone happy, it was Ryokun; now there was no need to say good-bye to his friend every evening.

'Used to look after the house properly when I was away, that dog. Never went to sleep till he saw I was back.'

'Slept with you, didn't he?'

'Mm—slipped in beside me as soon as I'd gone to bed. He must be lonely, now I don't go back in the evenings any more. Wanders around looking for me, I daresay. I did wonder about bringing him down here.'

'The old lady wouldn't like that.'

'I know. Ryokun would, though.'

'She hates creatures.'

'What's that dog doing now, I wonder. . . He's too old to go out and find his own food. Used to lie about sleeping most of the day.

I expect he can't even do that now, with those men turning everything upside down and teasing him all the time. His memory's nearly gone, too—probably he's forgotten me by now.'

'As if he ever could!' O-Sugi was emphatic, though she knew nothing of how the old dog would react to his master's disappearance.

'Father Soshu's calling a parishioners' meeting for tomorrow evening. I can't make out what it's for.'

'What's he want to talk about, I wonder.'

'The elders don't know, either. They got quite a shock when I called to give the message. It's always been them that did that kind of thing.'

'Must have made up his mind at last, I suppose.'

'What about?' said Shoju, pretending he had no idea.

'Get on with you! What the parishioners were so worked up about—his getting rid of the old woman, and agreeing to marry again.'

'I wonder. . .'

O-Sugi looked at him. 'What d'you mean, "I wonder"?'

'If that was it, you'd think he'd ask the elders to call the meeting.'

'Maybe he felt awkward about asking them, when it's about his own affairs he wants to talk,' O-Sugi answered after a moment's thought.

'I don't think so.'

'Then what *do* you think, eh, Shoju?'

'I don't know. . .'

'It's plain enough,' said O-Sugi confidently. 'Haven't you heard them talking about that Hoshina girl, the widowed daughter? Couldn't help noticing her myself two or three times lately; she's bigger than most, and fair. Everybody's hoping she'll marry the reverend.'

'It'd be a fine thing if she did. I can't see it happening, though. The temple would brighten up all right if she moved in. There'd be smiles and laughter all day long; the whole atmosphere would change. . . She'd be nearer twelve stone than ten, that girl.'

'The reverend went out a while back.'

'I didn't notice.'

'He was going to post a letter, I think.'

'Post a letter himself? That's strange.' The old priest stared into the blazing fire, thinking back over the years since Soshu had first come from Kyoto to Butsuoji. Little of what went on in the temple family had escaped him, and recently he had been obscurely aware that the time of reckoning of Soshu's long account was near. Perhaps tomorrow's meeting. . . He could not believe Soshu had summoned it merely to announce his willingness to live apart from Mineyo and acceptance of the parishioners' offer to find a new wife. That decision taken, the reckoning would still remain. . . An uneasy conviction grew upon him that the meeting had a significance none of the parishioners dreamed of, that it would determine the fate of Soshu himself and the whole future of their temple. Posting the letters had been his job, or O-Sugi's, as long as he could remember. Why should Soshu have gone out himself, unless this letter was of very special importance?

An aeroplane began to drone across the darkening sky, its tail-lights winking red and green.

Tomoko's plane was circling over Fukuoka, though she did not know this was where they were. Geography had vanished in the darkness, and even with her forehead pressed against the window she could not make out where the sea ended and land began. But the lights of a great city were unmistakable: innumerable scattered jewels of red and white and green, each shining purposefully with its own distinctive brilliance, yet together forming an unbroken sea of light. Yamaji kept looking at his watch.

'Wasting a lot of time circling today!'

To Tomoko, conscious only of flying through endless darkness, the remark was meaningless. She had never experienced this floating in the sky—that was how it felt, for all that a mere machine was carrying her—nor the sensation she had had at Itami of surrendering the choice of life or death into other hands, of stepping for a while outside her own identity and familiar reactions. Night had fallen while they were over the Inland Sea. The clouds were still visible, adding to the strangeness: their vast mass gradually darkening, yet edged with red and brilliant gold long after land and sea had vanished into black, empty space.

'Waiting for landing orders this time.'

'Where are we?'

'Over Fukuoka—still circling.' It dawned on Tomoko why the sea of lights had seemed interminable. A buzzer sounded; the stewardess began to give instructions. A moment later the lights came rushing up to meet them—they were diving straight into the ground, thought Tomoko in a panic; then, as they flattened out at three hundred feet, houses peered out from behind the lights. Two or three bumps, and they had landed.

'Do your ears hurt?'

'No.'

'People often get pain in their ears when they make their first landing. It goes off in a minute, though—swallowing's the best thing.'

Tomoko swallowed several times. Not that this would have any effect, since she wasn't conscious of any pain, but somehow the trivial physical action brought back normality and the sense that her life was in her own hands once more.

A bus took them to the rather shabby airport buildings. Yamaji briskly claimed their suitcases, then rejoined her by the rows of waiting cars.

'Anyone from the Shunshu Hotel?' he called out. A porter from the hotel appeared and showed them to a car. Soon they were driving along a gravel road through dark fields.

'You were thirty-five minutes late, sir,' said the porter.

'Thirty-five minutes circling the airport, you mean.'

'I suppose the passengers must find it upsetting too. It's worrying enough on the ground when you know the plane's arrived up there, and yet you have to go on waiting and waiting, without any sign of it landing.'

The road was paved now—a sign they were nearing Fukuoka City, Tomoko realised, her mind darkening with a sudden sense of loneliness. Soon it gave way to noisy, crowded streets. When the car stopped, she glimpsed a river, apparently quite broad, though it was too dark to see its flow; she could just make out the backs of houses on the bank opposite.

Settled in their room at the inn, Tomoko discovered how tired she was, which was hardly surprising, considering how far Tan'ami is from Kyushu, even by air. The return to normality at the moment of landing had not after all been quite complete; a thin film of strangeness still interposed itself between events and her physical and mental experience of them. A maid came to show Yamaji to the bath. Tomoko sat before the mirror. The face she saw was just noticeably pale, perhaps from weariness; it touched no chord of feeling. She got up and went to the bathroom, passing Yamaji on his way back. A modern tiled floor surrounded a defiantly traditional bath-tub of cypress wood, the scent of which mingled with the steam to fill the room. Unbelievable irony, that even while still longing desperately for Soshu, she could sit there letting the water lap so delightfully around her, enjoying the relaxation like any tired traveller—and in another man's company. . . The lie within her! No one knew her secret, but a mocking inner voice denounced her easy hypocrisy.

'This room remind you of anything?' said Yamaji as she was sitting at the mirror after her bath. She looked round the big room they had been given for the night, two rooms thrown into one; but nothing came to mind.

'It's like that room we had at the Shichisai Inn.'

Tomoko started.

'Hakurei Spa, do you remember?'

In fact there was no special resemblance. The rooms were only alike in sharing the standardised design to which most new hotel rooms are built nowadays.

'Just like, don't you think?' repeated Yamaji, smiling.

'I thought you would have forgotten.' The inn where she had first surrendered. . .

'Is that likely? When it gave me what I'd wanted so long? That was a red-letter day, if ever there was one. I don't suppose I'll ever forget that inn. Maybe I was a bit rough with you there—not deliberately, though: just excited, that's all.'

She turned, to see him staring at a group of beautifully-coloured Hakata dolls in a glass case in a corner of the *tokonoma*: a woman in a long robe reclining on an arm-rest, watching a little girl playing with seashells. The woman's face had something of Tomoko's pale, clear complexion. From the doll, Yamaji glanced back at her.

In his way, even he loves me, she thought, looking into the mirror again, and dabbing her nose with a powder-puff.

'Beppu tomorrow. We'll stay three or four days if you like it there, and take the boat back.'

Tomoko did not reply.

'The time we stayed at the Shichisai was a kind of honeymoon, I suppose, but it didn't feel much like it somehow. We'll have a real one this time.'

'How long will your business take?'

'I'll get it all done tomorrow morning. You'd better stay here till I come back; or if you want to see the city centre, take a taxi there and back—it's safer in a place you don't know.'

They soon went to bed, though it was still quite early, and after five or six minutes of talk Yamaji was already asleep. Tomoko switched off the bedside light. Darkness did not bring silence: they were evidently not far from the amusement quarter, and she could hear a jazz band playing. The hotel itself was quiet; outside, blended with the enveloping night, there was still the din of city streets that the ears do not register in daylight. Soon Yamaji began to snore, but Tomoko could not sleep.

Perhaps it was true that nothing but suffering could come from her knowing the priest, that she must give up all thought of loving him. . . she had longed for a different life, a life at peace with herself, and had turned to him to give it her—only to find that dependence on him had robbed her of all peace, of even the possibility of escape. If it had been anyone else, her dream might have been realised; but not with him. . . Yet she clung to it still. For years, so long as she remained a member of the Butsuoji congregation, there would be the certainty of their meeting each month. And even if he sent the old priest instead, she could always see him at the temple. . .

Yamaji's kindness bewildered her. When the car they had hired arrived at Hakata he wouldn't let her carry her case, and offered her the window-seat on the train, pleasantly conscious of the attention she was attracting. This kindness had begun, Tomoko remembered, as soon as they left Tan'ami, and the further away they travelled the more considerate he became. She wondered why. At home he was a bestial tyrant—how could a man change so easily into his own opposite? Did it mean he was ashamed of his other self, the Yamaji she was used to? If that was it, he would hardly go back to his brutal ways even when they were back in Tan'ami.

She was looking out of the window when she felt him lean towards her.

'What about it now, Tomoko?'

She looked at him, not understanding.

'The other man—what we talked about—' Yamaji was smiling pleasantly, confident of her reaction. She did not answer.

'Have you changed your mind?'

Again Tomoko did not answer.

'If you have, I want to know.'

There was nothing she could say. Yamaji had forced her to a crisis, but she was still free to refuse to recognize it as such; her life was still her own to decide, so the dilemma remained.

'We should have made this sort of trip before. I used to hate having anybody with me when I was travelling, even my secretary; you can't be free unless you're alone. I'll be going up to Tokyo soon; I'll take you with me, now I know what a pleasant travelling companion you make.'

'You're joking.'

'Nonsense—can't you see I'm enjoying your company?'

'But it doesn't make sense. . .' Tomoko paused, '—your treating me like this, as if I had never said what I did.'

'I haven't been acting, if that's what you mean.'

'It's frightening. . .'

'You don't know yet how kind I can be.'

'It's myself I'm frightened of.'

'Have you thought over what I told you then?'

Tomoko nodded.

'Reasonable enough, wasn't it?'

Again she nodded; but her thoughts flashed back to Soshu's sorrowful rejection of every appeal she had made. Both men wanted to destroy her dream.

'Isn't it time you gave me an answer? Not this moment, of course —you can tell me when you feel it's easiest. Some time during this trip, shall we say?'

The display of gentleness was obviously a deliberate attempt to win her over, the substitution of coaxing for brute force. Yet she did not have the impression he was thinking only of himself, or merely being perverse, trying to make her change her mind in order to save his own dignity. Only love could explain the completeness of the change. Nothing else could make a man as used to domineering as Yamaji treat a woman with such respect. He seemed even to enjoy being considerate, as a kind of release: as if he could afford to drop the mask of bluster and arrogance now they had left Tan'-ami, and behave like any other man. Their journey had affected him in the way she had least expected.

After changing trains at Kokura, they passed through Usa. Tomoko admired the station, built in the style of a Shinto shrine in honour of the famous Usa Shrine nearby. The station at Beppu, their destination, was surprisingly small: most visitors to the spa evidently came and left by sea. Soon their taxi was making its way through the busy streets.

'That's the famous Copper Palace.' Yamaji pointed. All she could see was a massive wall hung with the sign-board of an inn. 'It was built for Akiko Yanagiwara, the poetess they called the White Lotus. Now it's just an inn, of course, though the navy took it over during the war. A lot of American soldiers use it now, Korea being so close.'

Tomoko began to notice the many foreigners on the streets. They were nearing the edge of the town now, driving among tall pines, and soon passed an imposing gateway leading to what looked like a fashionable resort, with modern, American-style homes and a big hospital. The United States Army had requisitioned the whole area, the healthiest and most attractive in the whole town, and ran it as a kind of foreign concession.

'This used to be Beppu Park, until the Americans took it over. Makes you feel as if the Occupation was still on. . .'

Beppu being famous for its hot springs, soldiers wounded in Korea would be sent here for treatment, Tomoko supposed. Their car began to climb more steeply, leaving behind the gently sloping foothills on which the greater part of Beppu is built. A valley opened beneath them, the mountainside opposite dotted with inns. At last the car stopped. The inn Yamaji had chosen, she noticed, was one of the biggest. They were shown along a carpeted corridor to the back of the main building, then across a patch of garden to a small but beautifully designed and furnished annexe, consisting of four Japanese rooms and a western-style bedroom. From the verandah they looked out over the great sweep of Beppu Bay.

'It's like Atami, only bigger.' Yamaji was standing behind her, his hands on her shoulders. 'See the mountain over there on the right, covered with forest? That's Mount Takasaki, the one with the famous monkeys.'

'Monkeys?'

'There's a temple up there—the priest rounds them up and tames them.' Tomoko remembered having read about the monkeys somewhere. But 'temple' had startled her: 'priest' and 'temple', synonyms for her own despair... Not that any of her feelings had grown less vivid, or that she had thought of anything else but Soshu even on the train: if her mind ceased for a moment to remember him consciously, her body did not. His image was a constant presence, no longer needing the effort of memory to recall.

'You'd better come too, as soon as you're ready.' Yamaji entered the small bathroom with which the annexe was provided—there was no need to use the big public bath in the main building. Tomoko hesitated. The night before, at Fukuoka, she had waited till Yamaji had finished. Nor had they bathed together more than four or five times since she had known him—at Hakurei, for instance, in the beginning, she could not refuse; but that was in the morning, afterwards . . . she had avoided his eyes, hardly speaking. There was no reason for her to be shy now, not in that way, at least... Tomoko lingered in front of the mirror.

'Tomoko!' Yamaji called. Dismissing her reluctance, she opened the frosted-glass door into the dressing-room. Soap and toilet articles were laid out ready, by a full-length mirror. Near the little rug in the middle of the room she noticed two wet footprints: too impatient to wait, Yamaji must have stepped out of the bath to call her. At home, his calling her like that would have been a sign of irritation, or of anger sometimes, which he never took any trouble to hide. Tomoko grew suddenly tense, as if he had started abusing her already. Steam had moistened the sliding glass partition between the dressing-room and the bathroom; through it she could see the figure of Yamaji, pinker than usual, busily pouring hot water over his shoulders from a tiny wooden bucket.

'Wonderful bath—temperature just right!' Yamaji stared at her, devouring, as she stooped to shut the glass door. Kimonos made her look thinner than she was; in spite of having fed Shoko herself for as long as any mother, her breasts were still firm and swelling, like inverted rice-bowls, the skin fine-grained and moist.

'You can see the ocean from here, and Beppu, too.' Yamaji wiped the steam from the window, and pointed. Far below, a steamship hung motionless on a sea of clear blue. It was strange, thought Tomoko, to watch such magnificent natural beauty from the luxury of a bath. She had often seen wall-paintings of similar scenes in public bath-houses, but the real thing was different, purifying the mind as the water cleansed and refreshed the tired body.

'Enjoying the trip?'

Tomoko nodded, thinking how childish the look she gave him would appear.

'Like to stay another couple of days?'

'What about your business?'

'You're more important. Not that I'm trying to make you grateful; I want to stay on a bit myself, and if we do, I'll be the one that enjoys it most.'

'Why should you be so kind...'

'I've been rough with you, I know. There are only two ways a man can treat a woman like you—the brutal and the gentle, and nothing in between, because you never let him know where he is with you. You're a strange woman.'

'An ordinary one.'

'The more a man loves you, the more he tortures himself. You don't respond, or even tell him what you really feel; you keep everything locked up inside. When he does strike the right note for once, nobody's more passionate than you, but that hardly ever happens, and the rest of the time you're as cold as stone. A man needs to feel you want him, all the time; but you never give him a chance to know whether you do or not, and he starts worrying, because the only return he gets from loving you is a feeling he's making a fool of himself, anyway.'

Tomoko sat back, her arms across her breast. Still he did not know; she must be careful to give nothing away now. With Soshu she was a different woman, acting on her love with an intensity that frightened her. In neither case was her response deliberate, or merely selfish, it seemed to Tomoko, or anything but an unwilled reaction to the way each man treated her. With Yamaji, something living and sensitive within her receded, as if to hide: while Soshu excited her so, just by being what he was—probably without ever realising it himself. To them both her response was instinctive, inevitable.

'You're the kind of woman men love more than any other. Not the independent kind—you'd like to work, I suppose, run your life and all the rest, but you'd never make a success of it. Never. Being that sort of woman isn't something to grumble at, though, as it were a defect: it isn't. You were born with special advantages. Make the most of them, and you'll find life's really worth living; that's all it comes to. But isn't it time you told me the truth about yourself—for once? Can't hide anything much in the bathwater, either of us!'

Tomoko tried to smile. She was gazing at the blue unruffled water of the bay.

'How do you really feel, eh? About this trip, for instance?'

Quietly she faced him. 'You asked me to come, and I came. . . That's my answer.'

'What kind of an answer is that?'

'I've thought a great deal, of course. . .'

'Have you now? Been thinking about the talk we had, have you?'

'It's difficult not to think about what will determine the rest of one's life.'

'You've made up your mind, then?'

'Yes.' Her answer was unequivocal. Yet in making it she did not feel any the less bound by her love for Soshu, and the shock of revulsion at the deception was immediate. Of course it had not exactly been a lie, that brief answer.

'I knew you weren't so stupid,' said Yamaji, smiling. 'It's not always wrong to have an eye for your own comfort, you know. Everybody has to be a little mercenary at times, and it's a good thing you've realised it. Well! So you've decided. It'll give us something to remember, this night at Beppu; the start of our real honeymoon.'

Tomoko did not hear him. She was far away, listening to the melancholy fall of waves. . . while her body, the instrument of a duplicity in herself she could acknowledge but not resist, accepted—enjoyed—the company of a man she did not love. Her fingers bent and twisted a toe till it seemed it would break, the pain stifling other, nameless feelings. She had sunk back in the bath till the water played about her lips.

'It's going to be fine tomorrow.'

The weather report had forecast northerly winds and a clear sky with occasional clouds for that evening. Tomorrow would be cloudy with northerly winds veering to southerly at times. A glance at the weathermap in the newspaper showed the reason: tomorrow a trough moving eastwards from northern Manchuria would break up the big high pressure system now covering most of Japan and stretching down as far as the Yangtse.

In the Lute Room at Butsuoji Soshu sat reading the same forecast in an evening paper. It was nearly time for the evening service; the old priest was waiting in the hall. Soshu fetched his robe and stole and went across to the temple, as he had done on so many hundred evenings before—but wondering bitterly now, each step driving the question deeper home, how many more times he would walk the familiar connecting corridor.

Candles were already burning in the sanctuary. After pausing in the recess to bow before the portraits of the Seven Patriarchs of the Pure Land Sect, Soshu passed on to the sanctuary, where the old priest was already sitting, his head bent low over the sutra-table.

According to custom, he first lit a stick of incense and stood with clasped hands in front of the statue of Amida, then turned to repeat the same act of reverence before the portrait of Shinran. Memories of his long priesthood at Butsuoji came crowding in heavily upon his mind, jostling the unspoken prayers.

Finally he sat down facing the statue, clasped his hands once more, and began to murmur the *nenbutsu*. The old priest joined in, but in a louder, more urgent tone, as though with the words he were expelling some tangible inner impurity. Ryokun would laugh at the exaggerated, wave-like rise and fall the old man's voice took on when he was praying.

Then he stopped. Shoju followed suit instantly, so that their two voices died away in unison on the last syllable of the prayer, 'Namu Amida Butsu -u -u . . .' The old priest struck the sutra-bell as Soshu raised the book of scripture to his forehead in the gesture of devotion to the Holy Law—and caught his breath, for Soshu was still murmuring *nenbutsu* . . . oblivious of the sutra-book in his hand, of the bell, of the service he was there to conduct, he was repeating still the prayer of St Honen and St Shinran. 'Namu Amida Butsu. . . Namu Amida Butsu. . . Namu Amida Butsu. . .' The old priest was sitting at right angles to Soshu, not two yards away. In the younger man's face he could read the desperate intensity of his absorption in the words of the prayer; and was filled with a feverish, constricting sorrow, for he had glimpsed the conflict within. Knowing nothing of what was in Soshu's mind, sensing only the agony the struggle was costing him, he wondered what he could be going to propose to the meeting that night. During the day there had been no sign of anything unusual. But now the old man shivered; without looking, he knew that Soshu was weeping, no longer aware of his presence. Father Soshu weeping. . . he remembered how strained his face had looked recently, and how little he seemed to enjoy even Ryokun's company now. There had been other things: the hurried settling of odds and ends of temple business, the handing over to Shoju of the parishioners' death register. And he was murmuring *nenbutsu* still, his head bent over clasped hands. . . The old man wished he could have slipped away from the sanctuary and left him to his solitude.

Behind his praying lips Mineyo's words were echoing in Soshu's mind, taunting him with his weakness: 'if you did confess, I'd leave you, I promise—you'd have gone too far away from me then. *But it won't happen—you know it won't. . .*' Abruptly, the stream of murmured *nenbutsu* stopped. It was time, then, for the service? Soshu turned to look at the old priest: he was sitting with bowed head and closed eyes, no longer praying, but quietly waiting for Soshu to begin.

36

Always, when he had finished the last of the evening sutra-readings, Soshu would go up to the shrine and shut the gilded doors of the two feretories containing the statue of Amida and the portrait of Shinran, while the old priest continued to recite *nenbutsu*. Tonight, however, he paused before the portrait of the founder of the True Pure Land Sect, and turned to Shoju.

'These doors can stay open. And leave the shrine candles burning, please.'

The old priest looked up, wondering whether he had heard right, but Soshu had already left the hall. Still reciting *nenbutsu,* unconsciously now, as though the words of the prayer had merged with the rhythm of his breathing, he went round putting out the candles in the outer sanctuary one by one, then slid the night shutters into place. Darkness filled the hall, except for a small area in the sanctuary around the portrait of Shinran, looking out forlornly from behind its ring of tiny, flickering lights. As if Soshu wanted St Shinran to watch while he spoke to the parishioners. . . The solemnity of Soshu's determination awed the old man.

He noticed nothing unusual about Soshu's actions as he watched him in the house, except that Soshu himself recited the scriptures before the family shrine, a duty that was normally Mineyo's. When it was time for these readings, Mineyo had still not left her room; and the old man could not believe his ears when he heard the sutra-bell tinkle and Soshu begin to intone. This was the voice his parishioners loved, sacrificing pedantic clarity to a rich variety of tone, so different from the dreary mumble in which the scriptures are usually delivered. Such a voice was a great gift in itself. To its rhythms the congregation could respond as if to music, without needing to understand the archaic language in which the scriptures are written. Even in reciting the Pure Land hymns, which are in simple language and much easier to follow, Soshu's voice kept its special charm. Sitting by the brazier in the elders' room, the old priest listened. There was a sadness in the voice now, it seemed to him; a movement of profound emotion in its measured rise and fall. A pity there was no one beside himself to hear the scriptures recited so beautifully, he was thinking, when Ryokun burst into the room.

'A meeting tonight, is there?'

The old priest nodded.

'I'll stay up, then.' A late-night service or a parishioners' meeting always delighted Ryokun. There was such a bustle in the house that it was no good his going to bed at the usual time, and he would wander about among the women preparing food in the kitchen, running along the corridor every now and then to see what was going on in the temple hall. To the women he was a pathetic figure; the victim of an unhappy destiny, to be treated always with a gentle pity. Ryokun had long since realised this, and was quite at home in the role of the tragic child—adult notions of unhappiness meaning little to him yet, it gave him a distinction, he felt, which was even rather enjoyable. But the mere fact of an evening meeting at Butsuoji was enough to excite him.

'Is that Father praying in there?' Even Ryokun was surprised to hear his father's voice instead of Mineyo's. Jumping up, he ran into the shrine-room. The old priest imagined the scene: the father sitting erect before the miniature shrine, the son staring at him from the doorway, astonished. . . . The words of the sutra as Soshu intoned them seemed to speak directly to himself, filling him with a deep sense of acceptance of its truth. The words themselves were indistinct; the message, as it came to the old priest, was purely spiritual, yet none the less clear for being mediated only through the tone and rhythm of the voice. It was the first time he had ever listened to Soshu with such intense concentration—usually they intoned in unison, so that he could hardly distinguish Soshu's voice from his own. Suddenly he remembered the Getsudo blood in his veins. The only direct descendants of the ancient family that had provided Butsuoji with its priests for so many generations were Ryokun and himself. At once he found himself listening with a new attention—as a Getsudo, last adult representative of the temple's hereditary priesthood. Little by little the voice would fade, like a dying wind, then gradually swell once more, drawing after it in each flowing movement the old priest's listening soul and speaking to him with solemn, austere power. People differ, and some might have found Soshu's intoning monotonous, perhaps. But the note of sorrow was there; and if the old priest was moved so deeply, it was because it echoed an unspoken agony. So with his sudden awareness of his position as a Getsudo—that too was a response, as though through the intoning of the holy words he were hearing Soshu appeal to the house of Getsudo, to the living and to the long since dead. . . The voice was that of one who knew the depths of sorrow and of suffering.

Ryokun had stolen back on tiptoe.

'Why isn't Granny doing it?'

The old priest could not answer. Probably Mineyo was still in her room, listening like himself to the sutra-reading from the shrine-room. Soshu was not 'reading', picking out symbols from a printed page, though he had the text before him; the words flowed in a steady, purposeful rhythm, as if borne upon some irresistible current. Still the old priest listened to the voice with its burden of sorrow, the voice of a sinner laying the secret of his sin and suffering before the Lord of Light and the spirits of his ancestors, pleading with them for forgiveness. . . Ryokun darted off to Mineyo's room.

O-Sugi began preparing supper a little earlier than usual, on instructions from Soshu. A few minutes later the shrine-room service ended. The old priest stood up and was crossing the kitchen to the back door, when Soshu called.

'Is the bath ready?'

'Quite ready, Father.'

The old priest went round to the hole in the wall outside the bathroom and pushed another bundle of fuel into the fire. The water was already hot and the fire in the little stove burning vigorously, but a feeling that Soshu would take longer than usual over his bath kept him crouching by the fuel-hole. He wondered if there was any connection between this feeling and Soshu's unusual decision to read the service himself—and the suspicion that both had some bearing on the coming meeting prayed on the old priest's thoughts.

At supper he could see no change. Soshu was his usual self, even in his response to Ryokun's endless questioning and chatter. Mineyo spoke little. Paradoxically, Soshu's apparently normal attitude seemed to convey a sense of spiritual clarity, of light unobstructed. Mineyo, imprisoned in bitterness and hatred, could think of nothing but the meeting he had taken it upon himself to call.

'Evening, sir!' The wife of one of the parishioners appeared at the kitchen door, in working clothes; evidently she had come straight from the fields.

'Ah, it's Mrs Take. How good of you to come,' said Soshu, smiling. Bowing repeatedly, the woman edged towards the stove.

'I just came to say my husband's sorry he won't be able to get to the meeting tonight—'

'It's very kind of you. But you could represent the family just as well. Or Yasuichi—is he back from the factory yet?'

'Yes, he's home by half-past five.'

'He would be equally welcome.'

'If it wouldn't make any difference—he's only a boy.'

'He's twenty-two, quite old enough to take his father's place.'

He said he'd come, but with his being so young, we thought he wouldn't be of any use.'

'Please let him come. It's a special meeting I've called myself, and I want everybody to be there who possibly can.' Soshu spoke as if he had called the meeting to report some unexpected piece of good news. Promising to send her son after all, the woman apologised once more and left.

'It's wonderful to see how loyal these people are to their temple.'

'It's hardly surprising. In all these years you've never called a parishioners' meeting before, and they can't help wondering what it's all about. A special meeting, indeed—as if they weren't busy enough already. . .' broke in Mineyo accusingly, from the corridor leading to her room. She would have stopped the meeting if she could. If Soshu were suddenly to change his mind, she would have thought nothing of sending the parishioners home one by one as they arrived.

Soshu took no notice. After supper O-Sugi and the old priest set to work preparing the hall. The meeting being at Soshu's request, they had to do all the work themselves instead of sharing it with the elders and their wives, who would always come early and help them before any ordinary service or meeting. Mineyo sat warming herself over the foot-warmer in her room, pretending indifference; but the defiance of so many years was already near to crumbling, in the shadow of a retribution she was beginning dimly to foresee, though not yet to understand or accept.

The heavy outer door of the house slid back, and one of the elders announced himself. Others followed every few minutes. They had come early, as they would have done on any normal occasion.

'Anything for us to do?' said one of them after they had sat talking for a while in the elders' room. The old priest asked them to move to the hall, most of the parishioners having arrived by now.

Soshu was waiting in the library. Cold air from the dark wintry night seeped into the unheated room. It was cool even in the daytime, hemmed in on the two open sides by tall trees that shut out the sunlight and turned pale the face of anyone who entered the room. He sat erect, no longer at the mercy of his thoughts. A penitent criminal on his way to court would feel much the same, it occurred to him. To his surprise he found himself wholly at ease, even physically relieved, as if the sin of years had been some malignant, cancerous growth from which his body was at last free. Yet how he had suffered, wrestling alone with his sin. . . to struggle alone, in his own strength, could never make a man truly aware of sin as a part of his innermost being; it remained something apart from himself, to be fought against, not acknowledged and accepted. This he had understood at last.

And what of Mineyo, he wondered. She aroused no violent emotions in him now, nor any feeling other than compassion. Tomorrow, tragedy would lay its hand upon her: unavoidably, in the very act of freeing himself of his own sin, he would be involving her in fresh suffering, drawing on her the open contempt of the congregation. . . The memory of Tomoko Komiyama brought a sudden choking rush of despair, and for a brief moment he would gladly have wept. That she had gone to Kyushu with Yamaji he would hardly have believed, even if there had been anyone to tell him—still less that that night, in an inn overlooking the sea, the two of them were beginning what Yamaji called their 'second honeymoon'. . . He thought of her hair, so precisely arranged and perfectly combed; of the grace and harmony of every movement and gesture, even at the one moment—especially then—at which her love had broken through all constraint. . . He was glad she would not come to Butsuoji that night, he told himself. Yet if only she had—

Soshu was wearing a new silk robe of pure white, with a stiff white sash and white *tabi,* like a criminal summoned to appear for judgement.

Footsteps sounded in the corridor.

'Are you there, Father?' the old priest was looking for him.

'Here I am.'

'They are waiting for you, Father.'

'Thank you—I'll go along at once.'

The footsteps died away. Was he ready, Soshu asked himself—needlessly; he was surprised, even at his lack of fear. Before getting up, he thought once more of Tomoko. She had her own pilgrimage to make, apart from him. Neither he nor she could escape the sacrifice of self to which they were destined. What this meant for Tomoko was foreseeable, with a certainty for which they should even be thankful. But for himself—what was to be the object of *his* sacrifice? The contradictions in his own life remained unsolved, to torment him still. Tomoko—of this at least he was sure—was not the woman to let a transient extremity of passion destroy her.

Soshu did not move till such thoughts had ceased to echo in his mind. At last, conscious only of his own unrelenting purpose, he got up, turned off the light, and walked quietly down the corridor. Mineyo, sitting over her footwarmer, listened to his footsteps pass.

At the door into the temple Ryokun was standing, waiting for him.

'What's the meeting tonight?'

Soshu laid a hand on the boy's head. 'Temple business you wouldn't understand. Go to your granny, Ryokun—and make sure you keep warm; it's a cold night.'

'Don't want to.' Ryokun shook his head. 'I'll stay and listen.'

'No, Ryokun, children aren't allowed tonight. The elders wouldn't let you in.'

The old priest appeared in the doorway.

'Take him back, will you, Shoju?'

'Come along, Ryokun!'

'But I only wanted to watch—'

'You must wait till next month, when the big spring services start.'

Soshu and the old priest smiled mechanically at each other as Ryokun scampered off down the corridor. How worn, even weak, Father Soshu looked, thought the old priest; the bodily sign, perhaps, of newly-won spiritual strength? Standing in the shadows, he watched Soshu enter the sanctuary.

Instantly the conversation among the sixty or seventy parishioners gathered in the hall stopped, the silence focusing on the white-robed figure of their priest. Soshu bowed low before the portrait of Shinran, then turned to face the meeting. Kashimura had sent his secretary, as was his custom; next to him were Naota Ifukube, who had come to Soshu, with his story of the woman Tsuruko, and Tanemi Hoshina's father. There was Yosuke Tachi too, in his usual place at the back; and the youthful Yasukichi, sitting modestly behind everyone else. Most of the parishioners were older than Soshu, and knew more than he did of the history of Butsuoji. They knew well enough, they thought, what he would say. The long-awaited decision on his own remarriage and Mineyo's future could hardly be left to the elders to pass on like any routine announcement—courtesy demanded a formal statement to the congregation as a whole. No one guessed the public humiliation he was preparing for himself. No one, that is, except the old priest, standing out of sight in the corridor behind the sanctuary, who foresaw dimly the confession that was coming, and the unthinking disgust and hatred it would draw upon its author. . . The parishioners waited for the thin, obstinate lips to open, announcing acceptance of their wishes. Soshu sat erect, his hands upon his knees.

'I am grateful to you all for taking time to come tonight.' The voice was even, unemotional. Before continuing, Soshu glanced at the portrait of Shinran in the sanctuary. 'St Shinran will hear what I have to say to you tonight. It will be in his presence, as well as yours, that I shall make the confession I am going to make. For the concern all of you have shown for the good of your temple, and for the interest you have taken in my own future, I myself can offer no return other than this confession. You will remember our previous meetings; how stubbornly I refused to accept your advice. That was because I had not the courage to tell the truth.'

At the word 'confession' a ripple of astonishment swept through the meeting, as if his audience were wondering aloud what their reaction should be.

'Soshu!' Surely that was Mineyo calling. . . He turned towards the unlit room behind the sanctuary, from whose cave-like darkness the voice had seemed to come: a last imploring cry of agony and of weakness, at once a prayer and a plea for the help and compassion of the living. Half-drowned in a raging sea, Mineyo clung still to her boat, but with ebbing strength; soon, inevitably, the hands would slip. . . Soshu sighed, the breath cold in his throat. The illusion broke: the cry for help had come not from Mineyo but from himself, born of his own lingering fears. He pictured her where he knew she would be, sitting alone in her room, brooding, nursing her hatred for him and for his audience; and grew calmer. However conscious of her need, there was nothing he could do for her. He would not have flinched from telling her as much, even if she had in fact appeared at the meeting. She had no hold over him now, nor did he feel any longer the need to resist her directly. Not because of any sudden access of moral courage—he was utterly weak still, powerless to resist even himself. The grace of St Shinran was his only strength; this confession, made in his holy presence, would break the last bond between himself and Mineyo.

Soshu faced the parishioners once more, the sharp gleam of fever in his eyes.

'As a young man of nineteen I came to Butsuoji at your invitation, to be your priest. I was still a student, you may remember, but even then I was already committing a great sin, shamelessly and in secret. Thanks to you, I was able to finish my studies at the university. From that time on, so far from my repenting of my sin, in my weakness and folly I allowed it to become a habit; for twenty years your priest has sinned without shame. . . Misconduct with my mother-in-law, as she later became, first took place in my lodgings in Kyoto. If the initiative was hers, it is not for me to reproach her; half the guilt was mine. I know now, to my sorrow, that if I had been only a little stronger then, I could have lived through these twenty years without this burden of sin and the suffering it has brought. As it was, that one night in Kyoto made me what I have been ever since. In your generosity, you have allowed me to continue here as priest all through these years. You have long known something of the real relations between my mother-in-law and myself, and I have known that you knew. But for twenty years I have pretended innocence. . . To such depths has your priest fallen. For twenty years I have betrayed our holy founder, Saint Shinran.'

In tense, unbroken silence the parishioners listened and stared at the face before them, now visibly pale. They were not so much surprised at what he was saying—except for some of the younger ones, most of them had guessed at the truth long ago—as struck by his courage in confessing it. But there was surprise and shock too, inevitably: the impact of the story as they heard it from his own lips was different from any private imaginings, however well-founded. Of how they would finally react, they gave as yet no sign.

'My wife Renko left me, as you know. At the time I was adopted into the family I promised to marry her when the time came. The marriage was postponed several times. This was partly my mother-in-law's fault—she was jealous—and partly mine, because I let her decide everything the way she wanted it. Eventually we were married. But all the time I was weak. . . hiding my shame behind a mask of piety while I preached to you of the Way and the Law. Fine words in the temple—in the house, the sordid truth. Renko found out, of course. But there was no one she could tell, or turn to for help; it would have been too humiliating. So she started running after that actor in the touring Kabuki troupe. I saw what was happening to her, and eventually it made me realize what a terrible crime I was committing. But I hadn't the courage to lift myself up out of the dirt, and only grew even more brazen. My mother-in-law began to abuse Renko for her escapades with the actor; but it wasn't for me to blame her. I began to feel ashamed even to look at her. There's more space in a temple house than in an ordinary home, and life can easily be arranged so that the members of the family are not always together. Renko started sleeping in the annexe; I stayed in the Lute Room; and Renko's mother had her own room too—so that if I wished I could go for days on end without ever seeing my wife. Living in this way helped to keep the secret of our sin—and enabled me to ignore my own conscience. If we had been meeting constantly every day as most people do in a normal family, it couldn't have lasted so long; everything would have come out, there'd have been a flare-up, and then a solution of some kind. A weak man such as myself instinctively takes the easy way, so I found myself slipping into the habit of using the conditions of temple life for my own selfish ends—encouraging my own weakness instead of standing up to it. If only I had come to my senses when Ryokun was born. . . there were other opportunities, too: but I let them all go by. Eventually Renko couldn't bear it any longer, and ran away. There was nothing else she could do. Long before she left, I knew how she felt, and what it would come to. I watched her mother plotting to drive her daughter out of her own home. For that too I was half responsible; but for me, she'd never have dreamt of such cruelty. Only I could have stopped Renko going. I didn't even try—my sense of sin was so blunted by then. I can see my crime now for the enormity it was. . . forcing a young mother and her child apart, for no other reason but the easier satisfaction of my own lust. Of the wrong I have done to Ryokun I shall remain guilty all my life; it cannot be undone. After Renko had gone, the boy's very presence was a reproach, as it had been with his mother before. Yet even then I made no attempt to end the sordid cause of it all. . . I was steeped in sin, beyond salvation.'

Soshu spoke with an easy fluency, deriving not from any previous ordering of his thoughts in readiness for the meeting, but from the sheer force of the impulse that drove him to confess; sentence following sentence without hesitation or faltering, as if he were merely recording the words of an inexorable destiny. Silently the old priest came forward from behind the sanctuary and sat down on the steps leading up into the hall. There was no sign of movement in the temple, no sound save the even tones of Soshu's voice.

'When Renko was about to marry again, the gentleman's family sent a representative here to find out what her position was. Without consulting me, her mother told the messenger that by running away Renko had broken every tie, and the family would have nothing more to do with her. Again I did nothing. I let my wife go without a word—so that I could be free to commit adultery with her mother undisturbed. . . Your silence encouraged me; I no longer bothered even to pretend, more like a beast than a man. The bitterness and misery my wife must have felt made no impression on me, nor did Ryokun's loneliness when he lost his mother. I was not without some sort of conscience, even then, but the habit of sinning muffled its warnings, if it did not paralyse it altogether. There is no excuse or defence I can plead. The disgust and horror I felt for my actions did not stop me from repeating them. I grew desperate. . . Yet in a way, Renko's disappearance must have started me thinking more deeply than before—inevitably, because I was forced to think about marrying again and all that that would have meant. It gave me a little courage, at long last. My mother-in-law wanted things to go on as they were. I decided they couldn't. . . after twenty years, adultery at last began to revolt me, I suppose.

'I do not tell you this sordid story with any idea of defending what I have done; only that you should understand something of the depravity of your priest. . . Some kind of awakening I did experience. My mother-in-law was a very beautiful woman in her younger days, as many of you will remember, and even now, at fifty-four, she looks little more than forty. You must not imagine that I merely drifted apart from her because she was ageing; the truth is, it was only after twenty years that I woke up for the first time to the real horror of the sin. Sooner or later it would have to end, I began to tell myself. You and the other parishioners still pretended not to know. . . You were even kind enough to take up the question of my re-marriage; but the condition you implied, that my mother-in-law would have to leave Butsuoji—I was not prepared for that: to be told outright I was a common adulterer would have hurt less. But it was your way of telling me that you knew. I was frightened—or rather I saw even more clearly how utterly unworthy I was of your interest and good will. Suppose I were to send my mother-in-law away. . . I should marry again: she alone would be punished for a wrong of which we are both guilty—whatever private remorse I might feel, the world would see only grasping, unrepentant selfishness, taking advantage of your lenience to start afresh as if the past had never happened. It is not for me to accept such lenience. Both of us must submit to punishment, for both are guilty—and indeed, my own guilt is the greater of the two. By sinning within its precincts, Mineyo has defiled only the temple: I have compounded the sin by wearing in your presence a mask of priestly virtue which all my actions belied. . .

'As the first step in penance, I started to avoid my mother-in-law as far as I could, wanting sincerely to be firm in breaking her hold upon me. She did not understand why I had suddenly turned away from her, and pleaded with me, weeping, not to change. At this moment of penitence, when I was struggling for rebirth, the long habit of surrender overtook me and blotted out every good intention. It was then I began to know how a man can suffer, and to turn to Saint Shinran for help. I could hardly bear to continue wearing the robes of a priest. Many of you have come to me before now with your personal worries or those of your family, and I have listened to stories of every kind of trouble: but there have been none so squalid as my own. I am not the only man, I daresay, who has lusted after the woman who adopted him as her son. But there cannot be many others who have gone on to marry her daughter, let her bear his child, and finally drive her out of his home, without ever giving up adultery with her mother—let alone get rid of the mother as soon as she is no longer young, so that he can settle down comfortably with a new wife. . . The most brutish criminal would have stopped before going that far. And what I did, I did not once but for twenty years, long enough to corrupt a man in every part of his being. For the evil I have done I cannot hope to atone.'

Soshu was trembling now, and his gaze faltered, though his voice continued as controlled and even as before. A faint smile appeared on his lips, not of conviction but of relief, tinged still with regret.

'Mr Mosuke Yamaji once reproached me with a congenital

weakness of character, a feeble, indolent refusal ever to face facts. I have suffered for what I am, of course; but no doubt that is the kind of man I have seemed to you all. To have accepted one's own weakness so complacently, to have been content, even happy, to let one's life be ruled by it for so long in spite of the warnings one received . . . such a man does not deserve to be saved. It is myself I hate most.

'When I at last began to have less to do with my mother-in-law, I came to see more clearly that the struggle had to be with my own self, the deepest part of me, just as much as with her. The burden of guilt and misery crowded out any other feeling. Until then, I had been intoxicated with the passion, the sensual excitement she demanded and gave: befuddled into a stupor that enabled me to ignore the obvious. Now, it was different. I can imagine the revulsion you must have felt at the scandal in your temple—at having in your midst a priest with the mark upon him of guilt and hypocrisy. Yet in spite of everything, you have let me stay among you all these years, and have never shown me anything but kindness. For this I am more grateful than I can say.'

Memories of Tomoko flooded into Soshu's consciousness. . . Unless he spoke of her, his confession would be meaningless. He waited, anticipating the pain of this final self-inflicted wound.

'I must say, however, that I cannot agree that my mother-in-law alone should be asked to leave Butsuoji; and ask you, therefore, not to inflict upon her the suffering that would mean. To make this request is probably the last small service I can do her. Of my remaining here, of course, there can be no question now. Not that there would be any fear of past events repeating themselves; but I have taken advantage of your goodwill for so long, and now I must pay the price. After what I have told you tonight I can no longer continue as your priest. . . With this confession I return to your keeping the sacred office, and the dignity and good name that should go with it, and ask you to dismiss me from your temple.

'My one hope is that Ryokun may remain in Butsuoji, as the last direct descendant of its priestly family. And his grandmother—by the time he is old enough to serve you as his ancestors have done, age will have mellowed her into gentleness. Someday the boy will learn the truth. When that time comes he will understand, perhaps, something of his father's agony, and how he came to leave this temple.

'With this confession I shall take my leave of you and of Butsuoji. For what is past, I apologize to all members of this temple congregation, and thank you once again for the tolerance you have always shown to the worthless, evil man that I have been. But there is one more secret I have yet to confess. . .'

The parishioners continued to hear him in absolute silence, electrified now by this hint at a fresh revelation. Soshu's face was twisted with the bitterness of remorse and conflict.

'To my shame I cannot say that after such-and-such a date I had no more to do with my mother-in-law. I succumbed too often, I do not know how many times, even after the decision had been taken. But after a while resistance suddenly became easier; I found a courage and determination I had never known before—but not as the fruit of any spiritual growth in myself. . . I must tell you now of the source of this new strength of will.'

Far below, as if in some nether world, innumerable lights twinkled constantly, as if about to explode in a mass of sparks. Through the clear air, even the smallest was easily distinguishable from its neighbours. Some could be seen to be moving, others appeared suddenly from nowhere and darted from point to point like comets.

From the verandah of the inn at Kankaiji Tomoko gazed out over Beppu Bay. After a dip in the hot-spring bath and an excellent dinner, she was in a pleasantly tired, vegetative mood.

'Could we be any happier, Tomoko? Not many times in anyone's life when everything goes just how you want it. And that view, of course—ever seen anything like it? I shan't forget tonight in a hurry,' said Yamaji from the chair opposite, genuine feeling in his voice.

Tomoko nodded. She too would remember this night, though hardly for the same reasons. . . This was all, then, she could make of her life, of her womanhood. She had had longings, and had suffered for them; but that was over now. Heart-ache there would be—the sense of frustration at depending on Yamaji had not lessened—but no more than she was fitted to bear, instead of the torment endurable only in dreams.

There was nothing she could contribute to the conversation. Yamaji had never seen her looking happy, and now he enjoyed the forlorn expression on her face, assuming immediately it was her way of arousing the male in him. But she was thinking of a bird taking wing from its perch beside her, and soaring higher and higher, where only her eyes could follow. . . Soshu was like that; and in comparison, she herself, out here in Kyushu with Yamaji, falling. . . Suddenly Tomoko was aware of some great crisis facing Soshu.

Yamaji held out his arms across the table in a gesture of tenderness.

'Come, Tomoko!'

She smiled weakly. The lamps were out in their room and on the verandah. Only in the little hall outside a night-light burned dimly. Leaning forward, Yamaji drew her to him and sat her on his lap.

Conditioned by habit, her body responded to his embrace, the complexities of consciousness dissolving into a numbed awareness of sensual pleasure, even while a fragment of her mind remained aloof, registering the meaning of the instinctive physical act—that she was wholly Yamaji's. . . Not knowing where to look, she turned to gaze at the lighted street below the inn. Yamaji's face pressed against her side.

'There's been a kind of fate about us—I can feel it. Not just a casual man-and-woman affair. No, I won't let you go, as long as I live—or after I'm dead, come to that. . .' Yamaji whispered, half to himself. Tomoko did not answer. He enjoyed the pressure of her body on his lap, the gradual sensation of its warmth.

'One reason you've got such a hold over me is that you've never let me take you for granted. You never say what you really think or want. That annoys me, I can tell you! You don't talk, you never give yourself away. You're the kind that knows all the tricks—how to catch a man and keep him dangling—without ever having learnt them. Drives one crazy. . . You'd never play with a man deliberately: it just comes naturally.'

Suddenly Tomoko was seized with a strange, intense fear, that made her forget she was sitting on Yamaji's lap in the Kyushu inn. It had nothing to do with Yamaji—his manner towards her was still gentle, and nothing he had said had particularly excited or upset her. A premonition—if there is such a thing? Perhaps Shoko had been taken ill, or a fire had broken out in Kiyota-cho. . . Or Soshu. . . she thought of Butsuoji, where the day ended so early: already the temple buildings would be dark and silent as in the small hours.

Yamaji's arms caught her by the shoulders and pulled her towards him again. She turned away.

'Tomoko!'

His cheek met hers, forcing her to face him. Their lips met: slowly her arms folded about his neck in a gentle, almost reluctant embrace.

Neither of them moved or spoke.

In the temple hall the tense silence continued as Soshu prepared himself inwardly for his final confession. In his white robe he seemed more and more the prisoner facing judgement in some solemn court, yet the parishioners were visibly awed by the piercing whiteness of the figure before them, with its suggestion of the spiritual.

'Elders and parishioners of this temple!' His voice quivered in agony, though in spirit he had abandoned himself utterly to the grace of St Shinran. 'You who for twenty years have helped and supported me; who have given willingly of your time tonight to hear my confession. . . there is one more secret that must be told. What I have said till now was no more than a fuller account, or an explanation, perhaps, of what you already knew. I must tell you now of something you have not even imagined, and which nothing I can say will explain or justify. . . I have transgressed in a way that especially dishonours the priesthood of your temple. By comparison, my mother-in-law's sin is trifling. I came to love another woman. . . one of you, a lady member of this congregation. I have deceived you! It was my secret connection with this woman that kept me drifting, refusing to respond to the concern you showed on my behalf. This alone would have been enough to deprive me any right to continue as priest—put it beside the sin you knew of already, and what forgiveness can there ever be for a priest who commits both? The situation of the woman I am speaking of makes any thought of marriage impossible. From the beginning I knew this, but it did not stop me. The sin was all on my side; and the only result of it all was to cause her needless suffering, when she already had enough of her own. I tremble for the evil I have done. . . Soon I lost any detachment or peace of mind the priesthood might have given me: Under the eyes of the Lord Amida and of the holy saint our founder, from whom nothing is hidden, every morning and evening service here in this hall was a fresh reminder of my guilt.

'Sooner or later reality was bound to take its revenge, and shock me out of this double hypocrisy. Unsuspecting, you spoke of the need for me to remarry, and for my mother-in-law to leave Butsuoji. To me, those kind, considerate speeches of yours were the shock I needed.'

Whispers had begun to flit about the hall at the mention of the lady member of the congregation. Evidently some of the parishioners and this included the elders, had little difficulty in guessing her identity: and many eyes turned back to stare at him with a new curiosity.

'If I tell you frankly of what I went through then, it is once again not with any thought of self-justification, but that you should know how I came at last to break with my mother-in-law.

'For a long time after I began to be attracted to this lady, she knew nothing of my feeling for her. Yet even so it was she who gave me the courage I needed. One night my mother-in-law and I quarrelled violently—came to blows, even. Another night I spent wandering in the cemetery, another sitting here in the sanctuary till dawn. Soon the break was complete—but thanks only to the inspiration that the other lady—unknowingly—had been to me: nothing else could have saved me from own weakness. An old story, perhaps, this as much as the first, and as sordid—dropping an older woman for a younger. . . You may see in it no more than that. I can only say how profoundly I felt myself changed. But it is true that the change, the turning over of a new leaf, if one could call it that, is nothing to be proud of, since my own desires were at the back of this, too. In that sense I am as self-centred as before. If I could have helped my mother-in-law as well as myself, it would have been different; but I have only made her hate me. She will hate and curse me for the rest of her days, which is no less than I deserve in return for the misery she is having to go through because of me.

.'You will see now, I believe, why I could not agree that she should be sent away. I am the one that must leave Butsuoji. Her sin is common enough, one of those to which in the nature of things all women are liable at some time in their lives: little by little the bitterness will pass, and ten years from now she will be as placid and gentle as any other old lady. The past will be forgiven her, and forgotten, as it should be. But for me there can be no forgiveness, after the hypocrisy, the brazen-faced deception my life has been. . . neither forgiveness, nor even the salvation I have preached to others. This I know more clearly than anyone could tell me. I realised long ago that my presence here was an affront to this temple, but was always frightened to admit it publicly, or do anything but drift from one day's deception to the next. But then you began to let me know how you felt; and I had to think seriously about my mother-in-law's future and my own. In face of pressures like these—from outside, not from my own conscience—I was forced out of my silence. . . like a criminal making a deathbed confession. Such is the hypocrite you have known as your priest.'

The parishioners watched Soshu flush a deep red, in shame and in relief.

'If you will bear with me a little longer—' The truth drove him beyond the bare confession of his sin. 'You will forgive me if I do not name the lady of whom I have spoken. Names may occur to you; please—this is the only request I make—do not try to find out whether you have guessed right or wrong. She is blameless. . . Perhaps at one time she may have dreamt of marrying me; but that was impossible—too much was involved apart from any wishes we ourselves might have had. Knowing it was impossible, I let myself love her, destroying what peace there had been in her home and causing her pain she should never have been called upon to bear. But now, after this upheaval, her life is much as it was before—or so I believe and hope, though I do not know for certain—and outwardly at least will continue in the same quiet way: of that I am sure. But inevitably the deeper, inward wound will remain, with memory to keep the pain alive. Lifelong suffering—that is the return I have made her in my gratitude for the courage she gave me to raise myself from the mire. There are no words for sins such as these.'

'What do you mean to do now, Father? That's what we'd like to know.'

Soshu recognized the voice as Tachi's.

'Tomorrow morning I shall leave Butsuoji. Neither Ryokun nor Shoju nor my mother-in-law know anything of this. The boy is so young still, he would not understand any explanation I could give him—in any case, he will learn the truth from his grandmother soon enough. You will think such secrecy irresponsible: but I was too overwhelmed by the prospect of this public confession to think of anything else. . . Now that it is over, I am glad I have been able to confess—that in itself has given me fresh courage. The rest of my life will depend on what use I make of this chance of a new start; and the holy Shinran will be silently watching. For a time, as sinners always do, I thought of letting things go on as they were. The relationship with my mother-in-law was known to you already, without my telling you in so many words: I would be quite safe, I told myself, if I simply kept quiet and acted on the advice you gave me. My mother-in-law would be sent away, and I need have nothing more to do with her, while I myself would marry again—and provided the lady was good-natured and willing to look after Ryokun, there would be nothing difficult about that. What more could I want? The other lady understood how impossible it was for us to marry. I could have gone on meeting her secretly—in fact, she herself suggested it. With a little audacity on my part, all this would have been easy. In time my mother-in-law would have passed away, and by that time, in all probability, Butsuoji people would have had only the haziest memory of the temple scandal in which she had once been involved. Easy, perhaps, to imagine; but I could not do it. And now that I have spoken, I cannot remain in Butsuoji, not even if I wished to. . . but this is my own choice, made deliberately, even though it means leaving my son. The thought of Ryokun troubles me most—first robbed of his mother, and now abandoned by his father; he will grow up an orphan, and suffer so early—for the sins of his father. He will cry, of course, and feel lost and alone. I pray only that in time he will grow beyond this suffering, and know the ordinary, simple joys and sorrows of life.'

Soshu paused. For some moments he sat with bowed head, wrapped in the deep silence that had once more filled the hall.

'An old friend of my student days is priest of a temple in Kashiwazaki—I shall go to him first. But tonight I wish to spend here in this sanctuary, to meditate once more upon my sin, now that it is known to you all, in the presence of Saint Shinran. The holy Saint showed me his mercy when I was most desperate. He it was who taught me that if suffering is not to be barren it must be rooted far more deeply in the soul: who made hypocrisy no longer bearable, and gave me strength to confess before you tonight the sins of which you knew nothing, as well as the shame of twenty years. . . If any part of my secret had been left unsaid, I should have forfeited the one last hope of salvation.'

Soshu bowed low, as a sign that he had finished. Whispers here and there among his hearers gradually spread and swelled into a general murmur of excitement, as the parishioners wondered how they should react: whether Soshu's confession was really the end of the matter, and whether they should still pretend to ignore Mineyo's sin now that it had been publicly proclaimed.

In the corridor behind the sanctuary the old priest sighed, in awe and pity and sorrow. Tears stood in his eyes. But Soshu was breathing easily and deeply. There was no longer any tension in his motionless, image-like figure, only the peace that follows upon repentance and confession, the proof of a new life already begun. Behind him, the two candles shone their slender, flickering light upon the portrait of St Shinran.

Other TUT BOOKS available:

BACHELOR'S HAWAII *by Boye de Mente*

BACHELOR'S JAPAN *by Boye de Mente*

BACHELOR'S MEXICO *by Boye de Mente*

A BOOK OF NEW ENGLAND LEGENDS AND FOLK LORE *by Samuel Adams Drake*

THE BUDDHA TREE *by Fumio Niwa; translated by Kenneth Strong*

CALABASHES AND KINGS: An Introduction to Hawaii *by Stanley D. Porteus*

CHINA COLLECTING IN AMERICA *by Alice Morse Earle*

CHINESE COOKING MADE EASY *by Rosy Tseng*

CHOI OI!: The Lighter Side of Vietnam *by Tony Zidek*

CONFUCIUS SAY *by Leo Shaw*

THE COUNTERFEITER and Other Stories *by Yasushi Inoue; translated by Leon Picon*

CURIOUS PUNISHMENTS OF BYGONE DAYS *by Alice Morse Earle*

CUSTOMS AND FASHIONS IN OLD NEW ENGLAND *by Alice Morse Earle*

DINING IN SPAIN *by Gerrie Beene and Lourdes Miranda King*

EXOTICS AND RETROSPECTIVES *by Lafcadio Hearn*

FIRST YOU TAKE A LEEK: A Guide to Elegant Eating Spiced with Culinary Capers *by Maxine J. Saltonstall*

FIVE WOMEN WHO LOVED LOVE *by Saikaku Ihara; translated by William Theodore de Bary*

A FLOWER DOES NOT TALK: Zen Essays *by Abbot Zenkei Shibayama of the Nanzenji*

FOLK LEGENDS OF JAPAN *by Richard M. Dorson*

GLEANINGS IN BUDDHA-FIELDS: Studies of Hand and Soul in the Far East *by Lafcadio Hearn*

GOING NATIVE IN HAWAII: A Poor Man's Guide to Paradise *by Timothy Head*

HAIKU IN ENGLISH *by Harold G. Henderson*

HARP OF BURMA *by Michio Takeyama; translated by Howard Hibbett*

THE HAWAIIAN GUIDE BOOK for Travelers *by Henry M. Whitney*

HAWAIIAN PHRASE BOOK

HAWAII: End of the Rainbow *by Kazuo Miyamoto*

HISTORIC MANSIONS AND HIGHWAYS AROUND BOSTON *by Samuel Adams Drake*

HISTORICAL AND GEOGRAPHICAL DICTIONARY OF JAPAN *by E. Papinot*

A HISTORY OF JAPANESE LITERATURE *by W. G. Aston*

HOMEMADE ICE CREAM AND SHERBERT *by Sheila MacNiven Cameron*

HOW TO READ CHARACTER: A New Illustrated Handbook of Phrenology and Physiognomy, for Students and Examiners *by Samuel R. Wells*

INDIAN RIBALDRY *by Randor Guy*

IN GHOSTLY JAPAN *by Lafcadio Hearn*

JAPAN: An Attempt at Interpretation *by Lafcadio Hearn*

THE JAPANESE ABACUS *by Takashi Kojima*

THE JAPANESE ARE LIKE THAT *by Ichiro Kawasaki*

JAPANESE ETIQUETTE: An Introduction *by the World Fellowship Committee of the Tokyo Y.W.C.A.*

THE JAPANESE FAIRY BOOK *compiled by Yei Theodora Ozaki*

JAPANESE FOLK-PLAYS: The Ink-Smeared Lady and Other Kyogen *translated by Shio Sakanishi*

JAPANESE FOOD AND COOKING *by Stuart Griffin*

JAPANESE HOMES AND THIER SURROUNDINGS *by Edward S. Morse*

A JAPANESE MISCELLANY *by Lafcadio Hearn*

JAPANESE RECIPES *by Tatsuji Tada*

JAPANESE TALES OF MYSTERY & IMAGINATION *by Edogawa Rampo; translated by James B. Harris*

JAPANESE THINGS: Being Notes on Various Subjects Connected with Japan *by Basil Hall Chamberlain*

THE JOKE'S ON JUDO *by Donn Draeger and Ken Tremayne*

THE KABUKI HANDBOOK *by Aubrey S. Halford and Giovanna M. Halford*

KAPPA *by Ryūnosuke Akutagawa; translated by Geoffrey Bownas*

KOKORO: Hints and Echoes of Japanese Inner Life *by Lafcadio Hearn*

KOREAN FOLK TALES *by Im Bang and Yi Ryuk; translated by James S. Gale*

KOTTŌ: Being Japanese Curios, with Sundry Cobwebs *by Lafcadio Hearn*

KWAIDAN: Stories and Studies of Strange Things *by Lafcadio Hearn*

LET'S STUDY JAPANESE *by Jun Maeda*

THE LIFE OF BUDDHA *by A. Ferdinand Herold*

MODERN JAPANESE PRINTS: A Contemporary Selection *edited by Yuji Abe*

MORE ZILCH: The Marine Corps' Most Guarded Secret *by Roy Delgado*

NIHONGI: Chronicles of Japan from the Earliest Times to A.D. 697 *by W. G. Aston*

OLD LANDMARKS AND HISTORIC PERSONAGES OF BOSTON *by Samuel Adams Drake*

ORIENTAL FORTUNE TELLING *by Jimmei Shimano; translated by Togo Taguchi*

PHYSICAL FITNESS: A Practical Program *by Clark Hatch*

POO POO MAKE PRANT GLOW *by Harvey Ward*

PROFILES OF MODERN AMERICAN AUTHORS *by Bernard Dekle*

READ JAPANESE TODAY *by Len Walsh*

SALMAGUNDI VIETNAM *by Don Pratt and Lee Blair*

SELF DEFENSE SIMPLIFIED IN PICTURES *by Don Hepler*

SHADOWINGS *by Lafcadio Hearn*

A SHORT SYNOPSIS OF THE MOST ESSENTIAL POINTS IN HAWAIIAN GRAMMAR *by W. D. Alexander*

THE STORY BAG: A Collection of Korean Folk Tales *by Kim So-un; translated by Setsu Higashi*

SUMI-E: An Introduction to Ink Painting *by Nanae Momiyama*

SUN-DIALS AND ROSES OF YESTERDAY *by Alice Morse Earle*